About the Authors

Kate Hewitt has worked a variety of different jobs, from drama teacher to editorial assistant to youth worker, but writing romance is the best one yet. She also writes women's fiction and all her stories celebrate the healing and redemptive power of love. Kate lives in a tiny village in the English Cotswolds with her husband, five children, and an overly affectionate Golden Retriever.

Born and raised just outside of Toronto, Ontario, **Amy Ruttan** fled the big city to settle down with the country boy of her dreams. After the birth of her second child, Amy was lucky enough to realise her lifelong dream of becoming a romance author. When she's not furiously typing away at her computer, she's a mum to three wonderful children who use her as a personal taxi and chef.

USA Today bestselling, award-winning author **Lisa Childs** has written more than eighty-five novels. Published in twenty countries, she's also appeared on the Publisher's Weekly, Barnes & Nobles and Nielsen Top 100 bestseller lists. Lisa writes contemporary romance, romantic suspense, paranormal and women's fiction. She's a wife, mum, bonus mum, an avid reader and a less avid runner. Readers can reach her through Facebook or her website lisachilds.com

Royal Weddings

Royal Weddings
Saving His Princess

KATE HEWITT

AMY RUTTAN

LISA CHILDS

MILLS & BOON

First Published in Great Britain 2022
by Mills & Boon, an imprint of HarperCollins*Publishers* Ltd,
1 London Bridge Street, London, SE1 9GF

www.harpercollins.co.uk

HarperCollins*Publishers*
1st Floor, Watermarque Building,
Ringsend Road, Dublin 4, Ireland

PRINCESS'S
NINE-MONTH
SECRET

KATE HEWITT

To Laurie,
thank you for being such a fantastic editor!
Warmest wishes, K.

CHAPTER ONE

IN THE END it was surprisingly easy to escape. Abdul, the royal bodyguard posted by the hotel suite's door, dozed off around ten o'clock, his head nodding onto his chest, and Halina Amari, Princess of Abkar, slipped by him on her tiptoes, holding her breath.

She'd never done anything like this before, never once tried to escape whatever narrow confines she'd been put in—although she'd certainly tested the boundaries and stretched her wings as much as she could, which was very little indeed. But tonight she wanted to fly.

This might be her last chance. The world was closing in, getting smaller and smaller thanks to her father—and Prince Zayed al bin Nur, her fiancé. The realisation of how close she'd come to being even more of a prisoner than she already was made her heart leap into her throat. And as for Olivia…

But she couldn't think about Olivia, not now, during her one bid for an evening's freedom. Halina hurried down the hall of the elegant luxury hotel in Rome towards the lift. Abdul stirred and she pressed herself against the wall. She could hardly believe it had been so easy, but why not? The door to their suite had been locked from the inside, the guard posted outside as a matter of form. Her mother had been trying to keep people out, not in.

No one had expected her to escape. She could barely believe it herself.

The doors whooshed open and Halina stepped into the lift, her heart pounding, her palms slick. What was she *doing*? She'd spent every one of her twenty-two years hidden behind high walls—the palace, the convent school in Italy and then the palace again. Waiting, always waiting, for the fiancé she'd never met to regain his throne and become a suitable suitor. Waiting for her life to begin, or at least something to happen.

Three days ago, Zayed al bin Nur had mistakenly kidnapped Olivia Taylor, her sisters' governess and her school friend, thinking she was Halina herself.

Rumour was he'd married Olivia out in the desert before realising his grievous error. Zayed had sent a message to her father, assuring him that he had not in any way harmed Olivia, for which Halina was heartily relieved. But the whole episode had made her realise how precarious her own position was. How limited her own freedom. And it had infuriated her father, Sultan Hassan, who had sent Halina to Italy with her mother, away from Zayed's clutches.

Halina was glad for the escape; she'd never wanted to marry Zayed, a man she'd never even met, and she certainly didn't want to be kidnapped—although she doubted her fiancé was fool enough to try the same trick twice. But the walls around her were closing in.

After this, her father would make sure she was even more restricted, more guarded, than she already was. And that was something Halina could not stand. After twenty-two years of waiting, she wanted to live...even if just for a night.

The lift doors opened and from the hotel's opulent ballroom she heard the tinkling sound of piano music and crystal, the low murmur of cultured voices. When she and her mother had arrived that afternoon, she'd seen the notice in the hotel's lobby about the private party, a charity function hosted by some CEO, a glittering event for all of Italy's richest and finest. Her mother had given Halina a sympathetic smile.

'One day, such parties will be for you,' she'd said, steering Halina towards the lift. 'When you are wed. But as for tonight, a quiet night in while we wait for your father's further instructions.'

Halina had never been to a proper party. Since she'd turned eighteen she'd attended a few dire state functions, endless banquets with fussy old dignitaries, but never a *party*. She'd never worn a cocktail dress, flirted or drunk champagne. And that was what she wanted to do tonight—to be normal just for a little while, a young woman having fun, enjoying life.

Of course, there were a few obstacles to be overcome. She'd managed the first—escaping her room. She'd pleaded a headache and hidden in her room until her mother had gone to have a bath before making her getaway.

The second obstacle was clothes. She didn't have anything appropriate to wear. Fortunately the hotel had an upscale boutique, and after hurrying across the lobby Halina slipped into the elegant shop and picked the first suitable dress she saw—a knee-length sheath in black satin, simple, stark and very sexy. She found sheer stockings and high heels as well, and charged it all to her hotel room. She'd think about the repercussions later. Hopefully her mother would never look at the bill.

Holding the elegant bag with its embossed silver logo and thick cord handles, Halina snuck into the bathroom off the hotel's foyer and changed in a stall, her hands shaking as she stuffed her plain shift dress into the bag from the boutique. Was she really doing this? Was she *crazy*?

She'd always enjoyed pranks and dares, and had forever got into good-natured trouble at school. But this... this was something else entirely. If her mother discovered her...if her father found out... Halina trembled to think of their disappointment and wrath. Her parents were both genial, but they'd never had to deal with such direct defiance from her or her sisters. Still, she had to try. She'd just have to live with the potential consequences, whatever they were.

The door to the bathroom opened and Halina held her breath, one hand on the latch of her stall, fingers near to trembling. She couldn't be discovered now, not when her evening was just about to begin.

She heard the click of heels and from beneath the stall she saw the stiletto-shod feet of two women as they stood in front of the bank of sinks.

'Did you see him?' one of the women asked in Italian, in which Halina was fluent, as the other unzipped her make-up bag. Halina peered through the crack in the stall's door and saw the women, sleek and elegant, their lips pursed and eyes narrowed as they gazed at their glossy reflections.

'Falcone? Yes, he's just arrived,' the other woman answered with a toss of her head. 'The man's *cold*. Sexy as anything, but with a heart of ice. He's finished with his latest mistress, you know. Gave her the usual diamond bracelet as a payoff and now he's completely blanking her. She was crying her eyes out by the buffet.'

'That French supermodel? She didn't last more than a week.'

'They never do.' The other woman capped her lip-stick in one decisive movement. 'Would you fancy him?'

'Everyone fancies him. But would I *go* for him?' The woman tilted her head, considering. 'He must be fabulous in bed, based on everything I've heard, but I don't think I could warm up to someone that cold. One of his mistresses said that afterwards he always asks the woman to leave. And I mean, *right* afterwards. He's booting them out only seconds later.'

'There could be worse things.'

'And he insists on no personal questions at all. No asking, no answering, nothing. He just doesn't care.'

'But as long as you know that…'

'So it really would just be sex,' the woman finished with a sigh. 'And apparently that *is* amazing. That supermodel said she's been ruined for life, and it's only been a week.'

Halina's head whirled at the kind of gossip she'd never heard before. Whoever Falcone was, he sounded both appalling—and intriguing. Fabulous sex? She'd never even been kissed.

'Oh, well,' the first woman said as she zipped her bag up. 'Someone said he's already looking for his next mistress tonight—he doesn't like to have long in between paramours.'

'Mere minutes, it seems,' the other woman quipped. 'Well, it won't be me.' She sounded glum rather than determined.

With a swish of skirts and a click of heels the two women left the bathroom. Halina exhaled a huge sigh of relief. She was alone again—and it was time to make her own exit. She stuffed the bag with her own shift dress behind the toilet, hoping it would stay hidden for the evening until she was ready to return to her suite.

She hadn't quite figured out how she was going to return—would Abdul, her guard, still be asleep? And, if he wasn't, could she make something up about having taken a walk, gone for some fresh air? She'd just have to and hope Abdul—and her mother—bought her lie. This was her one night to shine, or at least twinkle a little.

Halina stepped out of the stall, her eyes widening at the sight of her reflection. The dress hugged her curvy figure, leaving little to the imagination. She'd never, ever worn something so flagrantly sexy. She'd never worn a dress so beautiful, so bare. She felt practically naked. The sheer stocking made her legs look long and slim, as did the sparkly black heels. She had no jewellery or make-up, and she'd have to leave her hair down, tumbled about her shoulders. She wouldn't look nearly as sophisticated as the women she'd just been spying on, but it would have to do.

One night. An hour, even. All she wanted to do was circulate among people, drink champagne, chat and maybe, *maybe*, flirt a little. And then she'd creep back to her bed. But for an hour—or two—she'd have fun. She'd live.

With her head held high, Halina walked out of the bathroom. She wasn't used to the heels and she stumbled for the first few steps before she got the hang of it, swinging her hips, sashaying a little. It buoyed her confidence, as did the admiring look from the man behind the concierge desk. She didn't even think he recognised her from when they'd checked in earlier in the day.

She followed the signs for the party and then paused as she saw a man on the door checking a guest list. She hadn't thought of that. The prospect of being turned away before she'd even put a toe inside the opulent ballroom made everything inside her shrivel with dismay and disappointment. She couldn't let that happen.

A couple glided past her, pausing in front of the man. Halina watched, nibbling her lip as they gave their names and he ticked them off his list. Another couple came by, and Halina watched as they followed the same procedure before going in.

Could she sweet talk her way in? She had a flair for the dramatic, but only in the safety of home or school. She'd never tried to charm a stranger, but she supposed she'd have to try.

Just then the man with the guest list caught her eye. He raised his eyebrows, managing to look both inquiring and a bit disdainful. 'May I help you, miss?'

Halina opened her mouth, her heart beating hard. 'Well…' she began, trying desperately to think of some credible reason why her name wasn't on the list but why she should still be allowed entrance to the party. 'As a matter of fact…'

The man's polite smile started to turn cool. 'Are you a guest tonight, miss…?'

Halina stared at him wretchedly. It was going to be over before it had even begun. Then she heard a voice from behind her, low and dark and rich.

'Yes, she is,' the man said. 'She's with me.'

Rico Falcone was looking for a woman, and he knew from the tightening in his gut that he'd found her. A startled gasp escaped the woman in question, her rosy lips parting as she whirled around to face him, dark hair flying about her shoulders in luxuriant waves and curls.

He'd caught a glimpse of her as he'd walked down the hall and his attention had been snagged immediately. A lush, curvy figure poured into a tight silk dress. Long, tumbling dark hair that she'd left loose and wild, like an open invitation. When she turned he saw dark-brown eyes widen, the colour of mahogany extravagantly fringed with soot-dark lashes.

'I…' she began in a breathy voice.

'*Cara,*' Rico purred, sliding a hand around her waist and enjoying the feel of his hip bumping hers. 'It was so good of you to wait for me.'

'I… I…' she stuttered again, looking shocked. Was she playing the innocent or was she just slow? She was obviously a gate crasher, so Rico would have expected her to play her part in this charade with a bit more alacrity. Never mind. He didn't bed women for their brains.

'Very good, Signor Falcone,' the man said, and ticked his name off the list, officious little nobody that he was. Rico moved into the room, his arm still around the woman's waist. She didn't resist, he noticed.

'Champagne, I think,' he murmured, and snapped his fingers. A waiter hurried forward and Rico plucked two glasses from the proffered tray before handing one to his next mistress. He'd already decided on that, although he didn't think she'd last too long. They never did. 'So. You obviously don't have an invitation to this party, but what is your name?' It was just about the only information he required of her.

'H— Lina,' she said, her fingers clenched tight around the stem of her glass.

'Lina?' He arched an eyebrow. 'You sounded as if you were going to say something else.'

She smiled sweetly, her eyes flashing dark fire, intriguing him. 'Lina will do for you.' So she had some spirit. He liked that, as long as she didn't start getting notions, thinking she could control him. Make him care. A few of the women he'd bedded had made that error, and it had been very tedious indeed. He'd had to make short work of them, when he would have enjoyed their attentions for a little bit longer.

'Lina,' he repeated, letting the syllables slide around in his mouth. 'And why were you so desperate to attend a party that you weren't invited to?'

She cocked her head, her smile teasing, her eyes alight, although he sensed a surprising nervousness underneath. 'What girl doesn't want to have fun?'

'Right answer,' he murmured, and clinked her glass. Her smile deepened, revealing a delightful dimple in one cheek, and she took a sip of her champagne.

'Oh, it's delicious!' she exclaimed, and he couldn't help but laugh.

'You almost sound as if you haven't tasted champagne before.'

She gave him a haughty look. 'Of course I have,' she said, and then, as if to prove the point, she drained her glass.

'Time for another, I think,' Rico said, and summoned a waiter with one imperious gesture. This woman, this Lina, was fascinating. Gate-crasher, definitely. Gold-digger as well, he was quite sure. He didn't mind, though; as long as women were upfront about what they wanted—as he was about what he didn't—the arrangement was usually satisfactory. He felt the tingle through his body of attraction and, yes, desire as he looked at her. Tonight, he hoped, was going to be very satisfactory.

She was certainly lovely, and unabashedly sexual with her tight dress and tumbled hair. She hadn't bothered with make-up or jewellery, as if she had no need for extra frippery for what was, after all, a very basic transaction. She'd come to this party looking for fun, and quite possibly a protector. Rico intended it to be him, at least for a short while.

He took another flute of champagne from the proffered tray and handed it to her. *'Cin cin,'* he murmured, and she smiled.

'Cin cin.' They'd been speaking Italian, and hers was flawless, although Rico suspected it was not her first language. He wondered what was. There was a faintly exotic cast to her features, her slightly tilted eyes and golden skin. He had no intention of or interest in asking her such questions or learning more about her. He'd long ago found that women started expecting things, emotional things, when he asked them even the most basic of questions. So he didn't. And he made sure they didn't ask any of him, either.

'Lina,' he said. 'This party bores me. Do you want to go upstairs?'

Surprise flashed through her eyes and her tongue darted out to moisten her lips, causing another painful arrow of desire to knife through him. 'Upstairs?'

'Yes, upstairs. I have the penthouse suite.' He let his mouth curve in a lazy smile. 'I think it would be a great deal more comfortable up there, and the champagne is of a far better vintage.'

'I don't even know your name,' she protested, her cheeks flushing. She looked uncertain but also excited. Perhaps he'd been a bit too abrupt. He was getting tired of the same old niceties.

'Rico,' he said, although he was quite sure she knew who he was. Everyone here did. 'I'm the CEO of Falcone Enterprises.'

'Falcone…' Recognition flashed in her eyes.

'You've heard of me, then.'

'Yes, in the bathroom just now.' Lina bit her lip, looking both guilty and amused. 'Two women were talking about you.'

'Were they?' Rico arched an eyebrow. 'Women's gossip in a bathroom—I can imagine what they said, and I assure you, it's all true.'

Her eyes rounded. 'All of it?'

Rico didn't even hesitate. 'All of it,' he drawled, and Lina let out a hiccuping laugh. She had, he noticed, already finished her second glass of champagne.

'They said you were cold. A heart of ice…'

'Pejorative, but essentially true.'

'Oh?' Lina tilted her head, her eyes sparkling, a small smile curving her lush mouth. 'How are you so cold, then?'

Rico took a sip of champagne, considering. 'I'm matter-of-fact,' he stated, deciding as always that bold honesty was by far the best policy. 'I don't dress up what is essentially a physical and very satisfying transaction.' He met her curious and impish gaze with a direct challenge in his own eyes, and he watched with pleasure as colour flared in her cheeks and her lips parted soundlessly.

'Do you mean…?' she began, and Rico cut her off.

'Yes,' he said. 'I do mean.'

She shook her head slowly, her pupils dilated, her cheeks still wonderfully pink. 'They said something else in the bathroom.'

'Did they?' Although he affected a bored drawl he realised he was interested. He wanted to know what Lina had heard, what preconceptions she might have of him.

'They said…they said…' She licked her lips, making his libido take a little leap. 'They said you were fabulous at sex.' She let out a little laugh, seeming almost incredulous that she'd admitted such a thing. Rico's mouth curved into a wicked smile.

'Also true.'

She laughed again, shaking her head, seeming embarrassed, almost shy. Was it an act, a rather obvious and unneeded attempt to snag his interest? A woman didn't pour herself into a sexy dress and try to gate-crash the party of the year without having some brash confidence and bold hopes.

'So?' Rico demanded in a low, sensual voice. He was tired of chitchat, of waiting. 'Shall we go upstairs?'

'Upstairs…'

'To my suite. A bottle of champagne is waiting.' It always was.

'I… I don't…'

Annoyance flickered through him. He didn't have time for this. Rico stretched out one hand and slid his fingers through hers, enjoying the shower of sparks that fired through him at that slight touch. He'd made the right choice, he was sure of it. 'Well?' he murmured. 'Are you coming…or not?'

CHAPTER TWO

HALINA COULDN'T THINK. From the moment Rico Falcone had rescued her from the box-ticking bouncer, she'd been ensnared. Bound body and mind by the sensual charisma of the man standing in front of her, so arrogant and self-assured and so very, very attractive.

She had limited experience of the opposite sex, and she had no experience whatsoever of the kind of man who stood in front of her now, one dark slash of an eyebrow arched, his mobile mouth curved into a smile of supreme self-confidence, his body radiating pure, muscular, sensual power.

'Are you coming with me?' he asked, and there was a note of challenge in his voice, as well as a hint of impatience. Halina hesitated. She shouldn't go with him, of course, this man whom she knew, from both gossip and his own gorgeous mouth, was a cold womaniser. A man who was fabulous at sex.

Not that she had any intention of having sex with him, of course. Her virginity was a point of honour, as well as a prized asset. As a princess of a desert kingdom, her chastity was of utmost importance. She'd never even *touched* a man before tonight.

But why did this have to be about sex? All she wanted was to drink champagne, perhaps even be kissed...

It was hard to resist such a beguiling invitation. And he was quite the most perfect specimen of a man she'd ever seen—dark hair cut close, silvery grey eyes that flashed like sunlight on metal as he remained with his hand outstretched, fingertips gliding along hers, his tall and powerfully built body encased in a top-end tuxedo, the crisp white shirt and black fitted jacket the perfect foil for his dark hair and grey eyes, his swarthy skin.

From the corner of her eye Halina saw the two women she'd glimpsed in the bathroom shooting her speculative and frankly envious glances. No matter what they'd said to each other, they wanted this man...this man who, improbably, *impossibly*, seemed to want her.

'Yes,' she said, flinging the word out the way a knight would fling down a gauntlet. It felt like a challenge, a dare, completely reckless but also brave. 'Yes, I will.'

'Excellent.' His fingers tightened on hers, causing a fizz of fireworks to go off in her belly. She was already feeling light-headed from two glasses of hastily drunk champagne, imbibed to steel her nerves. Now she felt utterly overwhelmed by the sheer, lunatic magic of the situation—she, the innocent Princess in her ivory tower being lured upstairs by the most magnetically sexual man in the world, never mind this room. *And he wanted her.*

Taking a deep breath, Halina followed Rico down the hall, away from the party, determined not to panic or even doubt herself. A little bit of flirting, another glass of champagne, maybe a kiss...and then she'd leave. Of course she would. And she wouldn't think about her mother, or Abdul, the sleepy bodyguard, and certainly not her father the Sultan who would be both furious and heartbroken to know she'd dared to go this far, never mind what she might get up to once they were in Rico's suite.

One night. One adventure. That was all she wanted, all she was asking for. Surely it wasn't too much?

Rico stabbed the button for the lifts and the doors whooshed open. Still holding her by the hand, he drew her inside, then the doors closed and they were alone, soaring upwards.

'So what made you decide to crash the party tonight?' he asked in a lazy voice. Halina tried not to blush. So it had been obvious that she hadn't had an invitation.

'An impulse decision.'

'Some of the best decisions are borne from impulse.'

'Are yours?' she asked. She was so nervous and hyper-aware of him that she wondered if he could see the hectic, urgent thud of her heart from beneath her dress. She resisted the urge to wipe her damp palms down its sides.

'My impulses are borne of instinct,' Rico answered. 'So they're always right.'

She laughed, incredulous and a little bit amused by his arrogance, despite her nerves. 'Is there anything you're insecure about?'

Something dark flashed across his face, so quickly that Halina almost missed it. She couldn't decipher what it was. Then his expression evened out and he smiled, his lips curving, showing a flash of very white, very straight teeth. 'No,' he answered. 'There isn't.'

The doors opened straight into the penthouse suite of the hotel, the one her mother had demanded but which the concierge had regretfully informed her was already booked. What kind of man was Rico Falcone, that the hotel had turned away even a queen?

'So, where's this wonderful champagne?' Halina asked as she stepped into the suite, her heels clicking the black marble floor. The space stretched on into the darkness, the only light coming from the floor-to-ceiling windows overlooking the city.

Rico threw her a darkly amused glance. 'Are you quite certain you want another glass?'

Surely he wasn't going to treat her like a child? Halina lifted her chin. 'Why wouldn't I?'

'I don't want you drunk when I make love to you.'

Everything inside her trembled, her internal organs reduced to a plateful of jelly. 'Who says you're going to—to make love to me?' Halina demanded with far more bravado than actual courage. An image slid through her mind like a sensuous snake—body entwined with body, candlelight gleaming off satin sheets—and a current of desire zinged through her, twanging all her senses, every nerve.

'I do,' Rico replied baldly as he retrieved a bottle of champagne chilling in a silver ice-bucket by a pair of white leather sofas. 'Why else would you have come up here with me?'

Nerves clamoured in her belly. Was she in over her head? The answer was obvious—of course she was. Yet she didn't want to leave. Not so soon, not yet. 'For the champagne, of course,' Halina quipped as she strolled through the sweeping living area of the suite towards the floor-to-ceiling windows that overlooked the Eternal City, its ancient, crumbling buildings now awash with moonlight.

'At least on that I can oblige.' With a satisfying pop he pulled the cork from the bottle and then filled two glasses right to the brim before handing one to Halina. She took a sip, relishing the crisp taste of bubbles on her tongue, and definitely needing the Dutch courage. *What now?*

'You really shouldn't be quite so arrogant,' she said as she lowered the glass. Her palms were slick and her heart thudded but she managed to hold his sardonic gaze. Just.

'Oh? Why shouldn't I?'

His utter, unapologetic confidence stunned her. She admired it too, because although she knew she could seem confident to her school friends or sisters, playing to familiar crowds with her trademark drama and humour, when it came to the real world she had nothing on this man. Nothing at all.

'It's not a particularly appealing trait,' she said at last.

'I disagree.'

His self-assurance was like a brick wall, high and wide, impossible to cross or find a chink in. Still, for some perverse reason, she tried. 'So you think it's an asset? Being so ridiculously self-assured?'

He shrugged, as if the answer was so apparent the question should not have even been asked. 'Of course.'

'Why? How?'

'Because there is a basis for it. I am the way I am because I know what I'm doing and, more importantly, I know what I want and I go after it.' His eyes flashed, a glint of silver like moonlight flashing off the blade of a knife. 'And do you know what I want right now, Lina?'

She swallowed. Hard. Excitement licked along her veins like the most dangerous fire. 'What?'

'You.'

Before she could form the words for a semi-coherent reply he'd crossed the room, swallowing up the space in a couple of strides, and plucked the champagne flute from her nerveless fingers. She opened her mouth to protest—she hadn't finished her drink—but then his hands were on his shoulders, warm and so very sure, and he was kissing her.

Her very first kiss, and it felt like diving head-first into ice-cold water, a shock to her entire system. She stiffened underneath the onslaught of his persuasive mouth, the sudden intimacy of it, even as heat exploded in her centre and stars shot from behind her eyes. Her knees buckled and she felt Rico smile against her mouth as he gauged her obvious and overwhelming response to him.

She clutched at the slippery, satiny lapels of his tuxedo jacket, lost in the sensation of his mouth on hers. Were all kisses like this? Did you always feel as if you were drowning, caught up in a whirlpool of pleasure, every sense singing? She'd never experienced anything like it, and all she knew was that she wanted more. Much more.

Her mouth opened under his and she stood on her tip-toes, straining to reach more of him. Feel more of him. Her breasts pressed against his chest and created even more arrows of sensations sizzling through her, making her whole being burn.

Rico slid his hands from her shoulders to her waist, anchoring her against him so her hips nudged his and she felt the hard throb of his arousal against her, shock-ing her to her core and thrilling her too. Even she, in her innocence, knew what *that* was. As much as it thrilled her, it also made a ripple of terror go through her. What was she *doing*? And did she want to stop?

Rico spread his fingers across her hip, each lean digit creating a burn even through her dress as if he were branding her by his touch. She was so achingly conscious of every part of him, from the hard planes of his chest and thighs to the sure movement of his mouth and the delightful press of his hands. He was everywhere on her, yet she still wanted more, a delicious and insistent ache of need starting at her centre and spreading outwards, right to her fingertips.

She felt so much, she was afraid she might combust, burst into flames right in front of him. How did people experience this and *live*?

Then, quite suddenly, Rico tore his mouth from hers and took a step away, raking his hands through his hair before dropping them to his sides. Colour blazed along his blade-like cheekbones and his breathing was ragged. He was, it seemed, as affected as she was, or almost, and that was an incredible thought.

Halina's knees wobbled and she grabbed onto a nearby table to steady herself. She felt the absence of him like a physical thing, everything in her all at once turning empty, cold and aching. For a little while she'd felt so gloriously alive. She couldn't let it end so quickly. She couldn't let it end at all.

Because she knew then, no matter how inexperienced and nervous she was, she wanted more. Needed it. She wasn't done with Rico…and she prayed he wasn't done with her.

Rico gazed at Lina thoughtfully, trying to ignore the hectic thud of his own heart. He'd been far more affected by her clumsy kisses than he liked to admit, even to himself. Even in love-making, in the highest heights of his pleasure, he kept his control. To lose it would be another form of weakness, one he despised. He would not be a slave to any emotion, whether it was love or its poorer but equally powerful cousin, lust. He'd decided that a long time ago, when he'd watched someone walk away from him and felt his heart break. *Never again.* Never again would he allow someone to break something inside him. He wouldn't even allow himself to be affected…at all. Never would he give in to the weakest emotion of them all, the torment of love.

And as for Lina… He let his gaze sweep over her, noting her flushed cheeks and swollen lips, her ink-dark, wavy hair falling in tumbling waves over her shoulders.

Her breath shuddered through her, and artlessly she pressed one hand to her pounding heart. She was just as affected as he was, and she wasn't even trying to hide it. He didn't think it had even *occurred* to her to hide it, to hide anything, and that made her very different from the women he usually bedded.

Those women were beautiful and hard in a sharply glittering way, as determined to get his money as much as they were eager to get into his bed. He gave them pleasure, of that he was certain, but they didn't respond as Lina just had—trembling and eager, unrestrained and artless, seeming to crave him just for him…which was an intoxicant in and of itself.

'What is it?' she asked, her voice a breathy whisper. 'Why are you looking at me like that?'

'How am I looking at you?'

'As if I'm a puzzle you're trying to solve.'

He laughed; he couldn't help himself. She was absolutely right and he wasn't used to that kind of perception, especially from a potential bed partner. 'Yes,' he said. 'That is how I'm looking at you. You intrigue me, Lina.' More than she should. He didn't want to be interested in the women he bedded, beyond their capabilities in that particular department.

Yet something about Lina, her utterly unrestrained response, made him pause. And then wonder. Because, he realised, she seemed the one thing he felt he'd never been, at least not since he'd been nine years old and realised that promises could be broken and dreams shattered. Easily.

What had given him pause just now was that Lina seemed innocent. And innocence was a quality in his bed partners he definitely did not want. He'd had enough dreams broken not to want to break anyone else's, which was why he was so upfront about his relationships, if he could even call the sexual transactions he enjoyed such a thing.

'I don't think I'm that complicated, really,' she said on a laugh, but the sound wobbled and she bit her lip, increasing Rico's curiosity…and his unease. Why was she acting as if this was all so *new* to her?

'Tell me what you were doing tonight at the party,' he said abruptly. Her eyes widened in surprise at the sudden change of subject.

'Trying to get into it,' she answered with a shrug. 'I didn't have an invitation, as you realised.'

'Do you do that often? Try to crash parties you aren't invited to?'

'Not…that often,' Halina said, keeping his gaze, but clearly with effort.

'But why that party?' Rico pressed. 'And why did you want to get into it so badly?'

A frown crinkled her forehead and something flashed in her eyes, something like unease. She was hiding something. But what? He'd already assumed she was a gold-digging mistress-in-expectation. What could she possibly be hiding that would bother him?

'Why not that party?' she challenged. 'It looked fun.'

'Were you hoping to meet someone in particular?'

She shrugged. 'I was hoping to have fun.'

Rico swung away from her, annoyed as much with himself for pressing the point as he was with her for her non-answers. What did he care why she'd shown up tonight or what her motives were? What did he care at all? He never had before. And he wouldn't now.

She was here in his suite for a reason. When she'd kissed him, as clumsily as she had, it had been with a genuine, eager desire. She was willing and so was he. That was all that mattered, surely?

And yet…it was almost as if she'd never been kissed before. She'd been so unrestrained, so open, and it had been that seeming innocence that had enflamed him. Yet surely she couldn't be as innocent as all that? Surely she wouldn't be in his suite now if she was?

'I've drunk all my champagne.'

Rico turned to see Lina clutching her glass, a determined tilt to her chin. She held it out and after a second's pause he reached for the bottle and poured her another glass, the fizz foaming over the top and onto her hand. She laughed and licked off the droplets, a move that seemed as thoughtless and uncomplicated as everything else she did. If it had been another woman, the kind of woman he was used to, he would have thought it a planned part of an attempt to ensnare him. Not that he could ever be ensnared.

'Cin cin,' she said again, a note of defiant bravado in her voice, and she lifted her glass to drink. Rico watched her, noting the sinuous movement of her throat as she swallowed, wondering yet again what was making him hesitate.

'Cin cin,' he answered automatically, even though he'd discarded his glass already. Slowly Lina lowered her glass, her eyes wide and dark above the rim as she stared at him.

'I… I should probably go now,' she said, and that surprised him even more. Was she playing hard to get? Or did she really mean it? And should he let her, considering how uneasy this whole exchange was making him feel? He felt strangely reluctant to watch her walk away, which was irritating and alarming in itself.

'Do you want to go?' he asked starkly.

She paused, her tongue darting out to dab a drop of champagne sparkling on her lips. Her gaze was wondering and transfixed as she slowly, so slowly, shook her head. 'No...no, I don't. But I probably should.'

'Should? Why?'

'Because you're a dangerous man, Rico Falcone.' She set the glass on a side table. 'And you're way out of my league.'

More honesty that took him by surprise. He wasn't used to such unvarnished truth. 'I'm not so dangerous if you know what to expect.'

'Which is?'

'A wonderful time and then a farewell.' He was absolute about that. He would never be left again, never watch someone walk away, leaving his heart in pieces. No, he would watch whomever it was walk away, a smile on his face because he was in control. He was always in control.

'Ah.' She nodded slowly. 'Just like the women said.'

'Those women in the bathroom?'

'The very same.'

He walked towards her, a long, loose-limbed, lazy stroll. 'Forewarned is forearmed, or so they say.'

'They said you kicked women out of your bed in rather indecent haste.'

'I suppose it depends on whom you ask.'

He stood in front of her so he could feel the heat coming off her, the desire. Her body trembled. He felt as if they were both on the edge of a glorious precipice; all it would take was for one of them to take that first tumbling step.

'I really should go.' Her voice was soft.

'Don't play games with me, Lina.' He met her gaze; her lids were half-lowered in dark challenge. 'I abhor any kind of dishonesty. If you want to go, go.' He swept one arm towards the lift. She didn't move, and if she had he didn't know what he would have done. Stopped her? Persuaded her to stay in any way that he could? Maybe. Probably.

But Lina stayed still, her gaze darting from the lift back to him. 'This is madness,' she whispered.

'Why?'

'Because…because I don't even know you. And you don't know me.'

'We know enough.'

'For you, maybe.' She closed her eyes briefly. He had the sense that she was battling with herself, and he wondered why it was such a momentous decision. She'd come to the party. She'd come upstairs. Was she going to cling to some outdated remnant of morality now? Still, it felt bizarrely important not to push her. This would be a decision she'd make on her own, though God help them both if she walked away now.

Then Lina opened her eyes. Stared him straight in the face. Took a deep breath and spoke. 'I'm staying.'

CHAPTER THREE

HALINA WASN'T SO innocent that she didn't know what she was agreeing to. Her heart tumbled in her chest and excitement zinged through her veins because, no matter how crazy this was, how nervous she felt, she wanted this. A lifetime of humble obedience and duty to her royal family and it had all shattered to broken pieces with Prince Zayed's foolish, desperate act. She would not marry him now; she might not marry anyone. So why not take one night? One night for herself, for pleasure? She'd deal with the consequences later. Maybe she'd be lucky and there wouldn't be any.

'Are you sure?' Rico's dark gaze searched hers, his voice a rumble in his chest. Halina had the feeling it was not a question he asked often. Did he know how innocent she was? Had he any idea that he was her first kiss, her first everything? Halina had no intention of telling him. She had a gut instinct that such lack of experience would horrify and perhaps even repel him. She wasn't like his usual women. Even in her inexperience, she knew that.

'Yes, I'm sure.' The words trembled through her and part of her, quite a large part, wondered what on earth she was doing. Losing her innocence, her prized virginity, to a man who had made it clear he had no expectations, no desires, beyond sex. Fabulous sex.

But perhaps that was better. This didn't have to be complicated. There would be no entanglements. And after a lifetime of waiting she wanted, *needed*, something finally to happen. To be the author of her own destiny, if only for an evening. Even if it ultimately led to heartbreak, or at least disappointment.

'Lina.' Rico's voice was rough. 'If you're sure, come here.' Her eyes widened but then she obeyed, walking towards him on trembling legs so she was standing before him. 'Take off your dress.'

Her heart was thudding so hard it hurt. Was he really going to ask her to do that right *now*? She swallowed hard and Rico's gaze seemed to burn into hers, his eyes like molten silver as he waited for her to obey his command.

'Well?' One eyebrow lifted arrogantly. This was a test, a dare; if she didn't do it, he would call her bluff. Accuse her of inexperience, and maybe even send her away. Taking a deep breath, her gaze never leaving his, Halina reached behind her and tugged the zip down her dress.

As the dress slithered off her shoulders, leaving her bare to the waist—her breasts encased in a serviceable white bra rather than the sexy lingerie she would have preferred—Halina could hardly credit she was doing this. Was it the champagne that lent the recklessness to the moment, or was it the urgency she felt? Or was it the man himself, Rico Falcone, his body radiating the most powerful sexual charisma Halina had ever experienced?

The dress pooled around her waist and Halina lifted her chin, resisting the impulse to cover herself. 'Well?' she demanded, and thankfully her voice didn't waver. 'Take off your shirt.'

With a low husk of laughter, Rico undid his tie and then the studs of his tuxedo shirt, tossing them aside heedlessly so they clattered onto the marble floor. He shrugged out of his jacket and shirt so his chest was bare and magnificent, his skin gleaming like bronze satin stretched over powerful muscles, the dark hair sprinkling his impressive chest veeing down to the waistband of his black trousers.

'Touch me,' he said softly, and it felt more like a plea than a command, surprising her, because for a moment Rico Falcone didn't seem arrogant. Gently she placed her hand on his chest, the dark, crisp hairs a sensual abrasion against her palm. His skin was warm, the muscles hard and flexed, and she felt the steady thud of his heart beneath her palm.

Rico encircled her wrist with his fingers, holding her hand there, against him. Neither of them spoke; the only sound was the ragged draw and tear of their breathing. Halina had never felt so close to a human being before, connected in a way that felt both intimate and intense.

Rico's fingers tightened on her wrist, and then he drew her slowly towards him so her hips and breasts pressed against him. The feel of his body in such close contact with hers made a thrill run through her, as if a live wire ran right through her centre and Rico's touch was the electric current.

He dipped his head, his mouth hovering over hers, their breaths mingled, everything suspended. Halina's eyes fluttered closed, waiting for his kiss, but then she opened them again when he remained where he was, his lips barely brushing hers.

'Rico...?'

Whatever he saw in her questioning gaze seemed to satisfy him, for in one swift movement he drew her even more closely to him, his hands on her hips, shrugging her dress down to her ankles as his mouth plundered hers with soft yet determined persuasion.

Halina brought her hands up to his head, her fingers threaded through his short, dark hair, her nails grazing his skull as she surrendered herself, body and soul, to that one endless kiss that demanded everything from her.

Her mind was a blur of sensation as Rico backed her towards the corridor that led to the suite's bedrooms; she stepped out of her dress, stumbling slightly in her unfamiliar heels, and when she did he swept her up in his arms as if she were an armful of feathers and, with her curled against his chest, he strode into the bedroom.

The room was swathed in shadows and moonlight as Rico laid her on the bed. She was dressed only in her stockings and plain bra and pants, and she felt shy but not uncertain as she lay sprawled on the black silken sheets for his thorough inspection.

And inspect he did, standing above her as he slowly unbuckled his trousers and then shucked them off so he wore nothing but a pair of navy silk boxer shorts that did little to hide the impressive evidence of his masculinity.

'You are very beautiful.' The words were stark and sincerer because of it. Rico was not a man to flatter; he was merely stating a fact. And Lina could tell by the silver blaze of his eyes that he meant every simple word.

'Thank you,' she whispered. Rico stretched out alongside her, the sinewy muscles of his body rippling with the easy movement. Halina held her breath as he hooked his fingers around the edge of her tights and tugged them downwards.

Her breath came out in a restless shudder as the tips of his fingers brushed against her sensitive core, igniting sensations she'd barely felt before. He tugged the tights lower, down her thighs, leaving fiery trails of sensation wherever his fingers brushed until he'd got rid of them completely and tossed them aside.

He loomed above her, his hands braced by her shoulders and his knees on either side of her hips. She felt caged by his body, but it felt protective rather than threatening, thrilling in a way she could barely articulate even to herself. She had no idea what he was going to do next.

Then he lowered his mouth and pressed a kiss to her navel, his tongue flicking inside her belly button and making her cry out in surprised pleasure. The cry turned to a moan as his mouth moved lower. Surely he wasn't going to…?

But he was. His breath fanned hotly on her underwear before he hooked his finger through the top of it and slid it down her legs so it went the way of her tights. She was bare and exposed before him, and it made her both tense and strain in expectation, incredulous and waiting, a little bit embarrassed and yet so eager.

Her body arched off the bed as he pressed his mouth to her centre, the feeling so intimately invasive that her mind blurred into nothing but sensation. His tongue flicked among her folds, seeming to know exactly what touch and pressure would make her writhe mindlessly, her body attuned to the exquisite pressure building within her.

'Rico.' His name was a moan, a plea. Her hips bucked with the restless ache inside her that she desperately needed to be assuaged. *'Rico.'*

He lifted his head, laughing softly, and then he slid his hands under her bottom, lifting her up so he had even greater access to her most intimate self. She felt too crazed with desire and need now to feel embarrassed or exposed, wanting only more from him.

And he gave it, his mouth plundering her centre until she felt as if she were shattering inside, breaking apart into glittering pieces, her hips arching under his knowing touch as her cries rent the still, taut air.

She'd never known anything like it, had never had such an experience so intimate, so intense, so overwhelming.

Rico rolled on top of her, braced on his forearms, his breathing ragged. 'Is it safe?' he demanded in a ragged voice and Halina blinked up at him, still dazed by an experience she could only describe as completely life-changing.

Safe? What, she wondered hazily, was safe about this? She was risking everything, including her very soul, by being here with him. It wasn't remotely safe. But she sensed that if she said as much Rico would exercise the incredible self-control she instinctively knew he had and roll off her, tell her to go. Their night would be over, and she couldn't bear the thought.

'Yes, it's safe.'

With a grim smile of satisfaction curving his features, Rico nodded, then Halina gasped as she felt him start to slide inside her. Her fingernails pierced his shoulders as she braced herself for what felt like a complete onslaught, an invasion of everything she was.

Before she could accept the discomfort and adjust to it, Rico stopped. His expression was one of complete and utter astonishment.

'You are a *virgin*?'

She couldn't be. Rico gritted his teeth, sweat breaking out on his brow as he held himself above Lina, calling on every shred of self-control he had to keep himself from sinking inside her velvety depths as he longed to do.

Lina looked up at him, her face pale, her eyes defiant. 'What does it matter if I am?'

Matter? He didn't deflower virgins. He didn't corrupt innocents. Having been heartbreakingly naive once himself, he had no desire to rip away the veil of inno-cence from someone else. Yet here he was, poised to do just that. If he was being completely honest with him-self, he'd ignored every neon warning sign that had been flashing at him tonight, every obvious example of the evidence of her innocence and inexperience. Her total naivety.

'It matters,' he gritted out and, though it felt like the worst form of torture, he started to withdraw from her welcoming, silken entrance.

'No.' Lina hooked her legs around his hips, pulling him back inside her. Her expression was fierce, her eyes bright with determination. 'You can't ruin me without fulfilling your side of the bargain.'

He let out a choked laugh, every muscle straining as they engaged in this absurd, exquisite push and pull. 'My side of the bargain?'

'You said you were going to make love to me, Rico,' she stated fiercely. 'So do it.' And with that she wrapped her legs more tightly around his waist and pulled him deeper into her, wincing as she did so, but not hesitat-ing for a second.

Rico muttered a curse as he sank deep inside her, his mind going hazy with the incredible feel of her body wrapped around his. His instinct was still to withdraw, to roll away from her and send her from the room. A *vir-gin.* A disaster.

Yet the tightly held shreds of his control were disinte-grating under the welcoming heat of her body, and with a groan he surrendered to her, knowing she was the vic-tor as their bodies began to move in that ancient, har-monious rhythm.

The least he could do for her was bring her back to that dazzling precipice, even as he climbed towards its heights. Rico watched in satisfaction as her face softened with pleasure, her eyes unfocused, pupils dilated, her breath coming out in a shuddery rush as her body convulsed around his. Then, and only then, did he find his own satisfaction, releasing himself inside her with a final groan of surrender.

For several moments afterwards his mind blurred and blanked as the last aftershocks of his climax pulsed through him. He rolled off her onto his back, one arm thrown over his eyes. Regret lanced him, a sword he threw himself on with bitterness—because he *knew* better. Of course he did.

He'd lost his self-control, he'd thrown it away with both hands, and for what? A single moment of pleasure? A damning *need*? He hated the thought. He didn't need anyone. He wouldn't let himself.

'Why,' he gritted out, his arm still over his eyes, 'did you come up to my hotel suite if you are—were—a virgin?'

She shifted next to him, pulling a sheet across her body. 'What does one thing have to do with the other?'

'You knew what I intended. I made it very clear, for a *reason*.'

'Yes.' She sounded calm and a little resigned, but not particularly regretful. Rico removed his arm from his eyes and turned to stare at her. Her face was rosy and flushed, her lips swollen, her eyes bright. She looked… She almost looked happy. He didn't understand it at all.

'Did you intend for this to happen?' he asked incredulously. 'Was that why you were waiting outside the party? Were you waiting for me?'

'Not for you in particular.'

His ego took a surprised bruising at that honest statement. 'So any man would have done?'

She bit her lip, her gaze sliding away from his. 'That sounds awful.'

'But that's what you're saying?' He felt outraged, even though he knew it was ridiculous. He'd had that very attitude countless times. He *preferred* that attitude…in himself. And one thing he was not was a hypocrite. Yet here he was, feeling offended by her honesty.

'No, that's not what I am saying.' Lina's eyes flashed and she scrambled up to a sitting position, her lush breasts on glorious display. She had the most amazing figure—curvy and womanly and round. Just looking at her made Rico ache all over again. Virgin or not, Lina still enflamed him.

She pulled the sheet up, wrapping it around herself as she glared at him, her chin tilted at a defiant angle. 'What does it matter to you?' she demanded. 'According to those women back in the bathroom, you should be showing me the door right about now.'

'Is that what you want?' Rico hurled back at her. He didn't even know why he was so angry, only that he was.

'It's what I *expected*. And wasn't that what this was all about? You warned me, Rico, about how little I could expect from you. Now it seems I'm getting more than I bargained for.' And she didn't sound very happy about it.

Rico stared at her in fury, wondering why he didn't just let her go. She was acting exactly the way he should want, but something compelled him to keep her here. He wanted answers. He also wanted her.

'It's different,' he ground out. 'Since you're a virgin.'

Lina rolled her eyes. 'That's my business, not yours.'

'You should have told me.'

'Why?'

'Because I never would have slept with you then!'

'And that's exactly why I didn't tell you.'

She was impossible. Rico rolled up to a sitting position and yanked on his trousers. A sudden thought occurred to him, terrible and profound. 'You said it was safe.' From behind him Lina didn't say a word and slowly Rico turned around. 'I asked you if you were on birth control…'

Her eyes widened a fraction and she hitched the sheet higher. 'That wasn't actually what you asked.'

'I asked if it was safe!'

'Which could mean something completely different.'

Cold dread swirled in his stomach, along with an anger fiercer than he'd ever felt before. 'Most women, when in the intimate situation we were in, would know precisely what that meant.' He took a deep breath and let it out slowly. 'Are you saying you're not on birth control?' Why would she be, if she was a virgin? Unless she'd taken it with the express purpose of losing her virginity tonight. The thought seemed so bizarre he didn't know what to do with it. 'Tell me you're on birth control.'

Lina shrugged, her ink-dark hair sliding about her shoulders. 'Fine. I'm on birth control.'

'You're lying.'

'You asked me to tell you—'

Rico swore loudly and viciously. 'I didn't mean for you to *lie.*' He raked a hand through his hair, his fingers pulling on the short strands, frustration now matching his fury and confusion. 'Lina, I don't understand you.'

'You don't need to.'

He knew she was right, and that infuriated him all the more. He should just send her away. By this point in an evening, usually he would already be in the shower, expecting his bed partner, whoever she was, to be finding her own way out. What was so different now?

'If you're not on birth control, you could be pregnant.' Lina lifted her chin another notch and said nothing. 'Damn it, Lina, that's a rather major issue, don't you think?'

A muscle flinched in her cheek. 'It's not your concern.'

'It is very much my concern,' Rico returned in a low, dangerous voice, certainty thrumming inside him. He would *never* abandon his own child, as he had once been abandoned. He would die first. 'If you are pregnant with my child, it is my paramount concern.'

Her face paled and she blinked slowly, seeming to absorb that statement. Rico shook his head, impatient as well as furious. 'Did it not even occur to you that you could become pregnant?'

'Not exactly.' She bit her lip. 'I wasn't thinking about that just then.'

'Then why on earth did you say it was safe? Did you lie on purpose?'

'I… I didn't understand what you meant.' Colour crept into her face and she looked away.

Rico stared at her incredulously. 'What did you think I meant, then?'

'I don't know.' Her voice rose in agitation. 'I wasn't thinking at all, to be honest.'

'Neither was I,' Rico returned grimly, hating that it was true. What a mess. And he had no one to blame but himself. He should have realised how naive she was. She'd given him plenty of clues.

Sitting in his bed, wrapped in his sheet, her hair everywhere, her eyes wide and her face pale, she looked very young and incredibly vulnerable. How could he have thought for a moment that she was experienced, a woman of the world? She was anything but.

'How old are you?' he asked abruptly and she gave him a look of scorn.

'Twenty-two, so you have no worries on that score.'

'Still—'

'I'm not your problem, Rico.'

'But you could be—' His words were cut off by a sudden buzzing. Lina looked at him questioningly.

'It's the lift,' he explained tersely. 'The doors lock automatically, since it opens right into the suite.' The buzzing sounded again, insistent. Whoever was in the lift wanted to get in. Who the hell was trying to find him now?

CHAPTER FOUR

HALINA WATCHED IN misery as Rico grabbed his shirt and strode from the room. She slid from the bed, still clutching the sheet to her, and reached for her dress. She needed to get out of here as soon as possible, before her mother or Abdul missed her. Before she broke down completely and burst into tears in front of Rico, appalling him even further.

How could she have been so *stupid*?

Hurriedly Halina snatched her underwear and yanked it on before wriggling into her dress. She managed to get the zip halfway up and decided that would have to do. She couldn't find her bra, so she just left it. She had to get out of here—now.

She needed to absorb everything that had happened tonight, everything she'd let happen, because she'd been so befuddled, besotted and bewitched by Rico Falcone. Those women had been right—he was fabulous at sex.

Too bad that didn't do much for her now, when she was facing a terrifyingly uncertain future. She looked back on the last few hours, blurred as they were, and marvelled that she'd been so reckless, with scarcely a thought for her future, her self. How could she have jeopardised everything for a single night's pleasure?

'What the hell are you doing?'

Halina's head jerked up at the sound of Rico's furious voice, and then her mouth dropped open in shock as the royal bodyguard, Abdul, strode into the bedroom. She'd thought things were bad enough but they'd just become a million times worse.

'Come now, Your Highness,' Abdul said in Arabic. He bowed his head so he didn't have to look upon her near-nakedness.

'Abdul…' Halina licked her lips, her mouth dry, her mind whirling. 'How did you…?'

'Please, Your Highness. Come now. Your mother is waiting.'

The balled tights she'd been clutching in one fist fell to the floor. 'Does my mother know…?' she began. Abdul's terse nod was all the confirmation she needed, and far more than she wanted. Any hope of creeping back into her hotel suite with no one the wiser crumbled to ash. Not only did she have to deal with the loss of her virginity and a possible pregnancy, but her parents' fury and disappointment. She swayed on her feet, sick with both fear and shame.

Rico stood in the doorway, looking furious. 'Who is this, Lina?' he demanded. His face was flushed, his shirt unbuttoned, his eyes blazing.

'I have to go,' Halina said numbly. She had to go now, before she passed out, or was sick, or burst into tears. She felt close to doing all three. With trembling fingers, she struggled with the rest of the zip. Rico muttered a curse and then crossed the room to her and did it up himself.

'Do not touch her again,' Abdul ordered in English, his voice flat and lethal, and Rico whirled on the man as if he'd been waiting for the chance to attack.

'*Excuse* me?'

'Please, Rico, just let me go.' Spots danced before her

eyes and a pressure was building in her chest. She needed to get out of here *now*.

Rico glanced furiously at Abdul, who was waiting by the door, his arms crossed, his face studiously blank. 'Who is he? What is he to you?' he demanded.

'No one,' Halina answered quietly. 'No one like that. He's one of my guards.'

'Guards?'

'We must go now.' Abdul stepped forward, six-foot-four of solid muscle, but he paled in comparison with Rico in all his glittering fury, who looked as if he was seriously contemplating throwing a punch at the body-guard.

'We aren't finished here, Lina,' Rico insisted in a voice that throbbed with angry intensity.

'We have to be,' Halina whispered, and she slipped by him towards the lift. As she stabbed the button she saw out of the corner of her eye Abdul block Rico's way. Rico looked mutinous, his fists clenched, his whole body taut with rage.

Thankfully the doors of the lift opened before he did something precipitous, and Halina stepped inside with a shuddery sigh of both relief and regret, Abdul following quickly... The doors closed as Rico strode to face them, fury and disbelief etched on every rugged line of his face. Then she saw him no more.

All the courage and defiance Halina had felt earlier in the evening, all the excitement from being with Rico, had all gone, leaving her flattened and empty. She was terrified too, yet she knew she deserved everything she was going to get, which she couldn't bear to think about yet.

She glanced at Abdul, who was stony-faced and silent. 'How did you find me?' she whispered.

'It was not so difficult, Your Highness.'

'But how did you know I was gone?'

'I check all the rooms of the suite throughout the night.'

And she'd thought she was being so clever. She hadn't realised Abdul was so thorough, never mind that he'd dozed off for a few minutes.

He must have seen she was gone and then looked for her downstairs. The bouncer at the party could have identified her, as well as Rico, and how he'd seen them leave together. No, it had not been so difficult. And she was even more foolish than she'd realised.

'My mother…?' she began, but Abdul just shook his head. It was not his place to say what her mother thought.

Soon enough they were walking down the hallway to their hotel suite, and Halina's heart began to thud in an entirely new and unpleasant way at the prospect of facing her mother. What would Aliya Amar think of her daughter's flagrant disobedience? What would happen?

She didn't have to wait long to find out. As soon as Abdul swiped the key card, her mother threw open the door. She stood with her shoulders thrown back, her face flushed with both fury and fear, her eyes narrowed to dark slits.

'Leave us,' she commanded Abdul, and he did so.

Halina closed the door behind her, her fingers trembling on the knob. She'd never seen her mother look so angry. Her mother was always carefree and charming, her light laughter tinkling through the rooms of the royal palace of Abkar. Yet now she looked like a woman possessed by rage. Halina shrank back. She couldn't help it.

'I cannot believe you have been so stupid,' Aliya stated in a cold, restrained voice. 'So utterly reckless. We leave

Abkar for one night—one night!—and you manage to completely disgrace yourself. How completely, I can see from the state of your dress.' She raked Halina with one up-and-down glance, taking in her rumpled dress, her lack of stockings, her tumbled hair and still-swollen lips. Halina felt as if the truth of her evening was written all over her, and she bowed her head.

'I'm sorry, Mama,' she whispered as tears gathered in her eyes. She couldn't even blame her mother for being so angry. She knew she deserved it, and more. From the moment she'd escaped her bedroom she'd acted foolishly, without a thought to her future. Now that it was all over, she couldn't believe she'd been so completely stupid.

'I always knew you were impulsive,' Aliya continued. 'Ever since you were a little girl, going after whatever you fancied. Doing whatever you liked.'

'That's not fair!' Halina protested, even though she knew it was unwise to argue. She'd been spoiled a little, yes. She could acknowledge that. But her life had been so restricted, with so little opportunity for fun or excitement. Halina knew it didn't justify her actions, but at least it explained them a little.

'Fair?' Aliya repeated, her voice ringing out. 'You want to talk to me about fair?' She whirled away from Halina, pacing the sumptuous carpet of the suite's living area. Then she stopped, her back to Halina, her shoulders slumping. 'Heaven help us both, Halina,' she whispered. 'What am I going to tell your father? He is going to be devastated. Heartbroken. This affects everything. All our plans…the political alliances that are so important…'

Halina swallowed, blinking back more tears. She hated the thought of disappointing her father so badly. She didn't even understand why she'd done it. Had Rico

Falcone really possessed that kind of hold on her? In the heat of the moment, he had. Even now she could recall a flicker of that intoxicating pleasure, the way it had blurred her mind and emboldened her actions.

Aliya turned slowly to face her. 'Who was this man? Why did you meet him? Was it planned?'

'I...' Halina stared at her helplessly. What answer could she give? 'It wasn't planned. I... I was scared,' she finally whispered.

'Scared? Did this man scare you?'

'No, not like that. I...' Her mind whirled. 'Olivia's kidnapping frightened me. It made me realise how little I've experienced, how little chance I've had to have fun...'

'Fun?' Her mother looked incredulous. 'This was about having *fun*?'

It made her sound so silly, so shallow, and in truth Halina knew she'd been both. 'I just wanted to go to a party,' she said. Aliya shook her head slowly. 'To see something of life, to feel...alive.'

'You are such a child, Halina. Do you have any idea what is at stake?'

'I never meant things to go so far.' Yet she'd chosen her fate. Halina knew she couldn't pretend otherwise. Rico had given her the opportunity to walk away and she hadn't taken it.

'How far did you go, Halina?' Aliya demanded in a low voice. 'As far as I fear, judging by the look of you?'

Halina said nothing. Her throat was too tight to speak. Her mother whirled around again, her fingers pressed to her temples.

'I cannot even believe...' she began in a throaty whisper. 'Could you be pregnant? Is that a possibility?'

'No.' The denial, the lie, was instinctive, and Halina

desperately wanted to believe it. She *couldn't* be pregnant. She just couldn't. Aliya turned around slowly.

'Because if you were,' she said, 'we would have to get rid of it. I know how heartless that sounds, but as a royal family we cannot endure the scandal. It would shame us all, and ruin your sisters' potential matches.'

Halina kept her mother's gaze even as she quailed inwardly at Aliya's total ruthlessness. Get rid of her child? No matter how much she'd wrecked her future, Halina knew she would never want that. But she hated the thought that what she'd done might affect her three younger sisters, who were still in the schoolroom and even more innocent than she was—or, rather, had been.

'There's no chance,' she said firmly, willing herself to believe it along with her mother. Inside her everything shook. Her future felt more uncertain than ever. She had no idea what was going to happen to her now.

Rico stared at the hazy landscape of Rome's buildings in the muggy summer heat, unable to concentrate on the property deal laid out on his desk. All he needed to do was review a few simple terms and scrawl his signature. Yet his brain had stalled, as it had many times over the last two months, ever since Lina had left his hotel suite in a cloud of confusion and shame.

It hadn't been difficult to find out who she was—Princess Halina of Abkar, known to be a spoiled pet of her father, a guest of the hotel where the party had been held and presently engaged to Prince Zayed al bin Nur of Kalidar. The fact that he'd deflowered a virgin promised to another man was like a stone in Rico's gut.

He might be considered cold and ruthless—he'd been called emotionless and even cruel—but he was a man of honour, and in lying to him Halina had made him violate his own personal code of morality. It was one he'd lived by staunchly since his days in the orphanage, determined to rise above the desperation and poverty, to be better than those around him, because that had felt like all he'd had. He didn't lie, steal or cheat. He never would. But in taking Halina to his bed he felt he'd done all three. It was something he could not forgive himself.

But, regardless of whether or not he could forgive her for lying to him, he needed to know where she was… and if she was pregnant. Because no matter what he felt for Halina he would take care of his child. His blood. That was a certainty. The very idea that he might be put in the position his mother had been in, a stranger to his own child, was anathema to him. His mother might not have cared about her own child, but he did. He would. Absolutely.

The day after Halina had left his suite Rico had hired a private investigator to discover where she was and what she was doing, determined to find her, and more importantly to discover if she was pregnant.

The possibility that she might be carrying his child and marry someone else burned inside him. He would never allow such a travesty; it would be even worse than her simply being pregnant. But as the days slipped by with no answer he knew he might have to; it might have already happened.

The thought of another man raising his child, passing him off as his own, made his fists clench and brought bile to the back of his throat. *Never*. But he'd had no word from the investigator who had flown to Abkar to ferret out information.

All he knew was that Halina had returned to Abkar the day after their encounter and hadn't been seen since, although she was believed to be residing in the royal palace. Attempts to get any information or gain entrance to the palace had been fruitless, so he had no idea if she'd married al bin Nur as planned or if she was pregnant.

Rico turned away from the window, pacing the confines of his luxurious office. For the last eight weeks he'd lived in a torment of ignorance and uncertainty, unable to focus on anything until he knew the outcome of his one night with Halina.

He'd told himself it was unlikely she was pregnant, that in all likelihood he'd never see her again and never needed to. His own history made that hope a faint one. His mother had been a waitress, his father a worker on Salerno's docks. They'd had one night together and he'd been the unwanted result. His mother had dumped him with his father when he'd been two weeks old and walked away, never to return. He'd been a mistake, a terrible inconvenience, and he'd never been able to forget it. He would not allow his own child to suffer a similar fate.

'Signor Falcone?' The crackle of his intercom had him turning. He reached over and pressed a button.

'Yes?'

'A Signor Andretti to see you, *signor*,' his assistant said, and Rico's heart leapt with fierce hope. Andretti was the private investigator he'd hired a month ago. 'Send him in.'

Moments later the neatly dressed man, slim and anonymous-looking, stepped into Rico's office.

'Well?' Rico demanded tersely. 'Is there news?'

'The marriage to al bin Nur has been called off. Apparently the Princess refused to marry him, and so he is remaining married to the governess he kidnapped.'

Rico had heard already, through the investigator, how Halina's fiancé had kidnapped the wrong woman and married her in so much haste that he hadn't ascertained her name first. A fool's mistake, one he would never make. He dismissed them both; they were irrelevant to him now that he knew Halina had called off the marriage. 'And the Princess?'

'I believe she is currently staying in a royal residence in the north of Abkar, a remote location.'

'Are you sure?'

Andretti shrugged. 'I bribed a maid in the palace, who told me the Princess had left about a month ago. It seems the Princess is going to stay in the north for some time...' Andretti paused meaningfully. 'At least nine months.'

Nine months. Shock iced through him, followed by a fiery rage. She must be pregnant and she hadn't told him. Hadn't even tried to tell him. Instead she'd gone into hiding...*hiding from him?* He took a deep breath, steadying himself.

'Thank you.' As his head cleared a new emotion took the place of that first lick of anger, something that took him by surprise. Hope. Joy. If Halina was pregnant...he was going to be a father. He was going to have a child. One he would keep by his side, for whom he would fight to the death Someone he would never, ever leave. Not as he'd been left.

'Do you have the location of the palace?'

Andretti withdrew a folded piece of paper from his pocket. 'Right here, *signor*.'

It took Rico only a few hours to make the necessary arrangements. By nightfall he was on a plane to Abkar's capital city, where the following morning he picked up the all-terrain SUV he'd bought over the phone. The palace where Halina was staying was three hundred miles north of the city through inhospitable desert, a landscape of huge, craggy boulders and endless sand. She really must have wanted to get away from him.

Of course, she could have been banished there but, judging from all the gossip Rico had heard through the private investigator about how the Sultan spoiled his four daughters, Rico doubted it. This was a choice Halina had made. A decision to hide from him.

He drove the first hundred miles before the sun got too hot, his body taut with suppressed energy, his mind focused with grim purpose on the task ahead.

When the sun reached its zenith he stopped the Jeep and sheltered under a rock from the worst of the midday heat. Along with the SUV he'd arranged for provisions to survive in the desert for a week. He always made sure to be prepared in every situation, even one as extraordinary as this.

As for when he arrived at the palace... His mouth curved grimly. He would be prepared then, as well.

He stopped again for the night and then drove as soon as the first pearly-grey light of dawn lightened the sky. The sun had risen and bathed the desert in a fierce orange glow by the time he arrived at the palace, a remote outpost that looked as if it had been hewn from the boulders strewn about the undulating dunes.

Rico parked the SUV far enough away that he wouldn't be noticed and grabbed a pair of binoculars. From this distance the palace's walls looked smooth and windowless; the place truly was a fortress, and the nearest town of any description was over a hundred miles away. Halina had chosen as remote a place as possible to hide from him, but it was no place for a young pregnant woman. The sooner he got Halina out of there, the better.

As the mother of his child she belonged with him— by his side, in his bed. As the mother of his child, she would raise that child with him, so he or she would never know a day without love, would never feel abandoned, an inconvenience to be discarded. A child needed both mother and father, and Halina would be there for their child and for Rico…as his wife.

CHAPTER FIVE

HALINA GAZED OUT of the window of her bedroom at the endless desert and suppressed a dispirited sigh. She'd been at Mansiyy Rimal, the Palace of Forgotten Sands, for nearly a month and it had been the longest month of her life. The prospect of spending several more months here filled her with despair, but it was better than contemplating what might come after that.

The week after her night with Rico was a blur of misery and fear. Her father, always so genial and cheerful, had become a complete stranger, cold and frightening in his fury, and Halina had shrunk before him, afraid of a man who had had only cause to spoil and indulge her until now.

He'd forced her to take a pregnancy test as soon as possible, and when it had come up positive the bottom had dropped out of Halina's stomach—and her world. She'd waited, barricaded in her bedroom, forbidden even to see her younger sisters, on whom she was now considered a bad influence, while her father negotiated on her behalf. He wanted her to marry Prince Zayed after all, now that she was spoiled goods and unsuitable for any other man. And Prince Zayed had seemed willing to go ahead, although reluctant.

Halina had used her last remnant of strength to resist

such a fate, especially when she'd seen how Zayed and Olivia had fallen in love with each other. She'd thought she could bear a loveless marriage, but not when her husband so obviously cared for someone else.

Her steadfast refusal was the straw that had broken the remaining remnant of her father's terse goodwill. Halina still couldn't bear to think of the torturous aftermath, those days of despair and fear. Eventually, in cold fury, her father had sent her here to this remote outpost in the cruellest stretch of desert, with only a few stony-faced staff for company, to remain until she gave birth.

After that she had no idea what would happen to her or her child, and that was something that filled her with terror. The Sultan had warned her that he would take her child away from her, but Halina tried to believe that once his grandchild was born he would relent. Her father loved her. At least, he had once. Surely he couldn't be so cruel, despite how she'd disappointed him? Yet he'd already shown just how cruel he could be.

Escape was an impossibility—she was constantly watched by the palace staff, and in any case there was three hundred miles of inhospitable desert between her and the nearest civilisation. She was well and truly trapped.

Halina turned from the window, surveying the spartan room that was to be her bedchamber for the coming months. The palace was a barren place both inside and out, without any modern conveniences or amusements. All she had were a few books, some drawing materials and endless time.

Halina pressed one hand to her still-flat stomach, trying to fight the nausea that had become her constant companion a few weeks ago. She felt lonelier than she'd ever imagined feeling, and far more grown up. She looked back on her evening with Rico and wanted to take her old, girlish self by the shoulders and give her a hard shake. What on earth had she been thinking? Why had she gambled her future away for a single, reckless encounter? The sex, fabulous as it had felt at the time, most certainly had not been worth it.

Restlessly Halina plucked a sketchbook from the table and a few charcoal pencils. She'd always enjoyed sketching, and now she had endless hours to hone her skill. Not that there was much to draw but craggy rocks and sand dunes.

A sudden commotion from outside her room had Halina stilling, the charcoal barely touched to the paper.

'You cannot, sir!' Ammar, one of the palace staff, exclaimed, then the door was thrown open so hard it rocked on its hinges, swinging back and hitting the wall.

Rico Falcone stood there, dressed in desert camouflage fatigues, his sharp cheekbones flushed, his eyes glittering. Halina's mouth dropped open and she found she couldn't speak.

'You,' he said in a low, authoritative voice, 'Are coming with me.'

Ammar burst in behind him. 'You cannot take the Princess!'

'The Princess is pregnant with my child,' Rico returned evenly, the words vibrating with taut anger. 'She is coming with me.' His tone left no room for disagreement.

For a second Ammar looked uncertain. He wasn't trained to defend the palace; it was remote, as forgotten as its name, and he was nothing more than a steward, meant to fetch and carry. Sultan Hassan had never anticipated anyone looking for Halina, much less finding her. She was here with a skeleton staff who were more used to cooking and gardening than wielding arms or defending the ancient stone walls.

'Halina.' Rico stretched out one hand. 'Come now.'

Halina would have resented his commanding tone if she'd felt she had any choice. But when the alternative to going with Rico was mouldering in this palace, and then in all likelihood having her baby taken away from her, she knew what she'd choose. What she had to choose. Wordlessly she rose from where she sat and crossed the room to take his hand.

The feel of his warm, dry palm encasing hers sent a shower of untimely sparks through Halina's arm and then her whole body. Quite suddenly, and with overwhelming force, she remembered just how much she'd been attracted to Rico. How he'd overpowered her senses, her reason, everything. And how completely dangerous that had been.

He pulled her towards him and then started down the steep, turreted stairs while Ammar made useless noises of protest.

'Wait—what about my things?'

'I will buy you whatever you need.'

A shiver of apprehension rippled over her skin. What exactly was she agreeing to?

'What am I to tell the Sultan?' Ammar demanded, sounding both furious and wretched.

Rico turned, his hand still encasing hers. 'You may tell the Sultan,' he said in a low, sure voice, 'That Princess Halina is with the father of her child, where she belongs, and where she will stay.'

Ammar's mouth opened silently and Halina had no time to ask questions or reconsider her choice as Rico led her out of the palace with sure, confident strides.

'How on earth did you get here?' she demanded as he strode through the courtyard and then out the front gates.

'I bought an SUV.'

'And how did you get Ammar to open the gates?'

'I told him who I was.'

'You mean—?'

'A billionaire with considerable power and the father of your child.' He turned back to subject her to a dark glance. 'He saw reason quite quickly. Why did you not tell me, Halina?'

'Not *tell* you?' Halina repeated in disbelief. 'As if—'

He cut her off with a slash of his hand. 'Now is not the time. We need to get back to Rome.'

'Rome,' Halina repeated faintly. 'You're taking me to *Rome*?'

Rico gave her another scathing look. 'Of course. Where else would we go?'

'I... I don't know.' She felt dizzy with everything that had happened so quickly. She didn't even know what questions to ask, what answers she was ready to hear. Why had Rico taken her? What was he going to do with her?

They'd reached Rico's SUV parked a short distance from the palace behind a cluster of craggy rocks.

'You know,' Halina said shakily as Rico opened the passenger door and she climbed in, 'Ammar will radio my father and he'll send out guards to find us. To take me back.' Her father would be furious that after everything she'd been kidnapped after all. And Halina knew he wouldn't leave her alone once her baby was born. He'd take away her child and then marry her to whomever he could find that was politically suitable and willing to take damaged goods.

'I am not worried about your father,' Rico dismissed.

'Maybe you should be,' Halina tossed back. She couldn't believe she'd forgotten how impossibly arrogant he was. 'Considering he is a head of state and he will send out trained soldiers who know this terrain far better than you do.'

'True, which is why I will not be traversing it,' Rico informed her shortly. He swung into the driver's side and then pulled away, choking clouds of sand and dust rising as the tyres peeled through the desert. Halina pressed back against the seat, every movement jolting right through her bones.

'Where are we going, then?'

'North, to Kalidar. I have a helicopter waiting at the border.'

'A helicopter?' Halina stared at him in disbelief. 'How did you arrange such a thing? How did you even find me?'

'I told you that if you were pregnant you would be my paramount concern.'

'Yes, but…' Halina shook her head slowly. Rico's steadfast determination shocked, humbled and terrified her all at once. What else was this man, this stranger, capable of? The father of her child. 'Where will we go after Kalidar?' she asked numbly.

'I told you, Rome. I have a private jet waiting to take us there in its capital city, Arjah.' Rico's face was set in grim lines as he navigated the rocky terrain. 'We should be at the helicopter within the hour.'

Halina lapsed into silence, still dazed by the day's events. To think only moments ago she'd been contemplating how bored she would be, stuck in a desert palace for the better part of a year. Now she didn't know what to feel.

The jolting movements of the SUV eventually lulled her into an uneasy doze, only to wake when it stopped as Rico cut the engine. The sun was hot and bright above, creating a dazzling sparkle on the undulating sand dunes.

In front of them was a helicopter bearing Kalidar's military insignia.

'How…?' Halina began, but then merely shook her head. Should she really be surprised at the extent of Rico's power? He was a billionaire, ruthless, arrogant and used to being obeyed. She had no doubt that he could get whatever he wanted…including her.

Rico helped her climb into the helicopter and then settled into a seat, putting on her headgear to muffle the powerful sound of the machine's blades as it started up into the sky.

Halina watched the desert drop away with fascinated disbelief, part of her still blessedly numb as she wondered what on earth her future held now—and how afraid she should be.

Rico stared straight ahead as the helicopter moved over the harsh and rugged landscape, a mixture of exultation and anger rushing through him. He'd done it. He'd found Halina. He'd brought her with him. Yet despite the triumph he felt at having accomplished that he couldn't let go of his anger that she would have hidden her pregnancy from him, his own child. Considering the nature of his origins and childhood, the possibility was even more repugnant to him. She would have turned him into a liar, the worst sort of man, without him even knowing.

He glanced at Halina who was sitting still, her hands in her lap, her gaze resting on the horizon yet seeming to be turned inward. Her face was pale, her figure slenderer than when he'd last seen her. In fact, now that he was looking at her properly, she seemed entirely different from the innocent yet knowing siren who had tempted him in Rome wearing a sexy dress and stiletto heels, everything about her lush and wanton.

Now she was wearing a drab tunic and loose trousers in a nondescript beige, both garments hanging on her gaunt frame. Her hair, once loose and wild, was now secured in a simple ponytail low down on her neck. She was as far a cry from the woman he'd made love to as was possible. But despite what she'd done Rico felt an inconvenient shaft of desire as he remembered the feel of her body against his, the silken slide of her limbs and the honeyed sweetness of her mouth. He looked away, determined not to give in to that unwanted emotion right now.

The next time he slept with Halina, it would be as her husband, their relationship made permanent for the sake of their child and the security he intended his son or daughter to know. The next time he slept with Halina, he wouldn't lose control. Even now the memory of how far he'd gone, how lost in her he'd been, made him grit his teeth with regret and shame. Never again.

The helicopter started to descend, and moments later they touched down in a remote and barren location where he'd arranged for another SUV to pick them up and take them to Arjah, from where they would fly to Rome.

Halina looked startled as she gazed around at the landscape, as inhospitable as at the Palace of Forgotten Sands.

'Where are we?' she asked as she took Rico's proffered hand and stepped out of the helicopter. The wind was kicking up, blowing sand everywhere, and she lifted one slender hand to shield her eyes from the dust.

'We're about a hundred miles from Arjah.'

Her eyes widened. 'So far?'

'Such measures were necessary.' He hadn't been sure how Sultan Hassan would respond, and he wanted to deal with the head of state on his own terms, back in Italy with Halina as his wife, not during some ill-advised skirmish in the desert.

Halina's lips trembled and she pressed them together. 'I see.' Her face was pale, and she swayed slightly where she stood. Rico realised, with an uncomfortable jolt, that she was tired. Exhausted, by the looks of it. And, of course, pregnant.

'Not too much longer now,' Rico said, even though it would be another three or four hours at least jolting across the desert in the SUV until they reached Arjah.

'Okay,' Halina murmured, and headed towards the car. She fell asleep curled up on the back seat, her dark hair spread over the seat. Rico had dismissed the driver, who had joined the helicopter pilot in a safe return to Abkar. It was just the two of them as the night fell, stars twinkling in an endless sky, until the wind started up again and obliterated nearly everything.

After another hour of painstakingly inching across the rugged sands Rico was forced to stop. He glanced back at Halina, who had risen sleepily as she'd felt the vehicle come to a halt.

'Are we there…?'

'No.' Rico's voice was terse. This wasn't part of his plan. This was out of his control, and he didn't like it. 'It looks like a sandstorm is brewing.' He'd known it was a possibility, but he'd hoped they could afford being caught in the crosswinds. 'We'll have to spend the night here.'

'Here? Where?' Halina pushed her hair out of her face as she looked around. There was nothing to see but dust and dark. 'But…where are we?'

'In the middle of nowhere,' Rico said with a humourless laugh. 'About fifty miles from Arjah.' Spending the night in the middle of a sandstorm was not a good idea, but he didn't have any others. It was too dangerous to keep driving.

'But it's a sandstorm,' Halina said, and she sounded

genuinely afraid. 'Rico, do you know how dangerous these are? People can be swallowed up in an instant—*consumed!*'

'I know.' Grimly he reached for a kerchief and tied it around his nose and mouth. 'Stay in the car and cover your face when I open the door.'

'What are you doing?'

'Going out to make us a shelter.'

'But shouldn't we stay in the car?'

'No, because it will be buried by the sand, and then we'll never get out.'

'Oh.' She swallowed, her fragile throat working, her face pale, eyes wide. 'All right.' Setting her chin with a determined courage that strangely touched Rico's hardened heart, she lifted her tunic to cover her mouth and nose.

Taking a deep breath, Rico opened the door. The wind and sand hit him full in the face, making his eyes sting and cutting off his vision. Despite the covering of his mouth and nose, the sand worked its way in, filling his mouth with grit and choking him.

Quickly Rico closed the door behind him and hunched his shoulders against the unforgiving onslaught. He gathered provisions from the back of the SUV—a tent, water, food and blankets. As swiftly as he could, his head bowed against the relentless wind and sand, he erected a tent against the partial shelter of a massive boulder. It wasn't much, but it would help a little against the wildness of the wind and sand.

Then he battled his way back to the car which was already becoming covered in sand and grit. He wrenched open the door and reached for Halina; she grabbed onto his hand with both of hers.

With his arm around her shoulders, their heads tucked

low, he led her to their shelter, pulling the flap closed behind them and taping it shut to keep out the blowing sands.

Halina fell onto the floor of the tent on her hands and knees, coughing.

'Are you all right?' Rico knelt next to her, one hand on her back as she shuddered and coughed.

'Yes,' she finally gasped out. "Although I feel as if I've swallowed half of the Sahara.' She looked up blinking, her hair tangled about her sand-dusted face.

'Here.' He reached for one of the plastic gallon containers of water he'd arranged to have packed in the SUV. Fortunately they would not suffer through the storm, as long as they could stay safe through the worst of the wind.

Rico poured a tin cup full of water and handed it to her. 'Slowly,' he advised, and she nodded and took a few careful sips. He held her gaze as she drank; he'd forgotten how lovely and dark her eyes were, how thick and full her lashes. Something stirred inside him, something half-forgotten and ever-insistent.

'Thank you,' she murmured as she lowered the cup. Rico dabbed the corner of a cloth in the remaining water and then gently wiped the sand from her face. Halina sucked in a shocked breath, staying completely still as he swept the cloth along her forehead and cheekbones, her dark, wide gaze tracking his.

What he'd intended to be expedient and practical suddenly felt erotic and charged. Desire throbbed through him as he continued to wipe the sand away, conscious of Halina's soft skin beneath his fingers, the pulse hammering in her throat, every hitched breath she drew.

'Rico…' His name was a whisper, whether plea or protest he didn't know. He dropped the cloth, not wanting the distraction of desire at this point, as insistent as it was. He needed to focus on their future...their child.

'You should eat,' he said roughly. 'You need to keep up your strength. You look as if you have wasted away to little more than skin and bone.'

'I've had morning sickness. All day sickness, really.' She smiled wanly but her eyes were dark and troubled. 'You're angry. Why?'

He was, but he disliked how she made this about his unruly emotion rather than her deliberate actions. 'Eat,' he said as he yanked out some pita bread and dried meat. 'Then we'll talk.'

Halina took the bread and nibbled on it, barely swallowing a mouthful. 'What are we going to talk about?'

'We could begin,' Rico said, an edge entering his voice, 'with why you dared to attempt to hide your pregnancy from me. Going all the way to that godforsaken place to keep it from me, even.' His eyes flashed fire and the pita bread dropped from Halina's fingers.

'Is that what you think...?'

'It's what I know.' He picked up the bread and pushed it towards her. 'But first, eat. There will be time enough to discuss the past...as well as our future.'

CHAPTER SIX

HALINA STARED AT Rico in disbelief, although why she should be surprised by his high-handed manner she had no idea. It was par for the course. Still, she struggled to find a suitable reply. Her mind was spinning and her stomach seethed. She was not at her best for an all-out confrontation.

'Eat,' Rico said again, and because she knew she needed the sustenance, she nibbled the pita once more. 'You look terrible,' he remarked after a moment and she let out a huff of humourless laughter.

'Why, thank you very much.'

'Why have you not been taking care of yourself?'

She lowered the bit of bread and eyed him with disbelief. 'Seriously? You're going to ask me that?'

'What else am I supposed to ask?'

She shook her head. 'God only knows. You blame me for everything, even being a virgin.'

'You should have told me.'

'Not that again. Are we going to revisit that particular argument now?'

'No,' Rico answered tightly. 'We are not.'

Which made Halina's stomach clench unpleasantly because she didn't think she wanted to talk about the other matters that might be on Rico's agenda. The courage that had been buoying her briefly, sparked by his sheer pig-headedness, trickled away.

She glanced at him from under her lashes, taking in the obdurate set of his jaw, the sharp cheekbones, the hard eyes. She'd forgotten how intimidating he was, especially when he wasn't trying to get her into bed.

The memory of just how easily she'd tumbled into that bed made her cringe with shame. She'd had nearly two months of public and private shame to deal with—her father's icy fury, her mother's heartbroken disappointment, her own inner torment. Even the lowliest of the palace staff had sensed her humiliation. No one had remained unscathed by her actions, least of all herself. When she thought of what she'd almost had to do...

She tossed the bread aside, her stomach too unsettled even to think of food. Rico frowned.

'I said you should eat.'

'I know, but I don't feel up to it. And I don't think you want me retching in this small space.' She wrapped her arms around her knees, feeling lonelier even than she had when she'd been at the Palace of Forgotten Sands, and the days had been endless and empty. Now she was in a tiny, enclosed space with a man who seemed to be taking up all the air and energy and she felt even more alone...and afraid. The relief that she'd been rescued was replaced by a greater fear. 'Frying pan and fire' came alarmingly to mind.

'Try the meat,' Rico said gruffly, handing her a strip of meat that looked as tough as leather. Halina couldn't tell if he was trying to be kind or just insistent. She took it reluctantly, because she really was feeling wobbly inside. Even though she didn't like Rico's methods or manner, she knew he was right. She'd lost nearly a stone since the nausea had hit. For her baby's sake, she needed to eat.

'Has your morning sickness been very bad?' he asked after a moment as she worried the salted meat with her teeth.

'Yes.' Halina swallowed. 'For the last month or so I've barely been able to keep anything down.' She managed a wry smile, her tone tart. 'Which is why I look so terrible.'

Rico, of course, did not look remotely abashed by her reminder. 'You need to take better care of yourself. Why hasn't your doctor prescribed something for the nausea?'

Halina stared at him, torn between fury and an exhausted exasperation. 'I haven't seen a doctor.' Not one she wanted to remember, anyway. The one doctor she'd seen… But, no. She didn't want to think about that.

'What?' Rico's mouth dropped open in outrage before he snapped it shut, his eyes narrowing. 'Why on earth not?'

She shook her head wearily. 'You have no idea.'

'Then enlighten me.'

Halina sat back, wondering whether she had the strength or will to explain to Rico about the last two months, and then no doubt be subjected to his scorn and condemnation—or maybe just his disbelief.

'Lina.' His voice was rough, urgent. '*Ha*lina. Tell me what you mean.'

'I was called Lina as a child,' she said inconsequentially. 'I didn't lie when I told you that's what my name was.'

'That is hardly my concern now.'

'But it was before.' She was splitting hairs, but she was too emotionally fragile to battle all this out now. 'Rico, I'm tired and it's raging out there. Can't we leave this for a little while?' Maybe another day she'd have the strength to admit everything she'd endured. As for now, she just wanted to sleep, if she could.

The wind had picked up even more and was battering

the sides of the tent, howling around them, a relentless monster eager for prey.

Rico gave a terse nod. 'Very well. As you say, now is not the time or the place—but I will have answers, Halina. Of that there is no doubt.'

'Fine.'

He unrolled two sleeping bags and shook them out. With an entirely different kind of queasy feeling, Halina realised how close they'd be sleeping to each other— shoulder to shoulder, thigh to thigh. Not that anything was going to happen in the middle of a sandstorm, and with her feeling like a plate of left-over pudding. But still... She was aware of him. Even now.

She adjusted the shapeless tunic and trousers she wore, as if they could offer her more coverage. As if Rico would even be tempted. She knew she looked terrible and he'd already told her so. Feeling silly for even considering such a possibility, Halina scooted into the sleeping bag and drew it up to her chin.

Rico eyed her for a moment, his mouth compressed, a look of cool amusement on his features.

'Are you worried for your virtue?' he drawled. 'Because, I assure you, it's not in any danger.'

'I don't have any virtue left to lose,' Halina retorted. 'You made sure of that.'

Rico's face darkened. 'Are you going to blame me for that now? Because—'

'No, Rico, I'm not. I should have told you. Trust me, I know. I wish I had, because then—' She cut off that unfortunate thought before she could give it voice. She would not regret her baby. It had already cost her too much, innocent life that it was. 'I just want to go to sleep,' she said. And then, pointedly, she turned away from him on her side and closed her eyes.

Sleep, however, felt impossible. Her stomach seethed, as did her mind. What was she doing here? And what was going to happen? Her life was in chaos, and the only sure thing was the baby nestled in her womb. But even that little one's life was being thrown up in the air like a set of dice... Rico was entirely in control, as he always was. Whether she was in a fortress or a tent, Halina acknowledged starkly, she was still imprisoned, her fate at the whim of another, and in this case a complete stranger.

Next to her she heard Rico moving around and then sliding into his sleeping bag. The rustle of fabric in the darkness felt intimate, and Halina inched a little bit away, not that there was much room.

Inconvenient memories were sliding through her mind in an all too vivid montage. The feel of Rico's body on hers. In hers. The way she'd given herself to him, utterly and overwhelmingly. It had felt as if she hadn't even had a choice, but of course she had. She'd just made the wrong one.

Then, even though it only hurt, Halina let herself think that treacherous *what if?* What if she hadn't been so stupid as to sacrifice her entire future for a single night with Rico Falcone? Where would she be now? Would Zayed al bin Nur have stayed married to her friend Olivia? Halina hoped so. She knew they were in love, and it would have been even worse to be married to a man who loved another than to be where she was now, pregnant and shackled to a man who regarded her with contempt and disdain.

So if Zayed stayed married to Olivia and she hadn't been pregnant...right now she might be free, the future stretched out in front of her, shining and brimming with possibility.

Of course, realistically her father would have arranged

another marriage to another suitable stranger, but Halina didn't want to think about that now. She had enough to deal with, sleeping next to *this* unsuitable stranger.

'Stop wriggling around,' Rico said irritably, his voice sounding loud in the enclosed space.

'I'm not wriggling,' Halina returned indignantly. 'I'm barely moving.' She'd been staying completely still, as if Rico might forget she was there.

Rico just sighed as if she were simply too tedious to deal with. It was going to be a long night. It was going to be a long life. What had Rico meant, 'their future'? She shuddered to think.

Eventually, simply because she was so utterly exhausted, Halina fell into a restless doze, only to wake suddenly, her body on high alert.

'What…?' she began, blinking in the darkness. Outside the wind was shrieking, and the sides of the tent sagged inwards from the weight of both the wind and the sand, and Halina felt as if she was being entombed. Perhaps she was.

A shudder of terror went through her and she whimpered out loud. The storm raged all around them, seemingly ready to consume their tent in its ravenous maw. Heaven help them both, was this going to be the end of them both?

'It will pass.' Rico's voice was low and steady, a thrum of comfort.

'How do you know?' Halina asked in a high, faltering voice. 'We could be buried alive.' She started to tremble, her teeth chattering with pure, unadulterated fear.

Then, to her shock, she felt Rico's hands on her shoulders and he pulled her against him, fitting her body next to his so she could feel the hard, warm press of his chest, his powerful thighs.

She stayed rigid with shock for a few seconds, then Rico began to rub comforting circles over her back with the palm of his hand, and Halina started to relax.

It felt so good to be held. It felt so safe. Until this moment she hadn't realised how much she craved both the comfort and security of another person's touch. She closed her eyes as she snuggled into him, telling herself this didn't count. Extraordinary measures for extraordinary circumstances—that was all this was. In the morning she would be back to keeping her distance and composure—and regaining her strength.

Rico continued to rub Halina's back as he felt her melt into him and he tried not to react. Even in her gaunt state she was pliant, warm and womanly. He desired her even now, with the storm raging all around them and their lives at stake.

'Have you never been in a sandstorm before?' he asked, trying to distract himself from his own demanding need.

'No, I've only seen them from a distance. From the safety of a palace.' She let out a choked laugh, her breathing fanning his neck. 'I've led a very restricted life, Rico.'

A very privileged life. Her upbringing was a world away from his on the docks of Salerno, a mother who hadn't wanted him at all and a father...

But why the hell was he thinking about his father now?

Seeing Halina, knowing she was carrying his child, had opened a need in him and, worse, a vulnerability that he struggled to contain. Control was paramount. He would provide for his child, he would love him or her, his own flesh and blood, he would make a stable family that his child could trust in absolutely. But he would not give in to this inconvenient and shaming need; he would never allow himself to be weak.

To make the point to himself, he inched a little bit away from Halina's soft, tempting body. Outside the wind howled and the tent continued to be battered mercilessly.

'Have you ever been in a sandstorm?' Halina asked, moving closer to him again, one fine-boned hand resting on his chest. Resigned, Rico put his arms more securely around her, telling himself he was doing it for her sake, not his own.

'No, I have not.'

'Then you don't know if it will pass.'

'I checked the weather before I set out on this journey. The high winds were only meant to last a few hours.'

'Somehow I don't think sandstorms bow down to weather reports,' Halina returned. 'They are entirely unpredictable, coming out of nowhere, sometimes lasting for days.' Her voice hitched. 'What if we're stuck out here for that long? What if we're buried alive?'

'We won't be.'

'You don't know that, Rico. You don't control nature, as much as you might like to.'

Of course he didn't, but he prided himself on living a life where he always maintained control. Where he was always totally prepared. Where nothing ever surprised him, because then he wouldn't betray himself, his doubt or his need. Yet, just as Halina had said, he could not control a sandstorm, and he feared this was just the beginning of all the things he would not be able to control.

His arms tightened around Halina. 'I admit, the storm is stronger than I anticipated, but I brought the necessary equipment and food, and we are well positioned to wait it out. We'll be safe, Halina. I will make sure of it.'

Halina relaxed a fraction. 'I'm sorry,' she murmured. 'I don't mean to overreact.'

Rico couldn't keep a wry smile from touching his lips as he stroked her hair. No matter his promises, they were in a life-threatening situation. He'd hardly call it over-reacting. 'You're forgiven,' he said, and Halina let out a little huff of laughter.

'Even when you're being kind, you're arrogant, do you know that?'

'It isn't arrogance when I'm right.'

She just laughed again, her lips brushing his neck, sending gooseflesh rippling along his skin. Desire arrowed through his body and he knew Halina felt it too by the way she tensed in his arms, shifting a little so she was looking up at him, her hair cascading down her back in an inky blue-black river that Rico could just make out in the darkness of the tent.

His mind blurred and he started to lower his head to claim her mouth with his own. He could imagine the kiss, the rightness of it. He could already taste it, like a drink of clean, sweet water. He heard Halina's quick, indrawn breath as she waited for him to close the space between their mouths and it shocked him into clarity. He lifted his head.

He could not complicate their relationship with sex. Not yet. Not until he'd made it very clear what he expected of Halina and their marriage. Of their life together, or lack of it. Until then, he'd keep his distance, for both their sakes.

He heard Halina draw another shuddering breath and knew she'd felt his withdrawal. She moved a little bit away from him, or tried to. Rico stilled her, keeping her close, although he wasn't sure why. Surely it was better to let her go, give them both a little distance? Still, he stayed where he was, and made sure she did as well.

'Go to sleep,' he said gruffly. Halina did not reply, but after a few endless moments he felt her body start to relax again, and then he heard the deep, even breaths of sleep as the storm continued to rage.

When he awoke the tent was hot and airless, awash in a greyish morning light, and the world was still. Halina was still snuggled in his arms and now he could see her properly—the luxurious spill of her hair, her lush lips slightly parted, her thick, spiky lashes fanning onto her cheeks.

He brushed a tendril of hair from her face and her eyes fluttered open. For a taut second they simply stared at one another, their bodies pressed close together, Rico's already responding.

Halina moved away first, wriggling away from him as her face turned fiery. 'The storm has stopped,' she muttered as she scooted across the tent, putting as much space between them as she could, considering the limitations of their environment.

'So it has.'

She peered out, as if she could see right through the dark canvas. 'Are we going to be able to get out?'

'I should think so.'

It took some doing, but after Rico had torn the tape from the entrance to the tent he managed to dig them out.

'Only half-buried,' he said with a smile, and then reached for Halina's hand to help her out.

Outside they both stretched and blinked in the glare of the morning sunlight, the landscape made even more strange by the ravages of the storm. Drifts of sand were piled on either side of the tent and the SUV was completely buried, no more than a large hump in the sand.

New dunes had formed, turning the once-flat stretch into a newly undulating lunar-like landscape.

'Goodness,' Halina murmured. Her arms were wrapped around herself, her face pale as she looked around. 'I'm amazed we're still here.'

'Yes.' Rico eyed the buried SUV. It would take him several hours to dig it out. 'We need to get going. Why don't you refresh yourself? Eat and drink something? I'll start digging out the car.'

'Why are we going to Rome, Rico?'

'Because that is where both my business and home are.' He rolled up his sleeves and started scooping the sand away from the car with his hands. Unfortunately he had not thought to pack a spade in his desert provisions.

'And what will we do when we get to Rome?' Halina pressed. Rico gritted his teeth. He didn't want to have this conversation, not until they were safely back in Rome, in his domain. But Halina seemed determined to discover his intentions, and Rico decided she might as well know them. It wasn't as if she could escape, anyway.

'We're going to Rome,' he said clearly, his gaze on the sand-covered car, 'because that is where we are going to live. Where my child is going to be born…and where you are going to marry me.'

CHAPTER SEVEN

HALINA STARED AT Rico in dawning realisation—and horror.

'Marry you?' she squeaked. *'That's* what you have in mind?'

'Yes.'

'But…but we don't know each other! And we don't even like each other.'

'I believe those statements are contradictory. And, in any case, you were prepared to marry more of a stranger to you than I am mere weeks ago.'

Halina flushed, not needing the reminder. 'I was prepared to do that out of duty,' she began, but fell silent when Rico gave a decisive shake of his head.

'And you will marry me out of duty as well. Duty to our unborn child.'

'We don't have to be married for our—'

'Yes.' Rico cut her off. 'We do. It is important to me, of paramount importance, that my child grows up in a stable and loving home.'

'Loving?' Halina repeated incredulously. 'But you don't love me.'

'I will love my child,' Rico stated flatly, his voice thrumming with certainly. 'But now is not the time to discuss this. We have more important matters to attend to.' He nodded towards the tent. 'Eat, drink and refresh yourself. We leave in an hour.'

Biting her lip, preferring not to argue with him when he was in such an intractable mood, Halina wordlessly turned and went back into the tent.

She choked down some more pita bread and dried meat, knowing she needed the sustenance, then washed her face with a sparing amount of water and rinsed out her mouth. With her hair tidied and her clothes straightened, she was as presentable as she was going to be, but she didn't feel at all ready for whatever lay ahead.

Marriage. She shouldn't have been surprised, she realised. Rico moved people about like pawns on his personal chessboard. Why should she, why should marriage, be any different?

Because he was the classic commitment-phobe who never kept a woman for more than a night. But with a sinking sensation Halina acknowledged that marriage to Rico Falcone was most likely not going to look or feel like a normal marriage. Not that she knew what that felt like. If she married Rico, she would just be exchanging one expedient union for another. One stranger for another. A loving, normal marriage had never been within her grasp, no matter how much she might have wanted it. Her life had never been her own.

Halina rolled up the sleeping bags and repacked their provisions in the canvas rucksack Rico had brought. Then, taking a deep breath, she went in search of her rescuer and captor.

He was hard at work digging out the SUV; he had shucked off his shirt and his tawny skin gleamed like polished bronze under the unforgiving glare of the desert sun. Halina blinked, trying not to let her gaze move slowly over his perfectly sculpted pectoral muscles, the six-pack definition of his taut abdomen. She failed and, even worse, Rico turned and caught her staring openly at his incredible physique.

His mouth quirked and something like satisfaction flashed in his eyes. He jerked his head in a nod towards their vehicle. 'I should be finished in another half hour.'

'Can I help…?'

'No, of course not. You're pregnant.'

'Pregnant, not an invalid.'

'Even so.' Rico turned back to the car. 'I do not wish you to tax yourself.'

With a sigh Halina wondered if Rico intended to wrap her in cotton wool for the next seven months. Then, with a jolt, she wondered why she was thinking this way. Was she just going to roll over and do whatever he said, including binding her life to his for ever? Would Rico let her do anything else?

Her choices, as ever, were limited. She'd never known what freedom felt like save, perhaps, for her one night with Rico. And look what had happened then.

Her mind in a ferment of indecision and uncertainty, Halina turned back to the tent. 'I'll pack up our things.'

Half an hour later the vehicle was clear and Rico had thrown their things into the back. His expression was grim and determined as he slid into the driver's seat. 'We have another two hours' drive to Arjah.'

'What if my father's soldiers are there? What if we're found?'

'We won't be.'

And if they were? Her father must have discovered her absence by now and most likely would have sent soldiers out to find her. And what then? Rico wouldn't give her up without a fight, but even he was no match against trained soldiers and weapons. Halina leaned her head back against the seat and closed her eyes. It was too much to think about on top of everything else.

'Any soldiers your father sent out would have been caught in the sandstorm, the same as we were,' Rico said. 'We have some time.'

Halina just nodded, not trusting herself to speak. In such a scenario she didn't even know what she'd prefer. To stay with Rico, or be rescued by her father? Both options seemed abysmal in their own way.

A bumpy few hours passed as they jolted along, the rough desert track gradually becoming a tarmac road, and then the low mud-brick buildings and handful of skyscrapers came into view—Arjah, the capital city of Kalidar.

Halina felt herself getting more and more tense as Rico drove through the city, his expression harsh and grim, his fingers tight on the steering wheel. They made it to the airport without notice, and Rico drove directly to a private plane waiting in its own bay.

Halina's breath came out in a shudder of relief that they had not been caught or detained. So she would prefer to stay with Rico. Her own reaction had betrayed her. That was why she'd left with him in the first place, she supposed—because she'd rather risk her future with this man than face the continuing wrath of her father, her baby taken away, her body given to a man she'd never even met.

Rico gave a grimly satisfied nod. 'It is just as I had arranged.' He parked the SUV and strode out to meet the plane's crew who were waiting for them on the tarmac. Halina followed, feeling exhausted and emotionally overwhelmed. If she got on that plane, it would take her all the way to Rome. And then where would she be? What would she do? What would Rico do?

'Come. There is no time to delay.' Rico beckoned her forward. 'You will be more comfortable on the plane.'

Halina hesitated, even though she knew there was no point. No choice. What was she going to do? Make a sprint for the airport? She had no money, no clothes, nothing. No resources at all, and no friends to help. For a second she thought of Olivia and Prince Zayed, who might be currently residing in the royal palace at Arjah. She could seek sanctuary with them perhaps, but did she want to do that—be the unexpected and undoubtedly unwelcome guest of her former fiancé and his new bride? She'd be putting them into an impossible position as well as herself, and that was assuming she could even get to the royal palace from here, which she probably couldn't.

'Halina.' Rico's voice was touched with impatience. 'Everyone is waiting.' On leaden legs Halina walked slowly towards him and as he took her arm she climbed the steps to the plane.

She'd been on Abkar's royal jet many times before, going to and from school, but it felt different now, walking into Rico's own plane. She glanced around at the sumptuous leather sofas and low coffee tables. Several crew members were waiting attentively, their faces carefully bland. Did they know who she was, that she was pregnant with their employer's child?

Rico strode in behind her and gestured for her to sit down. 'After take-off you can shower and rest. The flight will take approximately six hours.'

Numbly Halina nodded. She felt dazed, unable to process everything that had happened to her. Everything that was going to happen. *Marriage.*

She swallowed hard and looked out at the bright blue sky, the glare of the sun making the tarmac shimmer. The plane began to taxi down the runway and then they were taking off into the sky, away from all she had known.

As soon as they'd reached cruising altitude, Rico rose. 'I'll show you the bedroom.'

Halina followed him, aching with exhaustion, too tired even to think. The bedroom was even more luxurious than the living area, with a king-sized bed on its own dais, built in wardrobes and a huge flat-screen TV.

She gazed around at the adjoining bathroom, complete with a glassed-in shower and marble tub, the furnishings and amenities the height of luxury.

'This is amazing,' she murmured. 'I've never been on such a plane.'

'Not even the royal jet?' Rico returned with a quirk of his eyebrow.

Halina shook her head. 'Not even then.'

He stared at her for a moment, and Halina gazed back, uncertain how to navigate this moment. How to navigate every moment. She couldn't discern what he was thinking, what feelings, what fears or desires, lurked beneath his hard, metallic gaze, if any. Rico Falcone was a completely closed book and she had no idea what its pages held.

'When you're rested and refreshed,' Rico said implacably, 'we'll talk.'

Halina nodded and Rico walked back out to the main cabin, closing the door behind him. She sank onto the bed with a sigh of relief, glad to be alone for a few moments, away from the intensity of Rico's presence. She was desperate to wash, and also to think. To figure out what her next steps were…because Rico certainly knew his.

She spent far longer than necessary in the bath, luxuriating in the hot water and fragrant bubbles. The Palace of Forgotten Sands was forgotten in more ways than one; there had been no updating of its interior in over a hundred years, which meant her washing facilities, along with everything else, had been depressingly basic. A long, lovely soak went a good way to restoring her strength and spirit.

There were clothes in her size in one of the wardrobes, and Halina wondered if Rico had had them chosen specially for her. Or did he simply have a woman's wardrobe on hand for whatever mistress was his flavour of the week?

Pushing the thought out of her mind, she dressed in a pale-blue shift dress that, despite being her usual size, hung off her currently gaunt frame. She'd lost more weight than she'd realised in the last few weeks. Twisting her hair up into a loose bun, Halina squared her shoulders and then went to meet her fate.

Rico was sprawled on one of the sofas, a laptop in front of him, his forehead furrowed in a frown. He looked as sexy and as self-assured as ever, having changed into a knit shirt in charcoal-grey and dark trousers, both garments fitting his body to perfection and emphasising his incredible physique.

He looked up as soon as she entered, and then snapped his fingers. A staff member sprang forward.

'Sparkling water, orange juice and a full breakfast for both of us,' he ordered. 'And I'll have coffee as well.'

'Very good, sir.'

Halina watched as the man hurried to carry out his employer's orders. 'Are all your staff terrified of you?' she asked as she sat down opposite Rico, tucking her legs to the side to avoid his own long outstretched ones. She was determined not to be caught on the back foot, as she had been ever since Rico had stormed into her room at the palace. Now she would regain some control and all her composure. She knew she needed both for whatever lay ahead.

'Why should they be terrified of me?'

'Because you shout at them.'

'I didn't shout.' He looked mildly annoyed by her observation. 'I gave an order. There is a difference.'

'Is there? You don't seem to use "please" or "thank you" the way most people do.'

His mouth compressed. 'I do not like to waste time with useless fripperies, but I can be as polite as the next person.'

Halina looked away, wondering why she was baiting him over such a trivial matter at such a tense and crucial moment. Maybe because she felt so raw, chafing under his endless orders. He fully intended to command her life, and the truth was she didn't think there was anything she could do about it, except perhaps face it head on.

'So.' She squared her shoulders and met his narrowed look directly. 'What do you mean, you're going to marry me in Rome?' Rico regarded Halina and the way she was bracing herself, as if for bad news.

'Exactly that,' he informed her crisply.

'I have to say, your proposal could use some work.'

'I imagine it's a sight better than your last fiancé's,' Rico remarked with a touch of acid, nettled, even though he knew he shouldn't be. 'As I've heard it, you never even met him.'

'No,' Halina said slowly. 'I didn't. Not until a few weeks ago, anyway.'

Rico drew up short at that. He'd known the marriage had been called off, but he hadn't realised Halina had actually seen al bin Nur. 'You saw Prince Zayed recently? Since we…?'

'Yes, *since we.*' Her smile was tinged with wry sorrow. 'When my father found out I was pregnant, he tried to reopen marriage negotiations with Prince Zayed.' Fury flashed through Rico, a lightning strike of emotion he quickly suppressed. So his fears that another man might raise his child had been justified, making him realise how right he'd been to take drastic measures in finding Halina.

'And?' he asked, biting the word off and spitting it out.

'And I refused him, because I didn't want to marry a man who loved another.'

'Who does the Prince love? The governess he kidnapped by accident?' Contempt dripped from every word; how could a man be so unprepared, so foolish, as to abduct the wrong woman and, even worse, fall in love with her? Weakness twice over.

'Yes.' Halina's eyes flashed darkly. 'They fell in love with each other out in the desert, and I wanted them to be happy. And,' she added, flinging out the word, 'I didn't want to bind myself to someone who could never love me.' There was a challenge in her words, in her eyes, as if daring him to disagree, to disabuse her of such a notion—and so he would, without compunction.

'You were willing to do so before, it seems.'

'I knew Prince Zayed didn't love me before,' Halina clarified, 'but he could have grown to love me in time, as we'd come to know one another. To go into a situation knowing it will never happen…that the man you have bound yourself to for ever will never feel even the smallest affection for you…that is truly hopeless. It is total despair.'

Her words hammered through him, echoing emptily. Rico's mouth twisted. 'And yet here we are,' he observed.

She gave a small, strained smile, the knowledge of

their situation clouding and darkening her eyes. 'Yes. Here we are.'

He regarded her closely, trying to gauge her mood. Acceptance, resignation, or something else? 'I take it then you have no objections to our marriage?' he said after a moment, making it not quite a question.

'If you mean will I resist then, no, I won't.' She turned her head to look out of the window, acting as condemned as a prisoner in the dock.

'You will want for nothing,' Rico informed her, his tone harsher than he'd intended. 'I can promise you that.'

She turned back to stare at him, her expression bleak. 'No, you can't, Rico. You can't promise me anything. You don't know me, and you cannot presume to know either what is in my head or my heart. But if you meant I will live in comfortable circumstances...' She glanced around the plane, appearing deliberately unimpressed despite her earlier comments about the jet's luxury. 'Then, yes, I believe that.'

Rico stared at her, trying to suppress the ever-deepening twinge of annoyance her words caused. He shouldn't care what she thought or felt, only that she wasn't going to protest their inevitable marriage. Yet somehow her attitude of resignation rankled, as if he were marching her towards a noose rather than down an aisle.

'I'm glad to hear you will not attempt some pointless protest.'

She let out a huff of humourless laughter. 'Exactly. It would be pointless. My life has never been my own. I suppose it doesn't matter much whether it is you or my father who is pulling the strings.'

'I think it would matter at least a little,' Rico returned. 'As my wife you will certainly have some freedom and autonomy. More, I think, than you would have had otherwise, should you have married Prince Zayed or stayed in your father's home.'

Halina's eyes flashed dark fire. 'Prison is prison, no matter how gilded the cage.'

Although it wasn't an avenue of discussion he really wanted to explore, Rico could not keep from asking, 'What is the alternative, Halina? You are carrying my child. What would you propose, if not marriage?' He thought of the way she'd hidden from him. 'Would you really want to live the rest of your life out in the desert to escape me?'

She was silent for a long moment, gazing out of the window at the azure sky, her expression thoughtful and a little sad. Rico felt himself getting tenser and tenser. *What was she thinking?* And why did he want to know so badly?

'When I was a little girl,' Halina began slowly, 'I had this daydream. I wanted to live in Paris, in one of those tall, old houses, like Madeleine in the children's story. Do you know those books?' Wordlessly Rico shook his head. 'I had them as a child, given to me by my French god-mother. I loved them.' She lapsed into silence and Rico waited, having no idea where she was going with this.

'I pictured it all in my head,' she continued in a dreamy, faraway voice. 'I used to decorate it in my imagination. I'd live on the top floor, and there would be vines climbing outside and big French windows that opened onto a balcony with wrought-iron railings. I'd grow flowers and herbs in pots and I'd sit outside and sip my coffee and look at the world bustling below.' She smiled, caught in the memory, and Rico stared at her, bewildered. He had no idea what to say. What to think.

'And there was a piano in the living room,' Halina continued. 'A grand piano that I played on. I'd give music lessons as well, and I'd have a tin of sweets on top of the piano to hand out to children when they were good. And when I wasn't working I'd go outside and wander through the Tuileries Gardens—they were mentioned in the Madeleine books as well—and sketch.' She glanced up at him, a hint of a smile in her eyes. 'Do you know, I've never actually been to Paris? This is all just in my dreams.'

'Perhaps you'll visit there one day,' Rico said gruffly. 'With me.'

'Perhaps.' Halina turned back to the window. 'The thing is,' she said softly, 'I always knew I'd never live that dream. I'd never even have the chance. I've never had any say in my life, Rico. That's why I went to the party that night in Rome. The night I met you.' She drew a shuddering breath. 'I just wanted one evening to myself, to make my own choices.' She let out a hollow laugh. 'And look what a disaster that was. Perhaps my father was right all along in restricting my life so much. Maybe I'm not capable of making my own choices, or at least wise ones. But I've always wanted the chance. I still do.'

Her words resonated uncomfortably inside him, because in a strange way he could relate to them. His childhood had been entirely different to Halina's; she'd been cosseted, protected, privileged. He'd grown up first on the docks and then in the orphanage, both places of nothing more than grim survival. And yet he'd felt as trapped and restricted as she had, and his only choice had been to fight his way out. To be seen as cold, arrogant, ruthless. Because at least then he was in control. At least then he couldn't be hurt.

What was Halina's choice?

She didn't need one, Rico reminded himself. He would provide for her, protect her, give her every luxury she could possibly want. All this nonsense about an apartment in Paris was just a childish dream, meant to be discarded and forgotten upon adulthood.

Their breakfasts arrived, putting an end to any more whimsical conversation.

'You need to eat,' Rico reminded her as he watched Halina push the eggs around her plate. 'Keep up your strength.'

'I know.' She took a tiny bite of dry toast. 'I've just been feeling so ill.'

Which reminded him that she hadn't yet seen a doctor. 'As soon as we arrive in Rome, I want you to be checked over. I'm sure something can be prescribed for your nausea.'

'Hopefully,' Halina murmured, her gaze downcast. She took another bite of toast. Rico regarded her in growing frustration, unsure why he felt so dissatisfied.

He'd found her, he'd got her on the plane and they were now only mere hours from Rome. She'd already agreed to marry him. He was getting everything he wanted, and still he felt disgruntled and annoyed. *Hurt.*

The word popped into his head and he suppressed it immediately. He wasn't hurt. He never felt hurt. He'd never allowed himself to feel such a thing, not since his father had walked away from him while he'd watched. If he was bothered by Halina's lukewarm response to the idea of their marriage, then he knew just how to rev up her enthusiasm.

In bed.

CHAPTER EIGHT

HALINA TOOK A deep breath as she gazed at her pale reflection in the mirror the morning after her arrival in Rome. The last twenty-four hours had been a whirlwind of activity and movement: a limousine had met them at the airport and taken them to Rico's penthouse apartment in a sleekly elegant modern building near the Spanish Steps.

Halina had stepped into the sprawling luxury, too tired to be dazzled or impressed by the striking minimalist architecture and hand-crafted pieces of furniture. She'd felt as if she were a tiny boat being tossed on an endless stormy sea and Rico was the one controlling the wind and the waves.

As soon as they'd arrived he had shown her to the guest bedroom and practically ordered her to rest. For once Halina had been glad to obey. She was so tired she was swaying on her feet.

'Will you tell my father where I am?' she'd asked as she stood on the threshold of her bedroom. 'So at least he won't worry?'

Rico had given a terse nod, his expression flinty. 'I think he already knows, but I will inform him of our plans at a suitable time.'

'And when will that be?'

Rico had shrugged. 'When I decide it is.'

Of course. He decided everything. She'd turned into the bedroom and closed the door in Rico's face. At least she had control over that.

Six hours of sleep later, Halina was feeling refreshed physically even as her emotions remained wrung out. She lay in bed and relived the last twenty-four hours— the escape from the palace, the terrifying sandstorm, the flight to Rome. It all felt incredible, almost as if it had happened to someone else, scenes out of an action film or a melodrama. Until she'd met Rico Falcone, her life had been quiet, contained and definitely dull. Now, she acknowledged wryly, it was merely contained.

By the time she awoke from her nap, dusk was falling over the city. Rico knocked on her door, telling her she needed to eat, which seemed to be his constant refrain. Halina went out and managed to choke down some soup before retreating to bed before Rico could ask her any more questions or give her any more orders.

'I have made an appointment for you to see a doctor tomorrow morning,' he informed her as she headed for her bedroom. 'You need to start taking better care of yourself.'

She didn't trust herself to answer in a civil manner, so she merely nodded. Alone in bed that night, misery rushed over her. She'd thought being locked away in a palace in the remote desert of Abkar had been bad enough, but amazingly this actually felt worse. She was so alone. Rico was a hostile stranger who seemed intent on blaming her for everything, yet still intended her to marry him. What would her life be like with Rico? What would her child's life be like?

For a few seconds Halina imagined resisting. Running away, carving some kind of life for herself. But where would she go, and what would she do? She had no money, no clothes even, and her life skills were, she knew, pitiable. She could speak three languages, play two instruments and make sparkling conversation when required. They were not exactly qualifications for making her own way in the world.

She hated feeling so trapped. Yet her one bid to escape her gilded shackles had resulted in her ruin, so she hardly trusted herself to try again, even if she could have worked up the courage or the means.

'Halina?' Rico knocked on the door of her bedroom, startling her out of her gloomy thoughts. 'We leave in twenty minutes for the doctor.'

'All right.' She turned away from her wan reflection and opened the door. Rico stood there, looking both glorious and impatient, dressed in a pin-striped suit in deep navy, his eyes glinting like metal, his jaw freshly shaven and his hair spiky and slightly damp from the shower. He smelled of sandalwood, and the scent of him hit Halina like a fist squeezing her heart. She remembered his hands on her body all over again, the honeyed persuasion of his kiss.

With effort she yanked her gaze away from him and walked past him into the living room. 'I'm ready.'

'I sent out for some things I thought you might like to eat.' Halina turned, surprised to see a flash of uncertainty on Rico's rugged features. She didn't think she'd ever seen him look that way before.

'Thank you.'

'There are some pastries and fresh fruit, and also ginger tea. I read that ginger helps with nausea.'

Surprise rippled through her. 'You've been reading up on it?'

He shrugged. 'I want to know as much as I can. Information is vital.'

'Thank you,' Halina said again. She felt strangely touched by his concern, although another part of her acknowledged how little it was in the larger scheme of things. But maybe she'd just have to get used to little, at least in terms of affection or concern. Rico hardly seemed likely to offer anything else.

Rome was shimmering under a haze of heat as they stepped outside Rico's apartment. He held open the door of the limousine and she slid inside, edging to the far side as Rico sat next to her, seeming to take up all the space and air. Heat emanated from his powerful body and strength radiated from every taut muscle. The sheer power of his charisma left her breathless. She'd forgotten how overwhelming he was, and she was reminded again and again of that fact every time she went near him. It was no wonder she hadn't been able to resist him back at that party.

'So, do you live in Rome all the time?' she asked as the limo pulled smoothly into the traffic. 'I don't actually know that much about you.' Or anything, really, except that he was rich, ruthless and arrogant. *And fabulous in bed.*

'Most of the time.' Rico swiped his phone and slid it into his pocket, giving her his full attention, which felt like stepping into a spotlight. 'I travel for business to my various concerns and properties, most of which are in Europe.'

'Your penthouse isn't really suitable for a baby,' Halina said impulsively. 'Would I live there?'

Rico stared at her for a moment, his expression unfathomable. 'Of course we will need to work out the details, but I would most likely buy a house in Rome suitable for a family.'

For a second Halina let herself imagine it—a happy home, a place she could decorate and fill with music and art, books and laughter. A place of her own, of their own, where she and Rico could learn to live and maybe even love together. But of course it wouldn't be like that. How it would be, she didn't yet know.

'And when will we marry?' she asked eventually. The silence between them had become strained, tense, as it always seemed to.

Rico looked out of the window. 'Let's concentrate on today and making sure you and our child are both healthy. After that we can focus on the wedding.'

The doctor's office was upscale and comfortable, with a staff member fluttering around them making sure they had everything they needed, including fresh juice and coffee.

Halina's nerves started to jangle as she stepped into the examining room with Rico right behind her. The doctor smiled at her and introduced herself.

'My name is Maria Loretto. Signor Falcone has engaged me to be your obstetrician.'

Halina nodded and shook her hand. 'Thank you.'

'So the first thing we need to do is ascertain how far along you are.' Maria gestured for her to sit on the examining table, and nervously Halina perched on its end. 'If you know the date of your last period…'

'We know the date of conception,' Rico interjected flatly. Halina closed her eyes. Did he have to control this too?

Maria glanced up. 'If you're sure of it…'

'I'm sure. It was June twenty-fifth.'

Colour scorched Halina's cheeks and she stayed silent while Maria calculated her due date. 'So you are just over ten weeks along,' she said cheerfully. 'And your due date is March nineteenth.'

Halina let out a shaky laugh and instinctively pressed

one hand against her still-flat middle. Somehow just those words made it feel so much more real. For the last two months she'd been merely existing, feeling wretched and uncertain and afraid, barely able to contemplate what was ahead of her. But now the reality, the good reality, of her situation hit her with encouraging force. A baby. A child.

'Now we can check the heartbeat,' Maria continued. 'You're just far enough along perhaps to hear it with a Doppler. Would you mind lying down?'

Halina lay back on the examining table, feeling weirdly vulnerable as Maria lifted her top. She switched on the Doppler and then pressed the wand onto Halina's stomach, hard enough to make her flinch.

'You're hurting her.' The words seemed to burst out of Rico; he looked tense, almost angry, his jaw clenched. Unfazed, the doctor gave him a reassuring smile.

'Halina is fine, Signor Falcone, and babies are remarkably resilient.'

Rico still looked unhappy about it and Halina reached out one hand, almost but not quite touching him. 'I'm fine, Rico.'

He nodded once and then they heard it, the most amazing sound Halina had ever listened to. It sounded like a cross between the whooshing of waves and the galloping of a horse. Their baby's heartbeat.

'There it is,' Maria said with satisfaction. 'Nice and strong.'

'That's amazing.' Halina felt near to tears, but when she turned to look at Rico, instinctively wanting to share this moment with him, he'd turned away as if he wasn't affected at all.

The sound seemed to fill the room, rushing and strong, the sound of hope. Rico clenched his jaw, forcing the sudden and unexpected rush of emotion back. It was just a sound, yet it filled him with joy and terror in equal measures. Their child. A human being that they had created, that he would be responsible for. That he would love.

He glanced at Halina out of the corner of his eye and saw how moved she looked, her eyes bright with tears. No matter how much he wanted to keep things on a businesslike level between them, this was an emotional business for them both. How could it be otherwise?

'Halina's been feeling very nauseous,' he told the obstetrician, his voice terser than he meant it to be. 'As you can see, she hasn't been taking care of herself.' Halina sucked in a quick breath and belatedly Rico realised how that sounded. But he was *worried*, damn it, and he didn't like being worried.

'I can prescribe something for the nausea,' Maria said. 'But first I'd advise fresh air, plenty of rest and lots of good, wholesome food. Have you been able to have all those recently, Halina?'

Was there a knowledgeable glint in the doctor's eye? Rico hadn't informed her of their circumstances, and he didn't like the thought of her knowing.

'Not exactly,' Halina murmured.

'But she will now,' Rico said firmly. Taking care of Halina would be his priority. Taking care of his unborn child.

'Then I'd suggest you come back to me in a week or two, Halina,' Maria said. 'And we'll discuss medication then. You do look a bit run down.'

She smiled sympathetically and Halina nodded and rose from the table, pulling down her shirt. 'All right. Thank you.' Her head was bowed, her dark hair swinging in front of her face. Rico had no idea what she was thinking. Feeling.

Why did he care?

Because of their baby. For the sake of his child, he needed to care about Halina. About her moods as well as her health. It was all part of the same package. Satisfied with his reasoning, he took her arm as he thanked the doctor and then escorted her out of the building into the waiting limo.

'What now?' Halina asked listlessly as she stared out of the window at the city streaming by. Rico wished she didn't sound so damned downtrodden. When he'd met her, he'd been as intrigued by her humour and spirit as he had been by her lush, curvy body. Now both were gone and he wanted to bring back the Halina he'd only just come to know—bring back the sparkle in her eyes, the impish smile to her mouth and, yes, the curves on the woman whose body had made his palms itch to touch her.

But bringing a smile to her face felt like the most important thing right now.

'What would you like to do now?' Rico asked, seeming to surprise them both. She turned to him, her eyes widening, jaw dropping in shock.

'You're asking me what I want?'

'Why shouldn't I?'

'Because you're King of the World, Maker of All Decisions Ever?'

'That is a slight exaggeration.' His mouth twitched; he was heartened to see even that little display of spirit. 'But only slight.'

'Of course.'

'Perhaps I should put that on my business card. It's quite catchy, as a title.'

Her mouth curved just a little. 'You're joking with me.'

'Shouldn't I?'

'No, it's just…' Her smile faded. 'I don't know you,

Rico, at all. And yet you're the father of my child and soon you're likely to be my husband.'

'There's no likely about it,' Rico couldn't keep from saying, his voice hardening, that moment of levity vanishing like morning mist.

Halina sighed and turned back to the window. 'Exactly.'

Frustration boiled within him. Why could he never get this right? He wasn't used to feeling wrong-footed, unsure, wanting something he couldn't have. 'So what is it you'd like to do today?'

She shrugged, her face still to the window. 'I don't care.'

He found he hated her apathy. 'I'm giving you a choice, Halina—'

'Oh, that's right.' She whirled to face him, a sudden and surprising fury lighting her eyes and twisting her features. 'You're *giving* me a choice. I suppose I should trip all over myself to say thank you for that unimaginable kindness.' He opened his mouth to speak but found he had nothing to say. 'And tomorrow, perhaps, you won't give me a choice. Tomorrow I'll be informed of our plans without any discussion and expected to fall in line immediately *or else.*'

'You are talking about something that hasn't happened yet.'

'You don't get it, do you?' She shook her head in weary despair. 'You never will. I tried to explain before, but you're so used to ordering the universe you can't imagine what it feels like to be the one ordered about. And as privileged as my life has been—and I'm not stupid… I know it has—it's also always been ordered and arranged by someone else. So if you want to know what I want today, Rico, I'll tell you. I want my freedom, and that is something you'll never give me.' She broke off, breathing heavily, turning back to the window as she struggled to compose herself.

Rico sat back, stunned speechless by her outburst. Yes, he understood her life had been restricted and that she resented that, but he hadn't realised how bitterly she chafed against it, against *him*. How she now saw him as her captor, her commander. And he suddenly felt sympathy for her that was both overwhelming and inconvenient.

'Actually,' he said after a moment, keeping his voice mild, 'I do know what that feels like.'

Halina let out a huff of disbelieving laughter, her face still turned firmly towards the window. 'Yeah, right.'

'As you said yourself just a few moments ago, you don't actually know me. So how can you say whether I've felt something or not?'

She stayed silent for a long moment and then she turned towards him. Her face was still flushed, but that moment of furious rebellion had left her, and bizarrely Rico found he missed it. 'Tell me, then.'

But did he actually want to tell her? This was all becoming a bit too…intimate. Rico hesitated, debating the pros and cons of admitting something of his past to her. Then he decided he could tell her. He just wouldn't get emotional about it.

'Well?' Halina lifted her chin, a challenge in her dark gaze. 'Are you going to tell me or not?'

CHAPTER NINE

HALINA SAW THE indecision flicker in Rico's silvery eyes and knew he was regretting admitting even as little as he had to her. He didn't want her to know him. Didn't want to be known.

'For all my childhood, I had little control,' he said at last, his voice toneless. 'Over anything.'

'Most children have little control,' Halina answered with a shrug, determined not to trip all over herself in eager gratitude now that he was sharing something with her. 'Isn't that the nature of childhood?'

'I suppose it is.' His jaw was tight, his eyes flinty. Perhaps she shouldn't have been so dismissive simply because she was frustrated and feeling trapped. She did want to know more about the man she was going to marry, and if Rico was willing to open up even a little she wanted and needed to encourage that.

'How was your childhood different, Rico?' she asked in a gentler tone. 'What was it like?' She really did want to know, and she was sorry for her flippancy.

His lips compressed, his gaze turning distant. 'As it happens,' he remarked in a cool, matter-of-fact tone, 'I never knew my mother. She was a waitress who had a fling with my father. She didn't want the baby—me—and so she left me with my father when I was two weeks old.'

'Oh.' The word was a soft gasp of sorrow. She had assumed, she realised, that Rico was from as great a world of privilege as her own. He certainly acted as if he had always been entitled, had always expected obedience, or even obeisance. She'd had no idea that he'd been born in such lowly, unfortunate circumstances.

'Yes, oh.' His mouth twisted with wry grimness. 'My father worked on the docks, and I don't think he was best pleased to have a baby foisted on him, even his own.'

'Oh,' Halina said again, helplessly. 'That must have been… What did he do?'

'He kept me, to his credit.' Rico flicked his gaze away for a second before he turned resolutely back to face her, his face bland. 'Raised me himself, with help from some kindly neighbours who looked after me when I was small.' His lips thinned. 'It could have been worse.'

'So you never knew your mother at all? You grew up with your father?'

'Until I was nine.' Rico shrugged, as if to dismiss the matter. 'Then I ended up in an orphanage in Salerno. A convent, run by nuns who didn't like children very much, as far as I could tell. That's where I really grew up. I left when I was sixteen and never looked back.'

Sadness clutched at Halina's heart. It sounded like a truly miserable childhood—not a childhood at all. 'Oh, Rico, that sounds horrible. So lonely—'

'I've never been lonely.' He cut across her. 'I've never needed to feel lonely, because long ago I learned to depend only on myself.' He paused, adding a certain emphasis to the words, making her realise that he wasn't just talking about his childhood. He was talking about now, about not needing anyone now. Not needing her.

'But the real reason I told you all this,' Rico resumed,

'is to explain that I do know how you feel when you say you're trapped and want freedom.'

Halina flushed and looked down. It sounded as if Rico's life had been far more restricted than hers had ever been. She felt ashamed, a spoilt princess whingeing for even more than she already had. 'I'm sorry for doubting you. I never would have guessed… How did you get to where you are now?'

'Determination, hard work and a little bit of luck. Perhaps more than a little bit.' His eyes flashed with fire. 'I bought my first property when I was nineteen, a run-down warehouse near the docks, and turned it into a gym. I sold it for twenty times what I paid for it when I was twenty-one and then never looked back.'

Halina shook her head slowly. 'That is truly amazing, Rico. You're an inspiration.'

He gave a nod of acknowledgement and thanks. 'So, now I shall ask you again. What would you like to do this afternoon?'

Halina stared at him thoughtfully, wondering what she could suggest that Rico would agree to, that could be fun for them both. Because now that he'd shared something of his life, that surprising insight into a difficult childhood, she realised she wanted to spend time with him. To get to know him, to crack open the door into his mind, if not his heart, and gain another tantalising glimpse.

If they were going to be married, she needed to know this man. Understand him and hopefully even like him.

'What do you recommend?' she asked. 'I spent all my secondary schooling in Italy, but I've never actually seen any sights.'

'That's tragic.'

'Have you?' she challenged and his lips twitched.

'I'm too busy to sightsee.'

'Of course you are. But today…?'

He glanced out of the window, his expression as thoughtful as her own. 'We could see the Colosseum. That's something I've always wanted to visit.'

Halina's heart leapt with excitement and a strange hope. This was new, doing something together just for fun. Not sex, not squabbling, just simple pleasure, spending time with each other. 'All right,' she said. 'Let's see that.'

Rico insisted on lunch first, so they ate in the private garden of an elegant bistro only steps from the Colosseum. The food was fresh and delicious, a refreshing breeze ruffling the leaves of the plane trees that offered some much-needed shade.

Halina sat back as they waited for their food, feeling surprisingly happy for the first time in months. Maybe even longer. Her heart was light, anticipation burgeoning inside her.

'You're smiling,' Rico noted as he twirled his wine glass between long, lean fingers.

'I am, actually,' she admitted as her smile widened. 'This is very nice, Rico. Thank you.'

'You're welcome.' He tilted his head, his silvery, heavy-lidded gaze sweeping over her in assessment, considering. 'You're quite easily pleased, you know.'

'Do you really think so?' Halina took a sip of her sparkling water. 'I suppose, after the last few months, I am.'

Rico's eyes narrowed. 'What does that mean exactly?'

Halina bit her lip and looked away. 'It doesn't really matter.' She didn't want to drag up all those painful memories, only to have Rico question and doubt her and definitely spoil the fun but fragile mood that had begun to develop between them.

'And I think it does.' He leaned forward, as intent as

a predator on its prey, and just as lethal. 'You have never told me about the time between your visits to Rome. Why you didn't see a doctor. How you ended up in that remote palace.'

'I thought you believed I'd gone there to escape from you,' Halina returned. She'd meant to sound light but a note of bitterness crept in. How could he have made so many assumptions? But how could she be surprised that he had?

'It was the first thought that came to my mind,' Rico acknowledged. 'But perhaps that is because of my experience, not yours. Now I'd like to hear in your own words how you came to be at that palace.' He paused, gazing down into the glinting ruby depths of his wine. 'How did your family take the news of your pregnancy?'

'Not well.' The two words scraped Halina's throat and she took another sip of water. 'Not well at all, to be perfectly frank.'

Rico frowned. 'I thought your father doted on you.'

She laughed, the sound rather grim. 'Where did you hear that?'

'I hired a private investigator to find you. He found that the general sense was that your father doted on you, and that you were rather spoiled.' His gaze, when she dared to meet it, was steady and clear, without judgement or pity. 'Is that true?'

'It *was* true,' Halina said after a moment, when she trusted her voice to be as steady as his gaze. 'But it all changed when I ruined myself.'

Rico's eyebrows drew together in a straight line, his frown turning into a scowl so that he looked quite ferocious. 'Tell me what happened.'

'What I should have expected would happen,' Halina answered with a shrug. Even now she couldn't believe how stupid, how utterly naive, she'd been, and in so many ways. About Rico, about her father, about life. 'My parents were beyond furious with me. When the negotiations with Prince Zayed broke down, my father had been hoping to marry me to someone else, someone he deemed suitable, who would afford us another political alliance. My disgrace precluded that.'

'Surely in this day and age a woman's virginity is not a prerequisite, even for a royal marriage?'

'In my country, in my culture, it is. And I knew that.' She shook her head. 'All along I knew that, and yet still I acted as if the consequences wouldn't apply to me.' She tried for a twisted smile. 'I suppose you truly did sweep me away, Rico.'

'It was mutual,' Rico said after a brief pause. 'If I'd had any sense myself, any ability to think straight, I would have realised how innocent you were. And I wouldn't have touched you.'

'Was it that obvious?'

'In hindsight, yes. So what did your father do?'

'He was livid with me, first of all. Utterly enraged, as well as disappointed. I'm not sure which felt worse.' She shook her head, the memories assailing her like hammer blows. 'And when he found out I was pregnant…'

'How did he find out, as a matter of interest?'

'He made me take a pregnancy test,' Halina said simply. 'At the earliest opportunity. And then he tried to have Prince Zayed marry me, spoiled goods that I was, because he didn't think anyone else would have me. And when that didn't work out…' She gulped, not wanting to go on, closing her eyes against the harshness of the memory that still hurt her even now.

'What?' Rico demanded roughly. 'Whatever it is, tell

me, Halina. Surely it can't be worse than another man claiming my child?'

She saw how the skin around his lips had gone white, his eyes hard and metallic. He was angry, but with her father, not with her. Would he be even angrier when she told him the whole truth?

'You have to understand,' Halina said slowly. 'My father is a good man. A loving man.' She had to believe that, because if she didn't what did she have? A father who had never actually truly loved her? 'But,' she continued painfully, 'he was in very difficult circumstances…'

'It sounds as if you were in very difficult circumstances,' Rico interjected shortly.

Yes, she had been, but the circumstances had been of her own making. And she supposed she wanted to explain her father's actions—absolve him, even—because she still loved him and wanted to believe he loved her. Otherwise, what was love, that he could be doting one minute and damning the next? How did you trust it, if it could so easily turn into something else? What was love, if you couldn't forgive a mistake, an insult, an open wound?

'Halina,' Rico said, and it sounded like a warning.

'He tried,' Halina confessed in a low voice, 'To make me have an abortion.'

Rico stared at Halina, her pale face, her pain-filled eyes, and felt a whole new kind of fury sweep through him—a tidal wave of anger and indignation and, beneath those, a deep, soul-reaching pain.

'He tried?' he repeated in a growl. 'What do you mean by that?'

'He insisted, and he wouldn't listen to me at all. My mother agreed with him, and they took me to a discreet doctor. Forced me.' She blinked rapidly but a tear fell anyway, glistening on her cheek like a diamond. Rico's fists clenched on the table. 'I fought the whole way, tooth and nail.' She stared at him, her eyes huge. 'You have to believe that, Rico. I would never want to get rid of my child. I begged and pleaded, I cried and fought. I did.' She let out a choked cry, one trembling fist pressed to her mouth.

'I do believe it,' he said in a low voice. It was impossible not to when he could feel her desperation and grief like a tangible thing, a shroud covering her. 'So, what happened then?'

'The doctor refused to perform the operation,' Halina whispered. 'Because I was fighting against it so much. My father was furious, but in the midst of it all I think he saw where his own anger had led him, and he was ashamed.' She swiped at the tear still glistening on her cheek. 'I have to believe that.'

And Rico understood that too, because he'd felt the same about his own father for many years, trying to excuse the inexcusable, to give a good reason for cruelty towards a child. Towards him. You could twist the truth into knots to try to make it an acceptable shape, but it all came apart eventually, and he'd had to acknowledge the hard, unvarnished reality. His father just hadn't cared.

'So he sent you to the Palace of Forgotten Sands,' Rico said flatly. 'He banished you.'

Halina nodded, swallowing hard in an attempt to restore her shaky composure. 'Yes, I was meant to remain there until the baby was born.'

'And afterwards?'

'I… I don't know.' Halina bit her lip. 'My father said he would take my baby away from me, but I hoped… I hoped in time he would change his mind and let me keep him or her.' She pressed one hand to her belly. 'I can't believe he would have been so cruel to me or his own grandchild.'

Rico sat back, his mind whirling with all the revelations Halina had just levelled at him. He'd misjudged her badly, assuming she'd been acting on her own selfish whims, going to a remote location to keep his child from him. It had been a stupid assumption, founded on his own unfortunate experience and the ensuing prejudices he still had about mothers and fathers, about family, about love.

Because he'd never experienced a mother's love, a father's trust. Because he'd assumed Halina would act in as selfish and capricious a manner as his own mother had done. He'd been wrong. So very wrong.

'I'm sorry you went through all that,' he said finally. 'And I'm sorry I assumed...' He paused, realising how much he'd assumed. How much it must have hurt her, considering her true experience. 'I'm sorry,' he said again.

Halina nodded, pale-faced and spent now. 'That's why I didn't see an obstetrician,' she explained quietly. 'I wasn't given the chance.'

'I understand.' Rico spoke tautly, trying to control the raging anger he felt towards Halina's father. The man had no right to assume control over Halina's life, over their child's life. The thought that Halina might have been forced to terminate her pregnancy—end the life of his child—made Rico grind his teeth together. But his rage served no purpose now, not when Halina was looking at him so warily, as if afraid his anger might be directed at her. And why shouldn't she be afraid? Since snatching her from the desert palace, he'd assumed the worst of her at nearly every turn. Guilt, an unfamiliar emotion, lanced through him.

From the depths of his soul, a barren landscape until now, Rico summoned a smile. 'Let's put such unpleasant things behind us, Halina. The future will be different now—for you and for our baby, who will never know a day without the love of his or her mother and father. That is my promise.'

Halina nodded, but she didn't look much convinced, something which made guilt rush through Rico all over again. He could see now how arrogant and inconsiderate he'd been—announcing his dictates, never giving her a choice—and he vowed to do better in the future. He would provide for Halina, he would make her smile, he would see her blossom, so she could rediscover her old spirit and joy.

He just would do it without engaging any of his own emotions. Because even now, when his heart was nearly rent in two by Halina's sorrowful story, Rico steeled himself not to care. That was one place he could not go, and one thing he would never, ever give his bride-to-be. His heart. Even now, having shared and been entrusted with so much, he couldn't risk that much.

They spent the rest of lunch talking about inconsequential matters, then strolled through the sunshine to the Colosseum.

'Photographs don't do it justice!' Halina exclaimed as they walked through an archway, one of eighty. Although partially ruined, the Colosseum was still a magnificent and awe-inspiring structure with its high walls and many archways, the expanse of the old arena.

They roamed through its many corridors, reading each other bits from the guidebook—how it had been built by three different emperors and then had fallen to ruin a few hundred years later, much of its stone used to build other structures in Rome.

'It's horrible and beautiful all at once, isn't it?' Halina said as they stood on the viewing platform that overlooked what had once been the main arena. 'The architecture is so impressive, and yet so many people and animals suffered and died here terribly. It's awful to think about.'

Rico nodded. 'Beautiful things can be used for evil,' he said, feeling strangely sombre after their walk around the ancient archways and corridors. He felt as if he was sharing more than a mere tourist attraction with Halina; the way they'd talked together, reflecting on what they'd learned in the guidebook, was something he'd never done with a woman before, or really with anyone.

He didn't have friends, not beyond business colleagues, and women had been no more than mistresses, mere objects of sexual desire and fulfillment. Strolling in the sunshine on a summer's afternoon, sharing ideas, talking and listening, was all incredibly novel. And, he realised with a pang of unease, quite pleasant, which he hadn't expected at all.

He'd been viewing this afternoon as an expedient means to an end, a way to improve Halina's mood, gain her trust. But somewhere along the way it had turned into something else, something deeper and more meaningful, and he really didn't know how to feel about that because, the truth was, he didn't want to *feel* at all.

Halina glanced down at the guidebook. 'It says we shouldn't miss the museum in the inner walls of the top floor,' she remarked. 'It's dedicated to Eros.'

'Eros?'

'The god of love.'

'I know who Eros is,' Rico returned. 'I just don't know why they'd have a museum dedicated to him in a place that was used for torture and death.'

'Maybe that's why, to bring some light and hope to a place that has been the stage for so much darkness.' Halina's smile was teasing and playful, but her eyes looked serious and Rico felt a twinge of alarm, a deepening sense of unease.

Love did not bring light to the darkness; it wasn't the hope held out in a broken and damaged world. No, love was nothing but risk and pain, loss and weakness. He knew that because he'd made the grievous mistake of loving his father. A broken childhood might not be the best reason to avoid love, but it was Rico's, and it had affected him to the depths of his soul. It had made him determined not just to avoid love but revile it and all it meant. Because the alternative was unthinkable. Unbearable.

As he took Halina's arm and led her towards the stairs, Rico sincerely hoped that she wasn't holding out for some remnant of love from him. Surely she knew him better than that, even if their acquaintance had been limited so far?

If she didn't know it, he reflected grimly, he would certainly tell her as soon as possible, gently but firmly. He didn't want to hurt Halina any more than he already had, but the last thing he needed or wanted was a wife who was looking for that damnable emotion—love.

CHAPTER TEN

HALINA GAZED AT her reflection in the mirror, noting the colour in her cheeks, the new sparkle in her eyes. It had been two weeks since she'd arrived in Rome with Rico and the nausea was finally abating, thanks to plenty of rest, healthy food and fresh air, as well as simple time. She was nearly at the end of her first trimester, and her pregnancy—her baby—was becoming more real with every passing day.

The last two weeks had been surprisingly unpressured. Rico had been focused on restoring her health, and Halina had appreciated the chance to take long naps and baths, or simply sit out in the sun on the huge terrace off Rico's apartment. He'd hired a cook to make fresh, nourishing meals and had cancelled all his social engagements so he could be home as much as possible in the evenings after work.

He was acting every inch the loving, considerate husband except…he wasn't. After that first shocking conversation when he'd told her about his childhood, Rico had buttoned up, sharing no personal details, inviting no intimate conversations. Halina had missed it, had tried several times to engage him again, but any questions about his childhood, his feelings, his very self, had been firmly and sometimes brusquely shot down. Halina had a suspicion he regretted sharing as much as he had with her, and this was his way of retrenching.

That had been most apparent when they'd visited the museum dedicated to Eros at the Colosseum. They'd strolled through the galleries of frescoes and sculpture, terracotta vases and bas-reliefs, while Halina had read from the guidebook.

'The ancient poets describe Eros as an invincible force that can bring happiness but also destroy it.'

Rico had snorted, his hands shoved deep in his pockets. 'The latter is certainly true.'

Halina had glanced at him over the edge of the guidebook. 'You sound as if you've been in love,' she'd remarked, trying not to feel an inconvenient twinge of jealousy at the thought. Was that why he kept to mistresses, none of whom lasted longer than a week? To keep his heart from being broken again?

'Not *in* love,' Rico had corrected, then had refused to say anything more.

'I've never been in love,' Halina had remarked with an insouciant shrug. 'Never even close. Never had the chance.'

'Consider yourself fortunate, then.'

'What have you got against it?' She tried to keep her voice light, to disguise the hurt and, yes, the yearning she knew she felt. She might never have been in love but she wanted to be one day. And if she married Rico, *when* she married him, it seemed likely that she wouldn't be.

'You heard what the ancient poets said.' Rico paused to study a statue of Eros stringing his bow. 'It can destroy happiness. Who wants to tangle with that? And what about the whole concept of love being an arrow that hits you?' He nodded towards the marble figure.

'Something that is alleged to bring joy actually brings pain. That sounds about right.'

Halina stopped where she was and lowered the guide-book. 'Who hurt you, Rico?' she asked quietly. He jerked as if shot by the aforementioned arrow, his eyes narrowed.

'No one.'

'That can't be true, not with the way you're talking.'

He shrugged one powerful shoulder. 'It was a long time ago.'

'How long ago?'

'I don't want to talk about it, Halina.' His tone couldn't have been more repressive, and Halina didn't have the courage to press any more. But she wondered. Oh, how she wondered. What kind of woman had captured Rico's heart and made him as cold and closed-off as he was?

Because that was what she'd discovered over the last two weeks, pleasant as they had been. Rico had no interest in getting to know her, or being known himself. No desire to have a conversation that probed more deeply than the weather or the latest films. There was no need to deepen their relationship now that they were going to be married.

Tonight's party would be his way of introducing her to Roman society as his wife-to-be, and Halina quailed at the thought. She'd only been to one party before, and look how that had turned out. How was she going to be able to manage with everyone's eyes on her, and Rico remaining so solicitous yet so cold?

'Halina?' He knocked on the door of her bedroom. 'The limo is here.'

'All right.' Taking a deep breath, Halina gave her reflection one last inspecting glance. Yesterday Rico had taken her to the prestigious Via dei Condotti to shop in the city's most exclusive boutiques. She'd emerged from the various shops with half a dozen gold-corded bags filled with everything imaginable—lingerie, day dresses, casual clothes, evening gowns.

'I'm not sure what the point of all this is,' she'd told Rico. 'I'm going to start getting bigger soon and nothing will fit.'

He'd merely shrugged. 'You can wear them again after the baby is born. And you have a responsibility to look the part as my wife.'

A remark that had made her want to ask what their marriage was going to look like, what Rico expected from her in all sorts of ways. But she'd held her tongue because she wasn't ready for that conversation. Two weeks of rest had helped her a great deal in recovering both physically and emotionally from the last couple of harrowing months, but she didn't think she had the strength yet to tackle that emotional, explosive subject.

'I'm ready,' she called and, reaching for her gauzy wrap, she turned to the door. She took a deep breath and opened it to find Rico standing there, looking as devastatingly sexy and charismatic in his tuxedo as he had when she'd first laid eyes on him.

'Bella,' Rico murmured, his pupils flaring as his gaze travelled from the top of her head to the tips of her toes. He made no effort to disguise the heat simmering in the silvery depths of his eyes. 'Molta bella.'

Pleasure coiled within her like a tightly wound spring. She'd taken care with her appearance, styling her hair in a complicated up-do and applying make-up that was both subtle and effective, emphasising her lush mouth and dark eyes. As for the dress...

She'd chosen to wear one Rico hadn't seen during their shopping trip, an emerald-green full-length evening gown with a halter top and a plunging neckline. It was quite the most daring and sexy thing she'd even worn, and when Rico looked at her with so much unabashed desire she felt heady and powerful. She felt the way she had that fateful night two and a half months ago, and realised afresh how and why it had led her to abandon all common sense.

Rico stretched out one hand and drew her by the fingertips towards the living room and onto the terrace. The night was sultry and warm, the terrace lit only by a sliver of moon and the wash of lights from the buildings spread out before them in a living, breathing map.

'I want to give you this,' Rico said, and withdrew a small black velvet box from the inside pocket of his tuxedo jacket.

Halina's heart stuttered in her chest. 'Is that...?'

'Yes,' he replied as he opened it and showed her its contents. 'It is.'

Halina gazed down at the exquisite solitaire diamond that was big enough to reach to her knuckle. It glittered and sparkled in the darkness, its many facets catching the moonlight. 'It's beautiful,' she whispered. 'And huge.'

'Try it on.'

Wordlessly she held out her hand, unable to keep her fingers from trembling as Rico slid the massive ring onto her finger. It felt heavy, so much so that her hand faltered and Rico caught it up in his own, drawing her even more closely to him.

Their hips nudged and heat flared. This was the closest she'd been to him since the night of the sandstorm, when amidst the fear and uncertainty she'd almost lost her head. Again. Now dizzying sensation spiralled through her, and he was barely touching her.

'Now everyone will know you are mine,' Rico said as

he placed his hands on her bare shoulders and drew her even closer towards him. The brush of his lips against her was like an electric shock, twanging all the way through her as he deepened the kiss, turning it into a brand.

Halina swayed as Rico moved his mouth with firm, sure possession over hers, plundering its depths, taking control in this as he did in everything.

He broke the kiss first while stars danced behind her eyes and her knees nearly buckled. Blinking away the haze of desire, she saw his smugly satisfied smile.

'We will have a good marriage, Halina.'

'There's more to a marriage than that,' she returned shakily, and Rico's smile vanished, replaced by a wintry look.

'Not for us.'

She'd known it, of course she had, but it still hurt to have him spell it out so plainly. 'Why not, Rico?'

'What exactly are you asking me?'

'I guess I'm asking you what kind of marriage we will have,' Halina said slowly. Her heart had started beating with painful thuds. 'Because we've never even discussed it.' She held up her hand, heavy with the glittering ring. 'I don't even know when we're getting married.'

'In one month's time.'

'Have you told my father?'

'We'll send him an invitation.'

Halina cringed inwardly at his coolly dismissive tone. Despite the agonising way her father had hurt her, she still missed him and the rest of her family. She hated the thought of them not knowing how she was, or even where she was, but Rico had assured her Sultan Hassan knew she was with him—and that, Rico had said flatly, was all he needed to know.

Now she lowered her hand and gazed down at the ring.

'In one month,' she repeated slowly. 'And what about our marriage? What will it be like?' She hesitated, then dared to ask the question pulsing through her heart. 'I know you don't love me now, but would you ever, perhaps in time?'

She felt Rico stiffen as the seconds ticked on. 'I am not interested in love, Halina. It's an ephemeral emotion. It counts for nothing.'

Pain thudded through her. 'Yet you've said you would love our child.'

'That is different.'

'It's specifically romantic love you're talking about, then?'

A hesitation, telling, painful. 'Yes.'

Halina drew a deep breath. 'So you're telling me you'll never love me?'

'I'm telling you I will provide for you, protect you, seek your happiness above my own. What is love compared to all that?'

She stared at him sorrowfully, unsure of her answer but knowing with a leaden certainty that his wasn't enough.

Rico glanced across at Halina's thoughtful profile, wishing he could see into her mind, even as he acknowledged that he most likely didn't want to know what thoughts lingered there.

He'd planned for the ring—and the kiss—to seal the deal between them and bring her pleasure. What woman didn't like a nice piece of jewellery? And the ring he'd chosen was magnificent. But since the moment he'd slid it onto her finger Halina had cradled her hand as if it was too heavy, as if the ring were a burden or even a wound rather than a symbol of their forthcoming union.

His stomach cramped as he remembered how she'd

asked about the nature of their marriage, about whether he would ever come to love her. He'd been postponing such a conversation while Halina regained her strength; her health along with their child's was his main priority. But when asked so directly, he'd had to tell her the truth. He just hoped she could learn to live with it.

'So what is this party for?' she asked as the limo slid through Rome's traffic, the buildings blurring outside the car. She turned to him, looking so achingly lovely he longed to draw her towards him and kiss her lush, plump mouth. He could kiss away all her concerns and worries about the nature of their marriage; he was sure of it. What they would have together in bed would be far better than any tedious notions of love or affection.

He'd waited to reignite their physical relationship because he'd wanted her to feel better physically with her nausea and also because he'd wanted to gain her trust. But now he wondered if kissing away her concerns would be the most expedient option.

'Rico...?' Halina prompted, a frown crinkling her brow. Her eyes still looked sad, just as they had when she'd asked him earlier about their marriage.

'It's a charity event,' he replied. 'For street orphans.'

'Is that a charity you support?'

'Yes.' To the tune of millions of pounds, not that he would tell her as much. It was a charity that cut far too close to the bone, so he kept the amount of his giving secret. Few people knew the nature of his childhood, and no one knew about his father's rejection of him. He did not want to advertise his private shame, or cause people to pity him.

'And what will people there expect of me?' Halina asked, sounding nervous.

'The usual thing at parties. To chat and socialise.' He

smiled, wanting to lighten the mood and lift that sadness from her eyes. 'You surely know which fork to use with which course and other such matters?'

'Yes,' Halina allowed. 'But the socialising bit might be beyond me.' Rico looked at her in surprise and she let out a shaky laugh. 'Sometimes I think you have a completely skewed view of my life.'

'Oh?' He frowned, curious and a bit discomfited. He'd assumed, as she was a princess, she'd gone to plenty of parties, dozens of social occasions. 'Enlighten me, then.'

Halina shrugged. 'Before I met you, I'd been to exactly two parties, and they weren't parties the way you probably think of parties. They were diplomatic events at the palace—all I had to do was show up, bow my head and appear modest and subservient. I've never socialised beyond the schoolroom, and before the night I met you I'd never even worn a cocktail dress. This...' she gestured to the gorgeous gown that encased her lush body in a satiny sheath '...is the first evening gown I've ever worn.'

Rico's frown deepened as his wife-to-be surprised him yet again. Yes, he'd known Halina had had a sheltered and even restricted life behind the palace walls, but more and more she showed him just how small it had really been. And he wanted to make it bigger. 'What did you wear to the diplomatic events if not evening gowns?' he asked.

'Traditional dress. Very conservative.'

Something else he hadn't actively considered. 'Is this...these clothes, this lifestyle...difficult for you?'

She laughed, the sound crystalline and musical. 'Difficult? No, definitely not. I love these clothes. I love the freedom of going out to a party.' For a second something sad flickered across her face. 'Believe it or not, I have more freedom here with you in Rome than I did before in Abkar.' *But that's not saying all that much.*

Rico could practically see the thought bubble appearing over her head.

'Then I hope you enjoy tonight,' he said sincerely. 'It's your chance to shine.'

And shine she did as they stepped into the elegant ballroom of one of the city's best hotels. Halina was easily the most gorgeous woman in the room, looking like a brilliant green flame in her emerald evening gown. Rico steeled himself not to mind the curious and lustful looks slid her way by just about every male guest. The women looked too, just as intrigued by the woman on his arm. Rico waited until they'd attracted a decent-sized crowd before delivering the bombshell he knew would explode in the entire room.

'Please let me introduce Princess Halina of Abkar,' he said smoothly, his arm linked with Halina's. 'My fiancée.'

Murmurs of shock and surprise rippled through the room as Halina stiffened beside him. Rico pulled her a little closer, determined to stake his claim in every way possible. 'We will be married next month.'

'So soon?' a woman asked with acid sweetness. Rico didn't recognise her, but he certainly knew the tone. He held her gaze, putting iron into his own.

'Yes. Neither of us wish to wait.'

The woman's eyes narrowed and her mouth curved into a speculative smile. Halina put a protective hand over her belly and, from the ensuing ripple of murmurs that spread out through the crowd, Rico knew that just about everyone had seen that revealing action and judged it accurately.

'Let me get you some champagne,' he told Halina, and she gave him a wan smile.

'You mean sparkling water.'

Several people heard, adding fuel to the fires of speculation. Rico knew by the time the evening was at an end everyone there would know Halina was pregnant. Well, so be it. Halina's pregnancy would be physically apparent soon enough, and he would never be ashamed to claim his child.

He asked a waiter for a glass of sparkling water, then he began to move through the crowd, Halina pressed to his side.

As the hours wound down and the conversation and speculation swirled, Halina became quieter and quieter. At first she'd tried to enter into the various conversations, smiling and nodding, shyly offering her own opinions, but as time passed Rico sensed her withdrawing into herself.

After a five-course meal where they were seated on opposite sides of a table for twelve, she excused herself, disappearing for over twenty minutes before, both impatient and alarmed, Rico went to find her.

He strode down the hotel's opulent corridors, annoyed that he'd been compelled to leave the event to find his errant wife-to-be, even as he fought a growing sense of worry that something was really wrong with her. What if she was ill? What if, God forbid, something had happened to their child?

He asked the attentive staff of the hotel if they'd seen her, and finally tracked her down to the opulent women's powder room down one endless corridor. Not hesitating for a second, Rico rapped on the door.

'Halina? Halina, are you in there?' There was no reply, so he cracked open the door a bit and called again. 'Halina, please answer me if you're in there. Tell me you're all right.'

Two women came to the door, sidling past him with amused glances. 'So attentive,' one of them drawled, and the other gave an unpleasant cackle of laughter. Rico glared at them both.

'Is Princess Halina in the powder room?' he demanded.

One woman, looking spiteful now, shrugged a bony shoulder. 'Why don't you see for yourself?' she called as she walked off with the other woman, their angular bodies and raucous laughter reminding Rico of a pair of glossy, pecking crows.

He pushed open the door to the powder room and strode inside. The place looked empty—a row of gold-plated sinks, a plush settee and several opulent wood-panelled stalls. The room was completely silent, save for the drip of a tap and a sudden, revealing sniff from behind one of the stall doors.

'Halina,' Rico called, his voice rough and urgent. Another sniff sounded. 'Open the door,' he demanded. 'Tell me what's going on.'

After an endless moment Halina unlocked the door and stepped out into the bathroom. Rico gaped at her, taking in her dishevelled hair and tear-stained face, his heart lurching at the sight of her obvious distress.

'Halina,' he said and reached for her. 'What has happened? What's wrong?'

CHAPTER ELEVEN

RICO'S STRONG, WARM hands encased Halina's icy ones
as he drew her towards him, his brow furrowed, his expression somewhere between thunderous and terrified.

'Why have you been crying? Has something happened? Is it the baby...?'

'No, it's not the baby.' Halina pulled her hands from
his to dash at the tears on her face. She felt embarrassed
for falling apart so completely. This evening had been an
utter failure, and it was all her fault. She couldn't handle
a party. She couldn't handle being Rico's fiancée. 'At
least,' she amended, taking a steadying breath, 'it was,
in a manner of speaking.'

'What do you mean?' Rico's gaze swept over her, as
if looking for open wounds or broken bones. 'Are you
hurt?'

Halina let out a shaky laugh, torn between wry amusement and deep, abiding sorrow. 'Yes, Rico,' she managed
tartly, 'I am hurt. But you won't find any visible wounds
so you can stop looking at me as if you want to take me
to the hospital's emergency department.'

'I don't understand.'

'No.' She sighed. 'You wouldn't.' She moved past him
to study her reflection. She was even more of a wreck
than she'd realised, her supposedly waterproof mascara

giving her panda eyes, and her once elegantly styled hair falling about her shoulders in tangled ringlets.

'What is that supposed to mean?' Rico asked, his tone gruff.

Halina sighed and attempted to dab at her mascara even as she recognised a lost cause when she saw one. 'My *feelings* are hurt, Rico,' she said, deciding she needed to speak as plainly as she could. 'Feelings. You know those things you try not to have?'

Rico's mouth thinned. Clearly he didn't appreciate her pathetic attempt at humour. 'Why were your feelings hurt?'

She hesitated, her gaze still on her unhappy reflection. 'It doesn't matter.'

'Yes, it does.' Rico spoke with a force that surprised. 'Who hurt you? Did someone say something, do something? Because if they did it to you, then they did it to me.'

A feeling bloomed in Halina's chest, a mixture of surprise and warmth. It spread through her like sunshine or honey, warming her right down to the tips of her fingers and toes. 'Do you mean that?'

'Of course I do.'

Was that what marriage was? Maybe not love, but something just as fundamental? The question was, could it be enough?

'So what happened, Halina? Tell me.'

'Not here.' She glanced around the bathroom. 'Someone's liable to come in, and I can't cope with another snide remark.'

His frown of concern deepened into a positive scowl. 'So someone did say something to you. One of those women?'

'Not *to* me,' Halina clarified, and felt the tightening

of tears in her throat. The snippy, bitchy comments she'd overheard while in the bathroom stall had wounded her deeply, more than she cared to admit to Rico, because even though he wanted to know she knew he wouldn't understand. Not completely.

'Tell me,' he demanded. 'Tell me what they said.'

'Why, so you can punch them?' She let out a hiccupping laugh. 'I will tell you, but can we please go somewhere private?'

'Fine.' He slid his phone out of his pocket and quickly texted a message. 'The limo will meet us out front in five minutes.'

'We're leaving?'

'Do you really want to go back in to the party?'

'No, but I thought you would. This charity is important to you.'

He shrugged. 'Your well-being matters more.'

Which both touched her and made her feel guilty. She really had failed him this evening. Feeling miserable on so many levels, Halina followed Rico out of the bathroom. He took her arm as he strode away from the party so that Halina had to take quick, mincing steps in her tightly fitted evening gown and tottering heels to keep up with him.

'Rico, wait! I can't walk so fast. These shoes are killing me.'

'Sorry.' He glanced at her, contrite. 'I just wanted to get you away from here.'

The limo was waiting for them outside the hotel, and Rico opened the door before ushering Halina inside. She slipped into the luxurious leather interior with a sigh of relief. Every part of her ached.

'Are you in pain?' Rico asked, catching her wince, and Halina managed a laugh.

'No, I'm just not used to these stilettos. They kill my feet.'

'Take them off, then.' Before she could do so he reached down, undid the straps of her shoes and slipped them off her feet. Halina let out a gusty sigh of relief, then gave a little gasp of surprise when Rico took her feet and drew them up to his lap. When his thumbs began to massage powerful circles on their soles she wriggled with pleasure and couldn't keep a moan of delight from escaping her.

'Oh, my goodness, that feels fantastic.'

Rico laughed softly. 'I can tell.'

He reached over and tucked one of the throw pillows adorning the limo's seats behind her head. 'There. Now tell me what happened at the party.'

Halina's eyes fluttered closed as she surrendered to Rico's tender ministrations, his fingers continuing to work their magic on her aching feet. 'It wasn't such a big deal. I'm sorry I made it so.'

'That's for me to say, not you. What happened, Halina?'

She sighed and then wriggled again with pleasure as Rico's hands moved up to her ankles, his thumbs tracing the delicate bones.

'I was in one of the bathroom stalls and some women came in. They started talking about me—and you.'

His fingers stilled for only a second before he continued with the slow, rhythmic circles. 'And what did they say?'

'They knew I was pregnant. I don't know how...'

'You put your hand on your belly during our engagement announcement and then you asked for sparkling water.'

'Oh.' Now she felt stupid. 'Well, that explains it, then,' she said with an attempt at a laugh.

'I don't mind people knowing, Halina,' Rico said, his voice low and sure. 'I will never mind. You're going to be my wife and you're carrying my child.'

'Are you sorry?' Halina blurted, opening her eyes. In the darkness of the car she couldn't make out his expression.

'Sorry…?'

'That you slept with me. That I became pregnant. That I…that I ruined your life.'

'Halina.' Rico leaned forward so his gaze met hers and she could see how fiercely his silvery eyes glittered. 'You have not ruined my life.'

'But to be suddenly burdened with a wife and baby you didn't want… And you had all those mistresses…' A sudden, horrible thought occurred to her, one that now seemed appallingly obvious. 'Are you…are you going to keep on with them…after we marry?'

'What?' Rico's brows drew together in a ferocious frown. 'Of course not. Do you honestly think I would?'

'You didn't ask for this, Rico.'

'Neither did you. And, in any case, I believe I will be wholly satisfied in that department by my wife.' His hand slid from her ankle to her knee, his fingers splayed across her tender skin as his gaze remained hot and intent on hers. 'Perhaps I should remind you how good we are together, *bella*. How explosive.'

Halina's breath came out in a shuddery rush and the sensitive skin of her knee tingled. His fingers felt warm and very sure as they started to slide upwards. 'You've barely touched me in two weeks,' she whispered. 'Not since you saw me again.'

'I wanted you to rest.' His smile turned wolfish, his eyes filled with heat. 'To regain your strength.'

'Plus I looked like a worn-out dishrag.'

'You have always been beautiful to me. Never doubt that.' With his gaze still fastened on hers, he moved his hand to her inner thigh, his warm palm sliding upwards in a sure, fluid movement. Halina shuddered, every nerve on over-sensitised alert as his fingers skimmed along her skin.

'We're so good together, Halina,' Rico murmured as he continued to stroke her thigh. 'We always have been.'

'You mean the one time.'

'I am looking forward to many others. You have ruined me for other women.'

'That's what someone said about you.' Her breath came out in jerks and bursts as his fingers crept even closer to her feminine centre. If he touched her there, she thought she might melt—or explode.

'What do you mean?' One finger skimmed the lace of her underwear, making her shudder. Halina slid a little lower down on the seat.

'In the bathroom…that first night…some supermodel you'd slept with… The women said she'd been ruined for life by you, because you're so…' His fingers were becoming more insistent, more daring, sliding beneath her underwear, skimming her tantalised flesh and then going even deeper, with sure, knowing strokes. Pleasure swirled inside her, obscuring her senses so she could barely think, much less speak. 'They said…they said you were so good,' she half-moaned as her body arched upwards. 'At sex.' With a little cry she gave herself up to the pleasure crashing over her and felt herself go liquid and boneless.

As the last shudders of her climax rippled through her, Rico leaned over and pressed a hard kiss to her mouth. 'Which I've just proved, I think.'

She opened her eyes, dazed and more than a little embarrassed to be slouched on the seat, her elegant gown rucked up halfway to her hips, her wanton pleasure so very evident.

She struggled up to sitting, pushing her hair out of her face. 'I must look a mess,' she muttered.

'You look beautiful.' Rico touched her chin with his fingertips. 'Do you know how enflaming it is to see you come apart under my touch? Do you know what it does to me?' Wordlessly Halina shook her head, shocked by the admission, by the blatant need she saw in his eyes and felt in the tautness of his body. 'When we get back to the apartment,' Rico said, his voice roughening, 'I'll show you.'

Desire thrummed through Rico, a slow burn that threatened to ignite into a full conflagration. Seeing Halina respond to his touch, her face and body both suffused with pleasure, had been a severe test of his self-control. He'd wanted to take her right there on the seat of his limo, in the kind of helpless display of overwhelming need that he never gave into.

So he didn't. He wanted her—heaven help them both how much he did—but he still clung to his self-control, if only by his fingertips.

The limo pulled up to his building and without a word Rico emerged from the back, holding Halina's hand as he drew her along.

'My shoes,' she protested, and he saw she was barefoot.

'They don't matter. Forget them.' His self-control only extended so far.

With a little laugh Halina did, following him into the darkened foyer of the building and then into the lift. That was how far his self-control went; as soon as the doors closed, he pulled her into his arms, plundering her mouth as he backed her up against the wall.

She gasped, driving her hands through his hair as she surrendered to his touch, wrapping her arms around him and pulling him even closer.

It still wasn't enough. He yanked her dress up to her waist, needing to feel her against him.

'Rico…' His name was a soft protest and he stilled, shocked by his own urgent actions.

'Do you want me?' he demanded, unable to keep from saying the words. Voicing his fear. 'Do you want me as much as I want you?'

'You know I do.'

The doors to his apartment opened and with a sound nearing a growl Rico swept Halina up into his arms and strode to his bedroom. 'Then show me.'

'I already have,' she protested breathlessly as he peeled her dress off her and laid her on the bed. 'How could you doubt it, Rico? I've been putty in your hands since the moment I first laid eyes on you.'

'Good.' He pulled off his tie and tuxedo shirt, studs flying everywhere and clattering to the floor. 'That's how I want it to be.'

The self-control he'd been so determined, so *desperate* to hold onto was in shreds. All he could think of, all he could feel, was his need for her. Shucking off the rest of his clothes, Rico pulled Halina into his arms. The feel of her golden, silken skin against his was an exquisite torture.

'I've been dreaming of this,' he muttered against her skin, wanting to touch and taste her all at once. 'Dreaming of this ever since you walked out of my hotel suite all those weeks ago.'

'So have I,' Halina whispered, her body arching under his touch. 'Even if I tried to keep myself from it.'

Just as he had, because such need was weakness. But now he didn't care. Now he simply wanted—and took.

When he slid inside her velvety depths he felt a crashing sense of relief, almost as if a burden had been lifted. This felt right and true, the home he'd never had. Then she arched up to meet him, matching his thrusts, and he stopped thinking at all.

Later, when his heart rate had started to slow and he felt himself come back to his senses, Rico reviewed his actions as dispassionately as he could. Yes, he'd lost control. Completely. But so had Halina. The fact was they shared an incredible chemistry, and that was no bad thing. So as long as he kept the loss of control in the realm of the bedroom, he would be satisfied. He wouldn't be in danger of losing anything to Halina…such as the heart he'd always acted as if he didn't have.

Next to him Halina stirred sleepily. 'That was a nice way to end the evening.'

'Perhaps the evening is just beginning.' Rico rolled over to face her. 'But we never finished our conversation. What did those women say?'

'It really doesn't matter…'

He hated the thought of her being hurt. 'I think it does.'

With a sigh Halina rolled onto her back. 'They just said they couldn't believe you'd finally been snared— that was the word I think they used. And the fact that I was pregnant and a princess could be the only reason you'd ever marry me, because you were obviously way out of my league.'

Rico stiffened, a new fury starting to boil through

him. How dared those insipid, catty women say such things about his chosen bride?

'I don't know why you seem angry,' Halina remarked lightly as she rolled back to face him. 'It's all true.'

'What? No, it isn't.'

'Come on, Rico.' Despite her light tone, pain flashed in her eyes. 'Let's be honest. I know there are a lot of things we can't have in our marriage, but surely truth isn't one of them?'

'It's not true,' he insisted stubbornly.

'It is,' Halina returned, her tone just as stubborn. 'You know it is. You never would have married me if I hadn't been pregnant, and the fact that I'm royal no doubt has something to do with it too.'

'What are you saying? That if you'd been a nobody I wouldn't have married you?'

'Would you have?'

'I would always,' Rico said flatly, fighting back a tidal wave of fury, 'marry the mother of my child.'

'So I guess you didn't get a woman pregnant before.'

'No, I always took precautions, for a reason.'

She nodded slowly. 'And I'd told you it was safe. I'm sorry.'

He shook his head, annoyed and exasperated by the whole conversation. He didn't want to tread over this old ground yet again. He didn't want to be reminded of how he used to be, either. He was different now—just not *that* different.

'My point,' Halina said after a moment, 'Is that my pregnancy is what precipitated your proposal. How's that for an alliteration?' She gave him a teasing smile but Rico didn't have it in him to respond in kind.

His fury was fading, replaced by a far more alarming confusion as he realised that Halina was right, at least in part. He never would have married her if she hadn't been pregnant. He never even would have seen her again. It was blindingly obvious, but it didn't sit well with him. At all.

'I should go back to my own bed,' Halina said, starting to rise. Rico stayed her with one hand.

'You'll sleep here.'

Even in the darkness of the room he saw the surprise flash across her face. 'I thought you never slept with a woman—'

'You're going to be my wife,' Rico interjected fiercely. 'And we'll sleep together from now on. It's time,' he added, drawing her towards him so she was nestled snugly against his chest, 'That we started to plan the wedding.'

CHAPTER TWELVE

'THIS DRESS IS very discreet.' The sales assistant gave Halina a knowing smile as she gestured to a gorgeous dress of ivory satin with a convenient empire waist to hide Halina's small but growing bump. She was fifteen weeks pregnant and only just starting to show.

It had been three weeks since she and Rico had reconsummated their relationship, three weeks of virtually living as man and wife, even if they weren't going to say the vows for another fortnight. Three happy, hopeful yet so uncertain weeks, and with every passing day Halina felt more and more anxious.

She had spent every night in Rico's bed, as well as in his arms. He was a tender and attentive lover, awakening her body to sensations and desires she'd never experienced before.

As she'd grown in experience, she had also grown in confidence, daring to touch and explore his body as he did hers. It had brought an intense intimacy that left Halina breathless with longing for Rico to feel the same as she did...even as she forced herself to acknowledge that he didn't, he couldn't, not when he'd gone through a woman a week for most of his adult life. Sex was just a physical exercise for him, not the emotional, soul-shattering experience it had become for her.

As for out of bed… Rico was attentive then, too. Solicitous to her every need and comfort—often coming home with some treat she'd been craving, accompanying her to her doctor appointments and helping with the planning of their wedding which, according to the city's tabloids and gossip magazines, was going to be the event of the year.

Halina wasn't sure how she felt about that; in the weeks since that first, awful party they'd gone out on several social occasions and she'd managed to hold her head up high, despite several women's sneering looks and whispering comments.

'They're just jealous,' Rico said blandly, and Halina had laughed.

'That's a rather arrogant comment, you know.'

'But it's true.' And she knew it was.

As the wedding loomed closer, she veered between excitement and a growing terror. Excitement because part of her was looking forward to being part of a family again, to starting a new life with Rico. She'd enjoyed these last few weeks with him, more than she'd ever expected to, but the terror came from the creeping fear that it wasn't enough and it never would be.

His care, his solicitude, his thorough attentiveness in bed—none of it would be enough, because he didn't love her. He'd made that very clear in a thousand painful ways. He would never love her, and she had to accept that, learn to live with it, because she had no choice. As much freedom as she felt she had now, she still lived under the worst restriction of all.

'Would you like to try it on?' the assistant asked, and Halina nodded, needing a distraction from her circling and increasingly unhappy thoughts. She also needed a wedding dress; the church and reception hall had been booked, the meal planned, the champagne ordered and the guests, all six hundred of them, invited. Although she'd been looking for a while, she hadn't yet found a dress she liked—and it was getting late.

Halina went into the dressing room and slipped into the empire-waist dress. The bodice shimmered with crystal jet and diamanté, and the skirt fell in a drop of exquisite ivory satin, swirling around her ankles. It was simple and elegant and, as the assistant said, very discreet.

Halina tried to picture herself walking down the aisle in the huge church and inwardly trembled. She'd be walking alone; her father had refused to attend the wedding, or let her mother or sisters attend. Their absence made her relationship with Rico feel even lonelier and more lacking. He was all she had in the world, and he didn't love her.

'What does *signorina* think?' the assistant called, and Halina gazed at her pale face, her wide dark eyes.

'It's fine,' she called back tonelessly. 'Perfect. I'll take it.'

Her fingers shook as she fumbled with the hook-and-eye fasteners at the back of the dress. What was wrong with her? She'd been happy these last three weeks; she really had. There had been so much to enjoy, and yet…

Marriage. A loveless marriage. For ever. She closed her eyes and leaned her forehead against the cool mirror. Why did it matter so much? Why did it make her ache so?

'*Signorina?*' The assistant peeked through the curtain and Halina jerked back, embarrassed to be caught looking as if she were about to fall apart.

'I'll be straight out.'

The woman smiled sympathetically. 'Everyone gets cold feet, no? It is normal.'

It wasn't her cold feet she was worried about but Rico's icy heart. Quickly she slipped out of the dress and handed it to the assistant. 'Thank you.'

'You are sure…?'

'Yes.' She was sure about the dress, if nothing else at this moment.

Halina dressed quickly, as Rico was planning to meet her for lunch at a new upscale restaurant off the Via dei Condotti and she didn't want him sensing that she was worried or upset. He would just harangue her, demanding to know what was wrong and how he could fix it. Touching at times, but he couldn't fix this. He wouldn't want to.

'Did you find a dress?' Rico asked when she walked into the restaurant fifteen minutes later. He stood up as she came to the table and kissed her cheek.

'Yes, I have found one.' Halina sat down and smiled. 'I think it's very pretty.'

Rico scanned her face, a slight frown settling between his brows. 'What's wrong?'

He was so irritatingly perceptive, Halina reflected. A strange quality for man who claimed to have no use for feelings. 'Nothing's wrong,' she said and picked up her menu. Now that thankfully her nausea had gone, she found she was ravenous.

'Something's wrong, Halina. I can tell.'

Halina looked up from the menu, her eyebrows raised. 'How can you tell?'

Rico shrugged, seeming slightly discomfited by the question. 'I just can. There's something about you…it's like a sixth sense, I suppose. We're attuned to each other.'

Which could have been heartening, but wasn't. She didn't want to be *attuned*. She wanted to be loved. The realisation solidified inside her, although she'd been trying to talk herself out of it for weeks. Why did she care if Rico loved her or not, when he promised her so much else?

The answer came suddenly in a tidal wave of amazement and despair.

She loved him. She'd gone and fallen in love with him, even though she'd known it was foolish, the stupidest thing she could ever do. Yet she'd still done it. Her heart hadn't been able to resist because Rico was gentle, kind and fiercely protective, because he made her laugh and ache and sing.

This was love, then, that ephemeral emotion Rico dismissed out of hand. And it was so much more than that, because Halina knew what it meant. It meant she would love him no matter what; it meant she would love him even if he didn't love her back.

She'd wondered what love felt like, if she'd really know when it was missing or whether she'd found it, and now here was her proof. She loved Rico, and it filled her with both joy and despair because she knew, no matter what she felt, that he utterly refused to love her back.

'Well?' Rico demanded. 'Has something happened? Has someone said something? Tell me.'

'I don't want to, Rico,' Halina said wearily. She knew he wouldn't let it drop, just as she knew he'd hate to hear what was really troubling her—the realisation that thudded through her, a wonder and fear.

Rico's frown deepened. 'Why don't you want to?'

'Because there's no point, and it will just annoy you.' As much as it hurt her to say it. 'You don't have to be such a bull dog about everything, you know? I'm allowed to have some thoughts I can keep to myself.' Because it would horrify him to know she'd fallen in love with him. That much she knew.

'I'm hardly asking you to tell me your every thought,' Rico protested. 'But, if something is troubling you, I want to fix it.'

'Trust me, you can't fix this.'

That, of course, did nothing to appease him. 'There must be something I can do,' Rico insisted, and Halina almost smiled. Her husband-to-be hated the thought that he was not all-powerful.

'There isn't,' she informed him firmly. 'Shall we order?'

Rico looked unconvinced but he beckoned the hovering waiter over and they ordered their meals.

'You are happy with the dress?' Rico asked once the waiter had left them alone.

'Yes, it's very nice.' Although now she could barely remember what it looked like. It wasn't the way she had wanted to buy her wedding dress, alone and anonymous in a boutique. If she'd been at home, her sisters would have surrounded her, jabbering excitedly, and her mother would have been there to offer benevolent and wise advice. Even her father would have wanted to see the dress, and offer an opinion.

Sudden tears stung her eyes and she blinked them back rapidly, but not before Rico noticed.

'Halina,' he said, his voice low and urgent as he leaned forward. 'You must tell me what is wrong. I can't stand to see you so obviously unhappy.'

'I just miss my family,' Halina said, which was the truth, if not all of it. 'I wish they could be here for the wedding.'

Rico sat back, his lips pressed together. 'You are right, in that there is nothing I can do about that.'

'I know.' She sniffed and took a sip of sparkling water. 'I'm sorry. I'll be better in a moment.' She managed a wobbly smile. 'It's all these pregnancy hormones making me emotional.' But it was so much more.

'You don't need to be sorry.' Rico was subjecting her to one of his thorough, considering glances. 'But there's something else, isn't there?'

'Oh, Rico.' Halina let out a shuddery laugh as she rolled her eyes. 'What if there was?'

'Then I want to know.'

She stared at him for a moment, knowing he wouldn't let it go. Well, fine. She'd asked for honesty from him once; now he could have it from her, at least some of it.

'All right.' She took a deep, steadying breath. 'The truth is, I'm sad because I know you don't love me, and from what you've said you'll probably never love me. I'm trying to come to terms with it, but it's hard. I know I was willing to marry a virtual stranger, but a cold, loveless union is not what I've ever wanted for my life.'

Rico stared at Halina, trying not to let his emotions show on his face. His utter horror at what she'd just stated with such stark, bleak honesty. He must not have done a very good job because Halina let out a huff of humourless laughter.

'You don't have to look quite so appalled. Consider the bright side—I do know what I'm getting into.' She looked away, blinking rapidly, appalling him further. 'You made sure of that.'

'Yes, but I… I didn't realise you wanted…love quite so much.'

'Is it so surprising? Isn't it what most people want?' She turned back to give him a direct, challenging look. 'Perhaps you're the strange one, Rico, not me.'

'Perhaps.' He knew, on some level, she'd wanted love.

She'd said as much, but he'd been sure he could convince her otherwise.

What *was* love anyway? Nothing more than a feeling, as ephemeral as the morning mist. Halina could learn to live without it, just as he had. Everything would be better that way. Happier, even. He just had to convince her of it.

Rico eyed her carefully. 'Halina,' he began, choosing each word with delicate precision, 'Just because we do not love each other...we can still be happy together.'

'Can we?' Tears shimmered in her eyes and she blinked them back resolutely. 'I know all this emotion is appalling you, Rico. I'm sorry.'

'For heaven's sake, you don't need to be sorry.' Did she think he was that intransigent, that hard and unyielding? Perhaps once he had been, but now... He *had* changed, at least a little. Just not too much. 'You can't help the way you feel.'

'Just as you can't help the way you don't.' She forced a smile. 'So there we are.'

'It doesn't have to be all gloom and despair,' Rico persisted, trying to keep the impatience and urgency from his voice. 'What is love anyway, Halina? A feeling? A warm glow in your heart?'

She flinched at the scorn he'd unintentionally and instinctively put into those words. 'Maybe that's a sign of it, Rico, but it's not all love is.' Her lip curled, and now she was as contemptuous as he was. 'Love is so much more than that, which you should know, since you've loved someone before.'

He felt himself go still. 'What makes you say that?'

'You said it before,' she answered with a shrug, her pain-filled gaze sliding away from his. 'You told me it was a long time ago, but she obviously hurt you very badly if you can't bear the thought of letting yourself love someone years later.'

'She?' Rico repeated blankly, and Halina turned back to him with a frown.

'The woman, whoever she was.'

'There was no woman, Halina.' Perhaps it would have been easier, safer, to pretend there had been, but it didn't feel fair to Halina and he didn't want her to labour under the misapprehension that he'd loved another woman but wouldn't love her. 'I told you before, I've never been in love with anyone.'

'Then who was it who broke your heart?' Halina asked in a whisper. Rico flinched at the phrase.

Broke his heart. So trite, so real. 'It was my father,' he said after a tense pause. 'He hurt me very badly when I was a child and I never forgot it.'

'What did he do?'

'He didn't love me back,' Rico said simply. Even that felt like admitting way too much. Halina stared at him, her gaze both searching and yearning.

'And that's why you don't want to love anyone? Because of something that happened when you were a child?'

'It taught me a valuable lesson,' Rico said shortly.

'Which was?'

'That love isn't real. Whether it's a warm glow or not, that doesn't matter. It doesn't last. It doesn't change things, and you can't count on it or trust it. Frankly, we're both better off without it, Halina.'

'Of course you would think that.'

'Yes, I would,' Rico returned, his voice gaining force. He felt a deep-seated need, bordering on a compulsion, to prove this to her. To liberate her from such childish notions, as well as cement the foundation of their own future happiness. 'Think about it, Halina. You want me to love you. What does that even mean? What would it look like, practically?'

She flushed, looking as if she resented the question. 'If I have to spell it out to you...'

He reached across the table to cover her hand with his own. 'Humour me. Please.'

'Fine.' She pulled her hand away and folded her arms. 'It would mean I was the most important thing to you. That you couldn't bear to be away from me. That I made the sun shine more brightly and the sky look more blue. That I complete you.' She shook her head. 'How many clichés do I have to pull out of the book, Rico? Love just *is*. Either you love someone or you don't, and if you don't, then whatever you feel—whether it's affection or duty or something in between—is eventually going to fade and pale. At some point in the future it's not going to be enough, and that's what I don't want to have happen. I don't want to look up from my dinner or roll over in bed and see that knowledge in your eyes.'

'I swear to you,' Rico said in a low voice that thrummed with sincerity, 'that would never happen.'

'You can't make that promise.'

He put his hands flat on the table, a sudden fury coursing through him. 'And you think love is the failsafe guarantee, Halina? That, if I loved you, that feeling would never fade? Because, I can assure you, it would. Love is a guarantee of absolutely nothing. Haven't you learned that yourself? Look at your own father. You thought he loved you but he would have killed your own baby if he could have, and now he won't even come to your wedding. Is that love?'

Her face crumpled and he regretted his harsh words.

He'd been so caught up in the moment, in his own memories. He reached for her hands. 'Halina…'

'Maybe you're right, Rico,' Halina said, her expression composed now, although her voice trembled. 'Love can fade, or at least seem as if it does. But I choose to believe, and to hope. People make mistakes, they do unloving things, but at the core of their being the love remains. And I choose to believe that my father still loves me, and eventually he'll realise the mistakes he made. *That's* the difference. Someone who loves you can still let you down. They're only human. But because you love them, and they love you, you keep going. You forgive and you grow stronger, and you move on. Together. You asked me what love is. Well, that's my definition.'

Rico stared at her, humbled by her brave honesty and also by the gaping emptiness he felt in himself. Had he ever felt that, either to give or to receive? Did he even know what love was?

'So we're right back at the beginning,' Halina said with an attempt at a laugh. She shook her head sadly. 'There's no solution, is there, Rico? We're going to get married, but you will never love me. I just have to live with it.'

'I might not love you,' Rico said, 'but, as I told you before, I will protect and provide for you. Always. I will be loyal and faithful, and I will do anything in my power to make you happy. Isn't that enough?'

Her mouth curved in a sorrowful smile as she answered. 'I suppose it will have to be.'

CHAPTER THIRTEEN

A WEEK BEFORE the wedding Halina woke up in the middle of the night with terrible stomach cramps. It had been a week since her all-too-honest conversation with Rico, a week of learning to live without love and finding a way to be happy. At times she'd felt she was on the verge of finding it: when she and Rico could laugh together, when he reached for her in bed. But then memories would rush through her, or he would roll away, and she feared she'd always be searching for that ever-elusive feeling.

Now she lay in bed, blinking up at the ceiling as her stomach cramped, muscles contracting painfully. She was only four months along, and in the last few days she'd felt the first flutters of movement, which had filled her with joy. Now she feared something was wrong.

Quietly she slid from the bed and went to the bathroom, hoping that the issue was merely a spicy meal that had disagreed with her. But when she saw the rusty streak of blood on the toilet paper she knew otherwise.

Her soft scream had Rico bolting upright in bed. 'Halina?'

She came out of the bathroom, her whole body trembling. 'I'm bleeding,' she whispered. Her body throbbed with terror as her stomach continued to cramp. 'Rico, I'm bleeding.'

Rico's eyes widened as he got her full meaning. 'I'll take you to the hospital,' he said, already getting out of bed. 'To the emergency department, right now.'

Halina watched, fear hammering through her, as Rico pulled on a shirt and trousers. He was in the middle of buttoning his shirt when he saw that she hadn't moved from the doorway of the bathroom.

'Halina, we need to go.'

'I'm scared.' The two words fell softly into the stillness. She wrapped her arms around herself. 'I don't want to lose this baby. I can't. Not after everything…'

'You won't.' Rico took her by the shoulders and stared into her eyes, his expression both grim and comforting. 'You won't. The doctors will figure out what's going on. They'll help you and they will help our baby.'

She nodded, wanting to believe him, needing to. Her teeth chattered; she felt icy cold.

'Come on,' Rico said gently, steering her towards the bureau. 'Let's get you dressed.' Halina felt like a child as she stood there and let Rico tenderly strip her nightgown from her body. He found one of her new maternity tops and loose trousers and helped her shrug them on.

'I'm sorry,' she choked. 'I feel frozen…'

'Shh.' Rico brushed a kiss against her forehead. 'It's all right…it's going to be all right.'

He took her hand and together they walked out to his car, a luxury sports model that he used in his down time with a private parking space. Halina slid into the passenger seat and wrapped her arms around herself. Even though it was a balmy evening at the very end of September, she felt so very cold.

The emergency department of the local hospital was brightly lit and bustling despite the late hour. Several rows of hard plastic seats were filled with people with various ailments and injuries. Rico strode to the front to talk to the triage nurse while Halina sank into a seat, desperately trying to hold onto her composure as well as her hope. Her stomach still cramped, off and on, off and on.

Rico strode back to her then sat down next to her and took her hand. 'You're freezing,' he said, and chafed her hand between his own. Halina gave him a shaky smile.

'I feel like I'll never get warm. Maybe it's shock.'

'It's going to be okay, Halina.'

'I know you want that to be the case, but it might not be.' Her voice wobbled. 'It might not be. This isn't in your control, Rico, just like the sandstorm. I know you hate that, but it's true.'

'I do hate it.' Rico's voice was low and fierce. 'I hate it absolutely.' His hands squeezed hers. 'But I also believe it's going to be okay. It has to be.'

Looking at the agony written in harsh lines on his features, Halina knew he meant that with every fibre of his being. Rico couldn't take this not being okay. She couldn't cope with it, just as he couldn't, and it made her cling to him all the more.

'Signora Falcone?'

Halina gave Rico a startled glance as she heard the nurse call out her soon-to-be name.

'It seemed easier,' he muttered, and rose from the seat before helping her to her feet. 'We're here,' he called to the nurse.

Halina focused on staying calm as she followed the nurse to a cubicle in the hospital's busy emergency department. After a short wait a doctor bustled in, smiling in a slightly distracted way.

'What seems to be the problem?' she asked as he soaped her hands at the little sink.

Haltingly, Halina explained about the cramps and bleeding. The doctor frowned as he dried his hands.

'You're about sixteen weeks along?'

'Yes, just sixteen weeks.'

'It can be normal to have a little bleed during your pregnancy, but it can also be a sign of something wrong. Why don't we have a listen for the heartbeat?'

Halina nodded and lay back on the examining table, her mouth dry, her heart thudding. Rico stood by her, his hand still encasing hers.

The doctor turned on the Doppler and began to press Halina's belly, looking for the heartbeat. All they heard was the whoosh of her own body and blood, not the lovely, galloping sound of their baby's heart.

Halina closed her eyes, willing to hear that wonderful sound. This couldn't be the end. It just couldn't be. *Please, baby*, she prayed silently. *Please live.*

The doctor switched off the Doppler, looking serious. Halina risked a glance at Rico and saw his jaw was clenched tightly, his eyes dark and focused.

'I'll send you to the ultrasound department for a scan,' the doctor said. 'Sometimes it can be difficult to find the heartbeat.' He gave them both a sympathetic smile. 'But of course, it could also be that something has gone wrong. We'll only know when we see the scan.'

Halina nodded. She felt icy and numb now, too numb to be afraid any more. She'd feared the worst already, and it seemed likely. Wordlessly she pulled her top down and she and Rico went back to the waiting room to wait until she was called for a scan.

Neither of them spoke as they sat in the brightly lit room while people bustled and moved around them—children sleeping on mother's laps, babies crying. Halina looked away from the tear-filled eyes of a chubby-cheeked cherub. What she wouldn't give to have a baby in her arms right now, even one that was crying and in pain.

'It's going to be okay,' Rico said in a low voice, and Halina turned to him with a sudden, surprising spurt of fury.

'Stop saying that,' she returned, her voice just as low. 'You don't know. You can't know. And at the moment, Rico, it looks like things aren't going to be all right. The doctor couldn't even find a heartbeat—' She broke off with a shuddering breath and looked away.

'You're right,' Rico answered after a moment. 'I don't know, and I hate that, because I don't know what to do, Halina. I want to help you and I can't.'

Tears stung her eyes and she blinked them back. 'You can help me by just walking with me through this, whatever happens,' she said steadily. 'Don't try to fix it or control it, Rico—just be with me. That's what I want.' She turned to him, blinking back more tears that threatened to fall. 'Can you do that?'

He looked at her seriously, his mouth a firm line, an agony in his eyes. 'Yes,' he said. 'I can do that.'

He hated everything about this. He hated watching Halina's fear and pain, feeling it himself, twice the agony. He hated having their carefully constructed world break apart, shatter into pieces. He thought of the baby nestled in Halina's womb and willed it to live. He hadn't realised just how much he wanted this child until it was at risk. Until everything he'd shared and built with Halina was at risk.

The knowledge jolted him, like missing the last stair. This wasn't just about their baby; it was about him and Halina. Their relationship. Their marriage. Over the last few weeks he'd got used to having Halina with him; he enjoyed it, counted on it, even. And he wasn't willing to give that up.

But if their baby had died…there was no reason to get married. No reason at all, and with an uncomfortable, prickling sensation Rico realised that Halina would no doubt be glad to get away from him. She'd made it clear several weeks ago—hell, all along—that she was willing to marry him but she didn't actually want to… because she wanted someone who would love her. Who could love her.

And he couldn't.

'Signora Falcone?'

Halina looked up, her face pale, her lips set in a firm line. Rico reached for her hand and together they walked towards the nurse, braced for the worst.

The ultrasound room was dim and quiet as Halina lay back once again on the examining table and the technician squirted cold, clear gel on her bare belly, her baby bump barely visible. She looked so vulnerable lying there, waiting, worrying, and Rico's heart ached for her. Ached for them, because he was so afraid it was all slipping away.

He knew that fear. He knew it far too well, because he remembered feeling it when his father had dropped him off on the steps of the orphanage in Salerno, his face grim but determined.

'They'll take care of you here,' he'd said while Rico had fought tears as he'd begged for his father to keep him. Not to leave him. He'd cried like a baby; he'd clung to his father's sleeve and his father had had to push him off.

Then he'd watched his father walk away; he hadn't looked back once. And in that moment Rico had resolved never to let someone hurt him like that again.

'Rico, look.' Halina grabbed his sleeve, just as he had

with his father, and he blinked back the memories as he was startled into the present. 'Look, Rico. Our baby!'

He focused on the ultrasound screen, and the beautiful sight of their tiny baby wriggling around like a jumping bean.

'Baby looks fine,' the technician said with a smile, and Halina let out an incredulous, shuddery laugh of joy. Rico's smile nearly split his face. 'It looks, Signora Falcone,' the technician continued, 'as if you've had a subchorionic haematoma.'

'A what?' Halina asked, her voice filled with nervousness.

The technician gave her a quick, reassuring smile. 'Basically a bleed between your baby and the uterine wall.'

'Is it dangerous?' Rico asked, his voice harsher than he'd meant it to be.

'It doesn't have to be.' The technician gave them both a sympathetic smile. 'Of course, any bleeding in pregnancy can be a cause of concern, and a haematoma of this size is definitely something we need to keep an eye on.'

None of which sounded particularly good. 'So what now?' Rico asked. 'What do we do?'

'Signora Falcone can continue as normal,' the technician said. 'Which is what we'd advise. But we'd also advise slowing down a little if possible—not being on your feet too much, or carrying anything heavy, that sort of thing.' She smiled at Halina. 'Giving both you and your baby the best chance possible. And, if you have any more bleeding, don't hesitate to call.'

Rico's mind was still spinning as they drove back home, dawn lighting the empty streets of Rome and touching them with rosy gold.

Back in the penthouse Halina went straight to bed, and Rico tucked her in as if she were a child. 'See?' he said as he brushed a kiss across her lips. 'I told you it was going to be okay.'

Halina gave him a wan smile; she looked utterly exhausted. Within moments she was asleep.

Back in the living area Rico pulled his laptop towards him and spent several hours finding out everything he could about sub-chorionic haematomas. The information was mixed, with some specialists saying they heightened the chance of miscarriage, and others saying they had no effect.

His eyes gritty and aching, Rico stared out at the city and vowed to do everything he could to keep Halina and their baby safe. They'd come so close today to losing it all and it had scared him.

It had scared him even more how devastated he'd been at the thought of not losing just his child, but Halina too. He was starting to care for her and that prospect terrified him more than anything.

How could he make Halina happy, love their baby and yet keep the emotional distance from her he knew he needed? The lines were blurring more and more every day. Soon it would be impossible…and what then?

'What time is it?'

Rico looked up, startled out of his thoughts, to see Halina standing in the doorway, her hair in a dark cloud about her face, her expression still sleepy.

'I don't know.' He checked his watch. 'About ten in the morning. You should get back in bed.'

'I can't spend the next five months in bed, Rico.'

'You heard what the technician said.'

'Yes, I did. Did you?' With a wry smile she crossed the room and curled up on the opposite end of the sofa. 'She said I needed to take it a bit easier, not that I needed to be bedridden.'

'Still...'

She turned to him, her smile gone, her expression serious. 'Don't you think I'm going to do everything in my power to take care of this baby?'

Slightly abashed, Rico nodded. Yes, he believed that. Of course he did.

Halina drew her knees up, resting her chin on top. 'Still, it could all go wrong,' she said quietly. 'We have to be prepared for that.'

'Just as we have to do everything we can to make sure that doesn't happen,' Rico returned. 'I'm going to call off the wedding.'

'What?' She turned to him, startled, her eyes wide and dark.

'It's too much strain and pressure on you. We can have a quiet wedding later, or reschedule a big ceremony, if that's what you prefer.'

'But all the preparations...all the money you spent...'

'What does money matter? Your health is more important. Our child's health. Besides, perhaps if we wait a while your father will come round and decide to attend.'

Pain flashed across her face and she nodded slowly. 'Yes. Maybe.' She sounded so sad that Rico ached to hold her, but he didn't, because something about Halina right now was cool and brittle, as if she were trying to maintain a certain distance. Her next words confirmed it.

'But Rico...if I do lose this baby...we need to talk about that.'

He tensed, his jaw clenched. 'Let's not court disaster, Halina.'

'Let's also be prepared,' she returned evenly. 'Isn't that your motto? Wasn't that why you had all those provisions in the car when we were trapped in the sandstorm in the desert? Because you like to be prepared.'

'Yes, but—'

'So let's be prepared for this,' Halina said steadily. 'If I lose the baby, we don't have to marry. You're free.'

Why did he now hate that thought? 'And what about you?' he asked. 'Are you free?'

'Yes,' Halina returned after a pause. 'Yes, I will be. I told you before, I never wanted a marriage without love.'

He fought to keep his expression neutral when everything in him wanted to cry out, to resist and deny. 'So what will you do, in this worst-case scenario? Return to Abkar?'

She let out a small huff of sad laughter and shrugged. 'Maybe I'll get that apartment in Paris I always dreamed about, with a piano and a terrace.'

But how would she do that? She had no money, no resources, and if she was free from him, her father might plan another marriage for her. But maybe Halina would prefer that, rather than be shackled to him for the rest of her life. The knowledge hurt, far more than Rico wanted it to.

'Well, then,' he said in a hard voice. 'Now we're prepared for the worst. So let's hope for the best, hey? And keep you on bed rest.'

She smiled faintly. 'In control, as always.'

'Yes,' Rico answered, but he didn't feel in control at all. Now, more than ever, he felt as if things were spinning out of his grasp…especially his own heart.

CHAPTER FOURTEEN

TODAY WOULD HAVE been her wedding day. Halina gazed out of the window of her bedroom at the buildings and streets of the Eternal City, feeling more in limbo now than ever. The last week had been endless, lying in bed, waiting for the worst to happen.

Since the first terror-filled visit to the hospital, thankfully she hadn't had any more episodes of bleeding, but she still lived in fear, and so did Rico. They were both tiptoeing around each other, a constant strain between them, caused, Halina supposed, by the new uncertainty that had opened up like a yawning chasm, sending them both into tense isolation.

Any day, any week, and it could all be over. Their child's life, the little family they'd been creating, the marriage they'd both intended to embark on. All of it could be reduced to nothing. It was exhausting, living with that kind of uncertainty, and Halina spent most of her enforced bed rest sleeping, in part just to escape the strain. How long would it last? The next five months? Or maybe not long at all. Maybe today would be the day it ended. It was impossible to know.

What she did know was that she'd fallen in love with Rico and it was tearing her apart. At every turn her fears were confirmed and the knowledge that he didn't love her, didn't want to love her, reverberated through her all over again, a loss she could never get used to. A tiny, treacherous part of her almost wondered if losing this baby would bring its own bitter relief, because then she wouldn't be faced with a loveless future with Rico. She hated herself for thinking that way for even a single second, and guilt scorched through her, making her even more miserable.

Rico had berated her for not taking care of herself, and had tried to make her eat when she had no appetite due to fear and worry. She knew he was feeling it too, and she wished they could comfort each other in their shared anxiety and sorrow. But that never seemed to be the case; like the ninth circle of Dante's terrible hell, they were frozen in their own isolation, doomed to a life of loneliness.

The sound of the intercom of the flat buzzing had Halina turning from the window in surprise. Rico was at work, and no one called at the flat; deliveries were left with the building's doorman.

Cautiously she went to answer the intercom. 'Hello?'

'Signorina?' The doorman's disembodied voice came through the speaker. 'You have a visitor.'

'A visitor…?'

'Sultan Hassan Amar,' the doorman said in a tone of utmost respect. 'He says he is your father.'

For a few seconds Halina couldn't think. She couldn't even breathe. She simply stood there, blinking, one finger pressed down on the intercom.

'Signorina?'

'Yes, I'm here.' Her voice sounded strangely tinny and faraway. 'Send him up.'

As soon as she'd said the words she half-regretted them. What if her father was here to take her back home against Rico's wishes? What if she got kidnapped yet again? But then she reasoned that he wouldn't have come to do such a thing on his own. And in any case, if he was on his own she could resist. If she wanted to.

The treacherous flicker of wanting made her pause. Could she really be thinking that way, even for a moment?

The lift doors pinged open and then her father stepped into the open area of the penthouse. Halina turned to him, her mind spinning, her heart beating wildly as her throat dried.

'Father.'

'Halina.' His gaze dipped down to the gentle swell of her belly. 'You are looking well.'

'Am I?' She laughed uncertainly because lately, despite all the rest, she'd been looking as worn out as an old dishrag. 'I don't feel all that well.'

'You don't? Is something wrong?'

The note of alarm in her father's voice caught her on the raw. 'Why do you care?' she couldn't keep herself from retorting bitterly. 'You never wanted this baby to live.'

Her father's face contorted with a spasm of grief and he started towards her, his arms outstretched. 'Halina, *habibi*...'

'Don't.' Halina stepped back quickly, nearly tripping over her own feet. 'Why are you here, Father?'

'I was intending to come to your wedding, and then Falcone informed me he'd called it off.'

She flinched, in part because of the stark fact of her father's words, and in part because Rico hadn't even told her that her father had called, or that he'd changed his mind and had been planning on coming to their wedding after all. The relationship between her and Rico, if she could even call it that, had broken down even more than she'd realised… But perhaps nothing had been built up enough to be broken. It had all been in her head, the intimacy, emotion and love. All on her side.

'Why don't you sit down, Halina?' her father suggested gently. 'And let us talk.'

She wrapped her arms around herself, feeling cold despite the warm October day. 'What do we have to talk about?'

'There is much I wish to say to you. Much I sincerely regret.'

Halina hesitated, then she nodded. 'All right.' They moved towards a pair of luxurious grey suede sofas; she'd spent many happy evenings there curled up next to Rico, watching television or reading a book, pleasant hours they'd whiled away together. It felt like a dream world now.

'What is it?'

'I want to apologise for my conduct to you,' Hassan said seriously. 'I regret the way I acted very much.' He bowed his head, seemingly overcome, and Halina stared at him, too shocked to feel gratified or hopeful. Yet.

'Do you…do you really mean that?'

Hassan looked up, tears gleaming in his dark eyes. 'Yes, I do. Events overtook me, my daughter, and I let them carry me away. I couldn't think properly with everything that had happened. Prince Zayed's kidnapping attempt, your situation… There was so much to deal with.'

'I know,' Halina whispered. 'For me too, Father. And I… I know I acted improperly. Recklessly. I regret that very much. I do.'

'And I acted recklessly as well,' the Sultan returned seriously. 'But let us have no more regrets, Halina. Now that the wedding is called off, I am here to take you home.'

Halina stared at her father in shock, his words penetrating her overwhelmed state and leaving her cold. 'Take me home...?'

'Where you belong. Where you'll be happy. This is no place for you.'

'Rico Falcone is the father of my child.'

'I have had investigators research his past,' Hassan returned, his tone becoming cold. 'Do you know this man, Halina? Do you really know him?'

She loved him. 'What did you find out?'

'That he grew up a gutter rat, and then made his fortune in property investments, and has been known for years as being a cold, ruthless, heartless man. That he has had many women, more than you can imagine, and they never lasted for more than a week. That he has been quoted as saying he doesn't believe in love and he doesn't have time for marriage. This is not a man you want to marry, *habibi.*'

Nothing her father had said about Rico was a surprise to her, but to hear it spelt out so plainly, so terribly... It was hard to bear. Hard to accept. And yet Halina knew she had to.

'This is not the man for you,' Hassan said definitively. 'Or for your child.'

'Rico would never leave his child,' Halina said, unsure what she was really saying. That he would leave her? That she wanted to go but couldn't? She felt a welter of confusion and grief, and it didn't help that things had been so strained between Rico and her recently. She was filled with doubt and fear.

'Are you sure about that?' Hassan asked, his tone gentle. 'Has he said so?'

'He took me from the Palace of Forgotten Sands,' Halina reminded him bitterly. 'Where you'd left me to rot.'

'That is not true, *habibi*. I put you there to keep you safe.'

Her father had a penchant for viewing things through his own singular lens. He always had. It hadn't mattered when she'd been treated like a spoilt pet, but now it made a difference.

'That's what it felt like, Father,' Halina said quietly. 'And I don't have any desire to return to such circumstances.'

'That's not what I'm suggesting at all,' Hassan protested. 'Halina, I am asking you to return to your home, your family. Your sisters long to see you, and so does your mother.'

'You forbade me from seeing my sisters.'

Hassan bowed his head. 'An impetuous decision that I regret. Halina, come home. We all want you to come home. Falcone can't force you to stay here, and in all truth I suspect he would be relieved if you left. Such a man is not made for marriage and family.'

Halina flinched, because her father was only voicing her own terrible suspicions. What if they were both right? What if Rico secretly wanted her to go? Yes, he had a protective streak a mile wide, and he'd been determined to look after her and their baby. But she didn't sense any joy from him, any gladness that he had to do it, that she was here. In her darkest moments she'd even wondered if Rico would be relieved if things ended, if they had no child together.

'Halina,' Hassan said gently. 'I have the royal jet at the airport. We can be heading back to Abkar, to your family, in an hour.'

She ached to see her sisters, her mother. To feel safe and loved, instead of restless and uncertain.

'I can't leave without telling Rico,' she said, hardly able to believe she was saying the words.

'Telling me what?' Rico demanded as he stepped through the doors of the lift and surveyed them both with a dark glare.

Rico gazed between Sultan Hassan's impassive face and Halina's frightened and confused one and felt his stomach and jaw both clench. Whatever they'd been talking about, it hadn't been good.

'What do you need to tell me, Halina?' he asked in as mild a voice as he could manage. 'What's going on?'

'Tell him, *habibi*,' the Sultan said.

The endearment did not go unnoticed. So that was how Hassan was playing it. The doting father had returned. Rico had often wondered how he would act if his father had ever returned. What he would have said, whether he would have opened his arms to him. He'd known what Halina would do. He saw it in her face, in the unhappy guilt written on her delicate features.

She was leaving him. At least, she was thinking about it. God knew the last few weeks had been hard. He knew that; he'd felt it. Halina's admission that she wanted love from him, from their marriage, the terrible uncertainty shrouding her pregnancy…all of it had taken its toll. Had made her doubt, made them both doubt, if they were doing the right thing getting married. Because he was honest enough to admit he'd started wondering too, and somehow that made this moment all the harder to bear.

'Halina?' he prompted, an edge entering his voice, and she stared at him unhappily, her lips trembling.

'Let me talk to him,' the Sultan said, and Rico swung his gaze over to appraise his real adversary. He didn't trust this man. Not a single inch.

'I can…' Halina persisted, but she looked so pale and miserable that Rico took pity on her.

'Let him say what he wants to say. We can talk later if needed. You should rest.'

They stared at each other for a long moment, a world of yearning and regret spinning out between them, then she nodded and walked wordlessly to the bedroom. As the door clicked shut behind her Rico turned to face Hassan.

'Well?' he said coolly.

'The Princess is coming home with me.'

Rico kept his expression neutral, refusing to give the man the satisfaction of seeing him affected by anything he said. 'That was your suggestion, I presume?' he drawled.

'My suggestion and her desire.'

'She said as much?'

'I know it. She's my daughter.'

'And she's the mother of my child.' Rico stared at the man, refusing so much as to blink. 'We are to be married.'

'Yet the wedding was called off.'

'For health reasons only.'

'Come now, Falcone.' Hassan smiled, the genial expression so close to a smirk that Rico itched to wipe it off his face. His fists clenched and he forced himself to unclench them and relax. 'Let's be honest with each other, now it is just the two of us.'

'I am being honest.'

The smile dropped from Hassan's face like the mask Rico had known it was. 'I have had people look into you and your background,' he said in a low voice, his lip curling in an ugly sneer. 'Seen what a gutter rat you truly are. No matter how many billions you have now, you were born a beggar boy and you still are one now. I will never allow you to marry my daughter, a princess of the royal blood. How could I?'

'What you will allow is not my concern. Halina is of

age and in this country, my country, she is not bound by your archaic laws.' Rico spoke calmly even though the blood was boiling through his veins.

'So you would shackle her to you, all because of a child you've never wanted?'

'I'll always want my child.'

'Oh, yes, I understand that certain code of honour—'

'Do you?' Rico interjected, unable to keep the venom from his voice. 'Because, by all accounts, you do not possess it.'

'Halina has spoken to you about that unfortunate incident, I see.'

'You tried to make your own daughter get an abortion she didn't want.'

'I am King of a country, Falcone,' Hassan said sharply. 'With it comes responsibilities and expectations, some of them unfortunate. For my people to see my own daughter shamed in such a way…it would be disastrous. For them, for my rule, for the stability of my country and for Halina herself.' He took a step towards Rico. 'She sees things from her own view, a simple child's view. Trust me, the truth is much more complicated. But we are both men of the world. We know that.'

Rico stared at him, his jaw clenched so tight he thought he might break a tooth. He recognised the truth in the Sultan's words, a truth he had not wanted to see before. He didn't condone the man's actions; he could never do that. But he could understand them.

'Halina belongs in Abkar with her own people, her own family.'

'And would you marry her off to a man of your choosing, a stranger?' Rico demanded. 'Because those do not seem the actions of the loving father you are professing to be now.'

'Come, Falcone.' Hassan smiled. 'We both know that her marriage to you would be no different, and in some ways worse, for there would be no political benefit to you. You would tire of her eventually, whether you are willing to acknowledge it or not.' The Sultan levelled him with a starkly honest and challenging stare. 'Do you honestly think you could ever make her happy?'

Rico tried not to flinch at that question and the lack it revealed in himself. Because the truth that he'd been trying to avoid staring in the face for the last few weeks was that he didn't. And he knew in his gut, in his heart, that Halina deserved more than he could ever give her.

'Would you marry her off against her will?' he asked, the words dragged from him, scraping his throat.

'Against her will? No. In time, when she has recovered from this and longs for a husband and a family? We would make the decision together. That much I have learned.' The Sultan met his gaze unblinkingly; Rico knew he had no choice but to trust him.

'And the child?' he asked painfully, the sting of tears behind his lids, in the back of his throat.

'Would want for nothing. He or she would grow up in the palace, a member of the royal family.'

'Your people would accept that?'

Hassan smiled grimly. 'They will have to.'

Several moments ticked by; it took all of Rico's energy and effort simply to breathe. To keep standing. 'Fine,' he said finally. 'Leave us now. I want to talk to Halina.'

'I'll return in an hour.'

'An hour…'

'It will be better if it's quick,' the Sultan said, then walked towards the lift.

Rico stood where he was, waiting for the man to leave before he moved. Before he told Halina what he intended.

As the doors pinged open and then shut Rico let out a shuddering breath. So this would be the end. He would let her go, because he cared for her too much to shackle her to him. He saw that now.

And, in a jolt of sorrowful realisation, it occurred to him that he finally had a glimmer of understanding of what his father might have gone through in leaving him at the orphanage all those years ago.

Perhaps, just as Rico had, his father had come to the grief-filled conclusion that he could not make the person he loved most in the world happy. That he could not provide for them in the way he longed to. That leaving was the better, and harder, choice.

With a leaden heart, Rico walked towards the bedroom door.

CHAPTER FIFTEEN

HALINA HEARD THE rise and fall of low, tense voices from behind the door but she couldn't make out any words and she didn't think she wanted to. What was her father saying to Rico? And what was Rico saying to her father?

She paced the room in a ferment of anxiety and fear, wondering if the two men she loved most in the world were deciding her future without her. Here, then, was the ultimate loss of freedom. Her fate was completely out of her hands, even while she waited in the next room.

Then she heard the lift doors open and closing. She stilled where she was by the window, one hand resting on the sill. She couldn't hear a sound from the other room; had Rico gone?

Just when she was about to go and find him, the bedroom door opened and Rico stood there. The haggard and grim look on his face struck a cold note of fear in Halina's heart.

'Rico…'

'Your father will return in an hour.'

'Return? Why?'

'It's better this way, Halina.'

'Better?' She stared at him wildly. The doubts that had been festering in her heart burst into painful reality. 'What are you saying? You want me to go?'

'It's not a question of want or whim. It's what is best for you—'

'Best for you, you mean!' Halina cried, pain lancing every word.

'I can't give you what you need.'

'You mean you can't love me.' Even now it hurt to say it. Rico hesitated, his jaw tight, and then he nodded. 'And what if I was willing to live with that?' Halina asked painfully.

'Do you remember what you said to me? That if my loyalty or affection wasn't grounded in love it would eventually fade?'

'Yes, but—'

'Are you no different? Eventually you would come to resent me for not loving you. Hate me, even. And I would hate that. So would you. We'd end up living separate lives, festering in bitterness and resentment.'

She stared at him, hating the bleak, bleak picture he painted with his grim words. 'It wouldn't have to be like that.'

'Maybe not, but the risk is too great. I can't make you happy, Halina. I can't give you what you want.'

'And that is a reason to walk away?' she demanded, her voice shaking. 'You're a coward, Rico Falcone—'

'Do you think this is easy for me?' he cut across her, his voice a ragged roar. 'Do you think I am doing this lightly? I am talking of abandoning my child, as my father once abandoned me. Do you think I would ever want to do that?'

'Then don't—'

'I am trying to do the right thing, hard as it is for both of us. You have to think of the future, Halina. Your future. Perhaps one day you'll find a man you love, a man who can make you happy...'

'Perhaps,' Halina answered in a choked voice, 'happiness is overrated.'

Rico stared at her. 'Do you really mean that?'

Halina simply stared back, confused and miserable. She didn't know anything any more. She didn't understand why Rico was doing this, even as she feared she did. Because their relationship had been doomed from the start—forced into a marriage neither of them wanted for a child they never should have conceived. But even now she couldn't regret her baby, their baby, and she pressed a trembling hand against the soft swell of her bump.

'What of your child? What shall I tell him or her about you?' She shook her head slowly. 'You're really going to give up all your rights?'

'It's better this way,' Rico said. His face was as blank as his voice; it was as if he had already left her, emotionally if not physically. Halina knew she would never reach him.

'So that's it?' she said hollowly. 'After everything that's happened…the way you pursued me, how determined you were to marry me…that's it?'

A full minute ticked by as Rico stared at her, his jaw clenched, his eyes pitilessly blank. 'That's it,' he said flatly.

Everything happened in a fast, unhappy blur after that. Halina packed, leaving behind the couture gowns and outfits that she and Rico had shopped for together. She couldn't bear to bring away clothes that held so many memories, beautiful as they were. Her father arrived, nodding graciously to Rico before he turned to Halina.

'Are you ready, *habibi*? The plane is waiting. So is your family. I called your mother and she is eager to see you.'

Everything in Halina cried out to resist. She stood in

the living room, trying to work up the courage to turn to Rico and tell him she loved him. She'd never said the words. She'd never confessed how she felt about him, only that she wanted him to love her. Would it make a difference? Didn't she have a duty to try?

She opened her mouth, her heart beating hard, but before she could say a word Rico spoke first.

'Goodbye,' he said, and walked out of the room.

Halina stood there for a moment, stunned and blinking, then she followed her father out of the apartment.

She didn't talk much on the ride to the airport; grief swamped her, a fog surrounding her that made it difficult to think, much less speak.

Sultan Hassan was all gracious solicitude, asking how she felt, if there was anything she needed. Once they were on the royal jet Halina went to lie down; she couldn't face anyone, not even the servants. She slept the entire journey, only waking up when it was time to land.

She stared out of the window of the jet at the bleak, undulating desert of Abkar and her heart cried out for Rome. For Rico.

'Everyone is waiting for you,' Hassan said as he guided her from the jet to the waiting SUV. Halina slid inside, resting her head against the seat. She felt too listless to ask what was going to happen now, what her father intended.

Would she live in the royal palace? Raise her child there, under the benevolent eyes of her parents? It was so far from the fury and sick disappointment they'd shown her before, she couldn't quite believe in it. Somehow it didn't much matter any more, because Rico had rejected her.

Throughout the journey, even as she remained dazed, one hard truth had emerged from the fog of her mind.

His claim that he was thinking of her, of her happiness, was nothing more than an excuse. Of course it was. Rico would never give up his child unless he wanted to. Unless he'd decided that marriage and fatherhood wasn't for him, after all.

Bitterness rooted in her heart as she replayed their last conversation in her mind. He was a coward. He should have had the courage to tell her the truth—that he'd changed his mind, that he didn't want to marry her—instead of dressing it up with fine sentiments about thinking only of her happiness.

Back at the palace her sisters swarmed her, and Halina hugged each of them in turn, her heart emerging from its chrysalis of grief as she realised afresh how much she'd missed her family.

'Halina.' Aliya pressed her cheek against her daughter's. 'We are so glad you have returned home.'

'Thank you, Mother,' Halina whispered.

'We have much to do,' Aliya said as she gestured for Halina to sit down in the family's private living area. A member of staff poured glasses of mint tea.

'Much to do?' Halina's youngest sister was curled up on her lap and Halina put her arms around her, grateful for the easy affection.

'Yes, for the wedding.' Halina stared blankly at her mother and Aliya's eyes narrowed. 'To the Sultan of Bahari. Surely your father told you?'

'No,' Halina said numbly. 'He didn't tell me.'

'But the wedding is in a week! The Sultan wants to marry you before you show too much.' With her lips pressed together, Aliya glanced repressively at her younger daughters. 'You are lucky to have such a match arranged for you, Halina.'

'Lucky?' Halina stared at her mother in disbelief as

realisation bloomed poisonously inside her. Her father had duped her with his words of love and regret. He'd wanted her home only so he could marry her off again to his political advantage, this time to a man over three times her age.

She knew the Sultan of Bahari. She'd sat next to him at one of those stuffy diplomatic receptions; he had to be at least seventy, and he had two wives already. And it seemed she was to be the third. Bile churned in her stomach and rose in her throat.

'Mother,' she whispered, 'Are you really intending this for me?'

Aliya folded her arms. 'It is all you have left.'

'Rico Falcone, the father of my child, a billionaire in his own right, was willing to marry me,' Halina retorted, even as a treacherous little voice inside whispered, *Was he?* 'Surely he is more appropriate than an aging lecher with two wives already?'

'Do not speak so disrespectfully. Falcone is not appropriate because he does not offer any political alliances, and his reputation is quite beyond the pale. This is your duty, Halina. Surely you see that? After all your disgrace, this is the least you can do for your family.'

The *least*? She'd be giving up her whole life, and in far worse a way than any future she could have envisioned with Rico. But Rico didn't want her, and Halina was left yet again with no freedom, no choice, in the worst situation she'd ever had to face.

She turned from her mother, tears blurring her eyes. She could hardly believe she was right back where she started, only worse. So much worse.

Rico. Her heart cried out his name. She should have told him she loved him. Even if she had to marry the Sultan of Bahari, at least Rico would have known. It would have been small comfort during the bleak, barren years that stretched ahead of her now.

Three days had passed since Halina had walked out of his flat, his life. Three endless days. It was long enough for Rico to reconsider his decision, which now seemed unaccountably rash. What had he been thinking of, letting her go? Letting his child go?

Sultan Hassan had played on all his doubts, all his fears of inadequacy and commitment. The fear he had of risking his heart for someone, holding it there for her to crack or crush. Halina had been right. He was a coward. He'd chosen to let her go rather than fight to hold on. To tell her the truth, which had come to him in a shocking moment of naked realisation: that he loved her. He'd loved her for a while, but he'd been hiding it from himself because he'd been so afraid. Afraid to fall, to risk, to beg her to stay. So he'd chosen the cowardly option of walking away.

Now he would live the rest of his life knowing he'd loved and lost. It was the price of his cowardice, his shame. And all he could do was pray and hope that she had a better life without him.

Then, on the fourth day after Halina's departure, Rico read the headline in the society section of the newspaper: *Abkaran Princess to Marry Sultan.*

Everything in him stilled as he scanned the few scant lines.

Princess Halina of Abkar, recently engaged to billionaire tycoon Rico Falcone, is now poised to marry the Sultan of Bahari on Saturday. The Sultan has two wives already, and the Princess will be his third.

Rico's head jerked up from the newspaper, shock slamming into him, leaving him breathless. The *third* wife? He glanced back down at the article and saw a grainy black-and-white photograph of the Sultan, a paunchy old man with jowly cheeks and a smug smile. His skin crawled. He hadn't let go of Halina for this. He hadn't sacrificed his own happiness, his own heart, for her to be married off to some old lecher.

And he was sure, with a stony certainty, that she hadn't known what she was walking into when she'd returned to Abkar. Her father had tricked them both.

Rico swore out loud, viciously and fluently. His emotional cowardice had led to this disaster. He'd wanted the very best for Halina, and instead he'd dumped her in the worst situation possible. With his mouth hardening into a grim line of determination, Rico reached for his phone. He'd rescued Halina once before. He could do it again. Only this time it might take a little more finesse.

Several hours later, Rico had found his way forward thanks to a few crucial phone calls. He booked a flight to Bahari and within hours of landing he had a royal audience with the Sultan. Forty-five minutes later, their business was concluded and, after spending the night at a hotel in the desert country's capital city, he booked another flight to Abkar.

He stood in front of the royal palace, soldiers barring his way, the golden stone of the palace shimmering under the hot desert sun.

'You may tell the Sultan I am here in regard to Princess Halina's forthcoming marriage. I have crucial news that I know he will want to hear.'

The soldiers glared at him uncertainly before one gave a terse nod and spoke Arabic into an intercom. Several tense minutes later Rico was admitted to the palace and led to a small, spartan waiting room.

The Sultan kept him waiting for nearly an hour before he finally deigned to make an appearance. Rico didn't mind. He wasn't going to play the man's petty games, and he wasn't going to fall prey to them either. Not any more.

'How surprising to see you here,' the Sultan remarked, his eyes cold, any pretence at friendliness dropped. 'I cannot begin to imagine what you have to say to me in regard to the Princess's marriage, but I decided to humour you.' He folded his arms. 'So, say what you will and then be gone.'

'The Sultan of Bahari has called off the marriage.'

Hassan's eyes narrowed. 'You are talking nonsense.'

'I am not. If you wish for it to be confirmed, you may call him.' He held out his phone, his eyes glinting with challenge. 'I have access to his private line.'

'What have you done?' Hassan ground out, staring at Rico's phone as if it were a snake poised to strike.

'Why don't you find out?'

Wordlessly Hassan snatched the phone and swiped to dial. Seconds later they both heard ringing and then the Sultan of Bahari's unctuous voice. Hassan listened for several taut seconds, his expression becoming grimmer and grimmer, before he ended the call and flung the phone at Rico. Rico caught it neatly.

'Very clever, Falcone. Very clever.'

'It is too bad for you that the Sultan prefers racehorses to wives.'

'How much did it cost you to buy him that horse?' Hassan asked scornfully. 'Millions? Money wasted. I am not letting Halina go.'

'Yes, you are,' Rico said evenly. 'Because, if you don't, I will do everything in my power, give everything I have, to ruin you. And trust me, Hassan, it can be done. I've only just begun, and I enjoy a challenge.'

Hassan stared at him for a long moment, his eyes cold, his jaw tight. 'What does it matter so much to you?' he finally asked. 'You've had dozens—no, hundreds—of women. She's but one. Why can't you leave her alone?'

'If she wants me to leave her alone, I will. But that's her choice,' Rico returned. 'Not yours.'

Another minute passed, taut with suppressed tension and resentment. Then Hassan shrugged. 'Fine. She's damaged goods anyway, and I would be hard pressed to find someone suitable to take her now. Do what you like with her, but she will not be welcome back here.'

'That,' Rico answered, 'is your loss.'

A short while later he stood in front of the doors to a more ornate reception room, his heart beginning to hammer as doubt chased him yet again. He'd acted precipitously, out of concern for Halina, but what if it had cost her her family? What if she would have rather married the damned Sultan? There was only one way to find out.

Taking a deep breath, Rico opened the doors. Halina was standing on the far side of the room, once again looking pale and gaunt despite the roundness of her belly. She whirled around as he came into the room, her mouth dropping open in shock.

'Rico...'

'Did your father not tell you I was here?'

'No one's told me anything.' She drew a shuddering breath. 'I'm to marry the Sultan of Bahari...'

'No, you're not. The wedding's off.'

She stared at him in confusion. 'What?'

'I made a deal with the Sultan of Bahari. He agreed to call off the wedding, in exchange for a racehorse he has been wanting for many years.'

'A racehorse!'

'The owner wouldn't sell it to him, so I bought it instead.'

'How...?'

'It is done easily enough, when you know the right people and offer the right amount of money. But first, Halina, tell me you're all right. The baby...'

'The baby's all right.' She gave him a wan, tremulous smile. 'I haven't had any more bleeding and I've felt movement—tiny little flutters.'

'Thank God.'

'But why are you here, Rico? Why have you done this?'

'Because I read about your engagement in the newspaper and I didn't believe for a second that you wanted that. I feared your father had tricked you into coming home.'

'He did.' Halina closed her eyes briefly. 'I should have known better.'

'*Cara,* so should I. I will never forgive myself for jeopardising your life, your happiness, in such a way.'

'Let's have no more recriminations, please, Rico. There has been far too much regret already.'

'I need to ask.' Rico looked at her seriously. 'Is this what you want? Because your father made it clear that, if you left with me, you would not be welcomed back by your family. It's a high price to pay, Halina, and one I should have foreseen. Only you can decide if you wish to pay it.'

'And what is the alternative?' she asked, staring at him with wide, troubled eyes. 'To marry a man old enough to be my grandfather, and live in shame and seclusion as his third wife with an illegitimate child that would no doubt be taken away from me? Rico, it's a hard price to pay, but I pay it willingly. You need not fear that.'

'Good.' He took her hands, which felt small and icy, in his. 'Then it's time we departed.'

'Are we going back to Rome?'

'No,' Rico said, his heart full of both love and pain. He finally knew what love was, and he understood it was so much more than he'd thought. It wasn't an ephemeral emotion; it was life itself, duty and sacrifice, joy and feeling. He would do anything for Halina because he loved her. He would even let her go.

'Rico...? Where are we going?'

He smiled at her, his heart aching with both love and loss. 'We're going to Paris.'

CHAPTER SIXTEEN

YET AGAIN, WITHIN the space of a week, Halina found herself on a private jet, crossing the world. She felt such an overwhelming mix of relief and sadness that she could barely begin to process the emotions. To have seen her sisters, her family, again only to say goodbye so soon. It filled her with grief, even as she acknowledged the sweet and overwhelming relief at being rescued from a fate so grim she hated even to imagine it.

But what was going to happen now? She'd asked Rico why they were going to Paris, but he'd refused to be drawn. And, instead of seeming happy to have got her back, he'd withdrawn even more into himself, seeming so quiet and sad that Halina feared the cost her rescue was to him. Were they really better off than they'd been a few days ago before her father had arrived? It felt as if nothing had really changed; Rico was still remote and she still loved him. An impossible situation.

The plane finally touched down in Paris and, as they drove into the city, Halina gazed out of the limo's window in awe and wonder, her nose nearly pressed to the glass.

'There's the Eiffel Tower!' she exclaimed. 'I've only seen it in pictures…'

'You'll have time to do all the sightseeing you want,'

Rico assured her, and she turned back to him uncertainly. Why did he sound so resigned?

Realisation began to dawn when the limo turned onto a street of eighteenth-century townhouses, tall and elegant. It parked in front of number eighteen, a lovely old building covered in vines, just like in the children's story *Madeline*.

'What…?' Halina began in a disbelieving whisper. Rico drew a key from his pocket.

'Come,' he said, and she followed him out of the limo and up the stairs to the front door painted a shiny red. 'Sorry, there are quite a few stairs,' he remarked as he fitted the key in the door. 'But you did say the top floor.'

'My dream…' she whispered, feeling as if she were in one. She followed Rico into an old-fashioned lift with a grille for a door, up to the flat on the top floor. He unlocked the door and ushered her inside.

Halina stepped into the little hallway with its antique flocked wallpaper and colourful prints. She turned the corner and gazed in amazement at the living room—the squashy sofa, the grand piano, the shelves of books. It was as if he'd conjured it straight out of her head.

'How did you…?' she began, walking slowly around the apartment. There was a cosy kitchen with dishes in different colours and fresh flowers on the table. The bedroom had a double bed with a cover decorated in *broderie anglaise*, the window's bright-blue shutters open to the October sunshine.

And the balcony… She pushed open the French windows from the living room and stepped onto the tiny balcony with its wrought-iron railings and pots of herbs and flowers. Below her the streets of the Latin Quarter bustled and the smell of freshly baked croissants drifted up. Halina turned to Rico, shaking her head in amazement.

'It's as if you pulled this right out of my dreams.'

'Well, you did describe it to me in some detail.' He smiled faintly, but his eyes still looked sad.

'Yes, but how did you arrange it all?'

'It took some doing. I had very specific requests.' Rico's smile deepened. 'But it was worth it.'

'Rico, I don't know what to say.'

'The deed is in your name, of course,' he continued, and Halina blinked.

'What?'

'I've engaged a housekeeper to come once a week, but of course that's up to you. I thought you'd want your privacy.'

'I don't understand.'

'Of course this place might feel small once the baby comes, but we can cross that bridge when you come to it. If you'd like to move somewhere more suitable eventually, it can be arranged.'

'Now I really don't understand.' Her voice and body both shook. 'What are you telling me, Rico?'

He smiled sadly. 'I'm giving you what you've always wanted, Halina. Your freedom.'

Rico watched Halina's eyes widen in shock. Seeing her delight in the little flat had brought him such painful joy. She would be happy here. He'd make sure of it. Because, when you loved someone, you wanted their happiness more than anything. More than your own.

'My freedom,' Halina repeated slowly. 'You mean, you're leaving me again?'

'I'm giving you what you want,' Rico insisted. He'd thought long and hard about what to do when he'd been flying to Bahari and then Abkar. What Halina needed to be happy. 'You told me—many times you told me—

that you wanted your freedom, the chance to choose your own destiny. Well, here it is.'

'But I'm not choosing it,' Halina said, her voice growing in force and volume. 'Am I? You're still choosing it for me.'

Rico blinked, surprised by her fury. He'd thought she'd be pleased. He'd wanted to please her. Or, he wondered with an uncomfortable pang, had he been trying to assuage his own guilty conscience for backing out on her once before?

'If you don't want to live here, you don't have to.'

'I thought… I thought when you came for me you'd come to bring me back with you, because that's where you wanted me.' Her breath thickened. 'With you.'

'I'm trying to do the right thing, Halina—'

'Are you? Or are you trying to do the safe thing? Rico, I love you.'

The words fell into the shocked stillness.

'I've loved you for a while, and I should have told you sooner, but I was afraid. But I don't want to be afraid any longer. I've been batted back and forth like a ball in a game and I don't want that either. I want the freedom to choose, yes, and I choose you. If you'll have me.'

His stunned mind couldn't make sense of her words.

She continued determinedly. 'I know you don't love me, and I'm willing to accept that. I hope in time you might at least come to care for me a little, but in the meantime I want what we had before. I'll let it be enough. I want us, Rico. I want our family.'

'Stop.' His voice was so choked he could barely get the single word out. 'Stop, Halina. I can't let you say any more.'

Her eyes clouded and her lips trembled. 'You can't?'

'No, because you're wrong. So wrong. I won't come

to care for you a little in time, because I'm already completely, hopelessly in love with you.' Her mouth dropped open and he started walking towards her. 'I've been fighting it for a while, maybe even since we first met. Fighting it, because I was so scared of loving someone again, letting myself get hurt. Left. And so I did what I thought I'd never, ever do and I left you instead. I convinced myself I was doing the right thing, the noble thing, but really it was just cowardice. You were right to call me a coward, Halina. *Lina.* My Lina.'

He took hold of her hands, drawing her towards him. 'To hear that you love me…to know it and believe it… I wish I'd told you first. I wish I'd had that much courage. But I'm so honoured, so privileged, to be loved by you. I don't deserve it. I know I don't.'

'Deserving doesn't come into it, Rico,' Halina said softly as she came into his arms. 'Love is a gift, freely given, gratefully received. And that's how it is for me.'

'And for me. I love you so much. So much.'

'And I love you just as much.'

He kissed her then, because he needed to feel her in his arms, against his mouth. Halina wound her arms around his neck, her pliant body pressed to his as the sun spilled through the windows, and the whole world sang.

EPILOGUE

Six months later

'HE'S A HUNGRY little fellow, isn't he?' Rico gazed down at his son's rosebud mouth sucking greedily at his mother's breast. Halina stroked her baby's hair and looked up with laughing eyes.

'I don't mind.'

'As long as you're getting enough rest.'

'Plenty.' They shared a loving smile as he touched her hand, still incredulous, and so incredibly grateful, that she was here. That they shared this rare and precious happiness.

The last six months had been tumultuous, with their quiet wedding ceremony taking place when Halina had been seven months pregnant. Her friend Olivia, wife to Prince Zayed, had come, as had her husband, and Rico had found he liked the man. Halina's mother had come too, the first step of many to healing her fractured family.

After ten gruelling hours of labour his son, Matteo Falcone, had been born. Named after Rico's father, because all this had taught him that everyone made mistakes as well as hard choices. He didn't know which his father had made, but he knew he finally had it in his heart to forgive him. Because of Halina, and the light and love she'd brought to his life. The healing.

'I think he's had enough.' Halina lifted their sleepy son up to him. 'Do you want to hold him?'

'Of course.' Rico never tired of cradling his precious, tiny son. He marvelled that marriage and family had been gifts, treasures that he'd scorned, and he thanked God that he'd learned otherwise.

Now he balanced Matteo on his shoulder and gently jiggled him while Halina watched, a faint smile curving her face. She'd blossomed in the last few months through a difficult pregnancy, a tough labour, and then moving house to the villa outside Rome where they lived now, perfect for a growing family. Through it all she'd grown in grace and beauty, basking in his love for her, a love he'd never tire of showing and feeling…even when life was hard. Especially when it was.

'What are you thinking?' Halina asked softly, and Rico smiled.

'How blessed I am.'

'And I am, as well.'

'Yes, we both are.' He drew her up from the rocking chair and put his arm around her so they were together in a tight circle, the people he loved most in the world. His family. Their family. Together at last for ever.

* * * * *

ROYAL DOC'S
SECRET HEIR

AMY RUTTAN

For my Prince Charming, who swept me off my
feet twenty years ago when we first met
and who continues to do so.

CHAPTER ONE

IT HAD BEEN a long time since she'd been home. Jeena's heart beat triple time as the relief plane that was carrying medical supplies and her team of doctors and nurses approached the island kingdom of Kalyana.

She took a deep calming breath as the cloud cover evaporated and the jewel of an island set against the Indian Ocean came into view.

Her home.

Only Kalyana hadn't been her home. Not for a long time. Not since that night ten years ago when her father had woken her up and told her they were leaving Kalyana.

They were *all* leaving because they were in danger.

She hadn't wanted to go and didn't know where they were going, but her parents needed her and she needed them. So she'd left Kalyana for Canada.

She hadn't regretted it. It had been for the best. Still, she'd never thought she'd see Kalyana again.

She glanced down at her Canadian passport gripped tightly in her hand and *hoped* she'd be allowed in.

Her father had made it clear they couldn't go back. They should never go back. They hadn't been banished, but her father had said they weren't welcome in Kalyana. Because of her indiscretion, they would be judged. Harshly.

Jeena still found that hard to believe in this day in age, but her father had been adamant. He wanted to protect her and her unborn child.

The Canadian consulate had assured her that the visa had been cleared. That there shouldn't be any issues.

There shouldn't be a risk of someone waiting to pounce on her to ask her about her son and pry into her private life. She knew deep down there was nothing to fear. She hadn't done anything wrong.

All she'd done was become pregnant and decide to have her child. A lot of women were single mothers so there was no reason she would have to watch her back, but still those old anxieties were creeping into the back of her mind. The night her father had insisted they leave. He'd been so scared. He'd thought they were in danger and Jeena knew that someone had made him think that.

And it was all because of who her son's father was. If it had been someone else, they probably wouldn't have left...

"Why do we have to leave?" she asked.

"Lady Meleena said that the King will take your child!" her father said. "We have to go to keep our family together. Your child would be looked down upon. Do you really want that?"

"No." She shook her head. "But we can't afford to leave."

"Lady Meleena will help us. She just asks that we never come back. That we never contact anyone and keep your pregnancy secret. I promised her that for your safety."

"How does Lady Meleena know?" Jeena asked, con-

fused. "*No one but Mother and you know. Did you tell someone?*"

"*Of course not!*" *her father exclaimed.* "*Someone at the clinic told her.*"

"*Why would someone at the clinic tell her?*"

"*Because people know about who you were seen with and it wasn't long before Lady Meleena put two and two together. Meleena's father invests in my plantation. There would be scandal for all of us, and Lady Meleena wanted to take care of us.*"

"*I'm pregnant. I didn't commit a crime!*"

Her father hugged her. "*Of course you didn't, but Lady Meleena knows first-hand how an illegitimate child with a parent in the aristocracy can be treated. Look at her half-brother Kamal. He was treated so poorly by his peers and then he died in that terrible accident.*"

"*But—*"

"*No buts!*" *her father snapped.* "*We're leaving. It's the best thing for you and the baby. It will protect our family's name and avert scandal for all concerned.*"

Guilt coursed through her. "*Yes, Father. You're right.*"

Jeena shook the memory away and clenched her Canadian passport tighter in her fist.

The consulate might say that she was cleared to return and work in Kalyana, but was Lady Meleena, soon-to-be royal bride, okay with it?

They'd left ten years ago to save face and her father was indebted to Lady Meleena for her assistance, but then three years ago Lady Meleena had become engaged to the father of Jeena's unborn baby and a little part of Jeena couldn't help but wonder if Meleena had had her eyes set on a certain prize right from the start.

It had bothered her for years that Lady Meleena had taken such an interest in her.

Does it matter? He wouldn't have married you anyway. He couldn't. His family would have chosen his bride, and they wouldn't have chosen a farmer's daughter.

Her stomach twisted and she tried to relax on the last little bit of the long trip from Canada to Kalyana, only she knew she wouldn't feel at ease until they landed and she was cleared by customs. She was breaking her father's promise to Lady Meleena about never returning.

You didn't promise.

Jeena relaxed then. She was different now. She wasn't such a pushover.

This had been her home, whether Lady Meleena liked it or not. She was going to do her job here. She had no wish to interfere in Meleena or Maazin's life.

Even then, she wasn't sure she could relax, visa or not. She glanced out the window again and a lump formed in her throat, tears stinging her eyes as she saw the island get closer.

Home.

This was where her family had lived and thrived on the same vanilla plantation for generations and it was all her fault that it no longer belonged to her family. All because she'd got involved with and fallen in love with the wrong person.

"You okay?"

Jeena glanced at Teresa, one of the other doctors who had come to help with the relief efforts.

"Yeah, fine." Jeena forced herself to smile brightly. "Just missing my son."

Which wasn't a complete lie. She did miss her son. She'd never really been apart from him for this long and with this much of a distance between them.

He was safe in Canada with her parents. His competitive junior hockey team was in the finals and they were playing at Scotiabank Saddledome, which was a huge deal. He'd gone on and on about it for months. As had her father.

Syman was the reason her parents had taken Lady Meleena's aid and come to Canada, and why she needed them. She couldn't have raised him alone in Kalyana or Canada. She couldn't have become a surgeon without their help, and becoming a surgeon had been hard even with their help.

Still, there were things Syman would never know about Kalyana. Things she'd experienced that he'd never get to, like playing on the sand of a pearl-pink beach or swimming in a turquoise sea. Running through her father's vanilla fields or climbing a palm tree to stare out over the Indian Ocean.

Canada had been a good home for them and Syman loved his life there, even with the ice and snow that Jeena had never gotten used to. That she didn't miss.

If you'd stayed in Kalyana, Syman wouldn't even be interested in hockey.

Kalyana was near the Seychelles and was very traditional. Hockey wasn't one of the sports played in Kalyana. If she had raised Syman here, he would probably be into cricket.

Or polo?

Jeena shook that thought away. She didn't want to

think about Syman's father and how she had met him
during a divot stomp at a match she should've never
been at. She had only gone because her friend had
dragged her along and during the divot stomp she'd lost
her footing and been rescued by the man of her dreams.

Well, she hadn't been completely sure when she'd
first met him. Maazin had been a known playboy and
she'd known she should keep away, but when he had
been with her, he hadn't been the bad boy that everyone had said he was. He had been different.

So kind and caring.

And the more time they'd spent together, the more
she'd truly believed he'd loved her.

Her heart skipped a beat just thinking about him.
She'd been a fool. Young and naive.

Don't think about him.

Only it was hard not to. He was never really far from
her thoughts. The older Syman got, the more he looked
like his father, the more she saw the only man she had
ever loved. Syman was all the good parts of his father.
He was kind and caring. Also driven and stubborn.

Her heart may have been broken, but she loved
Syman and she was grateful that her time with Maazin
had given her her son.

"You'll see Syman soon. And I'm sure his team will
win the tourney," Teresa said brightly, interrupting her
thoughts of Syman's father.

Jeena chuckled. "They'd better or he'll be lamenting
it until next hockey season."

Teresa laughed and went back to her book.

Jeena glanced at the reading material she'd brought
for the long flight from Dubai, which was just one of
the flights she'd been on since they departed from Van-

couver. She really didn't know which way was up and given that there was a significant time zone difference, she couldn't help but wonder if Syman had actually won his tournament. Maybe he'd already played?

I should be there.

Only this was her job and her father had taught her and given her a work ethic she stood by. Kalyana needed her and her new country, Canada, needed her to represent them in the best possible light. She understood the customs. She knew the terrain and the people.

Even if it meant facing something that she wasn't sure that she was ready to face.

And when she closed her eyes she could still feel Maazin's arms around her, but then she was reminded of the pain when he'd turned his back on her, when Lady Meleena had told her he'd chosen his duty over her. When Lady Meleena had told her father that Syman would be an outcast. That Jeena would be an outcast because he would not marry her, even though he knew she was pregnant.

Then, a few years later, it had been announced that Prince Maazin had chosen his bride. None other than Jeena's supposed savior, Lady Meleena.

She shouldn't care, but it made her angry. Jeena knew her family had been manipulated.

Don't worry about it. Maazin isn't part of your life.

And she had to keep remembering that.

He hadn't been there for her when she'd had Syman. Neither had he been there when she'd scrimped and saved, worked odd jobs while attending medical school. That had been all her. She didn't need him. She was better off without him.

Syman was better off without him.

Are you sure?

"We're making our final descent into Huban. Please buckle up. It's a bit windy and there has been some damage to the airstrip from the cyclone so it might be a rough landing," the pilot said over the speaker.

"Here we go," Teresa said, setting down her book and buckling up her seatbelt.

Jeena nodded and pulled her seatbelt tighter. She kept her eyes focused on Kalyana as it got closer and closer. She could see the damage. Trees ripped from their roots, buildings along the coast destroyed, but there on the main terminal still flew the blue, green and gold flag of Kalyana. Untouched and fluttering in the strong winds in a clear blue sky. A sight she'd thought she'd never see again.

It helped tame the erratic beat of her heart.

She was home.

Maazin waited on the edge of the tarmac in a van to help transport medical supplies to the makeshift hospital that he and Farhan had set up between Huban and the southeast district, which had been the hardest hit when Cyclone Blandine had ripped through Kalyana.

Kavan, the bodyguard who also acted as chauffer-pilot, had seemed keen to accompany Maazin, but he'd eventually agreed it was best he stay with Farhan, Maazin's older brother, Sara, and her grandfather, Mr. Raj. Ever since the cyclone had hit, Farhan had been jumpy, fussing and fuming over his new bride.

Not that Maazin could blame him.

If he had someone he loved...

Maybe if he still had the one woman he'd once loved

he would've felt the same way that Farhan did, but he didn't have anyone.

He didn't deserve anyone. Not even the arranged marriage his father had set up three years ago. Not that he'd really cared for Lady Meleena. It had just been expected and since Maazin had lost the only woman he'd loved when she'd left in the middle of the night, he had settled for the bride his father had chosen. Or eventually settled. After everything that had happened when Jeena had left, he'd spent some time doing what good he could.

He'd served in the Royal Guard and earned his doctorate as a surgeon in the guard. It gave his life meaning, after all his past actions had caused so much pain. His service was the least he could do.

Which was why he'd agreed to marry Meleena. His father had guilted him into it and he had been tired of the nagging to find a wife. He'd had no interest in Meleena, so had had very little to do with her.

Of course, Meleena hadn't liked it too much when he'd devoted his life to healing others, to serving his country, and had ignored her. She'd left him, but no one knew about that yet and that's the way his father wanted it. There were diplomatic policies and contracts at play and his father wanted to wait until it could be properly addressed after Kalyana recovered from the devastation of Blandine.

So he had no one.

No one to worry about. No one to care.

Which was what he deserved.

It was best that he handle this. He was just as capable a doctor as Farhan and Sara were. This was what he lived for. This was all that had mattered since Jeena had left and his brother Ali had died trying to help him. The last thing he wanted to do was put Farhan or Sara in danger.

His mother had already suffered enough because of him. He wasn't going to put Farhan in harm's way when he had military training and could manage this kind of disaster situation with ease. Not that they were in much danger now. The cyclone was over. It was just a matter of picking up the pieces. Cyclone Blandine had done severe damage to the islands.

He couldn't remember such a storm ever hitting Kalyana.

His father King Uttam was all for Maazin helping with relief efforts. He should be a part of it. Farhan was an excellent doctor, but he didn't have the training Maazin had.

However, his mother Queen Aruna was a little more reluctant to hear a prince of Kalyana was out there helping with relief efforts and getting his hands dirty. She thought it was unsafe.

Of course, even if she didn't show it, Maazin worried his mother had never been happy with anything he'd done since Ali had died.

But Maazin wanted to help.

He *needed* to help.

Still, his mother had made her reservations clear...

"You're a prince!"

"So? What else should a trained surgeon be doing, Mother?"

"You're only a surgeon because of your time in the Royal Guard."

"So what would you have me do?" Maazin asked.

"You should stay in the safety of the palace."

"And tend to royalty? To aristocrats?"

"Perhaps. And perhaps if you had done more of your royal duties and spent time with your betrothed, Lady Meleena wouldn't have left!"

"I don't care that she left, Mother. I don't love her. I couldn't stand be around her."

"Ali did his duty!"

"I'm sorry that I'm not Ali."

His mother's had a faraway look as she murmured, *"You're right. You're not..."*

Maazin winced. He hadn't wanted an arranged marriage. Especially with someone his father had chosen only for the betterment of the country.

Your father chose for Ali and he'd been happy. Your father chose for Farhan and he's happy with Sara.

He ignored that niggling little thought.

Right now Kalyana needed him. When Ali had been alive, he'd always been out there lending a hand, and that was the least Maazin could do since he was responsible for Ali's death.

You're not.

Only he felt he was. And he was sure his mother felt that he was responsible for Ali's death. Ever since then his mother had been cold and distant. With him especially.

And he hated it that he was the cause of her grief, that he was just a living reminder of her pain. And he couldn't help but wonder if she wished it was him who'd died instead of Ali.

He pushed that thought aside and watched as the Canadian plane landed with much-needed supplies. Cyclone Blandine had done so much damage and they hadn't been very prepared. Storms had come and gone, but there had never been a cyclone like this. It had formed out of nowhere and so quickly and it had struck so hard.

There was no way they could prepare for quite how extreme it was and they were lucky that it hadn't done even more damage.

The plane from Canada that he'd been waiting for made its landing. Maazin had made sure that the airport runway in Huban had been cleared of debris so that they could receive assistance from other countries, like Canada, and he had his sister-in-law Sara to thank for that assistance.

The plane circled as the winds were high.

Maazin waited with bated breath as the plane came around again then touched down. He didn't know why he was so nervous about this plane landing, but something about this was eating away at him.

He hadn't felt like this in so long.

The last time he'd felt like this…well, he didn't want to think about her.

This was not the time to think about it. It was not time to think about Jeena. Of course, she was never far from his mind. He was always thinking of her, whether he liked it or not. Always wondering why she'd left him. It drove him mad.

"They're ready for us, Your Highness," his driver, Kariff, said.

Maazin nodded. "Let's go and fill this van with supplies and their doctors. The southeast region is in dire need of supplies and medical help."

Kariff nodded and drove the van toward the large plane that had dropped its rear door to make a ramp, ready to start unloading its precious cargo of medical supplies and doctors to aid them.

Kariff parked close and Maazin got out of the van. He opened the side doors and the back so that Kariff and a couple of the other men he'd brought with him could start loading up.

"Who should we be reporting to?" a female voice asked, which sent a shiver of recollection down his spine. He knew that voice. He knew it well because it was burned into every single neuron in his brain. Just the mere sound of her voice fired them off, bringing every bitter-sweet memory to the surface.

Maazin turned around and came face to face with someone he'd never thought he would see again.

His blood froze and everything around him stopped. He couldn't quite believe his eyes and he wondered if he was dreaming. It was like she had walked right out of his dreams, like nothing had changed, like time had stood still. She hadn't changed one bit. Her rich, dark brown hair was tied back in a braid, just like the first day he'd met her. Her skin was still a warm, rich tawny color.

Her deep brown eyes widened and her red lips, lips he remembered so well the taste of, dropped open for a moment and a subtle pop of coral colored her cheeks. She was just as shocked as he was.

Jeena.

In an instant he remembered when he'd first seen her. She'd looked so out of place and uncomfortable on the polo pitch.

She'd worn a long emerald dress and high heels as she'd teetered on the grass, trying to flip over a divot.

He'd been so entranced by her and had wondered who she was…

"You'll fall over, trying to flip those divots in those heels."

She looked up, embarrassed. "Pardon?"

Maazin knelt down and took her foot in his hands. "May I?"

She pursed her lips and nodded. He removed her shoe and pried off the large chunk of turf that had been impaled on the end of her stiletto heel. He replaced the shoe and then stood, steadying her in his arms, catching a scent of her perfume.

Jasmine and vanilla. It was intoxicating and he was instantly drawn to her.

"Thank you… Your Highness."

"Ah, so you know who I am."

"Everyone knows who you are," she whispered, and wouldn't look at him.

"Well, I am at a loss. I don't know who you are. I have never seen you at one of these events before."

She smiled. "My name is Jeena. I am here with my friend as her guest."

"And who is your friend?"

"Aishraya Raj." Jeena nodded in the direction of her friend. "Her husband is a diplomat, but I've known Aishraya for a long time."

Maazin smiled and bowed at the waist. "Well, allow me to welcome you to our little match…"

Maazin tried to calm the pulse that was now thundering in his ears. She had been the only one to truly *see* him.

The world thought he was this playboy and he let everyone believe that. The tabloids, his parents all believed it and it had got him off the hook of so many responsibilities, but Jeena had seen past that.

He had been so in love with her. He'd wanted to marry her, even though he had always been afraid and not interested in marriage because he'd felt it would tie him down, just like his royal duty.

And he hadn't wanted to drag Jeena into a life of protocol.

She had been free. Which was why he'd wanted her.

Jeena had left him. Left him without a word, and it was because of her leaving that he'd gone to that party to drown his sorrows and then called his brother Ali to get him.

And that had cost Ali his life, because after she'd left, Maazin had decided to take the bad boy road everyone thought he traveled. Ali came to sweep his indiscretions under the rug and died trying to cover up his mistakes.

It had destroyed him when Jeena had left. It was his own fault, though, because he knew he'd driven her away. He didn't deserve her and he certainly didn't deserve anything now. He knew that.

"Maa... Your Highness." And she curtseyed.

He was angry that she had almost addressed him with familiarity, like he wanted, but had then changed it to a formal address and curtseyed in deference to his station, which he hated.

Were they such strangers?

Yes. They were now. She'd left. He'd never left Kalyana. He'd never left in the dead of night, not telling anyone where he was going. And when he'd tried to find her there'd been no trace of her. It was as if her whole life in Kalyana had been erased.

She'd cost him so much.

You were the selfish one. She cost you nothing.

"I'm surprised that you've returned to the country you abandoned with such ease," he snapped.

Her expression hardened. "My apologies, Your Highness. I'm the lead surgeon on this relief mission. I'm representing Canada and I'm here to deliver your supplies and lend my services to *your* country." She turned on her heel and walked away.

She was a doctor?

Maazin was shocked, but as she stormed away he couldn't help but smile to himself. She still had that spirit he'd admired in her.

That fire.

That had been hidden under the surface, something she'd tried so hard to control, but he'd known what a strong woman had been under that demure exterior.

It's what he'd loved so much about her then.

Now, to see her standing her ground, it surprised him, but pleasantly so.

It woke up a piece of him he'd thought was long gone and as he watched her walk away, giving out orders, he knew that working with her would be a challenge.

One he hadn't expected.

CHAPTER TWO

JEENA DIDN'T KNOW what she had been expecting. She knew one thing, she hadn't planned on seeing him. Actually, she hadn't expected to see him at all. What was a prince of Kalyana doing at the airport, collecting medical supplies?

Not your concern.

And she had to keep telling herself that.

She was stronger now. She could handle seeing Maazin.

Can you?

She'd changed, but had she really expected a bad boy rebel prince to have changed in the last ten years?

No. Well, maybe? One could hope. Other than his engagement to Lady Meleena, Maazin hadn't really been in the papers. Perhaps he had changed? She'd always wondered if that image he'd projected before she'd met him had been an act. She knew one thing was for sure, his appearance hadn't changed at all.

It was like time hadn't even touched him at all.

When she'd seen him there, she couldn't believe her eyes. It was like all those years ago when he had knelt down in front of her on the polo field and stopped her from embarrassing herself in front of a social class that she had not been comfortable being around at all.

His ebony hair was shorter than it had been. Gone were the long curls that had framed his face when they'd first met and he was now clean shaven. He'd lost the neatly trimmed beard she'd loved so much. His skin was deep, lustrous gold and warmed by the heat and sun from Kalyana. And he'd lost some of that baby fat that came with youth, but those green-gray eyes were still the same as they'd bored deep into hers, totally riveting her to the spot.

Making her quiver with desire. Even after all these years apart her body still reacted to him. She remembered the feeling of those strong hands on her, the taste of his lips as he'd brushed kisses lightly on hers.

How safe he'd made her feel when his arms had been wrapped around her.

He turned his back on you and Syman, remember...?

"He knows," Meleena said in a scathing tone.

"He knows?" Jeena asked, stunned.

"Yes."

"How do you know that he knows?"

Meleena rolled her eyes. "My father is very close to the royal family. That's how I know. Prince Maazin can't commit to you."

"I don't believe that."

Meleena fished out a check and held it out to her. "Here. Compensation for your...situation."

It was like a slap in the face and her heart clenched as she stared at it.

This was all she was worth?

The fact he knew about her pregnancy and had

turned his back on her made her firm her resolve. She wouldn't be duped again by anyone.

She was no longer that foolish innocent who could be swept off her feet by a dashing Prince Charming.

He hadn't been there when her family had sold off everything to start a new life in Canada.

Neither had he been there when Syman was born.

Syman, who had those same eyes as his father.

Syman.

Her heart sank. He always was curious about his father and as he got older she knew it was something she would not be able to keep from him. Not when he could go online and look Maazin up.

He'd learn his father was a prince and a playboy. How his father had turned his back on her. His father's whole private romantic life had been splashed across tabloids around the world. The only romance not there and not known was hers. Lady Meleena's parents had paid people off to keep that secret.

"Dr. Harrak!"

She turned and saw Maazin coming toward her and her heart skipped a beat again.

Stand firm.

She crossed her arms and narrowed her resolve. How many people had tried to push her around when she'd been a resident and learning to become a surgeon because she was short at only five feet four? Too many and Jeena had had to rise above all of that and make sure that her voice had been heard above the others in a competitive medical program.

And on top of all of that she'd raised Syman.

She was stronger than some spoiled and pampered

prince who was coddled by parents who gave him everything and ruled a country.

She could handle him. She wasn't going to let a prince sweep her off her feet again. She didn't need saving or a knight in shining armor.

And she wasn't going to be sent back to Canada because he and his fiancée were uncomfortable with her presence in Kalyana.

"I have every right to be here," she snapped when Maazin caught up with her.

"What?" he asked, frowning.

"I have a visa and clearance from the consulate to represent Canada and assist in this humanitarian and relief aid effort. Kalyana may not be my home any longer…"

"I'm aware of that," he answered stiffly. "What I came over to say was sorry. I'm sorry for embarrassing you like that."

Jeena was shocked, but she didn't let him know that. That was different. The Maazin she remembered had been a bit arrogant with people he'd felt deserved it, but he had always been kind and gentle to her. She'd often wondered why he hadn't shown that side of himself to the public.

Of course he'd turned his back on her. She wasn't going to be fooled again.

It had been a painful lesson to learn that she didn't need a prince to come and save her and that she was more than capable of saving herself.

"No apology needed, Your Highness. I forgot myself for a moment, you are absolutely right, I left Kalyana for another country, because it was right for me. Now

I'm here on behalf of Canada. I'm home now and I'm here to help." She curtseyed again.

"Jeena, stop that." He was annoyed. She remembered how much he hated protocol. She knew she was getting to him.

Good.

"Stop what, Your Highness?"

"Curtseying and calling me Your Highness. Jeena, we know each other intimately."

"That's Dr. Harrak to you, Your Highness." She crossed her arms and leaned forward. "Perhaps we knew each other once, but a lot has changed. I prefer the formality, Your Highness."

His eyes narrowed. "Fine."

She nodded and felt a bit of satisfaction knowing that she had won that battle. It felt good.

Did it?

"Well, Dr. Harrak," he said, exaggerating her name. "My driver Kariff and I are to take you to the southeastern region, which was hardest hit by the cyclone. Our doctors have been working non-stop since the cyclone hit four days ago and they could use a break."

Jeena smiled. "Of course, Your Highness."

He stood there. "Well?"

"Well, what?" she asked.

"We have to leave."

"I'm waiting for you to lead the way, Your Highness. It's only proper."

He rolled his eyes and turned around and started marching stiffly toward the van, the tail of his blue kurta billowing out behind him.

If she really wanted to bite back at him, now would

be the time to tell him that he reminded her of his father, which had always used to annoy him as well.

She chuckled softly and kept that to herself.

Right now, there were patients waiting for help and that was all that mattered to her, but it was nice to have a little victory over the man who'd broken her heart.

A man who had ruined her for all others.

A man who still had a piece of her heart, whether she liked it or not.

The ride in the van was uncomfortable and tense. Maazin sat in the front next to Kariff while she and her team were crammed in beside medical equipment and gear. There would be another van coming soon to take the rest of the supplies and gear into Huban, but right now they were transporting what was most needed to the hardest hit region. That had been her plan. Get to work, help out and keep out of sight.

She might not really care about her father's promise to Lady Meleena but she didn't want the drama that would come with it.

The press didn't know about Syman or her romance with Maazin and she preferred it that way.

The only reason she was here was to save lives.

As the van navigated the damaged streets of Huban, Jeena's heart sank to see the destruction. The little wooden shacks of the poorest hadn't fared as well as the colonial buildings that had been built by the British over a century ago.

There were downed power lines, crumbled stone and debris everywhere.

"Hold on," Maazin said over his shoulder. "This part of Huban was flooded quite badly. The water has receded enough to allow passage, but it will be a bumpy ride."

Jeena bit her lip. Her head began to spin and her pulse thundered in her ears. A panic attack was coming on and she needed to center herself. She needed to gain control, but it was hard. She didn't like water too much. She was fine if she was on a large boat or had her feet firmly planted on the ground, but in a van going over a washed-out road, this she didn't like.

And she closed her eyes and tried to not think about that time when she had been a young girl and she'd wandered too far from her parents' home and down to the small creek that ran adjacent to the plantation.

She'd been playing in the water when it had begun to rain, but since there had been no lightning and it had been so hot and dry, Jeena had just stayed where she was and enjoyed not being hot for once.

It was then that a flash flood had ripped down the mountainside. She would have been swept away if she hadn't gripped that low-growing palm. She'd held onto the trunk of that tree for what had felt like an eternity as the water had rushed past her, trying to snatch her away and wash her out to sea.

And she remembered the terror of it all.

The water that had rushed over her while she'd clung to life, while she'd tried to breathe and not take water into her lungs. The weariness of trying to stay afloat had begun to set in.

And then she remembered the strong arms of her father reaching down to pluck her from the swollen creek and into the safety of his arms.

She'd gotten into trouble, but not too much as her father had felt that she'd learned her lesson about doing dangerous things and not listening to them, but really she hadn't learned her lesson. Not really.

And how had she repaid her parents?

She'd become involved with a prince of Kalyana, even though it was forbidden because he'd been destined to marry someone of his father's choosing.

Her parents had got her out of the country to protect her. Lady Meleena had helped before'd she got engaged to Maazin a few years later. Her parents had lost everything.

They love Syman, though.

Still, she should've learned to curb her reckless ways that day she'd almost drowned and maybe then her parents would still be in Kalyana and she could've been here with the cyclone had hit and she could've been helping right from the start.

But you wouldn't have Syman.

No. She wouldn't have had Syman and for that she couldn't regret her past mistakes. Even though she regretted everything about falling in love with a prince, there had been one bright spot to the whole thing and that was her son. And that thought made her feel guilty for wishing her mistakes away.

He was her world and she missed him. Especially at this moment when she could do with a smile and a hug. She really missed her son.

The van rocked, jolting thoughts of Syman out of her head. She gripped her seat as the van made its way through another washed-out section of the road. The rushing water caused the van to sway, but it wasn't deep.

It was deep enough for Jeena's pulse to thunder even more loudly in her ears and for beads of sweat to break across her brow. Her hands felt clammy as she dug her fingers into the upholstery of the seat.

She looked up and saw that Maazin was watching her in the rearview mirror. He looked concerned and she tried to shake it all off. The last thing she wanted was for Maazin to feel bad for her.

Or, worse, think that she couldn't handle this, because she could.

Jeena looked away and the van carefully made its way through the water and back onto dry road as they made their way out of the capital city of Huban. Jeena took a deep breath of relief and glanced out of the window. She could see the palace rising in the distance. It had sustained some damage, but it still stood there, like a rock, reminding all the people of Kalyana that the country was still strong.

And a blowhard loud-mouthed king ruling them.

Well, not really. King Uttam might not be her favorite person in the world, but he wasn't a terrible king. He was a fair ruler.

And she saw a lot of his stubbornness in Syman. When Syman set his mind to something, there was no convincing him otherwise. It made her laugh from time to time. At least Syman was strong.

He had a strong personality. One she hadn't had until she'd had him and had worked her way through medical school.

"We're nearly at the hospital," Maazin announced.

Jeena didn't respond. She just looked out the window toward the Indian Ocean, remembering precious days gone by and how it was all her fault that her son couldn't enjoy this with her.

* * *

Maazin watched Jeena as she and her team had a quick meeting and then started to move around the makeshift hospital that was set up in an old shanty town, or what was left of a shanty town now that it had been leveled.

Something had bothered Jeena in the van when they'd crossed through that water and he couldn't help but wonder what.

It's not your concern.

And it wasn't. She wasn't his and could never be his.

Still, he was drawn to her and he was worried that something had happened to her and he felt responsible.

"You all right?"

Maazin turned to see Farhan standing beside him. Farhan looked exhausted and Maazin couldn't blame him. He and Sara had been working hard to help since the storm had started. Farhan hadn't been here when Maazin and Jeena had had their torrid and short love affair.

So there was no need to explain it all now.

It was over.

And it wasn't Farhan's business.

It was Maazin's pain to bear.

"Nothing, just..." Maazin scrubbed a hand across his face. "Tired and relieved that help is here."

Farhan nodded. "So am I. Sara has been working herself to the bone and she needs her rest."

"Take her back to Huban and get rest. I'm going to stay and help the Canadians and help Kariff unload the medical supplies."

"You should rest too," Farhan suggested. "You've been working non-stop since even before the cyclone hit."

"What for? I have no wife and I like to keep busy."

"You're going to work yourself into an early grave, brother." Farhan turned and left and Maazin let out a breath that he hadn't even known that he was holding.

He glanced back over his shoulder to see Jeena sitting next to a patient's bed and talking with the elderly woman, who seemed to recognize her.

Why had Jeena left?

"She's left," his mother said with finality.

"What?" Maazin asked, stunned.

"Your paramour. She is gone. Now you can do the duty we all must, and marry someone of the lineage to be your bride."

"I don't believe you," Maazin said hotly. *"Jeena would never do that."*

His mother walked calmly over to her desk and pulled out a letter, handing it to him. It looked like Jeena's handwriting.

His mother held it out to him between two fingers. "Read it."

Maazin snatched the letter from his mother and quickly read the letter. It didn't sound like Jeena, but it was her writing.

"Where did you get this?"

"Meleena found it."

"Why would Meleena find it?" he asked.

"Her father has invested in the Harrak plantation and she's trying to prevent a scandal for a family her father supports."

Maazin read the letter again and couldn't believe it.

It stated that she was leaving him because she couldn't stand being linked to a prince who had a checkered past full of women and gambling. Even though she knew those things weren't true...even though he had never been unfaithful to her. He'd wanted to marry her.

Maazin crumpled up the paper. "She would never leave her parents. I'm going to find her."

He turned to leave but his mother cleared his throat and Maazin turned back.

"Her parents are gone too. They left Kalyana with her. This morning, in fact. They should already be in Dubai."

"Where are they going?"

His mother shrugged. "Who knows? They didn't tell me. Kalyanese people are free to come and go out of their country as they please."

Maazin had gone to her parents' vanilla plantation, which was on the westerly side of the main island. And his mother had been right. They had left and their plantation had been for sale. It had made no sense.

And he'd felt betrayed.

So he couldn't help but wonder why they'd left and why she was now back. She'd fled in the middle of the night like she'd been afraid. So why had she come back?

At least now he knew where she had gone and what she had done with her life these past ten years. She'd become a surgeon!

He hadn't expected that.

Why not? You became one too.

"You okay?"

Maazin turned around to see Jeena standing next to him.

"Perfectly," he said.

She cocked an eyebrow. "You sure?"

"Yes," he snapped, and then he sighed. "Sorry. I'm tired. It's been non-stop since we set up this hospital."

"I can see," she said gently, and then tilted her head to the side. "I thought the Royal Guard set up this hospital?"

"They did. I'm part of the Royal Guard."

Her mouth dropped open and then snapped shut. "You're a member of the guard? Since when?"

He wanted to tell her since she'd left and he'd had that drunken night, the night his brother Ali and his wife Chandni had died.

After the funeral he'd joined the guard to give back and try to appease the pain and guilt he'd felt for surviving when they hadn't.

And when he'd served his first year he'd decided to become a surgeon, to save even more lives.

It won't bring Ali back.

He cleared his throat. "I've been a member of the Royal Guard for almost ten years."

"That seems so unlike you."

His spine stiffened and he wanted to ask her who she thought he was. He hadn't been the one to leave. He'd stayed and made the most of the heartache she'd caused.

"Help!"

Maazin spun around as a man came in carrying a lifeless boy. He ran toward the man, who looked exhausted and sick. He scooped the boy up in his arms.

"Your Highness, please…my son."

"What's wrong?" Jeena asked, coming up beside Maazin and looking at the boy.

"He's burning up," Maazin stated, touching the boy's face.

"He started complaining of abdominal pain two days ago and there was blood…" The boy's father looked pale.

Maazin's stomach dropped and he felt sure he knew what it was.

The boy's father was probably a farmer who got water from the river. After the cyclone the water source had probably become contaminated.

"We need to isolate the boy and his father. I think it's dysentery," Maazin said to Jeena under his breath so as not to alarm the others in the hospital.

Jeena nodded and Maazin took the boy to the back of the hospital. There was a small building that they had the use of with a few rooms for cases such as this. Jeena led the boy's father to one of the rooms as well.

They had to get the two of them away from the other patients as bacillary dysentery was highly contagious, and since Maazin had picked the boy up without gloves he was going to have to go on a course of antibiotics as well and burn his clothes.

At least Jeena had on a surgical gown and gloves, as well as a mask. She was prepared and Maazin had been too busy thinking about the past and letting Jeena's presence unnerve him, so that he hadn't thought about dysentery being a problem after a cyclone. He hadn't changed into scrubs. He hadn't set up to deal with such a contagious disease, and he was kicking himself for not doing it sooner.

He was a fool, but right now he was going to try and save this young boy's life.

The boy winced and moaned in pain, but had a high fever and was completely out of it. Maazin set him on a bed and then got about setting up an IV with a bolus of fluids, electrolytes and antibiotics.

Jeena got the boy's father into the room beside him and through the small window that separated these two rooms he could see that she was doing the same and instructing a nurse, who had put on a hazmat suit, how to set up the quarantine.

Jeena then slipped out of the room and came to him. She looked at the boy and Maazin thought he saw a pained expression on her face.

"You're going to need to get out of those clothes and go on antibiotics in the other room."

"I know," Maazin said. "And you'll have to as well."

She nodded. "I know. I've changed and disposed of the gown, gloves and mask. I'll have the decontamination shower just to be sure, and then get the course of antibiotics."

"I want to make sure my patient's fever comes down." Maazin glanced down at the boy. So small and so sick. He hated seeing his people suffer.

"Your patient? I didn't realize you were a doctor." And he could hear the surprise in her voice.

"Yes. I'm a surgeon, a surgeon in the Royal Guard. My brother Farhan and I have been working here since the cyclone hit. I do my duty to my people!"

"Wow, I'm surprised," she said.

"What? That I'm a doctor or that I'm competent?" he snapped.

Jeena's cheeks flushed in embarrassment. "I'm sorry."

"Thank you," he said. He appreciated her apology.

"Either way, you need to take precautions. Princes are susceptible to dysentery too."

"I'm not leaving my patient!"

"I can take care of that, Your Highness." A Canadian doctor he was not familiar with came into the room in a hazmat suit. "I think you best go and clean up so we can keep the infection from spreading."

Maazin sighed. "Fine. You're right."

He followed Jeena to where the showers were. She slipped into one of the stalls and Maazin made his way to the other stall. As he passed by, he glanced down at her phone, which was buzzing, and was shocked to see a picture of a little boy on her phone. At first glance it reminded him of his late brother, but there were no pictures of Ali in a hockey jersey. And then it hit him.

The picture was of a little boy with gray-green eyes like his, looking back at him.

And suddenly he felt a bit dizzy.

CHAPTER THREE

JEENA WATCHED THE bolus of antibiotics dripping down and into her arm. It was unlikely that she had dysentery, but given the extremely infectious nature of it, she didn't want to take any chances.

People who weren't treated died.

And it was a painful way to die.

Maazin was in the bed next to her, he was wearing scrubs instead of the kurta that he'd greeted her in and he looked angry as he was hooked up to an antibiotic drip. He was brooding. This seemed to be more like the Maazin she remembered.

Of course she couldn't blame him. She'd be annoyed too if someone questioned her like she'd questioned him.

It just took her completely by surprise that he had served in the royal guard and become a surgeon too. He had never really talked about what he wanted to do because there was no expectation for him to do anything. He was a prince.

And she was impressed that he'd done something with his life.

I wonder what Lady Meleena thinks of his work?

Jeena was annoyed that she let that thought slip in

and she was angry at herself for questioning him. She'd apologized, but she knew he was still angry with her.

"We should find out if anyone else is in that farmer's home," Jeena said. "They'll all have to be treated."

"It's just the man and his son. I'm told the boy's mother died last year in a farming accident," he said.

"Oh, I'm sorry to hear that."

Maazin wouldn't look at her. The bolus of antibiotics was apparently far more interesting.

Of course, she couldn't really blame him. Their first meeting a couple of hours ago hadn't been the warmest.

She sighed and closed her eyes, trying to make the best of a tense situation.

"Who is that boy?" he finally asked, breaking the silence.

Her stomach twisted in a knot. "What boy? The farmer's boy?"

He turned and looked at her and then she knew. She glanced down at her phone on the bed beside her. She'd noticed that she'd missed a call from Syman when she'd gone into the shower and she was also very aware that when Syman called his picture showed up on her phone.

And she was also aware of Syman's striking resemblance to certain members of the Kalyanese Royal Family, but she was annoyed that he was asking her who he was.

Had he expected her to use that money to get rid of her pregnancy?

If he had and wanted the money back, she could pay him. The money was still sitting in an account. She hadn't spent a dime of his pity check.

"Who is the boy?" he asked again, his voice calm,

but there was a hint of anger in there and that sent a shiver of dread through her.

"My son," she stated. "Obviously."

"Your son? How old is he?"

"Nine. Again obvious."

Maazin's eyes narrowed and then he looked away. There was no sense in hiding the fact that Syman was his. She guessed by his expression, his tone and the fact that Syman was nine that he knew. And there was really no denying it. Syman had the same dark, long curls as Maazin had once had and the same stunning eyes.

He didn't say anything else to her, but she wasn't surprised as the nurses returned to check on them, which was good because emotionally, right now, Jeena didn't want to talk about it. She was afraid if she did she was going to break down and cry.

That was when her phone rang and Syman's face popped back up on the screen. Maazin's gaze locked on that picture.

Not now.

She had to answer it.

"Hi, Syman," she said, answering the phone and feeling Maazin's gaze boring into the back of her skull.

"Hi, Mom!" Syman's voice came from the other end. "We won!"

"You won. That's wonderful."

"Yeah, I'm so excited to get to play at the Saddledome. Grandpa said he's going to take me out for pizza."

"That's wonderful."

"You okay, Mom? You sound a bit weird."

"I'm okay. I'm here in Kalyana and you can tell your grandparents I'm okay."

"Actually, Grandpa wants to talk to you."

"No—" she began, but it was too late as Syman handed the phone over to her father.

"Jeena, are you okay?" her father asked.

She could hear the worry in her father's voice. She remembered how troubled he'd been when he'd found out she was carrying Maazin's baby. Her father had been so terrified Syman would be taken away or that they'd become outcasts.

"I'm okay, Dad. I'm fine."

"You're sure?"

"Yes. I'm working now, though." What she wanted to tell him was that Maazin was here and that he knew about Syman, but now was not the time.

"How bad is the damage?" her father asked. "Have you seen…? How much have you seen?"

Her father was asking about their plantation and whether she'd seen it. Even though her parents had left to protect her and even though her father insisted he didn't care for his old plantation, she knew he did. She knew her father missed his home country.

"I'm outside Huban, in the southeastern district that was hit the worst. I really have to go, but I'll talk to you later, okay?"

"Okay, Jeena. Be safe and avoid… Be safe."

"I will, Dad."

Her father had trailed off. She knew he'd been going to say avoid Lady Meleena and Maazin, but he hadn't.

Jeena ended the call. She felt like she was going to throw up. This was not how she'd planned this trip to go. All she wanted was to do her job and then head back to Alberta to be with Syman and her parents.

She wanted to lie low.

The last thing she'd wanted to do was run into Maazin but, of course, karma had had other plans. The nurses finished with Maazin and they were left alone again. He wouldn't look at her. He just stared ahead.

"Is he mine?" he finally asked, breaking the silence that had fallen between them again.

"What do you mean, is he yours? Of course he is." She swallowed the lump in her throat, one that had formed because of the tears she'd been holding back for so long. He acted like he didn't know about Syman. Maybe he'd forgotten and that wouldn't surprise her.

She and her unborn baby had been so insignificant to him, why would he give them a second thought?

"How can I be certain?"

"He's nine years old and you were my first." Jeena wanted to tell him that he was her only lover. That his betrayal of her, his abandonment when she'd needed him most had broken her so completely that she didn't trust anyone else with her heart.

And she had her son to look after. There was no time for romance. All she had was school, Syman and her parents.

The people who mattered most.

"Why didn't you tell me that I had a son?" Maazin asked.

Jeena snickered. "Really?"

"What do you mean, really? You obviously didn't want me to know or you would've told me."

Jeena rolled her eyes. How could she have been in

love with someone so stubborn was beyond her. "Don't be so precious. You knew. You've just forgotten."

He opened his mouth to say more but the nurses came back and they removed her IV as she had finished her dose of antibiotics. After she was cleared to go, she slipped off the cot and left the isolation area. She wouldn't be allowed to work on patients until she'd been clear for twenty-four hours and she was annoyed about that, but it came with the territory in emergency medicine. She walked out of the medical tent and made her way down to the beach.

The heat of the sun felt good on her skin. It was way better than the bitter cold Canadian winter that her mother still hadn't gotten used to.

She sat down on the beach and closed her eyes, drinking in the Vitamin D and listening to the sound of the waves lapping gently on the pearl-pink sand. Her mind drifted back to the last time she'd sat on a pearl-pink sand beach like this.

"Jeena, you are so beautiful," Maazin whispered against her ear.

A shiver of delight traveled down her spine and she couldn't quite believe that he'd taken her out on his yacht to Patang Island for a private dinner.

There were no guards here.

It was just the two of them on the sandbar, under the moonlight, with the ocean wind caressing their skin.

She knew that he had a bit of a reputation, but he hadn't been unfaithful to her. They'd been inseparable and she was so in love with him.

He kissed her again, cupping her face and making her melt into his arms. She was so in love with him that she couldn't remember a moment of what life had been like without him.

Life had been so dull and colorless until she'd met him.

"Be with me tonight," he whispered.

She nodded, and he scooped her up in his arms and took her to the private bower he'd built on the sandbar. Their own private retreat, where they were alone, with just the light from the moon reflecting on the ocean accompanying them...

"Jeena."

She opened her eyes and shook the erotic memory from her mind.

She knew it was Maazin.

"I know you have a lot of questions, but since I can no longer work on patients for the next twenty-four hours I have to figure out a way back to where we're being billeted and try to get some sleep."

What she really wanted to tell him was that she didn't have to time to play these games.

"I can take you there. I have my Jeep around back and maybe then we can have a meal together and we can talk about this in private."

She stood up. "Of course, because you wouldn't want a scandal."

"No. It's not that. It's for your protection and for his. Besides, we're the only two potentially exposed to the dysentery. We can't afford others to be exposed. We need all the help in the hospitals tending to the injured."

He was right.

And she felt silly. He was trying to offer her an olive branch and she was being cranky. She was better than this.

"Fine. I'd appreciate a ride."

Maazin nodded. "My car is over this way."

She followed behind. She knew it was for the best they talk this through, but she didn't want to. What was in the past was in the past.

Or at least she thought it was.

Maazin wasn't going to take her to the hotel where the relief workers were staying. Instead he was going to take her to his home. It was better that they didn't expose anyone else to possible infectious dysentery.

He'd sent Kariff out to warn the other farmers and plantation owners in that area who used that water source to avoid using water from the creek and he ensured the palace was made aware of the dire situation and that bottled, safe water would be provided to all who needed it.

He didn't say anything to Jeena as he drove back to Huban.

Thankfully he had also had a house that was not part of the palace. Maazin felt it was easier on his mother not to be under the same roof. So he'd chosen a colonial-built home just outside the city. He liked the privacy it afforded and what the two of them needed was privacy.

He was still in shock over the fact he had a son and he was going to find out who had kept this information from him and why. Maazin knew the mail and any correspondence to the royal family was monitored for their own safety, but he was so angry that someone could have done this.

His son.

His nine-year-old son. One that reminded him so

much of his beloved brother Ali. Except the eyes. The eyes on that boy were his.

A son he didn't deserve.

Ali's family had been taken from him and it was a cruel twist of fate that he, the one responsible for Ali's death, had a son.

"Where are we going? I thought the hotel was near the hospital?" Jeena asked, her voice rising in panic.

"It is, but I don't think it's safe that we stay close to the field hospital for the next twenty-four hours, so I'm taking you back to my place."

Her eyes widened. "Oh, I don't think so! I'm not going to the palace. You need to stop this vehicle right now."

"What is wrong?"

"I'm not going to the palace."

"I never said we were." And he couldn't help but wonder why she was so worried about going to the palace.

"You said we were going to your home."

"I don't live in the palace."

She looked at him in disbelief. "Right."

"No, really I don't. I bought a colonial home just outside the city. It was the old British consulate. It's walled and gated, so pretty secure. My father thought maybe letting me have my own place would curb some of my less desirable behavior."

"Did it?" she asked.

"No, not right away..." It wasn't the house that had given him a taste of being a responsible adult, it was the unbearable heartbreak Jeena had caused him by leaving him without any explanation and Ali's death.

Maazin had blood on his hands as far as he was concerned. And since Ali had died, he'd been trying so hard to right all his wrongs.

He hadn't had a drop to drink for ten years, but right now he felt like getting drunk.

Jeena seemed to calm down again once he assured her that they weren't headed to the palace. He turned off the main promenade that led to the palace and headed down the road toward the beach.

His home had sustained a bit of damage, but Maazin had made sure everything had been made secure when he'd known that the cyclone would definitely hit. He'd moved out all his staff and this was the first time he'd been back after Blandine. He'd been so busy with helping his people that he hadn't even thought about his home.

He parked the Jeep and then hopped out.

"Where are you going?" Jeena asked.

"The power to the gate has been cut. All power is being diverted to essential services only. Luxury items like powered gates are not essential." He unlocked the gate and then pushed on it to open it.

Once it was open he climbed back into the Jeep and drove it inside, then parked and repeated the process to close the gates.

He was relieved to see that only a few boards had been taken off and just one of the shutters was broken.

There were some fallen trees, but the larger ones still stood and no branches or trees had fallen on his house.

Jeena climbed out of the vehicle and looked at his home. "It's nice. I like the cerulean blue. It reminds me of the ocean."

He nodded. Pleased that she liked it. "It's what I was

going for. This place is peaceful and it's nice to come here and not be a prince."

"I'm sure it's so very taxing." She walked past him, her arms crossed as she looked all around his garden. He wasn't sure if she was commiserating with him or being sarcastic, but had a feeling it might be a mix of the two.

And he didn't care. He was going to make her a simple meal out of the supplies he had in the house and then he was going to find out more information about his son.

He climbed up the steps onto the covered deck and prised off the wooden boards and then unlocked the door.

"Right this way, Dr. Harrak."

Jeena followed him into the hallway and he flicked on the light, glad he'd had back-up generators installed last year.

There was a bit of water pooling on the marble floor, but for the most part everything looked to be in the same place as before the cyclone had hit.

"Wow, so this was the British Consulate?"

"It was moved to downtown Huban, but this is where the British had a seat for many years. Colonialism at its finest. Why don't you make yourself comfortable in the sitting room and I'll see what I have to eat."

Jeena nodded and found her way to the front sitting room. It was a cool room that he liked to use in the heat of the summer as it got breezes from the ocean and didn't have the direct sun.

In the kitchen there were bananas, which had gone bad, on the counter, so he tossed them and cleaned up the marble counter top so as not to attract insects or vermin, and then he looked in the fridge, which was still running.

He had absolutely no idea what to make.

He might like his independence, but he had staff who cooked and cleaned for him. When he'd been in England for medical school, his father had made sure that he'd been well taken care of and had wanted for nothing.

Even when he'd been serving in Kalyana's military and continuing his medical training to be an army surgeon, he'd had servants.

He knew how to make a few things, but he really didn't want to make toast for Jeena.

"Is everything okay?" she asked, peeking into the kitchen.

"No. I… Fine," he said, throwing up his hands. "I'm a pampered, coddled prince and I don't know how to make you anything that might be slightly edible. I can make toast and a pot of tea. Would you like that?"

Jeena bit her bottom lip, trying not smile. He'd always found that endearing, but right now he was slightly annoyed.

"Let's see what you have." She padded over to the fridge. "You have enough to make a nice Greek salad. Tomatoes, feta and olives. Would you like that?"

"That sounds wonderful." Now he was smiling and couldn't help but chuckle. "Would you show me?"

"How to make a salad?"

He nodded. "Yes."

"Sure." She pulled tomatoes, cucumber, feta and olives from the fridge and then wandered over to the pantry and pulled out olive oil, vinegar and oregano. He hadn't realized that he'd had all these things.

"Don't you need lettuce?" he asked. "It is a salad."

"If you want a traditional Greek salad then you don't have lettuce. You wouldn't happen to have any lemons, would you?"

"Yes, here you go." He handed her a couple. "Can we add lettuce too?"

"Why?" she asked.

"I like it and I think it might go bad soon."

Jeena wrinkled her nose. "Okay, let's see what we can salvage of it, but you know now it's not a true Greek salad."

"I'm sure I'll survive," he teased, pulling out the head of lettuce.

Jeena got to work and was washing the salad ingredients with bottled water. "Perhaps you should boil some water. If you're under a boiled water advisory, it would be safe."

"I have a lot of bottled water. I'm prepared for emergency situations. They wouldn't let a prince living on his own be without the essentials."

"Oh, good." Jeena finished what she was doing and then pulled out a cutting board and knife. "Do you have a big bowl?"

"Probably," Maazin said lightly. He went hunting through the cupboards until he found a large bowl. "Will this do?"

Her eyes widened. "That's massive, I'm sure it'll do."

"Too big?" he asked, glancing at it.

"For the two of us, yes, unless you have someone else coming over?"

He noticed there was a hint of apprehension in her voice and he wanted to ask her what she was so afraid of. First she'd been afraid of going to the palace and now she was worried about who else could be coming.

Did she know about the arranged marriage?

Of course she does. Who in the world doesn't?

The only thing people didn't know about was how the engagement was off and he couldn't tell anyone yet. He'd promised his father that. The people had loved Lady Meleena, or at least the idea of a fairy-tale wedding, not knowing that she was a spoiled and self-centered woman. Her father was from the Kalyanese dynasty, but they no longer lived in Kalyana and had made their home in Dubai. The last time Maazin had seen Meelena had been over a year ago. She'd been fed up that he'd chosen duty over her. But he'd never fancied Meleena. They'd been first introduced at that same polo match where he'd met Jeena, but the moment he'd seen Jeena all other women had paled in comparison...

"Your Highness," Meelena said.

She was very beautiful, but he could tell she was less than impressed to meet him. There was no spark or zest for life in her eyes and she seemed bored. Like every other debutante in his social circle.

Maazin bowed. "Excuse my dishabille."

She looked him up and down with no interest. "You're playing a match. I would expect nothing less."

Maazin tried to think of something else to say, but he couldn't. She turned and sipped her champagne and made it clear that she didn't really want anything to do with him.

Did his father really expect him to marry Meelena? She was not his choice and never would be.

His eyes then fell on a beautiful woman in the most

stunning emerald dress and ridiculous heels on the polo field.

Meleena followed his gaze. "What a fool," she snorted derisively.

"Excuse me," Maazin said quickly, and strode across the pitch to help her.

"So making a salad is extremely complicated, Your Highness," she teased, interrupting his thoughts.

"Oh?" he asked, crossing his arms.

"Yes." She smiled brightly at him and any tension that was between the two of them melted away. It was so easy with Jeena.

Why did she have to leave?

"You chop the lettuce like this."

He rolled his eyes and stifled a laugh. "Can I try?"

She handed him the knife and he cut the lettuce.

"You've done this before," she teased again.

"I'm not completely helpless," he said dryly.

"Just a moment ago you said the opposite, Your Highness."

"Call me Maazin."

A blush tinged her high cheeks. "I can't do that."

"Why?" he asked.

"It's not right. It's not proper."

"Well, we're alone."

"So?" she asked, nervously.

"You can call me Maazin. Please. I prefer it."

She glanced at him. "Fine, but only because we're alone."

He chuckled softly and finished chopping the lettuce and dumped it into the bowl. "Now what?"

"Let's chop the tomatoes." She handed him one.

He tried to chop it up correctly but ended up butchering it, spreading seeds and juice everywhere. Jeena chuckled and took the knife back.

"How about you go change and I'll finish here?"

Maazin nodded. "It's probably for the best."

As he left the kitchen there was a knock at his front door. Maazin cursed under his breath and went to answer the door.

"Yes?" he said, not thinking and opening the door. Thankfully it was just Joseph Malliot, his father's aide-de-camp, standing on the doorstep. He looked worried.

"I'm sorry for disturbing you, Your Highness. I went to the makeshift hospital and was told that you and another doctor had left."

"Yes, we were potentially exposed to dysentery. We have to be isolated for the next twenty-four hours, it's highly contagious."

Joseph worried his bottom lip and then stepped forward. "Your father got wind that it's a female physician staying with you and he's concerned about your upcoming marriage to Lady Meleena. Or rather…"

"That the doctor will find out and let it slip to the press that I'm no longer engaged to Lady Meleena."

Joseph nodded. "Yes, Your Highness."

"That's why he sent you to the camp?"

"Well, no. He wanted you back at the palace. Your mother is still a little concerned that you're working out there alone and without any kind of protection."

Maazin sighed. "I'm glad she's worried about my safety, but I can assure you that there is nothing untoward between myself and the other doctor. You can tell them I'm safe at my home and once I'm sure I'm not contagious then I will come and see them and assure them of these things myself."

Maazin shut the door on Joseph. He didn't meant to be rude, but he didn't want Joseph to get ill. His father would be lost without Joseph at his beck and call.

And if Joseph got sick because of him, it would just be one more thing his mother could blame him for.

"If it wasn't for your reckless ways then Farhan wouldn't have had to come back and step up as the next in line. I had been training Ali to be King since his birth. He was ready to be a great king. But because of your foolish ways he's dead."

Maazin swallowed the lump in his throat and his stomach twisted, he felt like he was going to be sick.

He was a failure.

He had killed his brother. The woman he loved had left and his son didn't even know he existed. It was too much to deal with and his eyes drifted to the locked bar, which he knew was stocked, but he turned his back on it. He wasn't going back down that path.

Not again.

CHAPTER FOUR

JEENA HAD FINISHED making the salad, but there was no sign of Maazin returning and she was worried. What if he'd passed out?

What if something had happened to him?

She crept out of the kitchen and made her way into the hall.

The large colonial house was eerily quiet.

And then she heard faint grunts coming from the far side of the house. She found another hall off the dining room, past the library and into what looked like a home gym.

Maazin had stripped off the scrubs and was in shorts and sneakers. He wasn't wearing a shirt and Jeena was taken aback. She knew that he was in good shape, but she wasn't prepared to see him standing there and doing a deadlift. The sweat dripped down his back and all of his muscles bulged as he arched his back and lifted what looked like a lot of weight.

His eyes focused on her standing in the doorway in the mirror he was facing. He finished his lift and then dropped the weights with a large clang on the mat.

"Jeena?" he said, surprised to see her there.

"You didn't come back," she said. "I was worried that maybe you fainted or were in distress."

"No, sorry. I was just… I needed to blow off some steam." He grabbed a towel and wiped his face.

And she couldn't blame him for blowing off some steam. She could do with some of that. She hadn't even been in Kalyana twenty-four hours and already her world was being turned upside down.

"There's some salad in the kitchen for you. I'm hoping you have a room for me and maybe I could have a quick shower? I feel pretty gross after that flight from Canada to Dubai and then here, then having to deal with dysentery."

"Of course. I'll take you to the guest room and I'll make sure you have a change of clothes."

"You keep women's clothing around?" And then she realized that was a stupid thing to say. Everyone knew that he was engaged to Lady Meleena. It had been announced to the world. Why they still weren't married was a mystery. Three years was a long engagement.

How would you know?

The Crown Prince Ali's death and Maazin's military service probably had something to do with it. But whatever the reason, it should not concern her. She would do well to remember that. Maazin had chosen Lady Meleena over her. He hadn't loved her at all and had made his feelings pretty clear when he hadn't come for her or fight for their love, even though he'd known she'd been pregnant. She was probably the only one who'd been in love in the first place.

"No, I don't have women's clothing on hand, but I can lend you one of my kurtas while your clothes are washed."

"I would appreciate that. Thank you."

Maazin nodded and led the way out of his gym and back out into the main foyer and up the stairs. He led her to a room that was above the gym and opened the door.

"This is the guest room and there's a private bath. It's the nicest guest room as it's under a shade tree and faces the pool out back. Though, until we're cleared of any infection, I wouldn't advise a dip in the pool. In the closet you'll find some plain kurtas that will fit you."

She nodded. "Thank you, Your Highness."

His expression softened. "Just Maazin. Please."

And it was sincere and gentle.

She nodded. "Maazin. Thank you."

He nodded and then left the room, closing the door behind him. Jeena let out a sigh of relief that she hadn't known she'd been holding. She walked over to the window and peered outside. The sun was beginning to set, the brilliant orange-gold light reflecting off the infinity pool that seemed to melt into the cerulean-blue ocean horizon.

Jeena sighed again.

She pulled out her phone and saw that she had an attachment of pictures. She opened it, not caring about the roaming charges at the moment, and smiled when she saw pictures her father had taken of Syman's hockey game.

Some were blurry, but there were a few good ones.

And there was a sweet one of Syman and her father after the game, enjoying a slice of pizza. Then there was a picture of Syman and her mother. Her mother was tucking Syman into bed and there was a caption that said they all missed her and loved her. Tears welled in her eyes.

She missed them too.

And she knew that her mother and father were very worried for her sake. Jeena couldn't help but wonder what would have become of her parents had they still been on the plantation. How would they have fared?

Would they have gotten sick like that boy and his father?

Would her mother have died from a farming accident?

Why was that family still getting their water from the creek?

Maybe it was good that her family gone to Canada. Canada had been good to them. Her father had learned how to farm in Alberta and had a small ranch of his own. Instead of vanilla, he'd built greenhouses and cultivated flowers.

Her mother would do flower arrangements and Jeena was a surgeon. Syman may not be able to experience the same childhood she'd had, but he still had so many opportunities.

And he was living on a farm, just a different one from the one she'd grown up on, and the best thing of all was that he was free to choose who he loved.

Who he married.

There was no protocol that decided his life for him. *Until now.*

Jeena worried her bottom lip. Maazin knew about Syman and she couldn't help but wonder what he'd do with that information. There was no more denying it. Would Syman be harassed by the tabloids? He was illegitimate, but he was Maazin's son nonetheless.

Prince Ali hadn't produced any children with his late

wife. Farhan didn't have any children, not yet anyway. Maazin had a son.

Syman was an heir, even if he had been born out of wedlock.

Yeah, but Maazin doesn't seem too interested in knowing about his son now, does he?

And Maazin was due to wed Lady Meleena. She had no doubt that Meleena would do her duty and produce a legitimate heir.

Until that time, though, Jeena was going to hold her breath and hope that Maazin didn't tell King Uttam about Syman's existence.

She couldn't lose Syman to Kalyana.

Jeena cursed under her breath.

She hoped that neither of them got sick, because she wanted to put as much distance between her and Maazin as possible, return to Canada and forget that she'd ever came back to the home that had turned its back on her.

Maazin paced and he was feeling a bit nervous, waiting for Jeena to come downstairs. He'd thought about this moment so many times. What he would say to her, but now that she was actually here, he didn't know what to say.

And they had a child together.

He felt deprived of that. It angered him.

Why did she hide it from me?

And he couldn't help but think it was because he was such a bad influence. He was the black sheep of the family. The rogue. The troublemaker.

Before Ali's death, he hadn't partied as hard as his family had always believed, he'd just wanted them to think that at the time so they wouldn't rely on him. So that he could be himself, so he could trick himself into believing that he was free.

He had, after all, been the third son at the time.

There hadn't been much expectation on him to settle down and produce an heir. And that had been fine by him. Then he'd met Jeena and had started to think about settling down. Until she'd left him, and he'd decided to actually live like everyone believed he'd lived. That's why Jeena had left him, so he'd indulged, just a hundred times worse than he should have.

Then Ali had died.

And Maazin had understood the errors of his ways, but it had obviously been too late. Ali was dead and he'd driven Jeena off, with their child.

He had to show her that he'd learned from his mistakes.

That he could be responsible, and maybe she would let him see the boy. To get to know him.

Do you really deserve that?

It was clear by Jeena's actions that she had no intention of returning to Kalyana permanently and Maazin had to help his country. They had to rebuild Kalyana and then break the news that he wasn't marrying Lady Meleena.

He turned around and saw that Jeena was standing uncertainly in the doorway, wearing one of his white linen kurtas. Her long dark hair was braided over her shoulder and he swore he had never seen a more beautiful sight.

Even though she'd broken his heart by leaving him all those years ago, he still thought she was the most breathtaking woman he'd ever seen.

The years hadn't changed that.

His heart may have hardened and he may have accepted his fate as a servant to Kalyana, but that didn't change the fact that he was still enraptured by her refined beauty. He was drawn to her spirit. She was a like a breath of fresh air. Still, after all this time.

"Won't you have a seat?" Maazin said, motioning toward one of the chintz couches was in the formal sitting room. The formal sitting room still had that old-world feel of the British colonies to it.

It wasn't furnished to his taste, but he only used this sitting room for visiting dignitaries. If he had his way, he would go with minimalistic.

Jeena took a wary step into the room. "This room doesn't seem to belong to you."

The corner of his mouth quirked up. She knew him so well. "You're right, but my father wanted me to leave it alone as it's part of our history. Winston Churchill came here when it was still the British Consulate. Would you like some tea?"

She nodded. "I would like that."

Maazin slipped out of the room and into the kitchen to grab the tray where he'd already prepared the tea, adding some sliced lemon. He brought it out to her.

"I'm impressed," she said as he set the tray on the table between the two overstuffed chintz sofas that were across from each other.

"With what?" he asked, handing her a cup and saucer.

"You're not completely helpless in the kitchen. You know how to put together a formal tea service."

He chuckled. "Well, teatime is still a thing here in Kalyana. I know it's not something that's done in Canada."

"We have tea."

"Do you have teatime? As in a meal?"

"No. Well, my parents do. They did continue with some of their old customs." She took a careful sip of her tea. "This is good."

"I know." He leaned back. "Your parents live in Canada now too?"

A strange expression crossed her face. "They do."

"They had a prosperous plantation."

"I know, but now they own a prosperous set of greenhouses just outside Calgary." Her eyes went wide and he could tell that she was annoyed that she'd let it slip. Let her location slip. He was relieved. Canada was a big country. You could get lost in a country that big.

"That's in Alberta, isn't it?" he asked.

"Yes," she said carefully, and set down her teacup. "Why?"

"I always wondered where you had disappeared to." He wanted to add, "when you left me all those years ago," but couldn't quite bring out the words to say it.

"Well, now you know. Just outside Calgary, but just outside Calgary is a large area."

"But given the agricultural industry of the Canadian prairies and indeed Alberta itself, how many large greenhouse operations are there in that area and how many grow and sell tropical flowers? Which I also find interesting, because I wouldn't think there was a big market for tropical flowers in Alberta."

Her dark eyes narrowed and he could tell that he was treading on dangerous ground.

"Poinsettias are tropical and need heat, but are much loved at Christmas, which is bitterly cold in Alberta."

"It's impressive they found such a niche market,

but that's not surprising given that they left their home country with basically nothing."

Her lips pursed. "What does it matter? People leave all the time."

"Your family left behind their prosperous vanilla plantation. I know they sold that plantation for peanuts. Way under value. They took a significant hit financially and I know that your father is a savvy businessman."

"So?"

"So? That I did not understand. I did not understand why he would sell for next to nothing a plantation that had been in his family for generations."

Jeena stood to her feet. "My father had to sell our beloved family home. There was no choice. I was pregnant by a prince who couldn't care less. What choice did I have?"

He was floored by her anger. He hadn't known she was pregnant, but she was acting like he had known. "What do you mean, I couldn't care less? I didn't even know!"

She crossed her arms. "Your fiancée is the one who helped my family leave. She said that you knew and she gave me a check to take care of my costs."

Maazin saw red. "Meleena knew?"

Tears filled Jeena's eyes and she worried her bottom lip, nodding. "She did."

"I wasn't engaged to Meleena then," he said, but he was angry.

He knew that Meleena was manipulative, but he hadn't known this. It made sense now why she'd supposedly found the letter that Jeena had left.

"I'm aware of that and I always wondered if she was

trying to get me out of the way so she could have you. I guess she won."

"She didn't win," Maazin said, shaking her head.

"You're engaged to her."

"No. No, I'm not."

Jeena's eyes widened. "What do you mean?"

"She's ended it and my father has kept it secret. There are some things to work out, but Lady Meleena ended it and I was quite relieved."

Jeena sat down slowly, looking a little pale.

Frankly, he was feeling a bit ill. Meleena had manipulated them both.

Still, that didn't bring back Ali or his wife. They were gone and Maazin still blamed himself for it all.

"So you really didn't know?" she whispered.

"No. I didn't. If I'd have known..." He trailed off, because he didn't know what to say. What if he had known? He would have gone after her? Of course he would have. He wished he had, not only for Jeena's sake but also for Ali and Chandni. But even if he hadn't gone out to that party, and Ali and Chandni hadn't died, he knew that the future for him, Jeena and their unborn child would still have been fraught with uncertainty. Would his family have accepted her? Would she have wanted this life? Would he have wanted his son to have the same life he'd had?

He wasn't sure.

But none of it mattered anyway. Ali and Chandni were dead, and he had to live with the guilt. Jeena and Syman had built a life in Canada that did not include him. And he had to accept that too.

It was too much to process and he felt awful. He hung his head.

"I think I need to rest," Jeena said quietly, her voice breaking slightly as if she was grappling with the same amount of emotion he was. "It's been a lot today."

He nodded. "I know."

She got up and left.

He didn't follow.

Maazin tossed and turned all night. It was all he could do not to go and see Jeena. He wanted to make things right, but he wasn't sure that he knew how.

It was early morning when finally he gave up any pretense of trying to fall asleep and got up, showered and dressed. When he got downstairs he found Jeena waiting calmly in the hall. She was dressed as well, in her now clean clothes. Her hair was braided back and she looked like she was ready to flee.

Again.

"Jeena?" he asked in surprise. "What are you doing up so early?"

"I need to get back to work. My team has been working all night and I've been lounging about here."

"You were hardly lounging about on purpose. We had to wait to make sure that neither one of us was infected."

"And we're not. We would've had symptoms by now, so I need to go back to work. My phone is dead, though, my charger is in my gear back with my team and your phone line is dead so I couldn't call a taxi to come and take me back to the makeshift hospital."

"The phone lines on this side of Huban are still out of order, but you wouldn't have been able to order any cab to come here and take you to the southeast district. No cab driver is equipped to handle that road. Only medical personnel and the army have permission to even try to traverse the roads."

Jeena sighed in resignation. "Will you take me, then?"

She didn't seem to want to rely on him. Not that he could blame her, he'd been hardly reliable in the past, but that was the past. This was different.

The only thing that wasn't different was that Ali was dead and he was responsible. That was his burden to bear.

The past is the past.

He nodded. "I'll drive you, of course."

"Thank you."

Maazin came down the rest of the stairs and grabbed his keys. He opened the door for Jeena while he finished locking up his home. He wasn't sure when he would get back here again and until the roads were open outside the city he wasn't sure when his small staff would make it back here.

They drove away from his home and back toward the southeastern district in near silence. He didn't know what to say. She'd had his child and he hadn't been there. He hadn't known about it.

Unless Syman isn't yours?

No. Syman was his. He knew that without a doubt.

It was one of the things he'd adored about Jeena when they'd first met. She had been so different from all the women in his social circle. She had been honest and good.

Or at least he'd thought she was until she'd left him.

One thing he did know, he had to get to the bottom of this. After he'd made sure that Jeena got back to the makeshift hospital and was reunited with her team, he was going to head straight to the palace and demand some answers from his parents.

"Have you heard from…?" He trailed off because it was hard for him to even think about the fact that he had a son. A son he knew nothing about.

There was so much he wanted to know about him but, then, there was so much he was afraid to know, and then there was a part of him that felt that maybe it would be better that Syman didn't know him or anything about this life.

Syman was currently free and he envied the boy that. Still, he was Syman's father and he wanted to know him.

You don't deserve to know him. You cost Ali his life. You don't deserve to have a child.

And he had to keep reminding himself of that.

"Syman?" she asked.

"Yes."

"I haven't heard from him since my phone died and I'm sure he's worried that he hasn't heard from me. I know my parents will worry."

Maazin nodded. "Well, they'll certainly be relieved when you tell them that you didn't contract dysentery."

She smiled. "Of course."

He hated that there was this awkwardness between the two of them, but he was the one to blame for that. He'd foolishly believed that she'd written that letter. It was clear now she hadn't. He hated that the both of them had been manipulated by Meleena.

At least Jeena hadn't destroyed anyone's life. She started a new life in Canada and prospered. He'd wallowed in self-pity and had caused his brother's death.

"So, why did you agree to marry Meleena?" she asked.

He almost lost control of the car. "What?"

"Maazin, clearly you loathe her or rather loathed her. Why did you agree to marry her?"

He sighed. "I didn't loathe her. I didn't particularly care for her but 'loathe' is a strong word."

She cocked her head to one side, studying him. "Fine. So why? Why get engaged to her and then let the engagement go on for so long?"

Because I couldn't get over you.

"It's my duty to marry and…" He had been going to say "produce an heir," but in reality he'd already done that. Illegitimacy aside, Syman was his heir.

Jeena's cheeks flushed with crimson. "I get it. You need a legitimate heir and, believe me, that's not why I wanted you to know about Syman. I don't need anything from you, Maazin. I haven't needed you."

That cut him to the quick.

I haven't needed you.

And he deserved it. He truly did.

No one really needed him.

Only his patients, which was one thing he never took for granted. His patients needed him, his people needed him and he would keep that promise he'd made all those years ago when Jeena had left and Ali had died, his promise to dedicate his life to his work and making sure everyone in Kalyana was taken care of.

Properly.

"Well, it doesn't matter now. It's done. The past is in the past," he said quickly.

He was done talking about this.

There was no point to discussing it further. The truth

was out and even though Meleena had ruined a life with his son, it had been his own actions that had killed his brother and sister-in-law. Jeena was right. She didn't need him in her life, and he truly deserved it.

That was karma for you.

CHAPTER FIVE

I WISH I had never said that to him.

It had been a couple of days since Jeena had last seen Maazin and had said those hurtful words that she was now regretting, even if they had been the truth.

She hadn't needed him in Canada. There were times she thought she did but, no, she didn't really need him. She was raising Syman to be a capable man.

And she'd learned that from the moment she'd walked through the doors of that first hospital in her intern year. A single mother in a foreign country. She'd had to rely on herself. Jeena had learned to rely only on herself.

Still, it wasn't his fault. He didn't know she had been pregnant. They had both been manipulated, but he didn't say whether he would've come to her aid. He'd trailed off, which made her believe he didn't want the responsibility.

Or that he was afraid of it.

And they weren't married. A prince had to produce a legitimate heir.

Still, she shouldn't have said that to him and she was regretting her words. She'd forgotten herself. When she'd been studying to be a doctor there'd been so many times that she'd had to really fight for her education. To be heard. Especially because she was a woman and she was a woman of color and an immigrant to Canada to boot. She'd had to become tough and fight for what she wanted and sometimes she was more brusque than she needed to be.

And that had been one of those times.

Maazin hadn't said much to her. He'd dropped her off so she could get checked out by her team and rejoin them in their relief work and then disappeared.

She would catch glimpses of him, but he was busy doing his work and wouldn't even look in her direction. He was acting like she wasn't even there.

It's for the best and what you wanted. He knows about Syman. You've done your part.

Which was true. From the moment she'd known she'd be returning to Kalyana, she'd been terrified about running into him again, but now that it hadn't been as bad as she'd thought it was going to be, she liked being around him.

She'd forgotten how charming he could be.

His charm is why you got into trouble in the first place.

And as she watched him across the hospital, checking on his people and being so tender and gentle with the sickest and poorest of the Kalyanese people, it warmed her heart. This was a different man from the playboy who'd swept her off her feet.

He seemed at ease and he was putting the poorest of the poor above himself.

He cared about something. He seemed passionate about something, instead of just coasting, like he had before.

Maybe he had changed?

How much could a member of the Kalyanese royal family change, though? They were bound by protocol and restrictions. They had everything, yet they weren't free. Maazin had told her that many times when they'd been together.

He was bound by duty and Jeena was very aware of the security personnel that surrounded the hospital. She didn't want this kind of life for Syman.

"So, you're the other Canadian Kalyanese doctor I've been told about."

Jeena startled and turned to see the bright smile of a beautiful woman, one who she recognized from photographs that had been plastered everywhere when Crown Prince Farhan Aaloui had wed his Canadian bride, Dr. Sara Greer.

"Your Highness." Jeena gave a small curtsey in deference to Sara.

A blush stained Sara's cheeks. "You don't need to do that."

"I do. I may be Canadian now, but I am Kalyanese and you are the Crown Princess. You will be my Queen one day."

"I'm really not used to all this bowing and scraping," Sara admitted. "I would like it if you just called me Sara."

Jeena nodded and smiled. "I would like that."

"Good," Sara said, relieved. "I was hoping that I was going to have a chance to run into you."

"Oh?" Jeena asked.

Sara motioned for them to head over to a quiet area, out of earshot of any patients, and now Jeena wondered if she knew about Syman too.

"I was wondering how long your team was planning on staying here? I asked, but couldn't get any definitive answers from anyone."

Jeena relaxed. "Oh, well…our work visas have been cleared for us to remain for at least two weeks minimum, but given the state that Kalyana is in after this cyclone it could be longer."

"That's what I was hoping for."

Jeena raised an eyebrow. "You were hoping we'd stay longer?"

"Well, not for that reason. I have been speaking to Farhan about the need to promote women in STEM programs and encouraging Kalyanese women to pursue STEM as a career. Especially in medicine, but there's no university here so young people have to study abroad, and a lot of families can't afford to send their children off-island for education."

Sara was right. Jeena had always had an interest in science and medicine, but her parents hadn't been able to afford to send her to a school to study abroad, which had been the only option.

Even though they hadn't wanted to go to Canada at first, it had worked out and Jeena had got her education.

"How do I fit in?" Jeena asked.

"I thought we could get together and work on a proposal to support young women in studying medicine abroad and returning to practice here. I'd also like to explore the possibility of Kalyana having its own university. As someone who grew up here, I would love to pick your brains. And maybe then we could speak to young women and inspire them. Let them know there are options for them. Both of us are successful Kalyanese doctors." Sara smiled brightly. "It's all just a bunch of jumbled hazy thoughts in my head, but I would love your input."

Jeena smiled. "I think that's a great idea."

"Right?" Sara crossed her arms. "I knew that I would like you. You think like me."

"I appreciate that. I don't find many people who think like me. Of course, living in Alberta I was the only one from Kalyana."

"I understand that. Where I grew up in London, Ontario I didn't really run into people from our country either. Of course, I was adopted and for a long time didn't even know that I was Kalyanese."

"That's a shame," Jeena said, and then quickly corrected herself. "Not because you were adopted, but that you didn't know anything about Kalyana. It really is a wonderful country and I've missed it."

"Can I ask something else?"

Jeena knew what was coming and she wanted to say no, but she couldn't. "You want to know why I left?"

"Yeah, it's obvious you love it here so much."

"I do. I love my parents more and my father had an opportunity to make his dreams of becoming a tropical flower farmer a reality. There wasn't enough land to fulfill his needs in Kalyana, so he moved to Canada when the opportunity came. I'm their only child and I wanted to become a doctor. As you say, there isn't really opportunity here in Kalyana for young women to do that, so I went with them. I haven't regretted it and I'm glad to be back here and helping the country of my birth."

It was all a lie, but Sara didn't need to know the sordid details.

Sara smiled. "That's lovely."

"Your Highness?"

Sara spun around to see a security guard waiting. She bit her lip and then turned back to Jeena. "I have to go. It was wonderful to meet you, Dr. Harrak."

Jeena bowed her head. "The pleasure is all mine, Your Highness."

Sara left with the security guard and Jeena let out of a sigh of relief that she hadn't even known she was holding. She was so worried that Sara had been told about her past, that Sara knew about Syman that...well, she didn't know what.

She was just so worried that others would find out about her and Syman. No one needed to know that Maazin was Syman's father.

Jeena had the feeling that someone was staring at her and she glanced over to see that Maazin was looking at her with curiosity.

Don't think about him.

She turned back to her work. He had made it clear that he was mad at her and she'd said something she completely regretted, but maybe this was for the best.

He leaned over, his breath on her neck making a tingle run down her spine. "I see that you've met Sara."

"I thought you weren't talking to me, Your Highness?" she replied.

"Yes, well I was curious when I saw Sara come in and introduce herself."

Jeena sighed. "Look, about what I said..."

He held up his hand. "I don't want to talk about that. What did Sara want?"

"She wanted me to help with her initiative to promote the STEM programs to young women in Kalyana. I told her that I would back her on that. Help her with her ideas for her proposal. Talk to other young women interested in the sciences."

"You're not here for long, how can you?" he asked, crossing his arms. "For that matter, why did she ask you to participate in this?"

"She asked me because I am Kalyanese and even though her heritage is Kalyanese, she was born in Canada and feels that I would have a better perspective of the needs here, as I grew up here."

Maazin cocked an eyebrow. "I can see that."

"I'm glad," she replied saucily. "Was that all you wanted to discuss?"

"Actually, there's a medical emergency on a small island north of Agung and I could use your help. We can take the royal yacht, which is loaded with supplies, and go and treat the village that has been cut off since Blandine hit."

Even though she knew it wasn't a good idea to be alone with Maazin and on his yacht, no less, she couldn't turn her back on patients who needed her.

"Okay." She nodded and set down the chart she was working on. "When do you want to leave?"

"Within the hour. Gather what gear you need, in case we have to stay overnight. I'll make the other arrangements and have a car come and get you to bring you down to the harbor." He turned and left before she had a chance to protest, before she had a chance to change her mind.

This is not a smart idea.

But, really, this was part of her mission to Kalyana.

She really didn't have a choice. This was what she was here for.

* * *

Maazin did the final checks on the yacht. Soon Jeena would arrive and he would set out on the hour-long sail to the island north of Agung. He would rather take the helicopter, but there was nowhere to land safely on the small island of Petrie because Blandine had damaged it so badly.

"Sara mentioned that you were getting your yacht ready to head out to Petrie."

Maazin glanced down onto the dock and saw that Farhan was standing there. Off in the distance were the security guards, ever-present when the Crown Prince was around.

"I am." Maazin walked onto the dock. "Is there an issue with that?"

Farhan shrugged. "Mother isn't happy about it. She thinks that you should send one of our doctors who is not royal blood, or the relief workers. You know Mother and how she worries."

Do I?

It didn't seem to him his mother cared much for him. Not since Ali had died. He knew his mother blamed him. She barely acknowledged him. It cut him to the quick. He'd managed to make his peace with his father. If only he could make things right with his mother, but he doubted that would ever happen. She was too hurt, too distant, and he felt responsible.

Actually, he was responsible.

He was certain she viewed him as a disappointment.

"You quite all right?" Farhan asked, cocking his head to one side. "You look out of sorts."

"I'm fine. A bit tired. I'm sure you heard about my little exposure to dysentery the other day."

"Yes. I did and don't worry, all that is being taken care of. The farmers in that area have been supplied with clean water and proper sanitation is in place."

"I'm glad to hear that."

"I know it's been a bit of an effort and difficult, but with the help of our allies we're getting the help that we need."

Farhan was ever the diplomat and Maazin had no doubt that he would be a great king one day. Even though it was Maazin's fault that Farhan had been put in that position in the first place.

"Did you want something else?" Maazin asked. "The other doctor will be here soon and we'll need to get going if we're to make Petrie Island before nightfall."

Maazin didn't mean to be so curt with Farhan, but he didn't want his brother around when Jeena arrived. Not that Farhan even knew who Jeena was. He hadn't told anyone about Jeena. The only ones who knew about her and the history he had with her were his mother and Lady Meleena apparently. No one else knew.

And no one needed to know about it.

Still, he didn't want Farhan meeting her and saying something to their father. And given the nature and turmoil that Kalyana was currently in, he wasn't sure how he was going to start that conversation.

"What, who, me?" Farhan asked.

"You didn't come here to see me off," Maazin said plainly.

"Fine. Mother wants you to return to the palace and Father is giving in to her." Farhan rubbed the back of his neck. "He says you don't need to be here."

Maazin could tell that Farhan felt uncomfortable telling him this.

Maybe go with Farhan and appease your mother?

Only he didn't want to. He'd promised to take Jeena to Petrie Island and this was part of his duty to his people. There were Kalyanese on Petrie Island who had lost everything and were in dire need. They needed him.

And that trumped his need to please his father.

"I can't," Maazin said quickly. "I promised those displaced people that I would take help and I will be there. Do you not think that's the right thing to do?"

Farhan sighed and nodded, rolling his shoulders. "I do."

"Thank you."

"Well, at least I tried, but…" Farhan trailed off and looked uncomfortable. "When you return I strongly urge you to return to the palace. Father is not well at the moment and it would be good if you returned. He's been asking you to come back to the palace since Blandine hit and you've been avoiding him. You need to go and see him."

"I know." Maazin knew that his father was feeling poorly. With his condition and the cyclone devastating Kalyana, it hadn't been good for their father, but he had a hard time being around his family. It was better to keep them at a distance.

It was easier that way.

"Good luck on your trip. If you need anything, please call and I will send for assistance."

Maazin shook his brother's hand. "Thank you."

Farhan turned and walked over to the dark SUV with tinted windows and Kalyana flags. A security guard held open the door for Farhan as he slipped into the back.

Maazin waved as the SUV drove away from the harbor.

Maazin knew there was security watching him, and he knew there would be an attaché of security following the yacht to Petrie, but Maazin didn't need as much of a detail as the Crown Prince did.

Of course, Ali had had just as much security and that hadn't helped him.

"You shouldn't have gone to that party. What were you thinking?" Ali lambasted him, yelling above the rain that was pouring down and the constant swish of the wiper blades. *"You left your security team behind. Do you know how foolish that was?"*

"So?" Maazin asked, but he could barely keep his head up. He didn't care much about anything. Jeena was gone and his pain wouldn't end.

"Don't be so hard on him, Ali," Chandni whispered gently. *"His heart is broken."*

"It doesn't matter. He's a prince. He should behave better."

Maazin snorted. *"I'm third in line to the throne and, unlike you, Ali, I can do whatever I want."*

"Or whoever," Ali snapped back. *"Honestly, Maazin, when will you grow up?"*

Maazin was going to answer, but before he could there was a large bang and the world turned upside down and went black...

"Hey, you okay?"

Maazin jumped and realized that Jeena was standing beside him. He hadn't even seen her arrive. She carried a duffel bag and his security team was unloading medical supplies, as well as food and water from the back of the van that had replaced Farhan's SUV.

"Fine." Maazin scrubbed a hand over his face. "I'm okay. Sorry, I just zoned out."

"If you're sure…"

"I'm fine." Maazin turned away from her. "We'd better get loaded up and get on our way to Petrie before it gets too late."

He just had to put it all behind him.

He had to put the memory of Ali behind him, just like he had to put the memory of Jeena and how broken he'd been when she'd left behind him as well.

It was all in the past and, wish it as he might, he couldn't go back and change anything.

The past was the past and his future was tied to serving his country and that was it. Maybe, just maybe then he could forgive himself for the damage he'd done.

Maybe.

CHAPTER SIX

THE WATER MADE Jeena a little nervous, but she felt safer being on Maazin's yacht and today was a beautiful, perfect day to be on the water.

Jeena raised her head to the sky and drank in the warmth of the late afternoon sun. Back in Calgary it was a bitter minus forty degrees Celsius and nothing like the beautiful eighty-degree weather that was here.

Just another thing she'd missed about Kalyana. She'd missed the warmth and sunshine. She was not a fan of winter or darkness. The only thing she liked about winter and darkness was the northern lights. That was something she was not sure she'd ever get tired of seeing.

She gazed out over the waters of the Indian Ocean, where all the islands that made up Kalyana lay. Beyond Kalyana lay the continent of Africa, Madagascar and then there was India, Yemen, Oman and the Maldives.

She'd forgotten what it was like to take a boat out to one of the far-flung islands of Kalyana. Looking east, she could make out the pearl-pink crescent of Patang Island.

On Patang Island had been the first time she had been with Maazin. She'd given her heart and soul to him that night, with no thought to the future and what it might hold for them.

Her cheeks heated as she thought of that night.

They had been on this yacht then too.

Their first time had been on the island, but then he'd carried her back to the yacht and made love to her again in his cabin. His arms around her, his hands in her hair and his mouth on hers. She'd been completely lost.

He'd been the only one to ever make her feel that way.

She'd been a fool.

And she had been such a fool to fall for a prince. What had she been thinking? She'd been so naive. So innocent. Well, she'd learned the hard way about trusting her heart to someone. The only one she could depend on was herself.

Jeena snuck a peak at Maazin at the helm, his white linen shirt billowing, his eyes focused on the horizon, and her pulse began to beat just a bit faster.

Damn him.

She hated that he still had an effect on her. Try as she might, she was still pulled toward him like a moth to a flame and she knew, just knew that if she allowed herself to get sucked in, she would get burned again.

This time she wouldn't let her heart lead her to disaster. When her work here was done she'd just leave and head back to Canada. There would be no struggle for her family. She wouldn't be as afraid. There was a life waiting for her in Canada. A damn good one.

Syman was her world and she was going to make sure that he was protected. She didn't want him sucked into this kind of life.

But Syman needs to know his father.

And it was that little voice she couldn't quell. Maazin deserved to know Syman and Syman deserved to know his father. She was just still afraid that Maazin would take Syman from her as Syman had royal blood. It's what her parents feared. She couldn't lose Syman, but she couldn't deny a father and son.

Maazin looked at her. "You seem lost in thought."

"Not really lost in thought." It was a lie. She didn't want to tell him what she was really feeling. "Just enjoying the warmth and the sun."

"It's not really that warm."

"For me it is. It's bitterly cold in Canada. I'd forgotten how hot and wonderful the weather is here when the dark of winter hits."

"Dark of winter?" Maazin asked, raising an eyebrow. "Surely it's not that bad."

"Yes. It's that bad." Jeena pulled out her phone and scrolled through the photos to find the picture she'd taken when her father had had the laneway to the greenhouse plowed out a month ago during a bad blast of snow.

"Look at this." She got up and walked over to him, holding up her phone to show him the picture. He looked at it, raising his eyebrows.

"Wow," he said. "That's a lot of snow."

"Right. It gets so cold and dark." She exited the photo app. "There was so much snow and Syman was so mad that hockey had to be canceled for the night."

She closed her eyes and groaned inwardly. She hadn't meant to mention Syman again, but then again Maazin hadn't really asked much about him either.

"You've mentioned that he likes hockey," Maazin said. "Does he like other sports?"

"Baseball in the summer. Soccer as well."

"Football, you mean," Maazin said with a smile.

"Yes, I suppose European football is known as soccer there. He doesn't play American football. Though he is a fan of the Saskatchewan Roughriders, which is CFL over NFL."

"What's the difference?" Maazin asked. "Or is there one?"

"Oh, there's a difference, and people get really tetchy about it if you don't know."

He smiled, his eyes twinkling. "Do you know the difference?"

"Of course."

He cocked an eyebrow. "Well?"

"Well, what?"

"What's the difference?"

"Does it matter?" she asked.

"Yes." He smiled at her, a lazy half-smile.

"Why?"

"Because," he teased. "You don't really know."

She chuckled. "Fine. I don't really know."

"So there's no difference, then?"

"Not really. I think it has something to do with field size. CFL is a bigger field size than NFL."

"Is there no cricket or polo in Canada?"

Jeena shrugged slightly. "They aren't really big in Canada."

"That's a shame. Perhaps..." He pursed his lips, as if he was going to offer to teach Syman cricket, but then thought better about it. It made her feel sad on one hand, but relieved as well. If he didn't want to be part of Syman's life or if he wasn't going to be around, she didn't want Syman to get hurt.

If he wanted out then he needed to say something.

She wasn't going to let Maazin hurt their son like he'd hurt her all those years ago.

Still, there was a part of her that wanted him to ask and know their son.

"You can ask me anything about him, you know. Anything you want," she said gently.

"I appreciate that."

She wanted to tell him that what she'd said the other day about not needing him didn't mean that she didn't want him to care about Syman. She just didn't want him to feel obligated to care for them, when he couldn't.

There was an almost palpable tension and she hated that it was so awkward around him. She remembered a time when it had been so easy between them. When they would talk for hours, laugh and make love.

Heat bloomed in her cheeks and she wandered to the starboard side of the ship to look out over the water. She leaned on the railing and sighed, trying not to think about the past, but everywhere she looked there it was. The past, calling to her.

Like a siren calling a doomed sailor to his death.

"You seem lost in thought again," Maazin said gently.

"Just...memories." She looked back at him. His expression was soft and he smiled at her, sending a thrill through her.

"I know. I was thinking the same thing. We took many a ride on this yacht."

"You liked the sea," she said.

"Don't you?" he asked.

"Yes... No. Water does frighten me. It's beautiful, but it's slightly terrifying."

"Then why did you come on yacht trips with me?" he asked.

"You liked it and I wanted to be with you."

He smiled gently at her, those gray-green eyes twinkling at her. "I thought you liked it and I wanted to please you."

"So you don't like it, then?"

"Yes and no. I like my yacht, but it wasn't because I liked cruising around on my own. I liked the privacy that it offered. Out here I can just be me. I'm not a prince. I'm no one."

She nodded. "I can understand that."

"I haven't asked much about Syman yet. I'm sorry. I'm processing it, but I want to know. I truly do."

"Look, I know I dropped this bombshell on you, but you had the right to know. I thought you did know."

"I understand. We were fooled."

She could hear the frustration in his voice.

"I am sorry."

"It's not your fault. And if I see her again…well, let's hope I don't."

"It's in the past," Jeena offered. Although she wouldn't mind taking a swift shot at Meleena.

"I am curious about one thing, though," Maazin said.

"What's that?" she asked.

"Why didn't you go to the press?" Maazin asked. "If you felt I hurt you, betrayed you, why didn't you tell the world what a vile, vicious man I was?"

"I'd never have done that. We were starting a new life away from Kalyana and didn't want to draw attention to ourselves. And I didn't want my child dragged into all of this. I didn't want him photographed or have the media follow us. There was so much going on when he was born. Your older brother Ali and his wife had died and—"

"I'm aware," Maazin said quickly, and a strange expression passed over his face. She had obviously touched a sore spot about Ali and she wondered what had happened. All she knew was that he and his wife had died in a car crash.

That was all anyone had ever been told.

"I'm sorry for your loss. I know how close you were to Ali."

Maazin nodded, but he wouldn't looked at her and she knew that whatever conversation they were having was over.

"For what it's worth, I'm not the kind of person who would ever go to the press, Maazin. I would never hurt you like that."

He nodded, but didn't look at her. "Thank you."

She sat back down and focused on the ocean. Off in the distance she could see dark clouds rolling in. It was fitting for how she felt. For how Maazin obviously felt, given the tension between them.

Or at least it felt fitting.

For the rest of the trip to Petrie Island the atmosphere was tense. Jeena didn't say anything and neither did Maazin. The dark clouds were still in the distance, but Jeena had a real sense of foreboding as she watched them.

Even Maazin seemed on edge about it. As they approached the island Jeena gasped in shock. She remembered coming to Petrie Island with her grandfather a lot. He would sell vanilla on the island every Sunday and often take her.

The little island just north of the larger Agung was always bustling on a Sunday when the market came in.

There were other smaller islands all around the main island of Kalyana and all these small communities would come together and congregate on Petrie. They would share stories and sell their wares.

She remembered a weaver living on the island who would weave beautiful saris the color of the sea shot with gold. Her mother had one still.

But as they got closer to the island and Jeena could see the devastation, her heart sank. Houses had been toppled, trees uprooted and the small harbor that housed the islands' boats had been destroyed. Boats were capsized or washed ashore and irreparably damaged.

It was like a war zone.

It was awful.

Maazin pursed his lips and frowned. "It's worse than I thought."

"No one from Kalyana has been out this way since Blandine?" Jeena asked in shock.

"No. We've been unable to get here. There were so many wounded and sick on the main islands. Then those in further outlying areas were coming to the main island to seek help. No one from Petrie came, but now I understand why, they were unable to."

Maazin docked his yacht at the main pier, where police officers and first responders who lived on the island were waiting for his arrival.

Jeena's stomach twisted in a knot as she watched Maazin greet the men and women who were waiting for him. There was a lot of deference and saluting, but Maazin was quick to shut that all down.

"I've brought medical supplies," he told the man who

Jeena assumed was the chief of police. "And a surgeon. This is Dr. Harrak."

Jeena climbed down onto the dock and shook everyone's hands.

"Jeena, this the chief of police on Petrie. His name is Mustafa. Mustafa, this is Dr. Jeena Harrak. She is Kalyanese, but is from Canada."

"We're so glad you've come, Your Highness," Mustafa said. "We have so many wounded. Our first aid and first responder teams have done what they can, but we have some who require surgical intervention."

"I'm here to help. Have all your buildings been damaged by the cyclone?" Jeena asked Mustafa.

"Not all. Those closest to the water have been. The city hall is standing as it was made from cement and cinderblock. We have moved all the wounded and sick there. It's sheltered and has a generator." Mustafa looked exhausted. "We have an elderly gentleman who was brought to us last night by his daughter. He lived on one of the smaller islands. He was a weaver and one of our medics said he suspects that the man has appendicitis."

Jeena bit her lip. "That's not good."

"No, he's very ill. The medics have set him up with an IV antibiotic drip, but if it's appendicitis he really needs to get off island and have surgery."

"There might not be time to get him off island," Maazin stated.

"You're right. We'll have to check him." Jeena frowned. "I could perform an emergency surgery if I had to."

"Can you?" Mustafa asked, surprised.

"Of course. It's what I'm trained for," Jeena replied. "You said the man was a weaver?"

Mustafa nodded. "Yes, and a tailor, the only one in Petrie. He's been selling his fabrics, saris, kurtas and lenghas here for over twenty years. He's very talented."

Jeena smiled. "Yes. My mother has one of his saris. She cherishes it."

Mustafa grinned. "Harrak is your surname?"

"Yes."

"Is your grandfather Rami Harrak?" Mustafa asked.

"Yes, that was my grandfather. My father took over his plantation, until…" She trailed off, trying not to think about the night she and her family had left their home. "My parents live in Canada now."

"Good for them," Mustafa said, and Jeena was thankful he didn't ask any further questions. "I'll take you to my truck and get you over to the courthouse. My other officers will make sure all your gear and supplies get there too."

Jeena nodded and then glanced at Maazin, who was staring at her with an unreadable expression on his face. She looked away quickly.

She didn't want to share that pain with him.

One for which she had blamed him for so long when it hadn't been his fault.

The drive to the courthouse that had been converted into a makeshift hospital didn't take too long. There wasn't much flooding and any rubble from the houses near the coast of the island had been cleared away. As had the trees. There were tents and a sort of makeshift shanty village the closer they got to the center of the town where the market was.

"Thankfully our water supply wasn't disrupted as it comes from a natural spring and because of our generator we're also able to have our desalinator up and running," Mustafa mentioned offhandedly as he drove through the streets.

"I'm glad. There was a small outbreak of dysentery on the main island that we were able to control," Maazin said. "I'm glad there is nothing like that here."

Jeena was glad too. Something like dysentery or another infectious disease would wreak havoc on the close-knit community of Petrie Island.

It didn't take long for them to get to the courthouse.

"We're here and I'll take you right to our most urgent patient, Mr. Patel." Mustafa parked and Jeena grabbed her duffel bag, which carried an emergency surgery kit. Something she always carried with her when she was going off into disaster zones.

Maazin followed Mustafa and Jeena followed them.

The medics had done a great job setting up the make-shift medical center. Jeena was impressed, but right now she wanted to take a look at Mr. Patel.

"He's in here. Our paramedic is with him."

"Thank you, Mustafa," Maazin said.

"Your Highness." Mustafa bowed.

Maazin held open the door for Jeena and she walked into the room. She could tell the man was very ill.

"Your Highness," the paramedic said with a curtsey.

"Please, it's okay. Can you tell us about Mr. Patel?" Maazin asked.

The paramedic nodded. "Mr. Patel was brought in early this morning. His daughter said he was complaining of lower right quadrant abdominal pain. Upon palpation we noticed he was guarding and his temperature was one hundred and two. He has been unable to pass a bowel movement and his blood test came back with a high count of white blood cells."

"So he's fighting an infection," Jeena said. She walked over to the bed and examined the patient. Mr Patel was just as she remembered him, slightly older, but he still looked the same.

"Yes," the paramedic said. "With antibiotics we've managed to bring his temperature down a bit, but it's rising again."

"Without an ultrasound it's pretty hard to tell if it's definitely appendicitis," Jeena said. "But from the description, it's not dysentery."

"There's no blood or mucus," the paramedic said. "It was our worry too, but Mr. Patel's daughter said he's been drinking bottled water. He's not a stranger to cyclones and storms."

"You've done an excellent job here," Jeena remarked, and she continued her examination. "You wouldn't happen to have certification in anesthesia, would you?"

The paramedic's eyes widened. "No."

"I do," Maazin said.

"That's good, but I do need someone to assist me."

"I can help with that. I'm training to be a surgical nurse," the paramedic said. "It's just been hard to get to a school, it's so costly..."

Jeena understood that only too well. There was no medical school in Kalyana and going abroad was very expensive, which was why her dream of becoming a surgeon hadn't been realized until she'd been banished and had moved to Canada.

"What's your name?" Jeena asked gently.

"Ayesha."

"Well, Ayesha, if you think you have a good handling of surgical instruments I would gladly have you assist me while Prince Maazin does the anesthesia."

"Thank you, Dr. Harrak."

"Please go prep a sterile room so that we can operate on Mr. Patel immediately."

"Of course." Ayesha left the room and Jeena went straight to her duffel bag to pull out her surgical kit.

"Are you sure this is wise?" Maazin asked, and she could hear the concern in his voice.

"If we don't do it, he won't survive the trip back to the main island. We have to."

"But with a paramedic assisting you?"

"She was smart enough to set up the IV and take his blood. You heard her, she wants to be an operating room nurse, a scrub nurse, but there's no little or no support available for her. This is what Sara was talking to me about so earnestly."

"I agree more could be done," Maazin said. "But this is a man's life."

"Exactly. I can do this, you'll be in the room and Ayesha is more than capable of assisting me."

Maazin looked uncertain. "What choice do we have? You're right. Very well, I'll be there and we can do this."

Jeena touched his arm. "Yes, we can do this."

Mr. Patel started to rouse and looked a bit surprised. "Your Highness?"

Maazin smiled at the man. "Mr. Patel, we're here to help you."

"Help me?" the patient asked, confused.

"You have appendicitis and Dr. Harrak from Canada and myself are going to take care of you."

Mr. Patel nodded and looked over at her. He smiled at her. "I recognize you."

Jeena smiled down at him. "I would say so. I saw you every weekend when I was a child."

"You are not Canadian," Mr. Patel said.

"I am now, but I'm back home to work and to help."

Mr. Patel closed his eyes. "Good. Good."

Jeena checked his pulse rate, which was racing. "We need to get him into surgery now."

If they didn't, Mr. Patel was going to get peritonitis and die.

Maazin thought that Jeena was foolish thinking about operating on Mr. Patel in a makeshift hospital on the small island of Petrie with a paramedic as her assistant and without ultrasound assistance or other specialized equipment to do the surgery.

Ayesha had done a great job in prepping a small, well-lit room. Jeena's instinct was right and Mr. Patel's appendix was on the verge of rupturing, which would have meant a bad case of peritonitis, and as he was over seventy, his chances for survival in a disaster situation like this would not have been good without surgery.

Maazin felt bad for wanting to wait to transport him to Huban. He wouldn't have made that journey.

Now, here they were in a small courtroom and they were saving a man's life. Not only that, Jeena was inspiring a young Kalyanese paramedic who had aspirations of doing so much more. Jeena was wonderful. There was no other word to describe it.

He couldn't help but smile from behind his surgical mask as he watched her.

She was so strong and she didn't even know it.

Or she hadn't known it when they'd been together. She had changed. She was fierce and it made him want her all the more.

You can't have her.

And that thought replayed over and over in his mind as he watched Jeena work and explain things to Ayesha as they removed the enflamed appendix and cleaned out the infection from Mr. Patel's abdomen.

He was also jealous of Jeena.

She had more hands-on practical knowledge than he did. Maazin had training and he'd done work in the field, but rarely. His father ruled Maazin's schedule and there wasn't much time to really practice medicine or teach it. He may have been a military surgeon, but he didn't get to practice as much as he'd like to. As much as she obviously did.

He'd moved away from medicine into politics and diplomacy, something Maazin hated more than anything.

If he'd not been born into the royal family, if he'd had the same freedom as Jeena, then she would've never left Kalyana. They would be together, married, and Syman would know who he was.

A lump formed in his throat as he thought about Syman. A boy who loved sport as much as he did. Not that he knew anything about ice hockey, but he could learn.

That's if Jeena would let him get to know Syman. He was so afraid Jeena wouldn't let him. She'd offered to talk about him, but he didn't quite believe she was actually going to tell him about Syman. She was determined to protect their son, and he understood why.

Maazin lived his life in the spotlight as a member of the royal family. Nothing of his was private. His whole life was on display.

Even if he did meet his son, he wouldn't want to burden him with this life. This horrible public life that he couldn't escape. That he was bound to forever, not only by birth but by his mistakes, which had made him second in line to throne until Farhan had an heir.

Still, he was a father. There was duty there. He'd never thought of having children, but now he had one he had to do the right thing by him.

He had to prove to Jeena that he could.

Do you deserve a second chance?

No. He didn't and that thought sobered him up.

"Now let's close up," Jeena remarked.

"This is an amazing opportunity, Dr. Harrak. Thank you," Ayesha said.

"You're very welcome and thank you for assisting me."

"Yes. Thank you, Ayesha," Maazin said, finally finding his voice.

"Thank you, Your Highness," Ayesha said nervously.

They finished closing up Mr. Patel and Ayesha promised to monitor him post-op so that Jeena and Maazin could go out and assess the rest of the Petrie Island villagers who had been hurt during the cyclone.

Jeena washed up and disposed of the scrubs and then placed the instruments in a biohazard container that was filled with antiseptic.

"That's a handy kit you had," Maazin commented as he cleaned up.

"This isn't my first time heading to a disaster area. Of course, this is my first one out of Canada."

"What have you dealt with in Canada?" Maazin asked.

"Mostly things like accidents or avalanches in the mountains. Sometimes a hiker falls down a cliff and you have to attend out in the field."

"Avalanches?" Maazin asked in amazement.

"Or mudslides. I know Kalyana has had its fair share of those." She shuddered then and shook her head as if shaking away a bad memory.

"Why are you shuddering?"

She sighed. "When I was a child, I was almost swept out to sea by a flash flood during a particularly bad rainstorm. It terrified me, but I've overcome that fear. Still, every once in a while when I think about it, the terror comes right back."

So that's why she isn't fond of water.

"I'm sure," Maazin said quietly. He knew exactly what she was talking about. There were times when that accident came back to mind, flooding back, and it sent him into a tailspin. He hated the helpless feeling that came with it.

He hated being reminded of that horrible night and its aftermath. How his parents had everything hushed up. People had been paid off and no one knew Maazin had been drunk and fighting with Ali as Ali had been driving during a rainstorm.

No one knew Maazin was the reason Ali was dead.

He was the shame of his family.

"You okay?" she asked.

"I'm fine. And I will help."

"I assumed you would," Jeena teased. "You are a doctor too, Your Highness."

"I don't have as much practice in the field as you."

"Aren't you an army surgeon?" she asked.

He nodded. "Yes, but royal duties outweighed a lot of my opportunity for really getting out there and saving lives. Though I lend a hand when I can, still it would be nice to have the freedom that you have. I would like to learn more."

"That's too bad."

"What is?" he asked.

"That you're so trapped by that royal title."

"It is. I much prefer my medical work and working with people to protocol and diplomacy."

She nodded. "Still, with your power you could advocate for change. I admire that power you have to make a real difference."

"I can do that. Yes. And I plan to."

"You do?" she asked.

He smiled at her. "I mean, with Sara's initiative to promote STEM sciences and medical sciences, in particular to women, and to bring a university to Huban. Kalyana needs this. I think you should help her and I will too."

Jeena smiled brightly, her lovely dark eyes twinkling with that sparkle he hadn't seen in so long. "You will?"

"It's clear that something needs to be done. You did a wonderful job with Ayesha and you saved Mr. Patel's life."

"Thank you."

"Now, let's go and help some others."

"Good idea." Jeena grabbed her medical kit and they left the small courtroom where they had just operated on Mr. Patel. Maazin sighed and ran his hand through his hair.

The panic in him was rising and his shoulder twinged where it had been dislocated the night Ali had died, as it always did when he was about to have a full-on panic attack.

Right now he had to calm himself down.

He felt useless, but if he didn't get his emotions under control he would indeed be useless to everyone.

"Your Highness?"

Maazin spun around, annoyed that he'd been interrupted. Mustafa stood there and Maazin could tell that he was nervous.

"What's wrong? Tell me."

Mustafa handed him a piece of paper. "This came in. There's a storm brewing. Not a cyclone like Blandine, but it's headed straight for Petrie. I've sent my crew out to bring those who are in the tent city here, but I need more help."

Maazin nodded. "I'll come with you. Let's go."

He hurried after Mustafa. Jeena and the first responders who were here could tend to the wounded, but right now he needed to help Mustafa bring in the others. It may not be a cyclone that was headed for Petrie, but a storm hitting an already ravaged island was dangerous enough.

And it appeared that he and Jeena were spending the night here, whether she liked it or not.

They were stuck.

Jeena walked among the cots that had been salvaged, along with the other mattresses and bedding that were scattered across the floor. The displaced and uninjured survivors were put in another courtroom. The little courtroom that they'd used to operate on Mr. Patel earlier in the day had been cleaned.

The storm had struck an hour ago. It was strong and the wind howled fiercely, scaring the small children who had already been through the turmoil of Blandine.

Jeena was exhausted, but she wanted to make sure that everyone was taken care of.

There was a quiet calm, broken only by the odd cough.

All the wounded and sick were stable. Mr. Patel was doing well and Ayesha was staying with him, as was his daughter.

Where did Maazin go?

Jeena had been looking for him since she'd heard that he'd gone out to collect the villagers and bring them to the safety of the courthouse. She'd seen him briefly helping Mustafa board up the windows, but now he was gone.

He was probably hungry and she had a bowl of jasmine rice and vegetable curry that Mustafa's wife was dishing out to everyone.

Maazin had to eat.

She wandered down another hall toward more offices, and found Maazin in one of them, sitting behind the desk, brooding in the shadows.

She knocked on the door. "I've been looking for you."

"Ah, I just needed a few moments and Mustafa thought that I would be comfortable in here." He rolled his eyes. "Apparently a prince needs a giant room all to himself."

"Do you?" she asked, amused.

"No. I would be more comfortable on my yacht, but my security team, which arrived just after us, advised that this would indeed be a safer location."

"I believe they're right," she said. "I have food. Mustafa's wife is making food for everyone and it's good. Very filling."

"It smells good." Maazin reached over and flicked on a small torch. The generator had been powered down to conserve fuel until the storm was over. Jeena came into the room and set the small metal plate down in front of him, together with a fork.

"Did you eat?" Maazin asked.

"I did. I wouldn't lie and say it was good if it wasn't," she teased, and she sat down in the chair on the opposite side of the desk.

Maazin took a bite. "That is quite wonderful."

"See, I don't lie."

He smiled at her. "How is Mr. Patel doing?"

"He's doing well." That was the truth and Jeena was relieved about that. He had been so close to death. "He's our most critical case and he's stable. Everyone else is in good shape too. For being such a small island with no doctor here, they're doing remarkably well."

"Well, let's hope they do eventually get their own doctor. My father listens to Sara and I'm sure he'll support her ideas."

Jeena snorted. "Right."

Maazin cocked an eyebrow. "My father does a lot of good."

"I know he does, but you can understand my derision, can't you?"

"No. I don't, actually."

"Kalyana is trying to be a modern country. Yet there's nowhere to teach people past high school. Your father has been King for a long time and that change hasn't happened yet."

"He has been King for a long time, but he isn't the ultimate rule-maker. There's parliament and procedures."

"So your father's ideas are not put through? Are you saying he's wanted a university?" she asked in disbelief.

Maazin sighed. "Fine. He can be stubborn and maybe not always think so progressively. He's getting better."

"You do agree with them anyway, don't you?"

Maazin sighed. "Yes."

"Like the marriage thing?" Jeena regretted asking him about it the moment the question left her lips, but she couldn't help it. She didn't understand why Maazin had agreed to marry Lady Meleena if he hadn't loved her. Maazin had always told her that he was against arranged marriage, even though his parents and Ali's arranged marriage had been successful.

He'd always told her that he wanted to marry for love and now he wasn't. It just didn't make sense.

Unless he actually had loved Lady Meleena.

"You weren't forced into it, were you?" Jeena asked, embarrassed that she was assuming that he was an unwilling participant.

"No. I agreed to it."

It stung, even though she didn't want it to sting.

It's because you still care about him. After all this time, you still care deeply for him.

"I'm sorry, then. I didn't mean…" She trailed off, not sure of what to say next, and she stood up to leave. "I'm sorry."

She tried to leave the room, before she continued to put her foot in her mouth. She really didn't know what had come over her, but as she tried to leave she felt a hand on her arm, pulling her back, and she saw Maazin standing behind her.

How had he got to her so fast?

His touch sent a shiver of delight down her spine.

And suddenly all she could hear was the sound of her pulse racing in her ears and the rain hammering against the roof.

She forgot everything else as she stared up into those eyes she'd loved so much. The eyes of the man that she'd loved so much, the man who haunted her dreams.

She looked away. It was too much.

"Jeena, it's not like that. I agreed to it because it made diplomatic sense, because it's my duty. That's it. I didn't love her."

Jeena looked up stunned. "You didn't?"

"No."

"Didn't you care for her at least? I mean, you agreed to marry her."

"Because it was my duty but, no, I didn't care for her because she wasn't you," he whispered. He took a step closer to her and touched her face, like he had all those years ago on Patang Island.

Her heart skipped a beat and her body shook, craving more of his touch. And then, before she knew what was happening, his hands were in her hair and he was pulling her close, kissing her, and she let him.

She let him kiss her, very gently, and her body began to melt, powerless.

There was a knock at the door and Jeena jumped back, embarrassed by what she'd let happen.

"Jeena..." Maazin pleaded.

She shook her head. "No. I'm not falling into that trap again."

"I'm not engaged," Maazin said.

"It doesn't matter. This can't happen."

"Why?" he asked.

But before she could say anything further, before she

fell into the trap of believing and trusting him again, she opened the door to find Ayesha there.

"Dr. Harrak, it's Mr. Patel. His temperature has spiked again."

"I'll be right there."

Ayesha nodded and left.

Jeena took a calming breath and looked back at Maazin. It was too late for them. Even if he was no longer engaged to Meleena, he was off limits. She couldn't be with him again, she was too afraid of being hurt, and when this was all over she was going back to Canada, back to her son, and would try to put this whole thing behind her.

CHAPTER SEVEN

THE STORM BLEW itself out overnight, although there was
a storm raging inside him. He knew he shouldn't have
kissed her, but he'd been unable to prevent it.

And even though no one else was supposed to know
that his engagement to Lady Meleena was over, he'd
wanted Jeena to know. And he was glad he'd told her.
He was just angry with himself for kissing her.

What had he been thinking?

At least no one had seen them. Jeena may know his
engagement was off, but the rest of the world didn't.

His parents would be furious if the announcement
was made now. Hadn't he done enough damage to his
family?

Still, he'd been unable to help himself. When he was
around her she made him feel alive again.

Maazin tossed and turned all night, guilt eating away
at him.

He was so selfish.

In the morning Maazin went out with Mustafa to sur-
vey the damage, which was minimal thankfully. The
last thing Petrie Island needed was to have more of the
small island torn apart.

Still it was clear to Maazin that Petrie needed more help than he and Jeena could offer. It would take a long time to repair the damage that Blandine had done. Thankfully not many lives had been lost.

Maazin got on the satellite phone in his yacht and called Farhan for assistance, and Farhan promised he would send more manpower and supplies needed to rebuild Petrie.

It only took about five hours for shelters, food and water, to arrive, as well as a relief physician who was a young doctor from Kalyana, which mean that he and Jeena could leave.

Her time was almost up. Farhan told Maazin that Jeena had been called back to Canada now that Kalyana was getting back on its feet. She would be leaving soon.

The thought of Jeena having to leave again struck him with a sense of dread that he wasn't prepared for. The official date hadn't been given by the Canadian consulate, but Jeena's time in Kalyana was coming to an end and he didn't like it one bit.

You should be relieved.

He should be happy to have this closure. He now knew what had happened to Jeena all those years ago so he would never have to wonder about that again. It had given him the closure he needed so he could move forward.

Really?

No, he didn't really believe that, because he knew deep down that he would never be *over* Jeena and that kiss they'd shared last night just proved how much he still wanted her. Even after all this time when he'd thought she'd betrayed him and left him.

When he'd realized Jeena had left he hadn't cared

about anything. And that lack of care had cost Ali his life and eventually set Maazin on the path to right his wrongs and save others by serving his country.

His dedication and passion for that had driven Meleena away and disappointed his parents yet again, but he didn't care that Meleena had left.

He'd never loved her.

He didn't even like her.

It was Jeena. Always Jeena.

He still wanted her. Wanted no other, it was just that he couldn't have her. He didn't deserve to have her.

And it was clear that Jeena no longer wanted him. She no longer wanted a life in Kalyana when Canada offered so much more for her. It was for the best.

And he wouldn't subject Jeena to this life of protocol, this shackle of being a member of the royal family.

He wouldn't do that to his son.

His son. As much as he didn't want this life for Syman, he wanted to be a part of Syman's life. Why did it have to be so complicated?

Perhaps it doesn't?

Maazin finished loading the yacht with the supplies the islanders didn't need and then saw Jeena coming toward him with her duffel bag on her back and carrying the biohazard container with her surgical instruments.

The duffel bag looked larger than her and he didn't know how she was carrying it all so easily. He met her down on the pier and held out his hand.

"What?" Jeena asked.

"Let me carry that for you."

"I can carry it. I'm used to carrying it."

"That must be heavy," Maazin remarked.

"I can deadlift over a eighty-five with ease and back-squat with the same. I think I can handle this."

He raised his eyebrows. "What?"

Jeena chuckled. "You think you're the only one who works out? I do strength training. I have to be able to manage out in the field on my own or with very little help. Who else is going to carry my gear?"

Maazin was impressed and he took the biohazard bucket. "Let me at least make sure this secure so we don't have a mess. The ocean is a bit choppy after the storm."

"Deal."

Maazin helped her on board and they secured everything and then cast off from Petrie Island, heading back south toward the main island.

Jeena sat beside him on the bridge and that tension that always seemed to be there settled in again. He hated that. Talking to her had once been so easy, but he'd been a different person then.

He'd felt more free. He hadn't necessarily been free, but he'd felt more free. Of course, that relaxed disposition had caused nothing but trouble. It had caused nothing but a world of hurt and pain that he was never going to be able to make up to anyone.

Not to his parents.

Not to Farhan.

Not to Jeena.

And not to himself.

He deserved his sentence. He deserved the unhappiness, and the best he could do was try and take care of his people.

"I want to thank you again for the work you did on Petrie," Maazin said, breaking the silence.

"You're welcome. That's why I'm here."

"Would you have come back had it not been for the cyclone?" Even though he knew the answer to that.

Jeena's expression was sad. "No. I didn't want him growing up here as an illegitimate lovechild."

Maazin flinched at her harsh words. "I am sorry. I wouldn't have let that happen."

Jeena shrugged. "I did what was best for myself and for Syman. My parents chose to give up everything to come with me. I can never repay them enough. They didn't have to come with me, but if they hadn't given up so much to support me, I wouldn't be a surgeon now."

"I am sorry. Your family shouldn't have had to give up so much just because of who I am."

Tears welled up in her eyes and she looked away. "Thank you."

"I have received word from the consulate that your orders have been changed and you will be called back to Canada in a matter of days."

Jeena brushed away her tears. "What?"

"Kalyana is getting back on its feet and Canada has called back its special services. Not to sound too cli chéd, but the British are coming."

"That doesn't make sense." She checked her phone and frowned. "You're right, my orders have arrived. In five days we'll be heading back to Canada."

"You'll be able to see Syman again," Maazin said gently. He was trying to give her something to be happy about because maybe if she was happy then he would feel happy too. Right now, he didn't feel happy about it.

Though it was for the best that she leave.

"Patang Island," Maazin remarked. "It looks so peaceful now."

Jeena nodded. "I wanted to go back. I wanted to visit all my old haunts before I left again, because it would probably be the last time I saw them."

"Well, let's go, then," he offered.

"What?" Jeena asked, confused. "We can't go to Patang Island."

"Why not?" Maazin asked, turning the wheel to head his yacht around to the lee side of the island, where they would be safe and wouldn't come up on a reef. From there they could take the small dinghy out to the sandbar and he could give her a short time of peace.

Later, he would take her back to her family's old home. He owned the plantation now and kept up the vanilla production. Jeena's old family home was used as a small bed and breakfast establishment now, but was currently empty because no tourists had been allowed to come to Kalyana since Blandine had hit, and any tourists that had been in Kalyana had been evacuated.

Not that many tourists took the long trip to Kalyana.

The Seychelles were much more popular, and didn't have quite the pomp and circumstance that Kalyana and his father demanded.

"Maazin, this is crazy," Jeena shouted above the wind as he sped toward the island. "Your security team will go bananas when you don't pass their certain check points in time."

"So let them. We're safe. Kalyana's waters are monitored. Let's just take this moment. You wanted to go back to Patang Island and we shall."

Jeena smiled. "Okay."

He came up on the lee side of the island and anchored in a safe spot where they wouldn't run aground from shifting tides but were safe from the waves or any surges.

"Why don't you change out of your uniform? There may be some women's clothing in the main berth. Farhan and Sara sometimes take the yacht out."

"That sounds good." Jeena disappeared below deck and Maazin let out a sigh as he listened to the gentle waves in the shelter of the island and the large reef that surrounded it lap against the side of his boat.

What're you doing?

He didn't know. He just wanted to give this to her. He just wanted to spend this time with her. When she left this time he didn't want her to leave and think about him or this country with bad thoughts.

And when Syman asked about him, if he did, then he would know that he was always welcome in Kalyana.

"Are you okay?"

Maazin turned around and took a step back when he saw Jeena in an emerald-green sari. It was the same color as the dress she had been wearing that first time he'd seen her. It took him right back to that moment.

And his breath was literally taken away.

"You look beautiful," he murmured.

A flush of pink rose in her cheeks. "Thank you."

"You ready?" he asked.

"Yes," she said nervously. "I think I am."

He smiled and took her hand. He climbed over the side first and down the ladder into the dinghy. She followed and he helped her, slipping his hands around her waist and guiding her safely down. It made his pulse quicken and the urge to kiss her, like he'd done last night, overtook him, but he held back.

He didn't want to scare her off.

This time on the island was to give her another memory of her homeland. It was something for her to cherish before she left again, and he wanted her to have that untainted.

He didn't want to make it any more awkward than it was between them. All he wanted at this moment was to give her a good memory. It was the least he could give her, especially when he'd missed so much.

He guided the little motored dinghy to the sandbar and cut the motor when he got close. He leaped over the side into the cool water and pulled the dinghy ashore.

Jeena stood up and without thinking he just lifted her up, gripping her waist and setting her down on the shore. She gasped when he set her down and he stared into her dark, warm eyes, lost for a moment.

"Maazin," she whispered.

"Yes."

"You can let go of me."

"Right," he said quickly. "Of course."

She blushed and took his hands in hers. Her hands were so tiny, so soft. "Come on, let's enjoy this moment of peace."

"Good idea."

Only she didn't let go of his hand and he didn't pull it away. He liked holding her hand as they walked barefoot on the sand. It was windy, but he didn't care. It was beautiful out here. The ocean and whitecaps. The sun reflecting against the water and causing it to sparkle. The sand seemed to shimmer like diamonds. They walked over to the lone piece of driftwood that Maazin had hauled up out of the water ten years ago. It was a place to sit.

"I can't believe that it's still here," Jeena said wistfully.

"Well, it was quite large, but I'm surprised it hasn't rotted away to nothing."

Jeena smiled and let go of his hand to run her hand along the rough wood. "I'm glad it's still here. That night…"

"The night we conceived Syman."

A blush tinged her cheek. "Yes."

"That was a magical night for me too. I'm sorry that I missed his birth, I'm sorry that I wasn't there for it all."

She nodded and sat down on the log. "Me too."

"Does he ask about me?" It was a question he'd been avoiding and he was afraid of asking it, but he had to know. It was eating him up not to ask.

"He does," Jeena said quietly, looking at her hands.

"What have you told him about me?"

"I told him you lived in Kalyana and I told him that I had lost touch with you, but that if you knew about him, you would love him."

Maazin nodded and sat down next to her. "That is true."

He wanted to tell her that if he had known it would all have been different, but he wasn't sure about that. He knew one thing—he was sad that this life with Jeena and his son had been taken from him. That he'd never got the chance to ask her to be his. He'd never seen his son as a baby. Never held him in his arms. He'd missed so much.

And you are responsible for taking Ali's life.

That thought grounded him. He didn't deserve it. Ali had never got a chance and he didn't deserve it either. It was fitting justice for his sins.

"Tell me about his birth. Tell me about Syman's birth."

Jeena looked at him like he was crazy. "What?"

"Tell me. When was he born?"

"June twenty-sixth. It was a Friday and he was born in the morning. He came out screaming and had all this dark hair, even on his bottom." She chuckled about that. "I thought he was going to be made fun of for being so hairy, but it was just lanugo and it fell out as he got older. Then he was this chubby, happy baby who slept all night in a bassinet by my bedside. Everyone who saw him loved him."

It cut him to the quick to hear about this. He'd been denied that precious time. He hadn't had a chance to hold him in his arms, to kiss his head and sing him to sleep.

"It must've been hard on you, getting a medical degree and having an infant."

"It was. My mother and father were my lifeline. If I didn't have them, I wouldn't be a doctor. They knew how much I wanted to be a doctor when we still lived in Kalyana and before I met you they were saving up all they could to send me to England or Australia to get my education, but then I attended that polo match and met you."

Maazin touched her face. "I'm sorry that I ruined your life."

Jeena touched his hand, still cupping her face. "You didn't ruin my life, Maazin. You gave me this great gift. Syman is a wonderful boy and my life in Canada is good. Do I wish that things could have been different and that I'd chosen my life in Canada myself, instead of it being thrust on me, yes, but my parents are better off there than they were here. We have a good life. Don't feel bad."

"You are too kind. Kinder than I deserve."

"What're you talking about?"

Maazin sighed. "I am the one who killed Ali."

Her eyes widened. "What're you talking about?"

"I'm telling you the truth. I am the one who killed Ali. It was my fault."

It took Jeena a moment to let the words sink in. What did Maazin mean that he was the one responsible for killing Ali?

"I thought it was a car accident?" she asked.

Maazin stood and was pacing on the sand, rubbing the back of his neck. "It was."

"Were you driving?" she asked.

"No."

"Then I don't quite understand how you're responsible for your brother's death."

"I was drunk. I had gone to a party that I shouldn't have been at. There was drinking and some drugs. I didn't do the drugs, but I was very drunk and I couldn't call security to come and get me. I was already splashed across the tabloids and when I called the palace, drunk again, Ali took it upon himself to come and get me. His wife came with him." Maazin closed his eyes and she could tell that it was hard for him to continue.

"Go on," Jeena urged gently. "What happened?"

"Ali came, of course. He was such a good brother." Maazin took a deep breath. "He came and got me. Both of them scolded me, of course, for being blind drunk and at a party I should not have gone to. Not that I did anything, I just got drunk with my friends. The house was up in the hills and while we were driving home a rainstorm hit. It rained very hard, or so they tell me, I don't remember. What I remember is Ali yelling at me, telling me that I had to pull up my socks and behave better.

"Then there was this loud bang and screaming and we were upside down, before it went black. I woke up in agony because my shoulder was dislocated and I was under the wrecked car. Ali and Chandni were dead."

Jeena gasped and she could see the pain in Maazin's eyes as he poured out his story to her. It was obvious that it weighed heavily on him and that it had been traumatic.

"Maazin, you were not responsible for your brother's death."

"Of course I was!" he snapped. "If he hadn't been such a good brother he would've sent someone to come and get me. But he didn't. He came himself because I begged him not to tell Father. I was terrified or… I really don't know. I don't remember much about the phone call. Only that I wanted Ali to come and get me. And if I hadn't been so insistent and he hadn't been such a good brother he would still be alive. And so would Chandni.

"It wasn't just his life I ruined. I ruined my parents' lives. Ali was my father's favorite. And then I ruined my late sister-in-law's parents' lives. They lost their daughter. And then Farhan was made Crown Prince. He had to come back from Australia and give up his life there…"

Jeena stood and walked over to him, and reached up and touched his face. "It's not your fault. Ali loved you, but it's not your fault that he and his wife chose to come get you that night. You are not to be blamed."

"Lady Meleena blames me for the end of our farce of an engagement."

Jeena's heart skipped a beat. "Oh?"

It shouldn't matter to her that his engagement was over. She shouldn't care, but she did.

"When Ali died I devoted my life to saving others and my duties. They took all my attention."

"Is that why the engagement went on for so long?"

He nodded. "Partly, but mostly I didn't care about her. There was only one person I cared about."

"I cared about you too," she said softly. She truly had never stopped caring about him.

There had been no one else.

Don't fall for him again. Don't do it.

He took a step closer to her. Those gray-green eyes twinkled as he caressed her face. Her body trembled like a traitor to her own mind under his touch.

And before she knew what was happening he wrapped his arms around her and kissed her, just like before, and she was lost to him. Her body wanted more.

She hadn't been able to stop thinking about that kiss that had snuck up on them in the office on Petrie. She wanted to forget that kiss because she was leaving and nothing could happen between them, even if that pull of attraction and feelings was still there.

It was off limits.

She couldn't give everything up for a chance with him. She didn't come from his world any more. She didn't want that kind of spotlight on her or Syman.

And as much as she wanted this kiss to continue, she knew that it couldn't. She couldn't let it continue so she pushed on his chest to move him away from her.

"We can't," she whispered, trying to calm the erratic beat of her pulse and quell the fire that was in her blood. "We can't."

"Why not?" he whispered, leaning his forehead down to hers. Their foreheads were pressed together, their arms around each other.

"You need someone to be your wife and I am not that woman. I can never be that woman."

Maazin nodded. "I understand. I'm sorry for kissing you. It's just that around you, I lose myself. It feels like all those years ago."

"I know, but it's not." She tried not to let the tears stinging her eyes spill down her cheeks. She wanted to tell him that she wanted to be his and that she'd never got over him, but that was selfish. Syman had a life in Canada. He had friends and loved his school, his hockey and his home.

Her parents had given up so much so that they could go with her and help her. Now they were prosperous and she couldn't ask them to give it all up to chase a whim.

Her mother had tried to warn her all those years ago that getting involved with Maazin was a bad idea, but she had been young and foolish then...

"You shouldn't get involved with the Prince," her mother said quietly. "Nothing good can come from that."

"What do you mean? He loves me. I know he does."

Her mother took her hands. "I have no doubt. Who could not love you? You are beautiful. But you are just a farmer's daughter and he is a prince."

"But Kalyana is a free country and he's the third son."

"Jeena, please be careful. I don't want you to get hurt..."

She should've listened to her mother back then. If she had she wouldn't have fallen in love with a man who was off limits. A man who had ruined her for all others. But she had been young and so foolish.

She wasn't going to make that mistake again. When she'd been sent to Kalyana, she'd promised herself that she wouldn't let herself be sucked in again.

She had to remind herself of that.

"We should go," she said, stepping away from him. It was safer to put some distance between the two of them.

Maazin nodded.

Jeena turned and walked back to the dinghy. There was a cool wind and it caused a shiver to run through her. The sun disappeared behind a cloud and suddenly things didn't seem so rosy and lovely on Patang Island.

It had lost its sparkle and magic.

It just reminded her of a life with a person she loved that she could never have. The best thing she could do now was walk away and try to just forget about Kalyana and Maazin's kisses, even if she knew that was going to be a hard, hard thing to do.

An impossible thing to do, but it was for the best.

CHAPTER EIGHT

THE MOMENT THAT Maazin docked in the harbor, there were several limousines waiting, as well as his brother's personnel. He had a bad feeling about what he was seeing.

He glanced over at Jeena, who had changed back into her medical uniform. She bit her lip, worrying about it, and he could see the fear in her eyes.

"Don't worry," he said. "They're here for me."

"Don't be so sure. We did take a detour and I am not Lady Meleena. Remember the world thinks you're still engaged to her."

"That I am aware of," he said quickly. "No one else knows about you, Jeena, and no one else knows about my broken engagement. You are a doctor, a Canadian doctor. It's all proper."

"If you say so." She didn't sound too convinced. She tried to walk past him, but he held her back.

"I won't let anyone hurt you," he said, and he meant it.

"Thanks," she whispered.

The moment Maazin's yacht was tied up and he helped Jeena down onto the pier, Farhan, flanked by two bodyguards, came quickly toward them. He was frowning and there were dark circles under his eyes.

A shiver ran down his spine.

Oh, God.

"Farhan?" Maazin asked, barely getting the words out.

"Maazin, it's Father. He took a spell this morning and we've been waiting for your return." Farhan glanced over at Jeena. "Are you Dr. Harrak?"

"Yes," she said nervously.

"Oh, good. We were looking for you. Your team said that you were able to perform a catheterization under less than ideal circumstances and that you were the best."

"I… I am, but…" Jeena was stumbling over her words and Maazin knew it was because of who his father was. His father was the King. She was terrified of operating on the King.

He knew what she was thinking. She thought she already had a bad reputation with the Kalyanese people.

"Jeena, nothing bad will happen to you at the palace, not while you are under my care."

Jeena looked at him and nodded. "Of course. Of course I can help His Majesty."

Farhan cocked an eyebrow. He was confused, but he wasn't about to argue about reasons now out on the public pier at the harbor. "Well, the royal motorcade will take you both to the palace."

Maazin put his hand on the small of Jeena's back and urged her to take a step forward. A bodyguard stepped forward and took her duffel bag from her.

Another took her surgical kit. Maazin stuck by her side as they were ushered into a limo where Farhan was already seated. Jeena chewed on her lip again and began to wring her hands.

Maazin wanted to reach out and comfort her, but Farhan was watching her with interest.

"Dr. Harrak, are you quite all right?" Farhan asked.

"Fine. It's just, I've never operated on royalty before. Never done a cardiac cath procedure on a king!"

Farhan smiled. "It'll be okay, I assure you. We have everything you need. I would do it myself, but I can't, as you know, being his son. So even Sara is unable to operate. It's driving her a bit mad, because she wants to help."

Jeena chuckled, but Maazin could still hear the nervousness in her voice.

"It'll be quite all right. You are a capable surgeon. You did an appendectomy in a courthouse and Mr. Patel is going to make a full recovery because of it, and you taught a first responder the ins and outs of being a scrub nurse. You are capable of this. Do not think about who he is, just think of him as any other patient."

Maazin's words were meant to calm her.

"Think of him as any other patient."

Which was easier said than done, but she was going to try. She had to try. They approached the palace and passed through Huban's gate and up to the palace. It sat on top of a hill and reflected the rich history of Kalyana's Eastern influence. It was like a fortress, but surrounded with lush, green vegetation. Or at least it had been, but when cyclone Blandine had blown through, the leaves had been stripped away and trees toppled. As they came closer to the palace she could see gardeners trying to clean up the mess that Blandine had left in her wake. The drive was littered with brightly colored petals that had been trampled down and crushed into the road.

It was sad.

The palace with its warm-hued stone walls and arched windows had been the center of Huban. It had been the heart of Kalyana and now it looked the worse for wear. As if Kalyana's heart had been broken.

At least her spirit hadn't been broken. Of that Jeena was sure.

The limo pulled up in front of two, large ornately carved doors that were immediately opened. Farhan slid out and Maazin followed, but Jeena felt frozen.

"Jeena?" Maazin asked. "Are you coming?"

"Yes."

She could do this. She'd sworn an oath as a doctor to do no harm and she was going to stick to that oath. She was not going to put her medical career in jeopardy because she was worried about operating on the Kalyanese King. And she wasn't going to embarrass her new country by being the Canadian doctor who couldn't save the life of the Kalyanese King.

Forget that!

She was going to save his life. For as much as she was nervous about operating on King Uttam, she loved Maazin and she knew that Maazin cared about his father. Even if he seemed to blame himself for Ali's death.

Maazin held out his hand, which was breaking protocol, and she smiled at him. She reached out and took his hand as he helped her out of the limousine. His hand was strong and he believed in her. She was going to do this for him.

Once she was out of the limo, he let go of her hand and she took another deep breath, calming her nerves.

Here we go. You've got this.

She straightened her shoulders and held her head high as she followed Farhan and Maazin through the large double doors into an entranceway of white marble and creamy stone walls that gleamed brightly.

"Maazin, so you've finally decided to grace us with your presence."

Jeena glanced up to see Queen Aruna standing there, regal and poised. She didn't smile and she didn't seem to look worried or have any kind of emotion as she looked at her sons.

Maazin walked over to his mother and took her hand in his, bowing over it.

"I'm sorry, Mother," Maazin apologized. "I was only doing my duty to my people."

"Yes. That's all very well and good, but we had to send Farhan out to fetch you. Your yacht was late getting in."

Jeena could sense the tension, the coldness and the detachment between Queen Aruna and Maazin. It was like they were strangers rather than mother and son. Perhaps Aruna did blame Maazin for Ali's death. There was a huge rift between them.

It was sad.

She was so close to Syman. She could never treat Syman with such aloofness.

"I'm sorry, Mother." Maazin stepped back and the Queen's hardened gaze fell on her.

Jeena curtseyed. "Your Majesty."

"Dr. Harrak, I am so glad you've come and I understand from my daughter-in-law that you're also Kalyanese."

Queen Aruna addressed her very politely, but Jeena

could hear the undercurrent of displeasure and Jeena realized then Queen Aruna knew *exactly* who she was.

"Yes, Your Majesty." Jeena straightened. "How can I be of assistance?"

"Farhan, you're a doctor—please explain it to our dear doctor and then take her to your father to perform the procedure. Please excuse me, but I haven't slept in the last twenty-four hours." Queen Aruna excused herself. She turned back up the stairs and disappeared out of sight.

Farhan turned to her. "Dr. Harrak, my father has a pulmonary embolus and he needs catheterization to remove it before it does further damage. My father has had a stroke in the past and he suffers from macular degeneration as well as atrial fibrillation."

"And none of your surgeons can perform it?" Jeena asked.

"Not under these conditions. In a hospital, yes, but we were told by your team that you were able to do it and you had done it successfully before." Farhan looked over at Maazin. "Again, none of us in the royal family can assist you, but there are some of the finest royal physicians in attendance. He is prepped and waiting for the procedure. He's had a sedative and is groggy."

Jeena nodded. "Take me to him."

Farhan bowed his head and gestured to show her the way. She was led down a hallway to a small antechamber and a room that was used a formal sitting room for visiting dignitaries. Only now it had been transformed into a procedure room.

Jeena glanced through the window and saw that King Uttam was laid out and prepped. They were just waiting for her.

You've got this. This is just another patient. He's not a king. He's a human being who needs your help. He's not your King right now. He's a patient. Just an ordinary, normal patient.

"There are scrubs in this room here and a place to scrub in," Farhan offered. "I'll leave you to it. Maazin, if you'll follow me."

"Just one moment," Maazin said. He took a step toward her and his presence was reassuring. She wished that he could stay with her. She wanted him to stay, she needed him there while she did this procedure on the King of her homeland.

She didn't want to be known as the doctor who killed the King of Kalyana.

"You can do this," Maazin whispered.

"I'm frightened," she whispered back. "This is your father...the King."

"He's just a patient. This is like any other patient you'd work on and try to save. You can do this." He took a step back and turned away with his brother.

Jeena took another deep breath and then went to get changed. She quickly changed into the scrubs that had been left for her, cleaned herself up and then headed into the makeshift procedure room.

Another doctor was there.

"Dr. Harrak, I'm Dr. Imran Patel, and I'll be your assist."

Jeena nodded. "It's a pleasure to meet you."

Jeena walked over to the King and looked down at him. He was mostly out of it, but not completely under. The King's gaze locked on to her and he smiled, as if she was an old friend and not some commoner who'd had his secret illegitimate grandchild. He probably didn't even know about Syman. Which was for the best.

"You look familiar," the King whispered.

"My name is Dr. Harrak. Jeena Harrak. I'm from Canada, previously from Kalyana."

The King's eyes widened. "I've heard of you. You have a son, don't you? A son who plays hockey."

Jeena's heart dropped to the soles of her feet and she felt faint. How did he know about Syman? How did he know that Syman played hockey? And then she realized that Kalyana had been keeping tabs on her for some time, even from as far away as Canada. She had been a fool to think otherwise.

It rattled her completely.

She wanted to turn and run. She wanted to run back to Canada and hide Syman, but she couldn't do that. She couldn't turn her back on a patient who needed her services, even if she felt like that patient posed a threat to her family.

She would save King Uttam's life and if he came for Syman, she would remind him how she'd saved his life and perhaps he would feel he owed her a debt and that debt would protect her son from this life of protocol and pomp.

Maazin was worried about Jeena. She looked so nervous, doing the procedure on his father, and he couldn't blame her one bit. If the situation had been reversed he would feel the same way. He couldn't stop pacing as he waited with Farhan in their father's office.

Maazin knew that his constant pacing was antagonizing his father's macaw Sophie, because she would squawk every so often when he got close to her perch.

"You're driving that bird crazy with your incessant pacing," Farhan remarked calmly. "Truth be told, you're driving me crazy too."

"I can't help it. I'm worried about her." And then he pinched the bridge of his nose and cursed inwardly for the slip.

"Are you having an affair with the Canadian doctor?"

"What're you talking about?" Maazin asked, trying to keep calm.

Farhan rolled his eyes. "I see the way you look at her. Be careful. The public thinks you are still with Lady Meleena."

"I'm not!" Maazin snapped. He was annoyed with his brother's questions.

"Having an affair?"

"I am not with Lady Meleena and not having an affair with Dr. Harrak. At least…"

"At least what?" Farhan asked cautiously. "You're not having an affair with Dr. Harrak, are you? Please tell me you're not."

"No, but… I did."

"When?" Farhan asked, confused. "You've been nothing but faithful to Lady Meleena. Even when you two were apart for so long."

"And look where that got me. She had her own countless affairs."

"I'm sorry she hurt you," Farhan said.

Maazin ran his hand through his hair. "Meleena did hurt me. But I couldn't care less about her and the men she saw. It was something else."

"Really?" Farhan asked.

"I never wanted to marry Lady Meleena."

Farhan rolled his eyes as if to say, *I know that*. "You promised Father."

"So?"

"I married who Father told me to marry."

"And I'm glad it worked out for you and I'm glad it worked out for Ali too and our parents. I'm glad for every arranged marriage that works out, but…" He scrubbed his hands over his face. "Ten years ago, before Ali died, I was in love with someone else and that's Jeena. I adored her, worshipped her and I wanted only her. Then she vanished. Mother told me she'd left and there was a letter Meleena found. I was distraught and hurt. Little did I know that Jeena left because she was pregnant and she was afraid of having the illegitimate child of a prince."

Farhan's eyes widened. "She was pregnant and Meleena knew? It all seems very odd."

"I know."

"Should we let Jeena be operating on Father, then?" Farhan asked with a frown, getting to his feet. "She's the mother of your child."

"She won't harm him. She takes her oath seriously. She came to Kalyana because of her love and respect for Canada and Kalyana. She is the last person to do him harm."

"How did you find out about…your child?"

Maazin nodded. "Syman. I have a son. A son I've never met and his name is Syman. He's nine."

"Why didn't she tell you about him? Even if she left for Canada with her parents she could've called or mailed a letter, even gone to the tabloids."

"She wanted to protect her son and Meleena told her that I didn't want our child. That I didn't want her."

"And clearly you did."

"Yes."

Farhan ran his hand through his hair. "And yet Father arranged for you to marry Meleena, who manipulated all this? If Father had known about his grandchild, he would have insisted you marry Jeena. Father loves his children."

"He loved Ali," Maazin said bitterly, and then his shoulders slumped. He hated bringing Ali up.

"When are you going to stop blaming yourself for that?" Farhan asked.

Maazin didn't answer him. Instead he looked back at the portrait of their father that hung on the wall. Next to it was a portrait of Ali.

Ali had been his parents' favorite.

And Maazin had destroyed that. His mother had made that all too clear to him.

I'm sorry, Ali. So sorry.

"Well, that explains her nervousness," Farhan said, breaking the silence that had descended between the two of them. "I thought it just had something to do with operating on the King."

"Well, I'm sure that's part of it," Maazin said.

"What're you going to do about your son?"

"I promised Jeena that I wouldn't hurt her and it would hurt her if I tried to claim him and bring him into this life. I don't want to do that to him."

"He has a right to know who his father is," Farhan stated. "He has a right to know where he comes from."

Maazin sighed. "I know, but…"

Do I really want him to know? Do I deserve to have him in my life?

He left Farhan standing there and walked out onto

the terrace. He didn't want to talk about it any more. He didn't want to dwell on the things he couldn't have. He'd hurt Jeena just as deeply as she'd hurt him.

There was no going back. Even if he desperately wanted to.

She'd made it clear that there was no going back for her.

Jeena pulled off her surgical mask and then walked out of the room. The King had tolerated the procedure well and she'd removed the clot. He was being moved to his own bed to recover.

Jeena slid down the wall and tried to take a few calming breaths.

She'd saved King Uttam's life, but he knew about her son.

He hadn't actually acknowledged that Syman was Maazin's but he knew about her son. How did he know about him?

She wanted to call her parents about it and ask their advice, but she didn't want to send them into a tizzy.

Jeena closed her eyes and tried to find her center, a place that had always calmed her. That place was standing out on her bedroom balcony overlooking the green lush hills, the fields of vanilla, and beyond all that she was tall enough to see the ocean.

How she wished she could go back there.

Even for a moment.

"How did it go?"

Jeena opened her eyes to see Maazin standing in the shadows.

"Are you supposed to be here?"

"Father's been moved. I'm allowed to be here." He smiled. "Are you all right?"

"No. That was… It was hard and I feel dizzy. I wish I could reach out to my parents and talk to them about it, but I don't want to worry them. That's the last thing I want to do, so I was trying to find my happy place."

"And where is that?" Maazin asked.

"My old home. The plantation."

"Then let's go," he offered.

"Shouldn't you be here or with your father?"

"It won't matter I'm gone. He won't care."

Jeena tilted her head to the side. She could see the pain in his eyes, the blame he bore. "Are you so sure?"

"Do you want to go or not?" he asked.

"I do, but my family doesn't own it any longer."

"I know," Maazin stated. "I went there after you left. I thought maybe your parents would be there and I could ask them where you'd gone. I saw that they had left too and the plantation was for sale, so I bought it."

Jeena's eyes widened and she couldn't believe what she was hearing. "You bought it?"

"Yes. I own it. It's still a plantation and during tourist season I rent it out as a little cottage. It's empty at the moment. There are no tourists in Kalyana. We can go there."

Even though she knew she shouldn't go with him, she wanted to go back home. Just for a moment, even if it was with him.

A man who made her lose all control.

A man she couldn't have but still cared for. A man who still owned her heart, even if she didn't want him to.

"Yes! Please."

Maazin nodded. "Go and change and we'll sneak out of the palace and head over there."

Jeena nodded and got up. She hurried off to get changed. She was shocked that Maazin had bought it. It had been his money that had allowed her parents to start a new life in Canada and she'd had no idea.

Why would he buy it?

She shook that thought out of her head, because all she cared about right now was that she got to go home. Even for a brief moment.

She was going home.

CHAPTER NINE

THE CLOSER THEY go to her home, the more excited and emotional Jeena got. She recognized the road they turned down, although it was a better quality road than she remembered. She closed her eyes and thought about all the times she had come down this road on her way home.

There had been some changes, but the scent of the fields and the sight of the orchids that she knew so well hit her, and a tear slid down her face.

Her father had liked to grow his vanilla orchids on wooden poles, as originally orchid vines had grown up trees and her father had always believed that the wood added to the productivity of the fruit.

And he had spent hours and hours checking on the flowers.

He had loved his plantation. He had known everything about it and he'd given it all up for her. She was still in shock that Maazin had bought the plantation. Why had he done that?

As they rounded a bend she cried out as she saw the fields. The vines were still growing on wooden poles. Some were old still and there were also fresh ones, but the fields were neat and tidy, just like she remembered.

She wiped away the tears as she drank in the sight.

"Can you stop the car?" she asked Maazin.

"Of course." Maazin pulled over to the side of the road and Jeena slipped out. She walked up to the fence and climbed up. Teetering precariously, she took a picture for her father. He was sleeping now, so she would send it to him later so it would be the first thing he saw when he woke up.

"We tried to keep it the same," Maazin said, coming up behind her. "Your father knew his stuff and he was admired around these parts. So I made sure that the man who farms this land now does it the way your family has always done it."

Jeena nodded, fighting back tears. "I still can't believe you bought it. Why did you buy it?"

Maazin shrugged. "I didn't want to see it ruined. You loved this place and I didn't understand why your family left. I know why now, but at the time I thought that maybe you would come back and I wanted it here, waiting for you."

"Thank you." She brushed away tears again. "Let's see the house. Please."

"Of course."

They climbed back into the Jeep. Jeena was swallowing back all the emotion that was welling up inside her. She drank in the sights. This was her happy place. This was the place she always came back to in her mind when she was scared, when she was hurt and when she was uncertain.

This was home.

And it was her fault that her family was no longer here.

Maazin pulled into the driveway.

And Jeena cried silent tears as she looked up at the house. The vines still grew on the outside. They weren't vanilla orchids, just plain orchids that her mother loved. The stone path was the same and there was the swing on the big old banyan tree that was said to have grown up through an original post of the first home that had been built when her ancestors had first come here from India in the seventeenth century.

It was all the same. Untouched.

Except it really wasn't the same. Her family wasn't here. It was her home, but the heart of it was gone. It seemed so lonely. So cold.

"Shall we go inside?" Maazin asked softly.

"Yes."

Maazin unlocked the door and stood back, letting her go in first. There were some changes, mostly modernizing to accommodate tourists, but the layout was still the same. Jeena closed her eyes and swore that she could hear her father singing as he came home from a long day in the fields.

She could smell her mother's cooking on the stove. The aroma of her saffron rice wafting in the air. And then the memory of her family frantically packing all their belongings, their sadness as they'd left this house for the very last time.

Jeena climbed the stairs to the room at the top that had been hers. It was no longer her childhood room, but had been converted into a loft space with a gorgeous balcony. A romantic getaway for lovers overlooking the vanilla fields. She opened the balcony doors and walked outside. The sun was setting in the west.

Shades of red and orange reflected off the blue water that lay beyond the rolling green hills filled with flow-ering vanilla. She could see the path to the creek where she'd almost drowned. And then she saw it, the palace in the distance. She'd forgotten that she would be able to see it from up here. When she'd been a child she'd dreamed of being a princess and wondering what it was like to live in such a palace.

Now she knew and she didn't want that.

Don't you? If you had it you could have Maazin.

It was all too surreal. She wrapped her arms around herself, hugging herself because she was overwhelmed. She'd never thought that she would be back here, that she would be able to see her childhood home again.

"I did make this change to your room. I'm sorry," Maazin said from the door, interrupting her thoughts.

"It's okay," she said, glancing back at him. "You've done a beautiful job and I'm thankful you kept so much the same."

He stood behind her. "I didn't want to change anything too much. I so wanted you to come back."

She looked up at him and her heart began to beat faster. "I wanted to come back too."

He touched her cheek, brushing his thumb across her skin. "I cared for you, Jeena. I still do."

"Maazin, don't say that."

"I can't help it, Jeena."

"Maazin, I… I cared for you too." A tear slid down her cheek. And it was true. She did.

I still love you.

Only she didn't say it out loud. She was terrified how quickly she'd let him back in.

"Jeena," he whispered.

"I know that you can't make a commitment to me and I have to leave again." And even though she knew she shouldn't, she just wanted this one night with him. This one last night to lay the ghosts to rest. To have the closure she needed, so that she could return to Canada and know that her life here was over. And there would be no pull, nothing to lure her back.

"I want you, Maazin. Please."

He pulled her into his arms and kissed her, very intensely.

His touch felt so good. She'd forgotten how wonderful it felt to be wrapped up in Maazin's strong arms. How safe he made her feel. How he made her body sing with pleasure. When she was with him everything else melted away. There was only the two of them.

Jeena wanted to forget all the pain, the loneliness, the anger she'd felt these last ten years. For once she wanted to feel like her old self again. She wanted to feel like that girl who had been swept off her feet by her Prince Charming.

She wanted to taste passion again. Hot, heady, sweet passion.

She wanted Maazin. He was all she'd ever wanted and if she couldn't have him forever then she wanted this one night.

Jeena melted into that kiss, pressing her body against him.

"Jeena," Maazin whispered huskily. "Are you certain?"

"Yes." She ran her hands down his chest, feeling his heart beating under her palm. It was racing, just like hers. "Please just be with me. Be with me tonight for one last time."

Maazin gave in with a moan and took her in his arms, scooping her up as he'd done ten years ago on

Patang Island. He carried her from the balcony into the room toward the bed.

Jeena's pulse was racing with anticipation over what was going to happen. She had missed this. She'd missed this intimacy, this connection that she had with him.

They sank onto the mattress together, kissing. His hands were in her hair. She wanted to just feel him pressed against her.

No words were needed because she knew that at this moment they both wanted the same thing.

Each other.

The kiss ended only so they could both undress each other, slowly, kissing in between because Jeena didn't want to break the connection between them. She didn't want to miss any stolen moment together.

"Jeena, I wanted you the moment I met you," Maazin whispered against her ear. "I still want you."

"I wanted you too." She was terrified of opening herself up to him. To be vulnerable to him again.

It was different this time, though.

Are you certain of that?

Jeena shook that thought from her head and let herself melt into the moment.

She wanted this.

They lay next to each other, both exposed and naked. She couldn't get enough of touching him, feeling his muscles ripple under her fingertips, running her hands over her skin and through his hair, but the most heady feeling was having his strong hands on her again.

Caressing her and making her body heat like it had been touched by electricity.

Maazin kissed her again, his lips urgent as he pulled her body flush with his.

This was it.

This was the moment. He pressed her against the mattress. His hands entwined with hers, his body so large over her she felt safe wrapped up in his arms.

Maazin gave her a kiss that seared her very soul. The warmth spread through her veins and then his lips moved from her mouth down her neck, following the erratic pulse points under her skin.

She let out a mewl of pleasure.

She wanted him inside her. Badly.

He stroked her cheek and kissed her gently again, his lips nipped softly at hers, one hand on her breast and the other stroking her between her legs. Desire coursed through her. It was overwhelming to let herself go with him.

Letting these wild emotions that she'd bottled up for so long come loose again.

He kissed her deeply as he entered her. She cried out as he slowly filled her, wanting more of him.

She couldn't get enough of him.

She wrapped her legs around him, urging him to go even deeper, to take all of her. To completely possess her.

Everything else, all her worries, her pain, her heartache melted away in that moment that the two of them connected again. It felt so right to be with him, yet it was wrong, but she didn't care right now.

It was just the two of them moving together in complete bliss.

It wasn't long before both of them came, close together in shared pleasure. A tear slid down her cheek as it ended.

Maazin wiped it away. "Did I hurt you?"

"No, no it's just… I don't want it to end."

He kissed her. "Neither do I."

He held her close and when he rolled over on his back, he brought her against him. His arm around her, holding her tight as if he was afraid to let her go. Jeena didn't mind. She clung to him just as tightly and she was just as terrified that he would let her go as well.

It frightened her that he still had this hold on her.

The Prince she could never have.

Beautiful.

She was so beautiful. Maazin couldn't believe that it had happened again. He couldn't believe that he was here, lying in Jeena's arms again. It was what he'd dreamed about time and time again, but had never thought would be a reality.

And he was so glad that it had happened, but he was worried about what this meant.

He wasn't sure that Jeena even wanted him in her life.

Or would want him to live in Canada. If he gave up his place in the line of succession he was pretty sure it would kill his father. And then he couldn't help his people.

Also, the winter and the cold did not sound appealing in the least bit.

It would be worth it to be with her, wouldn't it?

It would be, but he couldn't leave Kalyana. He couldn't do that to his father, his mother or his brother. He'd promised Sara too that he would help with her education plans.

And why did he deserve happiness? He didn't.

Yes, you do.

And he wasn't even sure that Jeena wanted him.

She'd wanted him this night, but she'd told him it was just for this one night.

He was torn.

Maazin slowly moved and got out of the bed. He pulled on his trousers and headed out on the balcony to enjoy the night breeze. The sky was clear and full of stars. He could see the distant glow of Huban and the palace all lit up.

Usually, he didn't mind looking at Huban lit up at night, but tonight he resented that he had been born to this life. He felt so trapped.

And he was selfish for thinking that way. Ali had never thought that way. Ali had been such a good brother and good son to their parents. He would've made a great king, but they would never know that now, thanks to him.

When will you stop blaming yourself for that?

Maazin turned his back on the palace and looked at Jeena, sleeping so soundly in the bed. There had been times in the ten years they'd been apart and his heart had been broken over losing her that he'd wished that he'd never met her. And he had no doubt that she'd felt the same way too.

But now he was glad that she did. Even if he couldn't have her forever, he was glad to be with her here at this moment.

He checked his phone and there were a few messages from Farhan.

Father is stable. Where are you? Where is Dr. Harrak?

Maazin didn't even bother responding. He'd told the security guards that he was taking a Jeep and going out to the plantation and that was all anyone needed to know. He was glad his father was stable, and that he was asking about the doctor who had performed the surgery.

All very good signs. Unless…unless his father found out he was romantically involved with Jeena and he was worried that Maazin would blow the secrecy about his engagement to Meleena being over. Perhaps Farhan had told their father about Syman.

If Jeena learned that his father knew about Syman she might flee again, and then he would never know his son.

Do you want to know him? Does he want to know you?

He knew deep down that his people would love Jeena, just as they loved Sara. And they'd be thrilled about Syman.

It was all just a dream, though. A fantasy he couldn't have, that he was afraid to have.

The sound of a phone vibrating on silent caught his attention and he noticed that Jeena had dropped her purse on the balcony floor. He picked it up and found her phone. When he touched it, it unlocked and a little boy's face looked up at him.

Oh, God. What have I done?

"You're not my mom," Syman said, confused.

"No. I'm not. Your mother is sleeping and… I heard her phone ringing."

The boy cocked his head to look at him better. "Who are you?"

"I am…" Maazin trailed off. He wanted to tell Syman that he was his father, but he couldn't. It wasn't his place. "I am Prince Maazin of Kalyana and you must be Jeena's son, Syman."

"Wow. A real prince? For real?"

"Yes," Maazin said, smiling. "Your mother has been helping out in her home country."

"I know."

Maazin could not stop staring at the boy. He saw himself in that face, but there were pieces of Ali and Farhan too.

"Well, I just wanted to speak to Mom, but if she's sleeping…" Syman trailed off as someone in the background called him. "Just talking to a prince, Grandpa. It's okay. Mom is sleeping."

There was some rushed talking in the background and Syman looked confused.

"Oh, Prince Maazin, my grandpa wants to talk to you, is that okay?"

Maazin's heart skipped a beat. "Very much okay. I will tell your mother you called."

"Okay. Here's my grandpa."

Syman's face was replaced by Mr. Harrak's and he was stunned to see Maazin.

"Your Highness," he said sternly. "Where is my daughter?"

"Sleeping. She worked very hard today on my father. The King."

Mr. Harrak's eyes widened. "What?"

"My father almost died today, Mr. Harrak, and your daughter performed a medical procedure on him at the palace. She's tired."

"She should not have been at the palace," he said worriedly. "I am sure you know why."

"I do now and I aim to find out what truly happened."

Mr. Harrak didn't look convinced. "My daughter

has a tender heart. Please, Your Highness. Don't hurt her again."

"I don't want to do that, Mr. Harrak."

"We all know you are to marry Lady Meleena."

Maazin sighed. "I will not hurt her and I want to show you something." He turned the phone around. "Do you see it?"

"It's pretty dark…" Mr. Harrak said. "Is that vanilla? Is that…?"

"It's your plantation." Maazin turned the phone back again. "I own it and I will return it to your family."

"You don't need to do that, Your Highness."

"I think I do."

Mr. Harrak said nothing at first. "Thank you."

"Goodbye, Mr. Harrak."

"Your Highness."

Maazin ended the call and hadn't realized how much he'd been shaking. How sweaty his palms had become and how he'd crossed a line he hadn't intended to.

"Who were you talking to?"

Maazin spun around and saw that Jeena had got dressed again and was standing in the balcony doorway, her arms crossed, and she didn't look too pleased.

"Your father." Maazin held out the phone.

Jeena took it from him. "You weren't talking only to my father. You were talking to Syman. This is his number. You were talking to our son? Why did you answer my phone? You had no right to do that."

"He's my son too," Maazin stated. "I went to get the phone to hand it to you, it unlocked and I accidentally answered it. I did not tell Syman that I am his father. Though I think he should know."

"He should, but are you going to be there for him?"

It was a valid question and he was stunned. Also, he was afraid. He didn't know the answer, he didn't have an answer for her.

Jeena looked unconvinced and she went through her messages. She frowned. "My flight home leaves in six hours."

"Six hours?" Maazin asked, his heart sinking. "I thought you had a few more days."

"The flight was bumped up. No doubt your father has regained his full faculties."

"Why do you think my father had a hand in this?" Maazin asked, confused.

"He knows about Syman! He knows about my son."

"Our son," Maazin corrected her.

Her eyes narrowed. "Would you want to keep around the former lover who bore your playboy son's illegitimate child? No, you'd ship her off so she didn't further endanger the reputation of the monarchy. You'd send her away and not have the scandal. Especially when the world thinks that son is still engaged to another woman!"

"You make my father sound like a despot. He's not. A bit of a stickler for tradition, but not a despot." It was a bad attempt at trying to lighten the mood and it only annoyed her further.

"Don't make light of this."

"I'm not. I'm telling you he had nothing to do with your orders being rescinded."

"Okay. Fine, but I'm still a threat to this secret." Jeena sighed, she shook her head. "I have to get back to my team. We have to pack to leave. You need to take me back to Huban."

"Jeena, we need to talk about this."

"What is there to talk about? I'm endangering the secret. I have to leave."

Maazin was stunned. "What're you talking about? I still don't understand how he'd know you or Syman. I didn't tell him."

"He knew me."

"He'd had sedation. People handle sedation in a very peculiar manner."

She shook her head. "He said my name and asked about my son that plays ice hockey. He knows about my son. How?"

"That I don't know."

Jeena sighed. "It's for the best I leave."

"Are you sure?" he asked.

"Can you promise me anything?"

"You said we didn't need to promise each other anything."

"Why do you push everyone away?"

"You're doing the same thing," he snapped.

"I'm protecting my son."

"Our son."

Jeena sighed sadly. "You think you don't deserve happiness, but you do."

"I don't! It's my fault Ali is dead. I don't deserve happiness. My family can't bear to be around me. They look at me and are reminded of it all. I'm the shame of the royal family. I have to do what they want, I took away too much."

"You didn't. You say you have to do what they say, but you don't always."

"What do you mean?"

"You became a doctor, you joined the royal guard. You're freer than you think."

"How would you know? You weren't here and you're the reason why I became reckless. Losing you destroyed me!"

"And you don't think it hurt me?" she asked, her voice trembling.

"No one died because of you. I killed my brother and his wife. You were free. You had a family who loved you. I have no one."

A tear slid down her cheek. "That's right. You have no one. Take me back to my team in Huban, Maazin."

He nodded. "Of course."

There was no point in arguing any further about this. She had her orders and she had to obey them.

She had a duty to her new country, just as he had a duty to Kalyana.

They collected up their things in silent tension. There was no convincing Jeena to understand his point, and she had to leave Kalyana anyway. She had to go back to Canada and he was going to get to the bottom of this. He found it very odd that his father knew who she was and that he knew about Syman.

As they headed outside there was a flash of light, several flashes that blinded him, and Jeena screamed as Maazin realized that it was paparazzi.

She turned towards him and he held her close, shielding her from the photographers. He didn't know how they had found them here.

Maazin got Jeena safely into the Jeep and pulled away as their vehicle was swarmed by photographers.

He sped away, leaving them far behind in the dust.

"What the heck was that?" Jeena asked, breathlessly.

"The popular press and the tabloids," he said in an undertone.

"How did they find us?"

"I don't know, but I do know one thing. If this reaches Canada, everyone will know that Syman is my son."

"This is why I shouldn't have come. This is why I should've just kept my distance from you and not told you about Syman! This is not what I want for him."

"You think I want this for him?" Maazin asked. "I don't want this life for him, but sometimes we have no choice."

"Yes. I understand that too well." Her voice shook and she didn't say more. He didn't know what to say to make it right either.

You know what to say.

He drove up to the Canadian consulate and thankfully there was no paparazzi there.

Jeena looked at him. "Please don't come to see me off tomorrow."

"Why?"

"This is going to spread everywhere and I just want to leave without drawing attention to my team. Or at least any more attention than is already being drawn. I want to leave Kalyana with my head held high."

"You can come back to Kalyana. I promised to give your father his plantation back."

"Come back to Kalyana and do what, Maazin? Have my son marked as an illegitimate son of a prince? Have the press hound me and Syman?"

"Jeena, please. I need you."

"You don't need me and you can't have my heart. Not until you stop blaming yourself for your brother's death. Not until you realize that it's your life to live.

You may be a prince, but Kalyana doesn't own you as much as you think it does."

"I'm a prince. Of course Kalyana owns me and I owe my country everything," he snapped. "You don't understand what I give up for this country."

"You're right I don't fully understand, but I do understand what you're giving up. I won't put my heart in jeopardy. I did once before and it nearly destroyed me. I'm not the same person I was all those years ago."

"Jeena—"

"No. No. Goodbye, Maazin."

She slipped out of the Jeep and up the steps of the Canadian consulate, leaving him heartbroken.

Alone.

She was right. Even if her family got back their plantation there was nothing really here for her or for Syman except shame and pain. Even though Jeena hadn't broken up the engagement the world would soon think she did.

He wouldn't be able to have Syman in his life.

Unless you tell your father you're done.

And that was what Maazin was going to do. He was going to drive back to the palace and tell his father. He wanted Jeena and it didn't matter if that meant his own banishment. He wanted his son and a family with Jeena. Only Jeena. Like he always had.

He wanted her by his side. Always and forever.

CHAPTER TEN

"This is outrageous!"

Maazin could hear his father raging from the other side of his bedchamber door. And he knew exactly what it was about. He knew that the press and the photographs of he and Jeena had come out.

Maazin knew this because he'd seen the headlines himself.

Seen the pictures of he and Jeena on the balcony, kissing and embracing. There were also photos that he hadn't been aware they'd taken, their stolen moment on Patang and when she'd stayed over at his place when they'd suspected they might have contracted dysentery.

Maazin didn't even knock when he opened the door to see his father propped up in bed and holding one of the trashy tabloid magazines in his hand.

"Father, you really shouldn't be over-exerting yourself."

His father dropped the magazine and glared at him. "What is the meaning of this?"

Maazin approached the bed and glanced at the magazine. It wasn't the only one that carried the story. Maazin and Jeena's faces had been plastered all over the national papers as well.

The headline was something along the lines of him betraying Lady Meleena. Still, they'd promised Lady Meleena that they wouldn't announce that the engagement was off for another month.

He'd broken that promise, but he was tired of taking on other people's problems. He was tired of keeping all these ridiculous secrets to avoid scandal. He was tired of blaming himself and of doing what made others happy.

Jeena was right, he had to stop blaming himself for Ali's death. He'd been so consumed these last ten years over losing her and then Ali dying that he was living in this perpetual hell of his own making.

He had to live his own life.

Ali was not coming back.

"I think you understand the meaning, Father," Maazin said calmly. "I'm sorry that the world knows I'm not marrying Lady Meleena before everything could be smoothed over."

His father waved his hand dismissively. "I don't care. That was her father's request. So we lose some trade deals. I have more important things to worry about. What I don't want is you returning to your old foolish ways."

"What foolish ways?"

"Sleeping around. Not taking care of yourself."

Maazin smiled. "I'm not, Father."

"Aren't you?" His father pointed to the photo in the tabloid. "This is my surgeon! The Canadian surgeon, yes?"

Maazin nodded. "I love Jeena Harrak. And I have for some time."

"What do you mean, you love Dr. Harrak?" Uttam asked, confused. "You've only just met her."

"Father, don't be obtuse. You know exactly who Jeena is."

His father frowned. "I know that she was the Kalyanese Canadian who performed my procedure and that she had a son who likes hockey."

"How do you know about her son?" Maazin asked curiously.

His father waved his hand in annoyance. "I always ask for the dossiers on my physicians. It's part of their security clearance. I was intrigued by the notion of ice hockey and I was pleased that someone from Kalyana had returned to help. I was making polite conversation."

"Father, do you know why Jeena Harrak left Kalyana."

"No."

Maazin scrubbed a hand over his face. "Jeena and I were involved in a romantic attachment ten years ago, before Ali died."

Uttam looked completely lost. "What?"

"She is the daughter of a vanilla plantation owner and we were in a romantic relationship for months. Then she left and I never knew why, until she came back to Kalyana. She left because she was pregnant with my child and believed Lady Meleena when Meleena told her I didn't want her, that we'd take away her child as he or she would be illegitimate."

"She had your child?" Uttam asked, shocked.

"Yes. I have a son. My son the ice hockey player!"

Uttam leaned back against the pillows, shaking his head in disbelief. "I have a grandchild? I would never have forced Meleena on you had I known Jeena was pregnant or that you were with Jeena. I would have allowed you to marry."

Maazin nodded. "That is good to know, Father, but too little too late. Her parents sold the plantation and took her to Canada, where she gave birth to my son, Syman. My son, who I didn't get to know. My son, the ice hockey player."

"I can't believe you have a son," Uttam said quietly.

"I do. One who was stolen from me because of Meleena's meddling. Do you ever wonder why I started drinking so heavily during that time? It was because Jeena had left me and I had no idea why. Maybe if she hadn't left we'd be together and I wouldn't be blaming myself for Ali's death. Maybe Mother wouldn't hate me so much for killing her favorite son!"

Maazin heard a gasp and turned to see his mother standing behind him. He had no doubt that she'd heard every word he'd said, but he didn't care. It was the truth.

It's how he felt.

It's how she'd made him feel for the last ten years and he was tired of letting her make him feel this way.

Maazin turned on his heel and left his father mulling all that over.

Right now he had to get to the airport and stop Jeena from getting on that flight to Canada. He had to tell her that he chose her and that he'd finally stood up for her. That he wasn't going to abandon her again. That he wanted her.

Farhan was pacing in the entranceway when Maazin came down the stairs.

"What was going on up there?" Farhan asked. "I heard all this loud talking and thought it best not to go in."

"It was for the best," Maazin said quickly. "I told

Father about Jeena. And I also told him about Syman, my son with Dr. Harrak."

Farhan's eyes widened. "Wow. I'm sure he took that well."

"Well, it certainly shocked him. I have to get to the airport. I have to stop her and tell her how I feel. I can't let her out of my life again."

"And if she doesn't want this life, this life of protocol?"

Maazin sighed. "I'll give it up for her. I'll live in Canada. I'll just disappear like Bhaskar did."

Farhan groaned. "That won't help anyone."

"I know and least of all you. I never told you that I'm sorry that you're in this position. That it was my fault you are now next in line to the throne."

Farhan took his arm. "I don't blame you. Even though you've been blaming yourself for ten years, I don't blame you for what happened to Ali. He made the choice to go and get you. It was a terrible accident. You have to stop blaming yourself for his death. You have to live your life."

Maazin clapped his brother on the back. "This is what I'm trying to do. I have to stop her from going back to Canada."

"You're too late," Farhan said. "I just saw the flight off. She was on it."

Maazin's heart sunk. "Well, then I need to clear this whole thing up and then I'm going to Canada to get her back."

Jeena knew that her team had seen the tabloids and the newspapers. They were friendly enough with her, but they were keeping their distance on the long flight home and that was fine by her. Even though Maazin and Meleena's engagement had ended some time ago, the world didn't know that.

In the world's eyes she was the other woman.

She was nursing her heart, which had been wounded again.

When she'd gone back to Kalyana, the last thing she'd wanted to do had been to let her heart be hurt again by Maazin, but of course that's exactly what she'd done.

She'd been a fool and the worst part of her being humiliated was that the press had caught wind of it all and it was everywhere.

When she'd talked to her father when they'd landed in Abu Dhabi to refuel, she'd found out that the press had located her parents' place and that they had been photographing Syman. Now Syman was afraid and confused.

He didn't know what was going on.

Her heart didn't matter, but Syman's heart did. This was not what she wanted for him. Her parents were disappointed and she was disappointed in herself too.

She craned her neck and could see Calgary airport coming into view. Her stomach clenched and she hoped that there wouldn't be any press there, but she didn't have high hopes of that. They would be around.

She just hoped her father wasn't being followed or harassed.

The plane landed and she closed her eyes, hoping and praying that she could just get home and be with her son.

Jeena hurried to get off the plane. She could see that there were people staring at her as she made her way across the airport and she could see from the corners of her eyes that her face was plastered everywhere.

Oh, God.

She went to the baggage claim and tried to ignore all the pointed stares. She picked up her gear bag and then spotted her father.

He gave her a sad, worried half-smile and then took one of her bags as he leaned over and kissed her.

"Father," she whispered. "I'm so sorry."

"None of that. Let's get out of here. There is press waiting so your mother is doing circuits and is coming up again to pick us up."

"And what about Syman?"

"He's staying with his friend Thomas for the night. Thomas's mother will bring him back tomorrow morning. Early, to avoid anyone seeing him."

Jeena's stomach did a flip-flop and she tried not to be sick. She hated this.

She followed her father out into the bitter cold. Jeena kept her head down as photographers snapped pictures and she realized that this was the first time she'd had to keep her head lowered in her new country.

For the first time since she'd come to Canada this was the first time she couldn't hold her head up high and she hated that. She was the other woman here too.

She climbed into the car and tried to hold back the tears that were threatening to spill. This was the worst.

Her mother drove away and for a few moments they didn't say anything.

"Tell us what happened, Jeena," her mother said. "The press is saying a lot of things, but I want to hear it from you."

Her parents exchanged a worried look in the rearview mirror as Jeena tried to explain what had happened between Maazin and herself, and how Lady Meleena had lied to them all.

"You are in love with him," her mother said. "It's understandable. The heart is forgiving when it's in love."

Jeena nodded. "I didn't want to forgive him. I didn't want anything to do with him, but we kept getting thrown together and it happened. The King knows about Syman."

"I had no doubt that he did," her father remarked. "Especially after the Bhaskar disappearances years before. The King keeps tabs on things. At least with Princess Sara that Bhaskar mystery was solved. It was a worry in Kalyana for so long and it did, eventually, have a happy ending."

"Well, I won't be going back to Kalyana. Maazin made it very clear that duty comes before the heart."

What she didn't say was that Maazin blamed himself. He thought he didn't deserve anything. Maybe he didn't want it and he was using his guilt as an excuse.

She didn't know and she didn't care. She was tired of caring.

Her father nodded but didn't say anything, and that was for the best. She was exhausted, both physically and emotionally. She'd thought she'd found her Prince Charming, but she hadn't. There was no happy ending for her after all.

There was no prince waiting to sweep her off her feet.

There was nothing but a heart that had healed and been broken all over again, and she had no one to blame but herself for that.

All she wanted was to see her son, but she was glad he was safe with Thomas's family.

That gave her some time to figure out what she was going to tell him about his father, the Prince.

CHAPTER ELEVEN

"WHAT DO YOU MEAN, you told everyone your engagement to Lady Meleena has been off for some time?"

Maazin winced as he heard his mother snap that across the room.

"It's simple, Mother. I told you that it's time to come clean so Jeena's name can be cleared. She's not the reason the engagement ended."

Queen Aruna took a deep breath. "I do understand that, but do you realize the embarrassment that you've caused us? They think you've gone back to your playboy ways! We paid off a lot of people when Ali—"

"I know, to cover up my indiscretions."

"No!" Uttam said. "To protect you from those papers. To protect Ali and Chandni's memories, but now they're saying all these awful things about you, Maazin."

"Yes. I've seen the tabloids."

His mother frowned. "The world should know it was Meleena who had the affairs. It was Meleena who drove off Jeena. All these years. We were all fooled."

Maazin was stunned. "Sorry, what did you say? Are you saying that you're angry with me because I did throw Meleena under the bus, as it were?"

His mother sighed. "I believed Meleena when she told me Jeena wasn't really pregnant by you."

"Wait, you knew she was pregnant?"

Queen Aruna nodded. "I did, but Meleena convinced me it was a hoax. Meleena told me that Jeena was going to blackmail us. You already had a bad reputation, so I was grateful to Meleena, and she said she would help take care of the problem. She would take care of the rumor...another one of your indiscretions. I thought Meleena was doing right by you in getting Jeena to leave, by paying her off and sticking by you."

"I still don't understand. How did you know Jeena was pregnant?"

"The doctor informed me. I knew you were in love with Jeena. I was happy, but then Meleena convinced me it was a lie and that Jeena was using you. I wanted to protect you."

"Meleena hurt us all," Maazin said bitterly.

"She may not have loved you but she wanted to marry you, Maazin, so she lied to all of us."

"I remember," Maazin said. "Now I remember that."

Uttam nodded. "She found out about Dr. Harrak's pregnancy and took it on herself to ruin your life. Meleena knew that you were going to choose Jeena and not her."

Seeing his son's furious expression, he reached out and placed his hand on Maazin's arm. "She's gone, Maazin. She's not worth your time. She's someone else's problem now."

"That's not good enough! She cost me ten years with the woman I love. She cost me time with my son!"

"I am sorry." Aruna motioned for Maazin to sit on the edge of the bed, where she was sitting next to Uttam.

It looked like his mother was about to cry. "No one should lose precious time with their child. I have wasted time with you, Maazin. I was scared your reckless lifestyle would cost me you as well, but I want you to know I don't blame you for Ali's death."

"You don't?" Maazin asked, stunned.

"No. I thank God every day you survived. Oh, at first I was angry that you had gone and done something foolish. That you were reckless again, but Ali did not have to go and get you, and it was an accident."

"That's what Farhan said," Maazin said quietly.

Uttam nodded. "He will make a fine king. One day. Not soon!"

Aruna smiled. "Stop blaming yourself, Maazin. You deserve to be happy. Ali would want that."

Maazin took his mother's hands. "And he would want you to be happy too."

Aruna's smile wobbled. "I will try. I am sorry if you've blamed yourself all this time. I don't blame you. I love you."

Maazin hugged his mother while she cried, and he felt a huge weight lift from his shoulders.

Maazin smiled at his parents. "So what do I do?"

"You go and you marry Dr. Harrak. You marry her and make things right. You may have lost those years with your son, but he's still young and you have time with him. Cherish that time with him and bring him to Kalyana." Uttam's chest puffed out. "Illegitimate or not, he is my grandson and I want him here with me. Life is too short."

"What do you think, Mother?"

Aruna brushed away a tear. "I want to know my grandson too. I want to know Syman and I want to apologize to Jeena. It's my fault as well. I am sorry my grief over the loss of Ali has made you feel that way, but when Uttam told me we have a grandchild, well…" More tears gathered in her eyes. "I want to meet him."

"I do too." Maazin stood up and kissed his mother on the cheek. "I'll have to take the private jet, then, to Canada. And we'll have to call the prime minster and get clearance to enter Canada."

"You leave that to me," Uttam said, and then he saw the stern look from his wife, which basically told him that he was treading on dangerous ground. "Or perhaps Farhan can arrange it?"

"Thank you, Father." Maazin bowed quickly and turned to leave.

"Maazin, wait!" his mother called out.

Maazin turned around and his mother held out a ring. "It was Queen Narubi's ring. Please give it to Dr. Harrak. Please let her know that we welcome her here. Explain to her it was not our doing. We were led to believe the wrong thing. Had we known the truth…she wouldn't have had to leave. She is welcome here and she would make a good wife for you. I'm sorry."

"That's right," Uttam shouted from the bed. "If I'd known that you were in love with her and that she was pregnant with our grandchild, I would've insisted you marry her straight away."

"Thank you." Maazin kissed his mother on the cheek again. "I will make this right. I promise."

And if Jeena didn't want to marry him and come to Kalyana, he would let her be, but he was hoping that in her heart she still loved him, just as much as he loved her.

He wanted her to know that she would be safe and

protected. That she wouldn't be trapped. Things were changing and they were changing for the better. Perhaps this was a life he would want for his son.

Perhaps it wasn't so bad after all.

Maybe together he and Farhan could change the face of the Kalyanese monarchy.

And if Jeena did agree to come and be his wife, he would have to go about building some kind of indoor ice rink so that his son could keep up with hockey. Just the thought of that brought a smile to his face.

The whole future lay ahead, bright and full of sunshine.

If only Jeena would say yes.

Farhan had worked with the Canadian government to make sure that no one got wind of Maazin's arrival in Calgary. He didn't want Jeena to know that he was coming. Or the media. He didn't want her to flee.

He wanted to let her know that she would've been accepted.

One petty person whose pride had been hurt had ruined their lives for the last ten years and Maazin only hoped that it wasn't too late. He only hoped that he hadn't ruined his chance with her.

Kavan, Farhan's bodyguard, had accompanied Maazin to Canada and was going to make sure that the press kept their distance, as well as drive him to Jeena's home. Farhan had insisted on it because Kavan had been with him when he'd gone to Canada to track down Sara, and he was familiar with the country and driving conditions there in snowy and icy conditions.

As the plane approached the runway at Calgary International Airport Maazin let out a shudder when he saw white on the ground. In the distance he could see the city and smoke rising from the buildings into the clear blue sky.

The large Calgary Tower stuck out in the skyline.

"It's very cold down there, Your Highness," Kavan commented.

"I agree," Maazin said. "Jeena told me it was cold."

"I think this is colder than those ski trips that you and your brothers took in Kitzbühel."

"I believe you're right." Maazin shuddered. "You made sure that customs has already cleared us and that the Canadian government is on board with our hushed operation?"

"I have the assurances from the prime minister himself. He's quite a charismatic man."

Maazin smiled. "I'm glad to hear he's so accommodating."

The plane landed smoothly and was directed to a private runway on the far side of the airport, reserved for foreign dignitaries, royalty and the prime minister.

There was a small fleet of cars waiting, which would accommodate Maazin's small staff and security. As requested, the Kalyanese consulate hadn't added the flags to the cars as it was a private visit and Maazin didn't want to catch any one's attention as they made their way north out of Calgary to a small ranch between Calgary and Airdrie.

It would be easy to locate the Harraks' ranch, because it was the only property in the vicinity that had a large number of greenhouses, and the Harraks were known for growing and selling poinsettias.

As Maazin stepped off the plane it felt like his skin was being cut by sharp knives. It was bitterly cold and he didn't like it one bit, but for Jeena he would brave anything. Even freezing cold temperatures and biting, nasty wind.

The Kalyanese ambassador to Canada was waiting and he was wearing a parka.

"Your Highness, I have a parka for you."

Maazin nodded and gladly allowed the ambassador to slip it on his shoulders. "This is awful!"

"Nothing like beautiful Kalyana weather." The ambassador smiled. "Everything is ready for all your people."

"Thank you."

The ambassador stepped back, the door to the SUV with tinted windows was opened and he slipped inside. Kavan took his place in the driver's seat. Maazin adjusted the temperature settings in the back and then slipped off the parka.

"Are you ready, Your Highness?" Kavan asked from the front.

"Yes. Let's go." Maazin touched the breast pocket of his designer suit to make sure Queen Narubi's ring was still there. His pulse was racing as Kavan punched in the co-ordinates on the GPS and then slowly drove away from the private jet. The rest of Maazin's people were going to the embassy in Calgary.

There would be a car following them for security, at his father's insistence. If Maazin had his way, he wouldn't, but then again, with the media pestering Jeena and her family and his son, he didn't want to take any chances.

He sat back and looked out at the scenery, which was very different from Kalyana's. They drove north on a large highway with cars everywhere. He noticed a lot of the vehicles on the highway were trucks and they were all white.

"Why do you suppose so many of the vehicles are white, Kavan?"

"Something to do with the oil fields, Your Highness, but I'm not certain."

"Oil fields?" Maazin really didn't know much about Canada, but one thing was for certain, the endless stretch of open plains without trees or sea to break the horizon was slightly unsettling. But if this was where Jeena was happy, if this was where she wanted Syman to stay, he would get used to it.

He would stay and do whatever she wanted.

He wasn't leaving without her. He wasn't walking away from her again, even though he didn't know that he had done that in the first place. He didn't know that she had been sent away. All these years he'd thought she left him.

And for all these years she'd thought he'd walked away from her.

Now it was time to make everything right.

It was time for him to claim his family, like he should've done ten years ago.

It felt like it took an eternity to drive forty minutes to the outskirts of Calgary and then on a side road off the highway that turned into a gravel road that had a sign pointing to the Harraks' greenhouses.

Maazin couldn't believe the large stretch of land that Mr. Harrak possessed. It put his small vanilla plantation to shame. Before they even reached the main house Maazin could see the greenhouses and through the fogged windows he could see the red of the poinsettias.

Kavan made another turn and they approached a raised ranch-style house. Kavan drove as close as he could. Maazin's pulse was thundering in his ears. To the side of the ranch house there was a small ice rink and there were kids out on it now, skating. He couldn't help but wonder which of those boys was Syman.

He was finally going to meet his son.

"Hey, Mom! There's a strange car parked in front of the house!" Syman shouted as he skated by her, gesturing wildly.

Oh, no.

Jeena turned around and was worried that the press was ignoring her father's restraining order and they were coming to get a glimpse of Syman again. Her phone was in the house because it was so cold out that the battery would die within minutes.

She hoped that her father had seen the cars approach and had the good sense to call the Royal Canadian Mounted Police about the restraining order violation. The RCMP had promised to protect her after a particularly intrepid paparazzo had gotten into one of the greenhouses and done substantial damage as he'd tried to get information about her parents.

Not to mention one photographer who had scared Syman senseless when he'd got off the school bus.

Since she'd got back three days ago there had been endless harassment.

And she was getting sick and tired of it.

She started marching in the direction of the SUV when she saw who had got out of the back. She froze in her tracks and her heart skipped a beat.

Maazin?

He was completely inappropriately dressed for this crazy cold snap that they were currently having.

"Maazin?" she called out.

He spun around and then started walking toward her.

"Jeena, thank goodness…"

"What're you doing?"

"I've come to see you."

"I get that. I mean, you're going to freeze to death standing out here without a coat on." She glanced behind her. "Why don't you have a coat?"

"I do. I left it in the car."

"Let's get inside and tell Kavan to come in as well. It's too cold to leave the car running."

"Well, if it's too cold, why are there children out there, playing on the ice?" Maazin asked.

"They're dressed for it and they'll be heading inside soon. They had to get their practice in. My father can manage the boys. He'll take them into the greenhouse staff lunch room for hot chocolate. Let's go into the main house."

Maazin nodded and motioned to Kavan, who was shivering as well.

Jeena opened the door and ushered them both inside.

"Mother!" Jeena called out. "We have guests."

"Oh, no. Not the press again!" Her mother came around the corner and then froze in her tracks when she saw Maazin. She instantly curtseyed. "Your Highness."

"Please. There is no need to do that, Mrs. Harrak."

Her mother stood up slowly and then looked at Jeena for an explanation. Jeena shrugged and took off her bulky winter gear. "Mom, will you take Kavan into the kitchen and give him a nice hot cup of coffee?"

Her mother nodded. "Of course. Follow me, Kavan."

Kavan waited until Maazin nodded and then followed her mother into the kitchen. She finished taking off her winter gear and then stood in front of Maazin, completely shocked that he was here in Canada and standing in her parents' front hall. It was surreal. Of all the scenarios she'd pictured in her mind of Maazin coming to get her, this had not been one of them. A royal prince of Kalyana, wearing an expensive suit and standing in a tiny front hall that was littered with twenty pairs of wet snow boots, not to mention a bunch of knapsacks.

"It smells a lot like feet here," he teased, obviously trying to break the tension.

"You're standing by the shoe rack and there are a lot of sweaty boots there."

Maazin glanced down. "So I see."

"What're you doing here?" she asked, still feeling stunned.

"I came to see you."

"Why?" she asked.

"Is there a place with more privacy where we can talk?" he asked.

"Sure. Follow me." Jeena didn't want to talk with him in the house because Syman might come bursting in after all his friends had been picked up. Attached to the house was her father's first greenhouse and it was a place where he still grew a small batch of vanilla orchids. It was quiet and warm in there.

She led him into the greenhouse and shut the door behind them.

Maazin looked around. "Your father grows vanilla here as well?"

"Just a small batch. He sells it on the weekends at a local organic market." She crossed her arms. Her heart was still hammering in her chest and she couldn't quite believe that Maazin was here, in Canada.

"So, will you finally tell me what you're doing here?" she asked.

"I came for you."

She blinked a couple of times. "Pardon me?"

"Jeena, you know I'm not marrying Lady Meleena. The moment I dropped you off at the Canadian embassy in Huban I went straight to the palace to have it out with my parents. I told them I was tired of hiding the fact I'm not marrying Meleena and I was going to marry you."

"I thought you couldn't promise me anything? I thought you didn't deserve happiness?"

"I was wrong."

She tried not to let her mouth drop open in shock. Her pulse was thundering in her ears and it was very hard to breathe. "How did your parents react to your news?"

"Not well at first."

"Of course. I'm the last person they'd want you to marry."

"No, you need to stop that. It's because my father didn't know Syman was mine. Meleena had them all believing you were going to blackmail us. They believed Meleena paid you off and saved the royal family from another one of my scandals. Meleena wanted to marry me, so she hurt us both. She lied to us both."

Jeena swallowed the hard lump that was forming her throat. "What?"

"My father wants you to know that he would never have forced me to marry Meleena had he known I wanted you. He would've been thrilled had he known you were pregnant with my child. My mother is thrilled too, but Meleena had convinced her you weren't pregnant. In fact, they're both very happy to have a grandson. They both want to meet him."

The room began to spin and Jeena didn't know how to take this information. She sat down on a bench and took a couple of deep breaths.

"I don't... I don't know what to say. We have a life here in Canada..."

"I know and if that is what you choose, then I choose it too."

"You choose it too?" she asked, confused.

Maazin dropped to his knees in front of her and took her hands in his strong ones. "You're trembling."

"I'm scared," she whispered.

"I am too, but if Canada is where you need to be then I will live here. What I can't do is live without you in my life. I can't live without Syman in my life. I've spent too many years thinking that I didn't deserve happiness or love because of my actions, but I was wrong. I was wrong about so many things. You were right, but I was scared. Scared to lose you again."

Jeena didn't know what to say. Tears stung her eyes, because he was saying all the right things. It was everything she'd wanted to hear ten years ago. It was everything she'd wanted to hear four days ago.

"How can you live in Canada? Your duty is to Kalyana. You're a prince."

"I can live wherever I want and return to Kalyana if I'm needed, but if you choose to come to Kalyana with Syman, you can continue your work there. My father has already passed the decrees and legislation to start the ball rolling on a university. A university that promotes the STEM program to women. Sara still wants your input."

"Are you serious?"

"Yes. The University of Kalyana will happen and it will happen in the next year."

"I'm glad to hear that." She was still shocked. "The world thinks I'm the other woman."

"No. My father straightened it all out and will make a formal speech soon. After the whole Bhaskar thing, the people don't want heirs running off. They don't want scandal for Kalyana. Everyone is thrilled we have a child."

"Oh." Jeena still couldn't seem to think straight. It was everything she'd wanted to hear ten years ago. She couldn't quite believe it.

Maazin reached into his pocket and pulled out a ring. One that she had seen on the hand of Queen Aruna. "Marry me, Jeena. Marry me like you were supposed to have done ten years ago."

Her pulse raced and she felt like she was going to faint.

"Yes," she whispered.

"Yes?"

She nodded. "Yes."

He slipped the ring on her finger and kissed her, and she couldn't stop the flow of tears. Tears that she had been holding back for so long they came pouring out of her. Maazin kissed away those tears and held her.

"I'm so sorry, Jeena. So sorry for it all."

"It's not your fault. I should've trusted you. I was terrified to be pregnant and alone in a country so far away from the one I knew. I blamed myself too. I blamed myself for letting you take my heart when I felt like I didn't deserve you."

"You deserve me, but I don't deserve you," Maazin said.

"Yes, you do."

They kissed again.

"And I would like to go back to Kalyana," she whispered.

"What about Syman and his life here?" Maazin asked.

"We can always come back and visit. My parents will stay here. I know that. They have found happiness here. And I wouldn't leave them behind unless I knew that there was a private jet to come and get them whenever they wanted to come home." She was teasing him.

He smiled at her. "Of course. Whenever they want to do that and whenever Syman wants to return to Canada, we will get him here. He'll just have to get used to bodyguards and security."

"Mom? Where are you?"

Jeena took a deep breath and stood up. Maazin followed her and she could tell that he was nervous.

"It'll be okay, Maazin. I've told him. He knows."

"He does?"

Jeena nodded. "It's okay. He wants to know you. You deserve to be in his life."

Maazin nodded. "Yes. Good. I want to be his father. I want him in my life."

"And he will be. It might take some time, but he wants to know you."

Syman came running into the greenhouse. "Mom, you won't believe—"

Syman stopped and stared up at Maazin. "It's you! The Prince I talked to over the phone."

"Yes. It's a pleasure to finally meet you." Maazin held out his hand and Syman shook it.

"What're you doing here?" Syman asked.

"I've come to ask your mother to marry me," Maazin said.

Syman looked at her. "Mom?"

"Syman, Prince Maazin is your father. You remember me talking about those newspaper men and other people following you around?"

"You mean that I'm a prince?"

"Yes," Maazin said. "I'm afraid so."

Syman nodded. "Cool."

Maazin knelt down to look Syman in the eyes. "I'm sorry I've been away for a long time."

"Mom said you didn't know about me."

"I didn't, and it's no one's fault, but know this, if I had known about you I would've come sooner. Do you forgive me?"

"Yes." Syman nodded. "You're here now for good?"

"I'm staying for as long as you need to, before I return to Kalyana."

Syman frowned. "Mom?"

"The thing is, we have to move to Kalyana for a while," Jeena said. "Are you okay with that?"

Syman worried his bottom lip. "Do they have hockey there?"

"No," Maazin said. "Not yet, but your grandfather the King promised that a hockey arena would be built and maybe you could show the other children there how to play."

Syman cocked his head to one side. "I like that, but

what about Grandma and Grandpa? Would we ever see them again?"

"Of course, whenever we wanted," Jeena said. "And they can come back to Kalyana and see you. For now, for a little while, we have to go back to Kalyana. You have to meet your other grandparents and your uncle and his wife."

Syman nodded. "So we get to go on a plane trip?"

Maazin chuckled. "Yes. A private jet, in fact."

"Cool. Okay, I'm okay with this. Can I go ask Grandma for a cookie?"

Jeena laughed. "Sure."

"Thanks!" Syman ran off.

"That was relatively easy," Maazin remarked.

"It'll take some time for him to process it," Jeena admitted dryly. "Then there will be a lot of questions."

"It'll take some time for him to get to know me. I understand that. I'm willing to wait." Maazin wrapped his arms around her. "I'm just not willing to wait ten years again to make you my wife."

"Neither am I. I love you, Maazin. I always have. There has never been any one else. I've only loved you. I've only ever wanted you."

Maazin tipped her chin. "I've only loved you and from that first moment that I saw you out on the polo field, you're all I've ever wanted as well. You're all I'll ever want. I was a fool to think otherwise."

Jeena laughed and kissed him gently. "Yes. Yes, you were."

Maazin ended up spending two weeks in Canada. There was a lot to do to prepare for the journey back to Kalyana.

Instead of staying at the embassy, though, he stayed at the Harraks' home, so that he could get to know Syman better. And though it took some time, Syman accepted Maazin as his father and was soon showing him the affection he so desperately wanted from his son. Affection he'd never thought he deserved.

Maazin reveled in those moments when he was able to tuck Syman in for the night and have the boy wrap his arms around him and call him Dad. That meant so much to him. The more that he got to know his son, the more of Ali and even his father he saw in him.

There was a stubborn, defiant streak in Syman that reminded Maazin very much of his father. And Ali too. And Maazin knew that deep down Syman and Uttam were like two peas in a pod.

Jeena, with the help of higher up government officials in Canada and Kalyana, was honorably discharged from her services to the Canadian armed forces. It was hard for Jeena to let go of her team, but she had plans to work closely with Sara and promote that program about women in the STEM program in the new university.

That gave her something to be passionate about and something to do beyond a life of protocol and charity events.

Maazin, Jeena, Syman and the Harraks had all watched King Uttam's speech to the media about Jeena and Syman. It was clear from the public's feedback that no one held any animosity toward Jeena. No one thought she was the other woman any more and Kalyana was excited to have another royal heir.

And although Maazin offered them their vanilla plantation back, Jeena's parents were much happier in Canada.

They hated being so far away from Jeena, but they were glad that they could return to their homeland with their heads held high and that their daughter was soon to be a princess.

Or rather she *was* a princess because before they left Canada Jeena and Maazin married in a civil ceremony at the Kalyana embassy and Syman was legitimized.

The line of succession would soon change yet again as Sara, Farhan's wife, was expecting a baby.

And that was fine by Maazin.

When they boarded the private jet at Calgary International Airport there was a lot of media waiting to get a glimpse of the new royal family of Kalyana, but Kavan and his team of security managed to keep the media at a distance.

It excited Syman that the prime minister of Canada had come out to see them off and that he was going on his first ever plane ride.

Of course, the novelty of a long flight soon wore off on Syman, but Maazin enjoyed having him on the plane and keeping him entertained by playing games with him and reading with him. Syman had a hard time sleeping but finally drifted off on the last leg of the trip from Abu Dhabi to Huban.

Maazin made sure he was secured on the couch portion of the private jet and covered him with a blanket, and he slept there for the last few hours.

"I hope we can wake him in enough time to see the welcome ceremony when we land," Jeena remarked. "I also hope he's not too grumpy for your father. He's a bit of a grumpy bear when you wake him up too soon."

Maazin smiled. "The same with my father. They're so alike."

"I hope that it goes smoothly." She was worrying her bottom lip again.

"It will. Trust me. My parents are thrilled."

"It's hard to do that. Even though I really should, because it wasn't your fault and it wasn't my fault. I'm glad that whole thing is behind us and I'm glad Meleena is no longer in Kalyana."

"Yes. She's safer away from Kalyana too, because if I ever see her again I'm going to— She's better off far away. She cost me too much." Maazin glanced back at Syman, who was rousing as the plane began to descend as they got closer to Huban.

"Well, we can't maim her we're both doctors and we've promised to do no harm." Jeena winked.

"That remains to be seen," Maazin teased.

Jeena started rubbing her hands together. She was wearing her mother's treasured sari, the one she'd managed to save, the one she'd bought on Petrie Island that the weaver, Mr. Patel, had made.

"That color suits you," Maazin said. "Your mother has good taste."

"I think so too. It's always been one of my favorites and I wanted to show my support for the people."

"Smart." Maazin took her hand and kissed it. "You will make an excellent princess."

The plane made its final descent into Huban and Jeena managed to wake Syman up. He was grumpy for a few moments, but when he realized they were landing and that soon he'd meet the rest of his family, he perked up.

The plane landed and Maazin could already hear the crowds cheering. As the plane taxied around he could see a sea of blue, green and gold flags waving and the red carpet, with the royal motorcade waiting at the end.

This was it.

The plane's engines stopped and Maazin took her hand, giving it a squeeze. Then he took Syman's hand and the door opened.

Maazin stepped out of the plane with Syman by his side. The cheers were deafening and Syman trembled.

"It's okay. They're happy you're here. Just wave."

Syman worried his bottom lip like his mother and then waved.

Jeena came behind them and they walked down the steps together. When they reached the red carpet King Uttam and Queen Aruna, followed by Farhan and Sara, came to meet them.

Maazin could see that his father was having a hard time hiding his emotions as he looked at the little boy who was so obviously his grandson.

And Uttam broke protocol to get down on one knee and hold out a Kalyanese flag to his little grandson.

"Welcome to Kalyana, Syman."

Syman smiled at him and took the flag and then did what Maazin had not expected and threw his arms around Uttam's neck.

Uttam was shocked, but then wrapped his arms around the boy and lifted him up in his arms, beaming with pride.

Jeena was fighting back tears.

Uttam turned to her. "Welcome home, Dr. Harrak. Or should I say Princess Jeena?"

"Your Majesty." Jeena curtseyed and Maazin bowed.

"Let's get out of here, shall we?" Uttam set Syman down and took his hand in his.

Maazin took Jeena's hand and both of them turned to the cheering crowds and waved.

"I'm a bit scared," Jeena whispered.

"Don't be scared. I shall protect you. I shall always protect you and I will never let anyone hurt you again. I love you."

"I love you too, Your Highness."

EPILOGUE

One year later

"Now!" BELLOWED UTTAM from across the cricket pitch. "Isn't this much better than ice hockey?"

Syman lowered the cricket bat. "No, but it's fun. I like it, Grandpapa."

Uttam laughed. "Good!"

"Good!" Sophie squawked from her outside perch, making Syman laugh, which in turn made Uttam laugh and then Aruna laughed from where she was sitting under an awning with her newest grandchild, Farhan and Sara's little boy, Ali, in her arms.

Jeena was wandering away from the cricket and the tent. She was hot and uncomfortable and still had a couple months left of her pregnancy.

Her parents were coming for a visit soon and she couldn't wait to see them again. They video-called most nights with Syman, and Maazin had taken Syman and her back once to visit them, but once Jeena had found out she was pregnant, with twins no less, she couldn't go anywhere and she was feeling a bit cooped up.

Maazin had been busy with the university plans and helping to get Kalyana back on its feet. New homes were being built. Homes and businesses on Petrie Island, and many of the other islands, were almost all rebuilt now and things were going smoothly.

Kalyana was thriving again and would be more than ready if another cyclone like Blandine hit. Jeena loved being back in her home country, though she did miss Canada, but she loved being with her people again and being with Maazin. If only she could get back to work.

She really hated not being able to work out in the field, but Maazin was being way too overprotective.

"Where do you think you're going?"

Jeena turned around to see Maazin strolling towards her, carrying a glass of iced tea. He handed her the glass and she gladly took a sip.

"I was uncomfortable. The canopy your mother had set up might keep the sun off everything, but it doesn't keep out the heat."

Maazin reached out and touched her belly. "You really should be sitting down. With twins you could be early. You're a doctor, you should know better."

"Haven't you ever heard that doctors make the worst patients?"

Maazin cocked an eyebrow. "No. I haven't heard that."

"Well, they do." Jeena sighed. "I promise I'll go and sit down again. I just wanted a little walk to see if I could catch a breeze."

Maazin kissed the top of her head. "Remember the cool breezes on Patang Island?"

"Yes. I do." She closed her eyes. "Are you offering to take me there?"

"No. Not in your condition, but tonight when we go

home we can go for a swim in the pool. Just the two of us."

"What about Syman?"

"He wants to spend the night with Grandpapa."

They both looked back to see their son finally catch a cricket ball on the end of his bat. The ball rolled over to Uttam who fell back, acting like he'd been hit, but really was hoping to catch Syman unawares to get a hug from him.

"They really are alike, aren't they?" Jeena asked.

"It's uncanny." And it was. She had always sort of suspected that Syman's stubborn streak and athletic side came from Maazin's side of the family. She'd just had no idea how well Syman would take to Uttam. Syman also loved Farhan and Sara. And since Sara was Canadian as well, she understood what it meant when he used words like "tuque" and "pop" to her.

And Syman doted on his newest cousin. Almost like a big brother would.

Syman fit in so seamlessly with his newfound family it did her heart good.

"So, what do you think? Do you want to go for a swim later with me?" her husband asked huskily, interrupting her thoughts.

Jeena stood on tiptoe. "How about we go back now? No one will notice if we leave."

"They'll notice if we leave. Father has this big meal planned with some dignitaries and… You don't look too impressed."

"I'm exhausted and I think if we told your father that I was he'd let us leave now. Do you really feel like having a dinner with all these stuffy people and talk politics in this heat?"

Maazin wrinkled his nose. "No. You're right. Not particularly."

"I think he'll understand if we slip away." She wrapped her arms around him. "We can go home and swim now. We can also swim later and then just spend the rest of the evening in bed."

"I think that plan is what got you into this condition in the first place," Maazin teased.

Jeena laughed. "What do you say, Your Highness?"

Maazin chuckled and kissed her. "That sounds like a good plan, my love. That sounds like a good plan indeed."

"Good." She kissed him. "Have I told you today that I love you?"

"No, but why don't you tell me now?" he said archly as he kissed her again.

"I love you. I didn't believe in all those old fairytales, the ones where a prince came and swept a girl off her feet, but now I'm a believer."

Maazin caressed her cheek. "I just wish my sweeping you off your feet had gone a bit more smoothly and in a more timely fashion."

"That only happens in movies. Real life is a lot messier and I wouldn't have it any other way."

Maazin kissed her again before taking her hand as they walked off together.

Happy that their happily-ever-after had come at last.

* * * * *

PROTECTING
THE PREGNANT
PRINCESS

LISA CHILDS

For my parents, Jack and Mary Lou Childs. Alzheimer's disease has stolen her memories of their long life together, but he is still her hero – loving and protecting her. While her mind doesn't always remember him, her heart will never forget that he is the love of her life.

Prologue

Heat scorched his face and hands, but Aaron Timmer ignored the pain and ran headlong toward the fire. His breath whooshed out of his burning lungs as his body dropped, tackled to the ground.

"You damn fool, what the hell are you thinking?" asked the man who'd knocked him down.

"We have to save her!" As her bodyguards, saving her was their responsibility. But she had become more than just a job to Aaron.

"It's too late." The house—the *safe* house—they had stashed her in was fully engulfed. The roof was gone, and flames were rising up toward the trees overhead. Leaves caught fire, dissolving into sparks that rained down onto the blackened lawn surrounding the house.

"We shouldn't have left her." But Aaron's partner, Whitaker Howell, had insisted that she would be fine—that no one could have possibly figured out where she was.

Obviously someone had.

He rolled over and swung his fist right into Whit's hard jaw. His knuckles cracked and stung as blood oozed from them. He shook off the pain and pushed away Whit's limp body. Then he turned back to the burning frame of the house, debris strewn wide around the yard from the explosion.

It was too late. She was gone.

Three years later...

BLOOD SPATTERED THE ivory brocade walls of the Parisian hotel suite. Holes were torn through the paper, causing plaster and insulation to spill onto the hardwood floor. Some of the holes were big, probably from a fist or a foot; others smaller and blackened with gunpowder. The glass in the windows was broken, the frames splintered. Shots had been fired. And there had been one hell of a struggle.

Aaron's heart hammered against his ribs, panic and fear overwhelming him as he surveyed the gruesome crime scene.

A whistle hissed through clenched teeth—not his but Whit's, the man with whom he'd vowed to never work again after that tragedy three years ago. But a couple of months ago he'd been offered an opportunity too good to pass up. Only after he'd accepted the position as a royal bodyguard had he learned that he was actually going to share that assignment with his former business partner and friend.

That safe house explosion had destroyed whatever bond they'd formed in war, fighting together in Afghanistan. After the fire, they had only fought each other. So Aaron should have walked away from this job. He should have known how it would end.

"She put up one hell of a fight," Whit said, his deep voice almost reverent with respect. "But there's no way they survived..."

Aaron shook his head, refusing to accept that they

were gone. *She* couldn't be gone. Charlotte Green was too strong and too smart to not have survived whatever had happened to her.

What the hell had happened to her?

To them? Charlotte Green was also a royal body-guard for the princess of St. Pierre Island, an affluent nation near Greece.

Aaron and Whit had retraced their steps from their missed flight home, back to the hotel they'd been booked into in Paris. The suite had been destroyed. But despite the amount of blood pooled on the hardwood floor, the Parisian authorities had found no bodies. No witnesses. No leads at all. And no hope for survivors.

King Rafael St. Pierre nodded in agreement with Whit Howell's statement of resignation. Aaron clenched his fists, wanting to punch both men in the face. He couldn't strike the king though, and not just because he was paid generously to protect the ruler of St. Pierre. He couldn't hurt the man because Rafael was already hurting so much that he probably wouldn't even feel the blow.

Whit, on the other hand...

For the past three years Aaron had wanted to do much more than just strike the man. He had damn sure never intended to work with him again. But when they'd both been hired, separately, to protect the king, neither had been willing to give up the job—a security job they'd been lucky to get after what had happened to the last person they'd protected together.

The king was fine, though. Physically. Emotionally, he was a wreck. The man, once fit and vital, was show-ing every year and then some of his age in the slump of his back and shoulders and in the gray that now liberally streaked his dark hair. Clearly Rafael St. Pierre was beside himself with grief.

Despite how far he and Whit went back, to a friendship forged under fire in Afghanistan, Aaron never knew exactly what his ex-business partner was thinking. Or feeling, or if Whit was even capable of feeling anything at all.

As dissimilar as they were physically, Whit being blond and dark-eyed and Aaron dark-haired with light blue eyes, they were even more unlike emotionally. Aaron was feeling too much; frustration, fear and grief battled for dominance inside him. But then anger swept aside those emotions, snapping his control. He shouted a question at both men, "How can you just give up?"

Whit's head snapped back, as if Aaron had slugged him. And the king flinched, his naturally tan complexion fading to a pasty white that made him look as dead as he believed his daughter and her female bodyguard to be.

Whit glanced at the king, as if worried that the once so powerful man might keel over and die. They could protect the ruler from a bullet but not a heart attack. Or a broken heart. Whit turned back to Aaron, his intense stare a silent warning for him to control his temper.

He had to speak his mind. "Charlotte Green is the best damn bodyguard I've ever worked with." Before she'd gone into private duty protection, she had been a U.S. Marshal. "She could have fought them off. She could have protected them both. She devoted herself to protecting the princess. She went above and beyond the responsibilities of her job."

And to extremes that no other guard could have or would have gone.

"It isn't just a job to her," Aaron continued, his throat

thick with emotion as thoughts of Charlotte pummeled him. Her beauty. Her brains. Her loyal heart. "She considers Princess Gabriella a friend."

"That's why she would have died *for* her," Whit pointed out, "and why she must have died *with* her."

Aaron's heart lurched in his chest. "No…"

"If they were alive, we would have heard from them by now," Whit insisted. "They would have reached out to us or the palace."

Unless they didn't think they could trust them, unless they felt betrayed. Maybe that was why it was easier for Whit and the king to accept their deaths; it was easier than accepting their own responsibility for the young women's disappearances.

"No matter how fierce a fighter she was," Whit said, "Charlotte Green is gone. She's dead. And if the princess was alive, we would have had a ransom demand by now."

The king gasped but then nodded in agreement.

Aaron shook his head. "No. We need to keep looking. They have to be out there—somewhere." He couldn't have been too late again. Charlotte Green couldn't be gone.

Chapter One

Six months later...

Like a sledgehammer shattering her skull, pain throbbed inside her head—clouding her mind. She couldn't think. She could barely feel...anything but that incessant pain. Even her hair hurt, and her skin felt stretched, as if pulled taut over a bump. She moved her fingers to touch her head, but she couldn't lift her hand.

Something bound her wrist—not so tightly that it hurt like her skull hurt, but she couldn't budge her hand. Either hand. She tugged at both and found that her wrists were held down to something hard and cold.

She forced open her eyes and then squinted against the glare of the fluorescent lights burning brightly overhead. Dark spots blurred her vision. She blinked over and over in an attempt to clear her vision. But images remained distorted. To her it looked like she had six arms—all of them bound to railings of a bed like an octopus strapped down to a boat deck. A giggle bubbled up with a surge of hysteria, but the slight sound nearly shattered her skull.

The questions nagging at her threatened to finish the job. *What the hell happened to me? Where am I?* Because she had no answers...

She also had no idea why she was being held down—restrained like a criminal. Or a captive...

She fought against the overwhelming fear. She needed to focus, but her head wouldn't stop pounding and the pain almost blinded her, like the fluorescent light glaring down from the ceiling. It was unrelenting, and reminded her of the light in an interrogation room or torture chamber.

That light was all she could discern of her surroundings. Flinching against its glare, she looked down, but she couldn't see more than a couple of feet in front of her—not because of the pain but because she couldn't see beyond the mound of her belly.

Shock turned her giggle into a sharp gasp. *I'm pregnant?*

No...

Her swollen belly must have been like her seeing six hands, just distorted and out of focus. She wasn't pregnant...

In denial of the possibility, she shook her head, but the motion magnified her pain. She closed her eyes against the wave of agony and confusion that rushed over her, making her nauseous. Or was that sick feeling because of the pregnancy?

How far along was she? When had it happened? And with whom?

She gasped again, her breath leaving her lungs completely. Not only couldn't she remember who the father of her unborn child might be but she couldn't even remember who *she* was.

AARON HELD OUT his phone to check his caller ID, surprised at where the call was coming from. Sure, as desperate as he'd been he'd reached out to everyone he thought might be able to help. He had called Charlotte's ex-partner with the U.S. Marshals. He'd tried calling her aunt, but there must not have been any cell reception in whatever jungle she was building schools or orphanages. And he'd called this man…

"Hello, Mr. Jessup." This man was America's version of royalty—the ruler of an empire of news networks and magazines and newspapers. Nothing happened anywhere without his knowing about it—unless a more powerful man, like King St. Pierre, had covered it up. "Thank you for calling me back."

Aaron was surprised that the man would speak to him at all. He was the last client of the security firm in which Aaron and Whit had been partners. He had hired them to protect the most important thing to him. And they had failed…

"Don't thank me yet," the older man warned him. "Not until you see if the lead pans out."

"You have a lead?"

"Someone called in a tip from a private sanatorium in northern Michigan, wanting to sell a story about Princess Gabriella St. Pierre being committed to the psychiatric facility."

From that destroyed hotel room to a private sanatorium? Given what she'd seen, what she must have gone through, it almost made sense. A tip like this was why Aaron had refused to give up. That and a feeling deep in his gut—maybe his heart—that told him Charlotte Green wasn't dead. She couldn't be dead—somehow he'd know if she was.

"Is she alone?" he asked.

"She's got a royal entourage," Jessup said, "including a private doctor and nurse."

Royal? But the king swore he knew nothing of their

disappearance. And a man couldn't feign the kind of grief he was obviously experiencing.

"And a security detail?" Aaron asked. Or at least one very strong woman.

Stanley Jessup grunted. "Yeah, too much of it according to the source."

Hope fluttered in Aaron's chest. Was it possible? Had he found them both? "Is one of the guards a woman?"

"I don't know." The man sighed. "I'm getting this third hand—from the editor of a magazine who got it from an ambitious young reporter. I don't have details yet, but I'm going to check it out."

"Why?" The question slipped out.

Stanley Jessup grunted again, probably around the cigar he usually had clamped between his teeth. "It's a story—a damn good one since it involves royalty."

If only Stanley knew the real story…

But the women had been checked into that Parisian hotel under aliases. To prevent the paparazzi from hounding the princess, Charlotte had developed several alternative identities for them. She had been that thorough and that good.

Still was—she couldn't be dead. Aaron had already lost one woman he thought he might have been falling for—Stanley Jessup's daughter.

"Why call me?" Aaron asked the newsman. "Why talk to me at all?"

"I don't blame you or Whit for what happened three years ago," Jessup assured him. "Neither should you."

Stanley, despite grieving for his daughter, might have found a way to absolve them of any culpability. But Aaron hadn't.

"Do you want me to call you back after I get more details?" Stanley asked. "I'm going to talk to this young reporter to verify he really has a source inside the sanatorium. Then I'll see if he can get a picture to prove it's actually her."

"No," Aaron replied. He couldn't trust anyone else to do that. No one else would know for certain which woman she really was. "Just tell me the name of this psychiatric hospital."

"Serenity House," Stanley divulged freely. "I'm going to have that reporter follow up with his source, too, Aaron. Anything Princess Gabby does is newsworthy, and this story is a hell of a lot more exciting than her attending a fashion show or movie premiere. And she hasn't even hit one of those in a few months— maybe longer. In fact, she's kind of dropped off the face of the earth."

Or so everyone had believed. But if it really was her…

"I know I don't have any right to ask you for a favor…"

"You said that when you called the first time," Jessup reminded him, "when you asked me if I'd heard anything recently about the princess."

"So I definitely don't have any right to ask you for a second favor," Aaron amended himself.

"That's BS," Stanley replied with a snort of disgust. "You can ask me anything, but I have the right to refuse if you're going to ask what I think you are."

"I'm not asking you *not* to run with the story," Aaron assured the man. He knew Stanley Jessup too well to ask that. "I'm just asking you to run in place until I get there."

"So hold off on printing anything?"

"Just until I get there and personally confirm if it's really Princess Gabriella."

Stanley snorted again. "Since she was ten years old, Princess Gabriella St. Pierre's face has been everywhere—magazines, newspapers, entertainment magazines." Most of those he owned. "Everybody knows what her royal highness looks like."

Everyone did. But unfortunately she was no longer the only one who looked like her. The woman committed to the private sanatorium wasn't necessarily Princess Gabriella.

"Just hold off?" Aaron asked.

Stanley Jessup's sigh of resignation rattled the phone. "Sure."

"And one more favor—"

The older man chuckled. "So what's this? The third one now?"

"This is important," Aaron said. "I wouldn't have bothered you if it wasn't…" If Charlotte wasn't missing, he would have never been so insensitive as to contact Stanley Jessup again. He hated that probably just the sound of his voice reminded the man of all that he had lost: everything.

"I can tell that this is important to you," the older man replied. "So what's this third favor?"

Maybe the most important. "If Whit calls, don't tell him what you've told me."

"About the explosion not being his fault?"

Aaron snorted now. It had been Whit's fault; he'd convinced him that the safe house was really safe. That was why he couldn't trust another woman's safety to his former partner. "Don't tell him about Princess Gabriella."

"He'll read it for himself."

"Let him find out that way, and let *me* find out first if it's really the princess." Or Charlotte.

"You don't trust Whit?"

Not anymore. Whit had always cared more about the money than Aaron had. Maybe he cared too much. Maybe he'd been bought off—three years ago and now. Both times there must have been a man on the inside. Aaron hated to think that that man was one he'd once considered a friend—a man at whose side he'd fought. But war had changed so many veterans. Whit had changed. Maybe he'd gone from killing for his country to killing for the highest bidder.

"Promise me," Aaron beseeched his old client.

Jessup grunted. "You make it all sound so life and death. She's just a spoiled heiress who's probably been committed to this private hospital to get cleaned up or dried out."

Aaron had only interacted with the princess for a couple of months before her disappearance. Even at parties she'd never had more than a few sips of champagne and she had never appeared under the influence of drugs, either.

If this really was Princess Gabby at Serenity House, she wasn't there for rehab.

SHE STARED AT the stranger in the mirror above the bathroom sink. The woman had long—very long—caramel-brown hair hanging over her thin shoulders. And her face had delicate features and wide brown eyes. And a bruise on her temple that was fading from purple to yellow.

She lifted her hand and pressed her fingertips against the slightly swollen flesh. Pain throbbed yet inside her head, weakening her legs. She dropped both hands to the edge of the sink and held on until the dizziness passed. She needed to regain her strength, but even more she needed to regain her memory.

She didn't even recognize her own damn face in the mirror. "Who are you?" she asked that woman staring back at her through the glass. She needed a name—even if it wasn't her real one. She needed an identity. "Jane," she whispered. "Jane Doe."

Wasn't that what authorities called female amnesiacs…and unidentified *dead* female bodies?

Drawing in a shaky breath, *Jane* moved her hand from her head to her belly. Her flesh shifted beneath her palm, moving as something—*somebody*—moved inside her.

She didn't recognize her face or her body. What the hell was wrong with her? Maybe that was why she'd been locked up in this weird hospital/prison. Maybe it was for her own damn good. Her belly moved again as the baby kicked inside her, as if in protest of her thought.

"You want out of here, too," Jane murmured.

A fist hammered at the door, rattling the wood in the frame. The pounding rattled her brain inside her skull.

"Come out now, miss. You've been in there long enough."

The gruff command had her muscles tensing in protest and preparation for battle. But she was still too weak to fight.

The door had no lock, so it opened easily to the man who usually stood guard outside her room. Unlike the other hospital employees who wore scrubs, he wore a dark suit, and his black hair was oily and slicked back on his big, heavily featured head. His suit jacket shifted, revealing his holstered weapon. A Glock. As if familiar with the trigger, her fingers itched to grab for it.

But she would have to get close to the creep and if she got close, he could touch her, probably overpower her before she ever pulled the weapon from the holster. A cold chill chased down her spine, and she shivered in reaction.

A nurse moved around the guard. "You're cold," she said. "You need to get back into bed." The gray-haired woman wrapped an arm around Jane and helped her from the bathroom to the bed. The woman had a small, shiny metal nameplate pinned to her uniform shirt. *She* had a name: Sandy.

Jane found herself leaning heavily against the shorter woman. Her knees trembled, her legs turning into jelly in reaction to the short walk. With a tremulous sigh of relief she dropped onto the mattress.

"Put the restraints on her," the gruff-voiced guard ordered. He spoke with a heavy accent—some dialect she suspected she should have recognized if she could even recognize her own face right now.

"No, please," Jane implored the nurse, not the man. She doubted she could sway *him*. But the woman... "Sandy, please..."

The nurse turned toward the man, though. "Mr. Centerenian, do we have to? She's not strong enough to—"

"Put the restraints on her!" he snapped. "You remember what happened to her the last time you didn't..."

Deep red color flushed the woman's face and neck. But was her reaction in embarrassment or anger?

What had happened the last time Jane hadn't had on the restraints? She hadn't simply fallen out of bed...if that was what he was trying to imply.

Jane doubted the bruise on her head had come from a fall since she had no other corresponding bruises on her shoulder, arm or hip. At least not recent ones. But she had a plethora of fading bruises and even older scars.

More than likely the bruise on her face had come from a blow. She glanced again at the holster and the gun visible through Mr. Centerenian's open jacket. The handle of the Glock could have left such a bruise and bump on her temple. It also could have killed her.

From the loss of her memory and her strength, she suspected it nearly had. This man had attacked a pregnant woman? What kind of guard was he? He definitely wasn't there for her *protection*.

The nurse's hands trembled as she reached for the restraints that were attached to the bed railings.

"Sandy, please…" Jane implored her.

But the nurse wouldn't meet her gaze. She kept her head down, eyes averted, as she attached the strips of canvas and Velcro to Jane's wrists.

"Tight," the man ordered gruffly.

Sandy ripped loose the Velcro and readjusted the straps. But now the restraints felt even looser. The nurse snuck a quick, apologetic glance at Jane before turning away and heading toward the door. Sandy couldn't open it and leave though. She had to wait, her body visibly tense, for the man to unlock it.

Mr. Centerenian stared at Jane, his heavy brows lowered over his dark eyes. He studied her face and then the restraints. She sucked in a breath, afraid that he might test them. But finally he turned away, too, and unlocked the door by swiping his ID badge through a card-reading lock mechanism. The badge had his intimidating photograph on it, above his intimidating name.

Jane Doe was hardly intimidating. What the hell was her real name?

Once the door closed Jane was alone in the room,

and she struggled with her looser restraints. She tugged them up and down, working them against the railings of the bed, so that the fabric and Velcro loosened even more. But she weakened, too.

Panting for breath, she collapsed against the pillows piled on the raised bed and closed her eyes. Pain throbbed in her head, and she fought to focus. She needed to plan her escape.

Even if Jane got loose, she didn't have the ID badge she needed to get out of the room. But then how could she when she didn't even have an ID? Of course she was a patient here—not an employee.

But the slightly sympathetic nurse didn't have one, either. The only way Jane would get the hell out of this place was to get one of those card-reading badges off another employee.

The guard was armed, and Jane was too weak and probably too pregnant to overpower Mr. Centerenian anyway. So whatever employee or visitor stepped into her room next would be the one she ambushed.

Images flashed behind her closed eyes, images of her fists and feet flying—connecting with muscle and bone, as she fought for her life.

Against the guard?

Or were those brief flashes of memory of another time, another fight or fights?

Who the hell was Jane Doe really?

Chapter Two

A sigh of disappointment came from the man standing next to Aaron. "It's not Charlotte," he said.

The guy wasn't Whit Howell. Aaron had managed to leave him behind on St. Pierre Island. But this man had met him at the airport in Grand Rapids, Michigan. Once Aaron had dealt with his anger over the guy flagging his passport to monitor his travel, he had made use of him...for the fake credentials that had gotten Aaron on staff at Serenity House. Problem was that the U.S. Marshal had insisted on coming along.

Jason "Trigger" Herrema pushed his hand through his steel-gray hair. "Damn, I'd really hoped she was still alive."

"You and me both." The only difference was that Aaron wasn't entirely convinced that this woman wasn't Charlotte. Through the small window in the door of hospital room 00, he couldn't see much more than her perfect profile: slightly upturned nose, delicately sculpted cheekbone, heavily lashed eye.

Charlotte's partner didn't think it was her because Charlotte Green hadn't had a perfect profile...until she'd taken on the job of protecting the princess and had plastic surgery to make herself look exactly like the royal heiress. Because they had already shared the same build and coloring, it hadn't even taken much surgery to complete the transformation.

Aaron had seen a before photo of Charlotte; she'd had one of her and her aunt on the bedside table in her room in the palace in St. Pierre. She'd had a crooked nose from being broken too many times and an ugly, jagged scar on her cheek from a wanted killer's knife blade. It was no wonder her old partner didn't recognize her now.

But it had to be Charlotte.

Aaron couldn't look away from her; he couldn't focus on anyone but her, which was exactly how he had reacted the first time he'd met the tough female bodyguard. Even more than her beauty, he'd been drawn to her strength and her character. And even lying in that bed, she was strong—she had to be to have survived the attack in the hotel room in Paris.

"I need to talk to the princess," Aaron said. Obviously Charlotte hadn't told her old partner about her surgery, so neither would Aaron. If she had wanted the U.S. Marshal to know about her physical transformation, she would have informed him already. Maybe she hadn't trusted this guy. And if she hadn't, Aaron didn't dare trust him, either. "Someone needs to keep an eye out for the goon that was guarding her door."

They'd waited until the muscular man had slipped outside for a cigarette. "And maybe check around to see if Charlotte's been visiting her." He doubted it. If this was the princess and Charlotte knew she was here, she would have broken her out of this creepy hospital long ago.

Unless Charlotte wasn't who Aaron had thought she was. Unless she was the one keeping Gabriella here…

The Marshal nodded in agreement. "I can ask some of the nurses about her visitors and keep an eye out for the big guy."

"The princess knows me," Aaron said, "so I'll talk to her."

Trigger glanced inside the room again. "Just because she knows you doesn't mean you're going to get any information out of her."

"Maybe not," Aaron agreed. "But maybe she can shed some light on what happened in Paris—"

Trigger interrupted with an urgent whisper, "And what happened to Charlotte!"

"Exactly," Aaron said with a nod. "I have to try to find out what she knows."

Trigger's shoulders drooped in a shrug of defeat, as if he was already giving up. "Don't expect much. I doubt that girl knows anything. I worked with Charlotte for four years, and I never knew what was going on with her."

"I had a partner like that, too," Aaron muttered beneath his breath as the U.S. Marshal headed toward the nurses' station.

Was it possible that Whit had sold out? Was he the one behind what had happened in Paris?

And what about Charlotte? Had he been wrong about her, too? Maybe she'd had her own agenda where the princess was concerned.

Only one way to find out…

He clutched his fake ID badge and swiped it through the security lock beside the door. After a quick glance around to make sure no one was watching him, he slipped inside the room and shut the door at his back.

She didn't awaken; she didn't even stir in her sleep

or shift beneath the thick blankets covering her. Was she all right? Or heavily sedated?

If she was Charlotte, then whoever had brought her here would have had to keep her subdued somehow. Drugs made sense.

He stepped closer, checking for an IV, but there was nothing. However, her arms were strapped to the bed railings.

"Are you all right?" he whispered, reaching out to touch her. He tipped her face toward him. He'd been able to tell the women apart—because Gabriella was younger with a wide-eyed innocence. And because Charlotte had made his heart race. But now his heart slammed against his ribs when he noticed the angry bruise marring her silky skin. "Oh, my God…what the hell happened to you?"

This injury was not from the struggle in the hotel room. Much of the bruise was still brilliant with color; it was a recent wound.

Despite his hand cupping her face, she didn't react to his touch. Her lids didn't flicker; her thick lashes lay against her high cheekbones. He ran his fingertips along the edge of her jaw toward her throat to check for a pulse. But as he leaned over her, his arm brushed against her stomach and beneath the blanket, something shifted, almost as if kicking him.

It wasn't just her body beneath the heavy blankets. Or at least it wasn't the shape of her formerly lithely muscled body; it had changed due to the rounded mound of her stomach.

"Oh, my God!" He felt as if he had been kicked—and a hell of a lot harder than that slight movement against his arm.

This woman was pregnant. So she couldn't be Charlotte, who had been adamant about never becoming a mother. She had to be the princess. But he hadn't known…he hadn't realized…that the princess must have already been carrying a royal heir when she and Charlotte disappeared.

While he stared down at her stomach, she moved. Suddenly. Her hands wrapped tight around his throat, pushing hard against his windpipe. Despite the pressure he managed to gasp out one word, "Charlotte."

He had no doubt now—he had found *Charlotte*. And if her death grip was any indication, she wasn't happy that he had.

"CHARLOTTE…" she whispered the name back at him. It felt familiar on her lips. Was it her name? Or had she used it for someone else?

She wanted to ask the man, but for him to reply, she would have to loosen her grip. And then she wouldn't be able to overpower him. She'd caught him by surprise, playing possum as she had; otherwise she never would have managed to get her hands on him.

He was nearly as big as the other guard. But his body was all long, lean muscle. His hair was dark, nearly black, and his eyes were a startlingly light blue. His eyes struck a chord of familiarity within her just like the name he'd called her.

Did she know him? Or had she just seen him before in here? He had one of those name badges clipped to what was apparently a uniform shirt. It was a drab green that matched the drawstring pants of what looked like hospital scrubs. So he obviously worked here.

She needed that badge to escape. She needed to escape even more than she needed to know who the hell she was. But her grip loosened, as his hands grasped hers and easily pulled them from his throat. She cursed her weakness and then she cursed him. "You son of a bitch!" She wriggled, trying to tug her wrists from his grip. But his hands were strong. "Let me go!"

"I'm trying to help you," he said, his voice low and raspy—either from her attack or because he didn't want to be overheard.

"Then get me the hell out of here!"

"That's the plan."

Her breath shuddered out in a gasp of surprise. "It is?"

"It's why I'm here, Charlotte."

"Why—why do you think I'm Charlotte?" The question slipped out, unbidden. And now she silently cursed herself. If Charlotte was the woman he'd intended to free, then she should have let him believe she was Charlotte.

Hell, maybe she was.

His eyes, that eerily familiar pale blue, widened in surprise. "You're not?"

God, now he wasn't sure, either.

She should have kept her mouth shut, but maybe she had done that as long as she had physically been able. Her voice was raspy, as if she hadn't used it much lately. Or maybe someone had tried choking the life out of her, too.

She needed to get the hell out of this place. But should she leave with a stranger? Maybe he posed a bigger threat than the man with the Glock.

He studied her face, his gaze narrowing with the scrutiny. "Princess Gabriella?"

"Pr-princess?" she sputtered with a near-hysterical giggle. "You think I'm a princess?" Maybe it wasn't that ridiculous a thought, though. It was almost as if she had stumbled into some morbid fairy tale where the princess had been poisoned or cursed to an endless slumber.

Except she wasn't sleeping anymore.

"I don't know what the hell to think," the man admitted, shaking his head as if trying to sort through his confusion.

Maybe it wasn't the blow to her head that had knocked out her sense since he couldn't understand what was going on, either.

"Please," she urged him, "get me out of here." She glanced toward the window in the door, where the burly Mr. Centerenian usually stood guard. "Now."

"I need to know," he said. "Who are you? Gabby or Charlotte?"

Gabby? The name evoked the same familiar chord within her that Charlotte and his eyes had struck. It must have been a name she'd used. "Does it matter?" she asked. "Would you take one of us but leave the other?"

And why couldn't he tell the difference between the women? Was she a twin? Was there someone else, exactly like her, out there? Hurt? In danger? As freaking confused as she was?

He shook his head. "No, damn it, I wouldn't. You know I wouldn't leave either of you here."

Either of you...

Where was the other woman? Locked in another room in this hellhole? Jane's breath caught with fear and concern for a person she didn't even know. But then she didn't even know herself.

"But why won't you be honest with me?" the man asked, and hurt flashed in his pale blue eyes. "Don't you trust *me?*"

It was probably a mistake. But the admission slipped

out like her earlier question. "I don't even know who you are."

"Damn it, you have every right to be pissed, but it was the king's decision to make that announcement at the ball. He wouldn't listen to me…" he said then trailed off, and those pretty eyes narrowed again. "You're not talking about that. You're not just mad at me."

Maybe she was.

He definitely stirred up emotion inside her. Her pulse raced and her heart pounded hard and fast. Her mind didn't recognize him, but her body did as even her skin tingled in reaction to having touched his. An image flicked through her mind, of her hands sliding over his skin—all of his skin, his broad shoulders bare, his muscular chest covered only with dark, soft hair.

Then her fingers trailed down over washboard abs to…

Her head pounded as she tried to remember, but the tantalizing image slipped away as a ragged breath slipped between her lips. Despite the pounding, she shook her head and then flinched with pain and frustration. "No. I really don't know who you are."

He sucked in a sharp breath, as if her words had hurt him even more than her hands wrapped tightly around his throat had.

"Don't feel bad," she said with a snort of derision. "I don't know who I am, either."

"You don't?" His dark brows knitted together, furrowing his forehead. "You have amnesia?"

She jerked her head in a sharp nod, which caused her to wince in pain again. "I don't know who I am or why I'm here. But I know I'm in danger. I have to get the hell out of here."

Even if leaving with him might put her in more danger...

The door rattled. And she gasped. "You waited too long!"

While this man was probably stronger than the one who usually guarded her, this man was unarmed. He would be no more a match for the Glock than she had been.

The door creaked as it swung open. The man spun around, putting his body between hers and the intruder—as if using himself as a human shield.

"Timmer, we gotta go," a male voice whispered. "He's coming back."

A curse slipped from Timmer's lips. "We have to bring her with us."

"There's no time."

Anger flashed in those pale blue eyes. "We can't leave her here!"

"If we try to take her out, none of us will be able to leave."

The man—Timmer—nodded.

She grabbed him again, clutching at his arm. "Don't leave me!" she implored him.

"I'll be back," he promised.

"Hurry!" urged the other man, who hovered yet outside the room. "He's coming!"

Timmer turned back toward her, and taking her hand from his grasp, he quickly slipped her wrists back into the restraints and bound her to the bed.

He obviously hadn't intended to help her at all. Maybe it had all been a trick. Some silly game to amuse a bored guard...

As her brief flash of hope died, tears stung her eyes. But even in her physically weak state, she was too strong and too damned proud to give in to tears. She wouldn't cry. And she damn well wouldn't beg.

"I will come back," he said again, so sincerely that she was tempted to believe him.

But then he hurried from the room. Before the door swung completely shut behind him, she heard a shout. Voices raised in anger. Maybe even a shot.

She flinched at the noise, as if the bullet had struck her. As if they had sharp talons, fear and panic clutched at her heart. She was scared, and not just because if he were dead, he wouldn't come back and help her.

She was scared because she cared that he might be hurt, or even worse, that he might be dying. She'd had only a faint glint of recognition for him—for his unusually light eyes and for his skin…if that had been his body in that image that had flashed through her mind. However, she didn't remember his name or exactly how she'd known him.

She had known him very well; she was aware of that fact. Her stomach shifted as the baby inside her womb stirred restlessly, as if feeling her mother's fear and panic.

Or her *father's* pain?

AARON HAD STEPPED into it—right into the line of fire. The burly guard had caught him coming out of the room. The door hadn't even closed behind him yet, so he couldn't deny where he'd been—where he had been ordered never to go. Only a few employees were allowed into the room of the mysterious patient. Room 00.

Since he probably couldn't talk his way out of the situation, especially with the guy already reaching inside his suit jacket for his gun, Aaron tried getting the hell *out* of the situation. He ran away from the guard, in the direction that Trigger Herrema had already disappeared.

Some help the U.S. Marshal had proven to be…

With that guy as her partner, it was no wonder that Charlotte had left the U.S. Marshals and become a private bodyguard.

Was she now, despite her adamant resolve not to, about to become a mother? Or was that pregnant woman actually Princess Gabby?

He needed to know. But even more than that, he needed to get her the hell out of this place. He couldn't do either if he were dead.

Shouting echoed off the walls, erupting from the guard along with labored pants for breath. But he was either too far away, or the guy's accent too thick, for Aaron to make out any specific words. But he didn't need to know what the man said to figure out that it was a threat.

He skidded around corners of the hospital's winding corridors, staying just ahead of the lumbering guard. With a short breath of relief, he headed through the foyer to the glass doors of the exit. He would have to slow down to swipe his name badge through the card reader in order to get those doors to open.

But he never made it that far. Shots rang out. That was a threat he understood. He dropped to the ground. But he might have already been too late. Blood trickled down his face and dropped onto the white tiled floor beneath him.

He'd been hit.

Chapter Three

"You could have killed him," the woman chastised the guard, her voice a hiss of anger. "You could have killed other employees or patients. You were not supposed to use that gun. Again."

Through the crack the door had been left open, Aaron spied on the argument. Despite the man's superior height and burly build, he backed down from the woman. She was tall, too, with ash-blond hair pulled back into a tight bun. The plaque on her desk, which Aaron sat in front of, identified her as Dr. Mona Platt, the hospital administrator.

"That man is not an employee," the guard replied, his accent thick.

Aaron tried to place it. Greek? St. Pierre Island was close to Greece.

"He's a new hire," she replied, "who passed all the security clearances."

She had checked. She'd used her computer to pull up all of his fake information. He needed to know what other information was on her system, like the identity of the woman in Room 00. Or if not her identity, at least the identity of the person who had committed her to Serenity House.

Keeping an eye on the outer office where the two of them argued, Aaron moved around her desk and reached for her keyboard. He needed to pull up the financials. A place like this didn't accept patients for free. Someone had to be footing the bills.

Dr. Platt hadn't signed off her computer before leaving the room. And not enough time had passed since she'd left her desk that the screen had locked. He was able to access the employee records at which she'd been looking. But he needed *patient* records. However, he didn't know the patient's name. And if she was telling the truth, neither did the patient.

"He's not a nurse aide," the guard argued. "He could be a reporter."

"Not with those credentials," the administrator argued. "They're real. He passed our very stringent background check."

"Then he's not a reporter," the man agreed with a sigh of relief.

"That isn't necessarily a good thing," she warned him. "Since he had a legitimate reason for being here, he's more likely to go to the sheriff's office to report your shooting at him."

Aaron couldn't involve the authorities—couldn't draw any media or legal attention to the woman in Room 00. No matter who she was, it was likely to put her in more danger if her whereabouts became widely known.

"He can't go to the police if he can't leave," the man pointed out.

Aaron suppressed a shudder. Maybe instead of looking for information, he should have been looking for an escape. There was a window behind the desk, but like every other window in the place, it had bars behind the glass.

"We can't hold him here," she said. "Someone could report him missing, and we don't want the state police coming here asking questions. Or worse yet, with a search warrant."

"It is too dangerous to let him go," the man warned. "He could still go to the police."

"Yes, because you shot at him," she admonished him. "That was dangerous—for so many reasons!"

"I couldn't let him get away!" the man replied. "He was in *her* room."

"And she couldn't have told him anything," the administrator assured him. "*She* doesn't know anything to tell."

"But he must have recognized her…"

Aaron had but he still wasn't certain which woman she was. Her trying to strangle him had convinced him she was Charlotte. But part of Charlotte going above and beyond, besides plastic surgery, to protect the princess had been teaching the royal heiress how to protect herself. And Princess Gabby had never needed more protection than she did now.

So as not to draw their attention back to him, he lightly tapped the computer keyboard. But he wasn't certain what to enter. To pull up patient records, he needed the patient's name.

"All our employees sign a confidentiality agreement," the administrator reminded the guard. "He can't share what he saw with anyone without risking a lawsuit from Serenity House. Shooting at him was totally unnecessary."

"I still need to talk to him."

"You will only make the situation worse," she said. "If he does go to the authorities, I will be informed."

So she had a contact within the sheriff's office.

"Will you have enough warning for us to get her to a more secure location?"

"I don't know."

"You were paid handsomely to keep this location secure," the man said, his already gruff voice low with fury. "And since you have failed, I will handle this, and him, in my own way."

The guard wasn't going away. Instead of punching keys in the computer, Aaron needed to figure a way out of Serenity House—first for him and then for the patient in Room 00.

Room 00. He typed it in and the screen changed, an hourglass displaying while the computer pulled up records. He was almost in…

"What the hell are you doing?" the woman demanded to know as she slammed open the office door with such force it bounced off the wall and nearly struck her.

Aaron hit the exit key as he leaned across the keyboard, reaching for the box of tissues. He pulled one out and pressed it to his head. "I'm bleeding. That crazy son of a bitch was shooting at me."

He glanced behind her but the man was gone. Somehow she'd gotten rid of the goon—apparently with just a look as he'd overheard no words of dismissal. Maybe Aaron would have been in less danger if he'd gone with the guard because there was something kind of eerie about this steely-eyed woman.

"Yes, that was bad judgment on his part," she said, sounding nearly unconcerned about the shots now. "But maybe it wasn't uncalled for."

"Dr. Platt, I've done nothing to warrant an *execu-*

tion." He edged around her desk, toward the door. She blocked it, but as a trained bodyguard, he could easily overpower her—physically. Mentally, he didn't trust her—given the doctorate of psychology degree on her wall and her overall soulless demeanor.

"You entered a room that every employee," she said, "newly hired and long-term—has been warned is strictly off-limits."

He hadn't actually attended an orientation. But the guard posted at her door had certainly implied Room 00 was off-limits. "I thought I heard a yell for help. I was concerned—"

"Then you should have summoned the guard or the nurse who are authorized to enter that room. That is protocol," she stated, her voice cold with an icy anger. "By going inside yourself, you violated protocol."

"I wasn't thinking," he said. "I just reacted."

"You reacted incorrectly," she said. "And because of that, you can no longer be on staff at Serenity House." She held out her hand.

He moved to shake it, but she lifted her hand and ripped the ID badge from the lanyard around his neck. "You're fired, Mr. Ottenwess," she said, addressing him by the name on that ID badge.

"I would appreciate another chance," he said. "Now that I'm fully aware of the rules, I promise not to violate them again."

She shook her head. "That's a risk I can't take. And frankly, Mr. Ottenwess, staying here is a risk you can't take. I talked the private security guard out of interrogating you. But if he sees you again, I'm not sure what he might do to you."

Shoot at him again. And maybe the next time he wouldn't miss. The only thing that had nicked Aaron's cheek had been a shard of a porcelain vase that the guard had shot instead of him.

The burly guy had disappeared, but Aaron suspected he hadn't gone far. How could he get past him again to access Room 00?

"That's why I'm having my own guards escort you off the premises." As silently as she'd dismissed the private guard, she must have summoned her own because two men stood in the doorway.

"This isn't necessary," Aaron said. "I can show myself out."

"Actually you can't," she reminded him, "without your badge you can't open any of the facility doors—not to patients' rooms and not to exits. They will show you out." She barely lifted an ash-blond brow, but she had the two men rushing forward. Each guy grabbed one of his arms and dragged him from her office.

Aaron could have fought them off. They weren't armed. But he didn't want to beat them. He wanted to outsmart them. Or he had no hope of helping the woman in Room 00.

JANE HAD JUST resigned herself to the fact that the man, that the voice in the hall had addressed as *Timmer,* wasn't coming back…when the lock clicked and the door opened. She fought to keep her eyes closed and her breathing even, feigning sleep as she had when he'd entered the first time. Or at least the first time that she remembered.

"Is she really out?" the gruff-voiced guard asked someone.

Soft hands touched her face and gently forced open one of Jane's eyes. She stared up at the gray-haired nurse who dropped her lid and stepped back before replying, "She's unconscious."

"Did he hurt her?" Mr. Centerenian demanded to know.

"Who?" the nurse asked, her voice squeaking with anxiety. Over Jane or over lying to the guard?

"Someone was in her room," the man explained.

"He wouldn't have been able to talk her," Nurse Sandy easily lied again. She obviously hadn't been anxious about lying to him. "I gave her a sedative earlier, like you requested. She's completely out and oblivious to her surroundings."

Jane fought to keep her lips from twitching in reaction to the nurse's blatant lie. Wouldn't the guard remember that the nurse had given her no medication?

If only this woman had access to a door-opening name badge, Sandy could prove an even more valuable ally because Jane suspected she would help her escape if she could.

Of course the other man—*Timmer*—had promised he would return. Could he? Was he physically able to return?

"Good," the guard grunted. "And he won't get another chance to talk to her."

She held in a gasp as fear clutched her heart. Had one of those shots struck the man?

"Why—why won't he?" the nurse nervously asked the question burning in Jane's mind.

The guard did not answer, just issued another order. "Leave now."

"But—but I should stay to monitor her—"

"Leave now," Mr. Centerenian repeated.

The lock clicked again and the door opened with a creak of hinges and rush of cool air from the hall. It closed again, shutting in the stale air that smelled faintly of the cigarette smoke that always clung to the guard.

Had Mr. Centerenian left with Nurse Sandy? Was Jane alone again?

She nearly opened her eyes but then the guard spoke again. Since the older woman had left, he wasn't talking to the nurse.

Jane peered through a slit in one lid and saw that his cell phone was pressed to his ear. He spoke in a language she couldn't place but somehow understood. She interpreted his side of the conversation.

"There is a problem," he said. "Someone got inside her room tonight. He saw her…"

Mr. Centerenian grunted in response to whatever the person he called told him and then agreed, "Yes, it is no longer safe to keep her here. I will bring her and your unborn child to the airport tomorrow night to meet your private plane."

Who the hell was the guard talking to? Who was the father of her unborn child? She had suspected it was the man who'd snuck into her room. If not him, then who?

She barely restrained her urge to attack the guard and demand that he tell her who he was talking to, who he was bringing her to meet. But she couldn't risk getting hit again. An apparent blow had already cost her too much—of her strength and her mind.

And she needed all she had of both to escape before the guard brought her to the airport. She feared that if she got on that private plane, that she would have no hope of ever regaining her freedom.

She couldn't trust that the man who had snuck in would keep his word to return and help her. She didn't know if he even could—if Timmer had survived his confrontation with the guard. She waited but Mr. Centerenian said nothing of the man he'd caught in her room.

Was he alive or dead?

And who the hell was he or *had* he been to her?

PAIN EXPLODED IN Aaron's stomach, sending his breath from his lungs in a whoosh. He doubled over, hanging from the arms holding him back. Not that he couldn't have broken free had he wanted to fight. But as he writhed around in an exaggerated display of pain, he lurched forward and *accidentally* fell against the guard who was using him as a punching bag.

"And don't come back unless you want more of that," the man warned as he pushed Aaron back. He pushed him through the gate he'd already opened that led from the building to the employee parking lot.

The lot was behind the big brick building and dimly lit. The few parking lights flickered and cast only a faint glow that reflected off the windshields and metal of the cars filling the lot. Darkness was gathering, pushing the last traces of daylight into night.

The gate snapped shut behind him and the lock buzzed. That gate and the one between the guest parking lot and front entrance were the only ways through the sixteen-foot-high fence surrounding the building.

Serenity House was a freaking fortress—more prison than hospital. If Charlotte was the woman in Room 00, it was no wonder that she hadn't managed to escape yet—despite her skills. Of course if she'd been telling him the truth, she'd forgotten all those skills…except for how to strangle him. Only she hadn't been as strong as the woman he remembered—as the woman with whom he'd made love one unforgettable night.

Images flashed through his mind. Moonlight caressing honey-toned skin and sleek curves. His hands following the path of the moonlight. Then his lips…

And her hands and her soft lips, touching him everywhere. Passionate kisses, bodies entwined…

His breath shuddered out in a ragged sigh as he shook off those skin-tingling memories. That had been one incredible night. And even though they'd used protection, it wasn't foolproof.

Was that baby she carried his? The dates would probably be about right. But was the woman?

He would find out soon. For the sake of the guards who watched him yet from behind the gate, he stumbled across the parking lot with the drunkenlike stagger of a boxer who'd taken too many hits.

Aaron had driven separately from the U.S. Marshal, which was good since Jason "Trigger" Herrema had left him without a backward glance. Some partner Trigger must have been to Charlotte. No wonder she was so strong and independent. And no wonder she had resigned from the U.S. Marshals for private security.

But Charlotte Green wasn't the only one with skills. Aaron clutched the ID badge he had lifted from the guard who'd hit him. The guy had seemed too arrogant an SOB to admit or even realize that Aaron had taken the badge off him. At least not right away. But he might eventually figure it out. So Aaron had to act quickly.

But not too quickly that they were waiting and ready for him to try something. He also needed backup. Obviously he couldn't count on Trigger, the man, so he needed another kind of trigger—one on a gun.

He hurried toward his vehicle, which was a plain gray box of a sedan that he'd rented at the airport. His gun wasn't inside but back at the cottage he'd found in the woods near Serenity House. He hadn't rented it; he hadn't needed to—it had looked abandoned or at least out of season for the owners. The cottage was close enough that he'd figured they would be able to run there if they weren't able to reach his vehicle.

But now that he had seen Charlotte or Princess Gabriella or whoever the hell she was and realized how weak she was, he suspected that outrunning anyone was out of the question.

He needed wheels and a very powerful engine. Maybe he should have gone for fast rather than nondescript when he'd rented a car. Just as he was considering his choice, shots rang out—shattering the rear window. He ducked down, easing around the trunk toward the driver's side. Maybe if he kept the car between him and Serenity House, the guards wouldn't have a clear shot—if they were the ones shooting. But he'd seen no weapons on them. Then the driver's side windows shattered, bullets striking first the rear window and then the front window.

"I'm not getting the deposit back on this rental," he murmured as he clicked the key fob to unlock the doors. He could have just reached through the shattered window and unlocked it himself, but he didn't want to raise his head too high for fear that it might be the next thing a bullet hit.

He didn't even know where the hell the shots were coming from. Serenity House? Or somewhere in the parking lot behind him?

He ducked down farther, suspecting the shots might have been coming from behind him. Maybe he had his answer about where the hell the private security guard had gone. Instead of standing sentry outside Room 00, he'd set up an ambush outside Serenity House.

With the door unprotected, Aaron had the best

chance to free Charlotte or Princess Gabriella. But he couldn't go back inside. Shots kept firing, and he knew it was just a matter of time before one struck him. He had to get the hell out of here while he still could.

Chapter Four

Shots rang out, echoing inside Jane's aching head. She reached for her gun, but it wasn't on the holster. Hell, she wasn't even wearing the holster. Instead her fingers encountered the soft mound of her burgeoning belly. Of her baby...

She jolted awake, as if fighting her way out of a nightmare. But she awakened *to* the nightmare, not *from* it. She still couldn't remember who she was or how she had wound up trapped in this strange hospital jail. But she hadn't forgotten that she needed to get the hell out of here.

And not to that private airport. She couldn't let the surly Mr. Centerenian take her there. When? Tomorrow night? Tonight? She had no idea how long she'd been asleep. She wore no watch, and there was no clock for her to mark the seconds, minutes or hours.

Given the urgency of her situation, how had she fallen asleep? Was she the one to whom the nurse had really lied? Had Sandy actually slipped her a sedative? But Jane didn't feel groggy from drugs. She was just tired—either because of the concussion or the pregnancy.

The baby shifted inside her, kicking against her ribs

as if trying to prod her into action—reminding Jane that she had someone besides herself to protect now. No matter who the father was—*she* was the mother. Something primal reared up inside her, clutching at her heart and her womb. A mother's instinct, a mother's love. This was *her* child.

Her baby girl. She felt it with a deep certainty that the baby she carried was a girl. Had she had an ultrasound? Even though she didn't remember the process, maybe she remembered the results.

"Okay, baby girl, I don't know how we got here," she murmured. "But that doesn't matter right now. What matters is that we're getting out."

She just had to figure out how. She tugged on her wrists, fighting to loosen the restraints. Maybe that man—Mr. Timmer—hadn't tightened them as much as she'd feared. Or maybe the nurse had returned and loosened them while Jane had been sleeping. Either way, she had enough play to slip one hand free. Just as she reached out to undo the other strap, the lock beeped. And hinges creaked as the door opened.

Damn it! Maybe she had slept too long. Maybe she'd slept away a day and any chance she'd had of escaping this nightmare of captivity.

S*HE WAS STILL HERE*.

Aaron's breath shuddered out with a sigh of relief. He had worried that they might have moved her already, that they probably had just minutes after he'd been discovered in her room. But then maybe they didn't realize those last shots—fired at him in the parking lot—had also missed him.

As he studied her, his relief ebbed away, and his concern returned. She lay, her body stiff and unmoving beneath her blankets. Maybe when they hadn't managed to get rid of him, they'd decided to get rid of her instead. Was she dead? Or just playing dead like she had the first time he had come into her room?

He moved toward the bed, hoping that she would reach out to strangle him as she had last time. She wasn't strong enough to hurt him but it proved she was still strong enough to fight.

He opened his mouth to whisper her name but had no idea what to call her. Was she Charlotte or Princess Gabriella? He wished he knew. Since he wished she was the woman he had already begun to fall for, he called her, "Charlotte…"

Her eyes opened wide with shock, but probably at the sound of his voice rather than any recognition of her name because she said, "I thought you were dead."

"So did I," Aaron admitted.

If the Marshal hadn't shown up in the parking lot when he had, those shots probably wouldn't have stopped until Aaron had been hit. And killed. But Marshal Herrema's car pulling into the lot had sent the shooter into hiding. Aaron suspected he would come out again—just hopefully not until Aaron got *her* to safety.

"We have to get out of here," he said, reaching for her restraints.

But she already had one arm free and quickly freed her other arm. "I thought you were shot," she said. "I was sure I heard gunshots."

"You did," he confirmed.

"The guard with the Glock?" She swung her legs over the bed but hesitated to stand.

"Yes." She knew guns. She had to be Charlotte, or had Charlotte taught Princess Gabriella to identify firearms? "He caught me coming out of your room."

She glanced toward the door, her caramel-colored eyes widening with fear. "After catching you, I'm surprised he would leave my side for a second—even for his nicotine fix."

Her fear made him think she was the princess. Because he'd never seen fear on Charlotte's face. Passion. Anger. But the fear had been Gabriella's.

"I came up with a distraction to get him away." Trigger, in a short dark-haired wig that made him, from a distance, look like Aaron. "But we don't have much time." Before the guard either gave up trying to catch Trigger or caught him and figured out he wasn't Aaron.

She gestured at her hospital gown. "I won't be able to just walk out of here dressed like this, and I don't think I have anything else to wear. There's no bureau or closet in here."

He'd noticed that the first time he had broken into the room. There had been no sign of her belongings—nothing to provide a clue to her identity or a wardrobe for her departure. So he had come prepared. He handed her the wad of clothes he'd had clenched under his arm. She unfolded the drab green shirt and pants. He'd stolen the scrubs from the employee locker room. He reached for her arm to guide her from the bed, so that she could change.

She stood but swayed on her bare feet.

Aaron grabbed her. "Are you all right?"

The blow to her head had obviously stolen more than her memory. Would he be able to get her out without assistance? Maybe he should have brought along a wheelchair.

She drew in a deep breath and, using his arm, steadied herself. "I'm fine."

"Do you need help getting out of the gown?" he

asked. And images flashed through his mind of another time he'd undressed her...

"No. I can manage myself." She hadn't lost her stubborn independence. She had to be Charlotte.

"Turn around," she ordered him, her modesty misplaced. If she was Charlotte, he had already seen every inch of her naked. He had already caressed and kissed every inch of her naked skin.

But he obliged her and turned back toward the door and kept watch through the small window to the hall. For a big building—three stories of brick and mortar—the place was surprisingly quiet and nearly deserted. Where were all the other patients and visitors? Locked up and locked out?

"Actually I can't manage," she corrected herself. "These damn ties are knotted in the back. Can you undo them?"

He drew in a deep breath to steady his suddenly racing pulse, and then he turned to face her again. She stood with her back toward him, her long hair pulled over her shoulder so it would be out of the way. She had already pulled on the pants and stepped into the slip-on shoes. Her arm over her shoulder, she contorted as she tugged on the straps binding her inside the hospital gown.

"You're making it worse," he observed and gently pulled away her fingers. Forcing his fingers to remain steady, he unknotted the ties and parted the rough cotton fabric.

Baring her back reminded him of lowering the zipper on another kind of gown—one of whisper-soft silk that had slid down her body like a caress—leaving her bare but for a tiny scrap of lace riding low on her hips. She wore no bra now, either. Maybe she thought turning away from him protected her modesty. But he could see the side of her full breast and the nipple puckered with cold. But the rounded mound of her belly drew his attention from the beauty of her breast.

This was another kind of beauty.

One that stole away his breath. Was the baby she carried his? That was only possible if she was Charlotte. While he suspected that she was, he wasn't certain if that was merely wishful thinking on his part rather than fact. Hell, not even she knew for certain who the hell she was—if he could believe her claim of amnesia.

She tugged the scrubs shirt down over her breasts and burgeoning belly. The cotton stretched taut. He should have found her a bigger size, but he'd grabbed what he could from the first accessible locker. He'd acted quickly then because they didn't have much time.

"Are you ready?" he asked, the urgency rushing back over him. Trigger might have already been caught. Time was running out. "Do you have everything?"

"There's nothing here," she said. "We shouldn't be here, either." As she turned toward him, she swayed again and clutched at his arm.

"You're not fine," he said, disproving her earlier claim. "You're weak and dizzy."

"I will be fine," she amended herself. "Once we get out of here. Let's go." And then instead of holding on to his arm for support, she was tugging on it to pull him toward the door. "You still have your badge?"

He shook his head even as he pulled the ID from the lanyard around his neck. "Not mine."

This was probably better. Since it belonged to one of the Serenity House security guards, it had access to more areas than Mr. Ottenwess's badge had.

"I was fired."

"Then how did you get back in?" she asked, her golden-brown eyes narrowing with suspicion.

He lifted the badge toward the lock. "I grabbed this off the guy throwing me off the premises." His stomach clenched in protest of the blows it had taken to provide the distraction. He could have fended those off and would have had he not needed that damn badge.

Her brow furrowed now—with suspicion. "Who are you?"

He sucked in a breath of disappointment. "You still don't remember me?"

"I don't remember anything before I woke up in this place." But she looked away from him as she said it, as if unable to meet his eyes.

Why? Because she lied? But why lie about having amnesia? Was she playing him for a fool?

What the hell was going on? Was this whole disappearance just a way to get the princess out of the obligation the king had announced at the ball? That was what Rafael St. Pierre and Whit had suspected until they'd seen the hotel suite.

But Aaron had believed Charlotte too honest for subterfuge. Had he been wrong about her?

It wouldn't be the first time he had let his attraction to a woman cloud his judgment. The last time his lapse had cost that woman her life.

He had to be more careful—had to make certain that nobody died this time. Because, given all the bullets that had already been fired at him, it just might be him who wound up dead this time.

JANE HELD HER breath as she waited for him to swipe the badge he'd stolen through the lock. But he hesitated, his gaze fixated on her. Even though she wasn't looking at

him, she knew those pale blue eyes were staring at her.
He wasn't touching her, but yet she *felt* him. Her skin
heated and tingled as it had from just the brush of his
fingertips as he'd untied her gown.

She closed her eyes and drew in a steadying breath.
But that was a mistake because that fleeting image she'd
had earlier of him returned—even more vividly. She
not only felt him. She *saw* him. Naked.

Her face heated with embarrassment over that being
the only thing she remembered about her life before she
had woken up in this place. That was why she'd lied to
him. How could she admit to knowing what he looked
like naked—*magnificent*—but not what his name was?

She'd only heard that voice from the hall refer to
him as Timmer. But she didn't even know if that was
really his name or a cover he'd used to gain access to
this creepy place.

Hell, she didn't even know what *her* name was.

But none of that mattered right now.

"We have to get out of here," she urged him. "Mr.
Centerenian, that armed guard, called someone—I don't
know who—earlier, and they made plans to take me to
some airfield—to get me out of the country." She had
no idea what country they were in, but that didn't matter, either. What mattered was not getting on that private plane to a new prison.

He nodded, either in understanding of the guard's
plan or in agreement with the need to get out of here
because he swiped the badge through the card reader.

She held her breath until the lock buzzed and a green
light flashed on the card reader. She reached for the
door, but his hand was already on the handle. Her fingers connected with the back of his hand, with his hard
knuckles and warm skin. And she tingled again from

his touch, just as she had when he'd undressed her. Attraction had chased chills up and down her spine then. Now apprehension did as he opened the door to the hall.

Would the guard catch them as he'd caught this man last time?

Now that Timmer had unlocked the door, he was done hesitating. His hand wrapped tight around her arm. Maybe just to steady her. Or maybe to make sure that she didn't get away from him.

He pulled her down the hall behind him, as if keeping himself between her and whatever threat they might encounter. As she followed him, she noticed the bulge beneath the scrubs at the small of his back. He wasn't unarmed this time. Since she'd seen him last, Timmer had acquired a gun. Was it his or had he taken it off the burly guard?

Was that where Mr. Centerenian had gone? Disarmed? Or dead?

Maybe this man, whom she'd once known intimately, was just resourceful. Or maybe he was dangerous.

The threat actually came from behind them as someone yelled, "Stop!"

The man increased his speed, nearly dragging her as Jane obeyed the command and tried to stop. It wasn't a male voice yelling but a familiar female voice. Nurse Sandy caught up to them and clutched at Jane's free arm.

"Stop!" But the older woman spoke to the man. "You can't take her."

"I can't stay," Jane told her. "That guard—the one who hurt me—he's going to take me out of here. Out of the country. I can't leave with him."

"You can't leave with this man, either," the nurse

said. "Unless…" Sandy stared intently into Jane's eyes. "Do you know him?"

"I—I—"

"Of course you don't," the woman answered her own question. "You don't even know who you are."

"Tell me," Jane implored the nurse. "You know. Tell me!"

She shook her head. "I can't. And I can't let you leave." She held on tightly to Jane's arm as the man tugged on her other arm.

Feeling like the rope, pulled taut to the point of fraying, in a game of tug-of-war, Jane summoned all her strength and wrestled free of both of them. "I have to get out of here!"

"Don't leave with him," the woman implored again. "You don't know him."

As if the adrenaline coursing through Jane had awakened the baby, she shifted inside her womb. Or maybe she was trying to send her mother a message. "I think I knew him—that I would know him if I had my memory."

"That doesn't mean you should trust him," the nurse said. "If he was on the up-and-up, he would have come here with the police—not all by himself."

"I didn't come alone," the man replied. There had been the other one in the hall, warning Timmer to leave before the guard came back. "I brought a U.S. Marshal with me."

At the mention of a Marshal, Jane shivered—her blood chilling. Who the hell was the Marshal? And how would she know one? Was she a wanted criminal?

"You don't have a warrant or any legal reason to take her," the nurse said with absolute certainty.

"There's no time to get before a judge and get one," he replied.

"There isn't," Jane agreed. The guard had already made plans to take her away. This man wouldn't have had time to obtain a warrant.

And then whatever time they had had ran out because someone else shouted. The burly guard lumbered toward them. Mr. Centerenian wasn't alone—two other, slighter men followed close behind him. When they caught sight of Jane with Timmer, they surpassed the guard.

As he had before, Timmer stepped between Jane and the threat—bracing himself as if to take a blow. But he dodged the fist thrown at him and instead threw one of his own with such force that he dropped his would-be assaulter to the ground.

The guy grunted and clutched his head while his co-worker stepped over him, his arms already swinging. Jane's protector braced himself with a wide stance, but instead of throwing another punch, he kicked out. His foot connected with the man's jaw, sending him backward over the guard already sprawled on the ground.

Who the hell was Timmer? What kind of experience had equipped him to break in and out of secure facilities and beat up men nearly as big as he was?

But before Jane could ask him any questions, the guard usually posted outside her door lifted his weapon and stared down the barrel at him. Mr. Centerenian wouldn't shoot her—not when he had plans to take her away.

His intent was clear. He was going to kill the man who had tried to help her escape. And if he succeeded, her chances of ever regaining her freedom would be dead, as well. But she cared less about getting away than she cared about Timmer. No matter who or what he was—he had mattered to her.

Chapter Five

Aaron reached for his gun, but he was too late. Metal scraped his spine as someone pulled the weapon from the waistband of his drawstring pants. He'd been so focused on the guards rushing him that he'd forgotten about the nurse. But it wasn't her. The older woman had flattened herself against the corridor wall to avoid the fight and the bullets that would inevitably fly.

The barrel of the guard's gun pointed right at Aaron's face—his own gun probably pointed at the back of his head. Either way, this wasn't going to end well for him.

A shot rang out, reverberating off the walls. He flinched at the noise and in anticipation of the pain. But he wasn't the one who cried out with it. The burly guard uttered a foreign curse as he dropped his gun from his bleeding hand. One of the Serenity House guards reached for the discarded weapon, but another shot rang out. And another curse as blood spurted from torn knuckles.

"What the hell!"

Aaron repeated the sentiment. "What the hell—" He whirled toward the shooter who stood beside him. Recognition and relief clutched his heart, squeezing it tight in his chest.

Charlotte.

"Let's go," she said as she backed quickly down the hall.

He shook his head at her and then addressed the guards. "Toss your ID badges over here."

Their eyes hard with rage and hatred, they just stared up at him.

Another shot rang out and Charlotte gestured at them with the gun. "Do as he says or the next bullet I fire will do some serious damage!"

They tugged off their badges—the two who still had theirs—and tossed them onto the floor.

"You, too," she warned the other.

"I don't have it!" the man exclaimed, casting a vicious glare at Aaron.

Charlotte's lips curved into a small smile. "You took his?"

Aaron nodded. He leaned over and grabbed up the badges and the gun.

"Now let's go," she said.

He wanted to, but he couldn't leave yet. Trigger might have taken off on him earlier, but he had returned. "Where's the Marshal?" he asked the first guard she'd shot—the man who wore the suit instead of hospital scrubs.

The man was still cursing beneath his breath while he clutched at his bleeding hand. "Who?"

"We have to get out of here," Charlotte urged him. Clutching his arm with her free hand, she tugged impatiently.

"The Marshal," Aaron repeated. It wasn't the only question he wanted to ask the man; he wanted to know who the hell he was working for, too. But first he had to know if the Marshal was all right. "The man wearing the wig to look like me—where is he?"

The guard shrugged. "He's gone…"

"We should be gone, too," Charlotte said.

She was right. More guards or the police could have been called and were already on their way. His other questions and answers would have to wait until he got Charlotte safely out of Serenity House.

Aaron agreed with her—with action. Keeping an eye on the guards to make sure no one followed them, he steered her through the lobby to the exit doors. A quick swipe of his badge had the doors sliding open, but then an alarm blared. The noise was louder even than the shots that she had fired, causing him to flinch and for his heart to slam into his ribs.

The doors stopped and began to close. Aaron gently pushed Charlotte through the narrowing gap. Then he turned sideways and tried to squeeze through behind her. The metal edges of the glass doors scraped against his hip and shoulder, threatening to crush him as the doors continued to close. But he made it through the narrow space just before it closed completely.

Alarms sounded outside, too. Aaron swiped his badge through the card reader in the gate, but the red light kept blinking. And the alarms kept blaring.

Charlotte squinted and grimaced—probably in more pain from the bruise on her head than in fear. She'd been almost too weak to stand up back in her room. The physical exertion might be too much for her. But before Aaron could reach for her, she lifted her gun toward the lock and fired at it—in sheer frustration and anger. Sparks ignited from the machine, glinting off the metal. "It won't open."

Not now. He couldn't even try another badge since

the reader caught fire. And there was no way he could get Charlotte over the gate—not with the men rushing through the lobby behind them.

He glanced through the fence, to where a car idled in the front lot. "Stand back!" he shouted at her, as the engine revved.

Tires screeched as the car headed right toward the gate. And them.

JANE LIFTED HER gun and aimed it at the windshield. It was already broken, the glass shattered. She couldn't get a clear target, only the vague shadow of a man behind the wheel. This shot might not be as nonlife-threatening as the other shots she had fired. But before she could squeeze the trigger, a hand closed over hers and shoved down the gun.

"Don't shoot!"

The car kept coming, right at them. She struggled to lift her arm, but her strength wasn't back yet. She couldn't overpower a man like this—one so strong he'd easily fought off two men. Timmer's arms closed around her, lifting her off her feet. Her legs flailed, but she didn't kick at him. He was already moving, carrying her away from the fence.

Metal crunched as the car careened through the gate, crumpling it and the fence around it. She screamed—more with frustration than fear. Would she ever be able to escape?

Then the man changed direction, carrying her toward the car instead of away from it. Timmer opened the passenger's side rear door and pushed her inside, onto the backseat. Had the nurse been right? Had Jane been a fool to trust a man she didn't know, or at least that she couldn't remember?

Before he could climb in beside her, the guards reached him—tugging him from the car as it backed away from the building. The gate tangled beneath it, sparks flying as the car dragged it across the asphalt.

"Stop!" she screamed at the driver. "Don't leave him!" Her mind couldn't recall more than how he looked naked, but her heart—which beat frantically with panic—remembered him. Had she loved him? And if she had, how could she have forgotten him?

And if the man behind the wheel was the partner of the other man, why wasn't he helping him? Instead he glanced into the rearview mirror and studied her. "Charlotte?"

It felt more familiar—more right—than it even had the first time that Timmer had called her that name. But was it hers?

She remembered the weapon clenched in her hand and lifted it again, training it at the back of the man's head, she told him again, "Stop!"

"Charlotte," he repeated with the same certainty she had heard from Timmer when she'd tried to strangle him.

She cared less about who she was than his safety right now, though. Ignoring the driver even while she kept her gun trained on him, she turned back to the fight going on inside the gate. The man didn't need her help this time. Hell, he wouldn't have last time if she hadn't pulled his weapon before he'd had the chance.

He had the guard's gun, but he used his feet and fists, knocking down the guards as easily as he had inside the building. Then he ran toward the car, jumping inside the door she'd left open for him.

"She's Charlotte," the driver told him, turning from behind the wheel to look at his backseat passengers.

"How the hell is she Charlotte looking like that—looking exactly like Princess Gabriella?"

"Get out of here!" Timmer ordered him, pointing toward the guards rushing toward them.

As the car backed away, a tall woman ran out of the building. It wasn't the nurse but another woman, one who shouted with an anger that was more intense than Mr. Centerenian's. Her shouts were clearly audible through the broken windows. Had every window of the car been shot out? When?

The woman yelled, "Don't let them get away!"

Jane shivered.

Timmer pulled the door shut and wrapped an arm around her shoulders. "Are you all right?"

"Not yet," she murmured. "Not until we're far away from this place."

But they didn't go far—just a few sharp turns on dark back roads and the car pulled up in front of a cottage. Headlights glinted off dark windows. The place looked abandoned.

"Where are we?" she asked. "Are we still on the grounds of that horrible place?" She shuddered at the thought. She wanted—she *needed*—to be much farther away.

"They'll be checking airports and train stations," Timmer replied as he opened the back door again and stepped onto the driveway, gravel crunched beneath his shoes. He held out his hand for her. "This'll give us some time…"

"Time for you to explain what you're up to this time, Charlotte," the driver said, his voice gruff with bitterness. He reached over the seat and caught her arm before she could slide out.

Her fingers were grasped in the other man's hand—

leaving her feeling again like that rope in a demented game of tug-of-war. And that rope was getting even more frayed as exhaustion overwhelmed her.

"You're not going anywhere until you tell me what I want to know," the driver said. With his free hand he dragged off a dark wig, revealing coarse-looking iron-gray hair.

The man was threatening despite or maybe because of the fact that he seemed vaguely familiar. She may have known him before but definitely not as intimately as she had known the younger man. And she had certainly never trusted this man.

It was nothing—*what she remembered*—so damn little that it made her laugh. She wasn't all that different from the baby she carried—starting out all over again—with no past.

At least no past that she could clearly recall...

"You think this is funny?" the man asked, a vein beginning to bulge in his forehead with frustration that she wasn't taking him seriously.

No. But now that she had started laughing, she couldn't stop. It was all so ridiculous—how could she have forgotten *everything?*

"What's so damn funny?" he demanded to know, his voice sharp with anger.

She gasped for breath and tears rolled down her face. But she couldn't stop.

"What's wrong with her?" the driver asked the other man.

"She doesn't remember anything, Trigger."

Like his roughly lined face, the name struck a chord with Jane. A very unpleasant chord that had her breath catching in her throat.

"What do you mean?" Trigger asked. "You don't even know what I was going to ask her."

"The only thing you should be asking her about is what happened in Paris or where she's been the past six months." Timmer's light blue eyes narrowed with suspicion. "Unless you're here for some other reason than breaking her out of that psychiatric hospital?"

Paris? Six months lost? Timmer had also mentioned some things earlier—about princesses and kings and announcements. Jane wanted to know about those things and so much more. But she didn't want to talk in front of this man—this guy named Trigger. She tugged on her arm, but he held tightly to her yet, refusing to release her.

"I—uh," he stammered, "there is some other information I need from Charlotte."

Timmer tugged on her other arm, trying to pull her free of the driver. "She's not Charlotte."

"I know she doesn't look exactly like her," Trigger said. "But her voice…"

Timmer chuckled. "The princess is so adept at learning languages that she picks up the dialects of the people she spends the most time with. So of course she picked up her American accent from Charlotte and sounds just like her."

So there was another woman out there that not only looked like her but sounded like her, too?

Trigger shook his head, obviously still unwilling to accept Timmer's explanations. "But the way she holds a gun…"

"Charlotte taught her how to shoot. She taught her how to defend herself."

So despite the certainty with which Timmer had said her name, he wasn't really sure who she was. Or at least he now appeared positive that she was the princess when earlier he'd seemed convinced she was Charlotte. Until Jane reclaimed her memory—and all of her memories—she had no idea which of these two women she actually was.

"Since they were that close," Trigger persisted, "maybe Charlotte talked to her about some of our old cases."

Timmer groaned in obvious frustration with the other man's stubbornness. "You yourself said that Charlotte kept everything to herself. You doubted the princess would know anything."

Jane dragged in a deep breath as her own frustration overwhelmed her. "I don't know *anything*. I don't even know who I am."

The guy studied her face intently. "Then it's possible she's Charlotte and that Charlotte had a nose job and that scar fixed…"

Jane wanted to reach a hand up to her nose and her cheek. But she couldn't move her hands. She was trapped, her arms bound as effectively as the restraints had tied her up and made her helpless.

But Jane wasn't helpless. While her memory was gone, her common sense was not. She moaned and sagged against the seat, faking a faint.

AARON'S HEART SLAMMED against his ribs as he watched her go limp. He reached inside the car and caught the woman up in his arms, tugging her free of Trigger's grasp. Careful to not hit her head against the roof, he lifted her through the door and carried her toward the house. She was light but she wasn't limp. Her body was still tense. With fear? Was she so frightened that she couldn't relax even in unconsciousness?

Her actions back at Serenity House hadn't been fearful. More fearless.

But maybe the fight she'd put up had exhausted her to the point of passing out. He needed to get her inside. He needed to get her away from Trigger.

The car headlamps illuminated the entrance to the tiny clapboard and fieldstone house. Aaron didn't bother searching for a hidden key to the front door, and he didn't waste time walking around to the back door that he'd unlocked earlier that evening. Instead he lifted her higher in his arms and kicked open the front door.

"I could've gotten that for you," Trigger said, as he hurried inside after them. He pulled a sheet from a couch and stood there, waiting for Aaron to lay her down.

Aaron didn't want the U.S. Marshal anywhere near her, so he held her yet in his arms. "Why did you really flag my passport?" he asked. "What was your real reason for wanting to find Charlotte?"

"You called *me*," Trigger reminded him. "You wanted *my* help to find her."

Because he'd thought that if she was in trouble—or hiding the princess from her controlling father—that she would have reached out to friends. It was only now that he realized she and Trigger may have been partners, but they had probably never been friends.

Not like he and Whit had once been friends. But that seemed like a lifetime ago now.

"I know why I called you," Aaron said. "But why did you agree to help find her? What information did you want from her?"

Instead of answering Aaron's question, Trigger asked one of his own. "You really don't think she's Charlotte?"

Aaron finally settled her onto the couch. The headlamps shining through the open door illuminated her flawlessly beautiful face. "Look at her. *Really* look at her. What do you think?"

"She's been missing for almost six months. She could have had plastic surgery," Trigger said, stubbornly clinging to that possibility.

She'd actually had the surgery long before she'd disappeared, but Aaron felt compelled to continue lying to the Marshal. "Is Charlotte the kind of woman who would ever get plastic surgery?"

"What I knew of Charlotte, no," Trigger admitted. "The woman had no vanity. She cared about nothing but keeping people safe. And because of that, she might have had it, so she could protect the princess."

Charlotte's former partner knew her better than he thought he had.

But then Marshal Herrema shook his head. "That would be extreme, though, even for Charlotte. But even if it's Princess Gabriella, she might know something. Maybe Charlotte talked about…"

"About what?" Aaron asked. "What do you want to know about?"

Trigger shrugged. "An old case."

"If it's old, why does it matter now?"

"The witness is missing."

"Just now?" Could that case have had something to do with what had happened in Paris? Had someone gone after Charlotte to find out where the witness was?

Trigger sighed. "The witness has actually been missing for a while, and it's important we find her."

If she'd been missing before Charlotte disappeared, wouldn't he have already contacted her? And if Charlotte hadn't told him then, she must have had her reasons for keeping the witness's location secret from her former partner.

"Charlotte left the Marshals a few years ago," Aaron recalled. "How would she know anything about where this witness is now?"

"They got close."

Like she and Princess Gabby had.

"If anyone knows where she is, Charlotte does," Trigger said.

Aaron gestured at the unconscious woman on the couch. "That's not Charlotte," he lied. At least he was pretty damn certain he was lying.

"But since that woman was her friend, Charlotte might have talked about her. Or maybe the princess overheard Charlotte talking to the witness…"

"It wouldn't matter if she had," Aaron said. "She has amnesia. She doesn't remember anything now."

"Not even you?"

He shook his head. "No. She may never get her memory back." That was another lie because he was determined for her to remember. Him.

"Amnesia is her excuse for forgetting," Aaron continued. "What's yours?"

"What?"

"We had a plan," he reminded the Marshal. "After we got her out, you were going to go to the police and have them get a warrant to seize Serenity House records to find out who the hell put her in that place."

Trigger stared at the sleeping woman for another minute, as if he was having an inner debate about whether or not she was Charlotte. Aaron recognized the look since he'd been having that debate within himself since he'd found her in Room 00. Finally Trigger shook his gray head, turned away and walked toward the open door. "I'll go to the county sheriff and see what I can find out," he agreed. "Do you want me to bring anything when I come back?"

He didn't want the Marshal to come back. "I have everything we need in the trunk." He followed the Marshal out to the rental car and groaned when he saw the fresh damage on it. "I'm definitely not getting my deposit back," he murmured as he got the box of food and clothes. Then he told the Marshal, "You've got my number. Call me as soon as you talk to the sheriff."

Trigger nodded and got back behind the wheel of the running car. When he drove off, he left the cottage and property in total darkness. Aaron stumbled his way to the open door and stepped into the blackness inside the home. As he did, a cold barrel pressed hard against his temple. Had the guards already tracked them down?

Maybe they should have followed Charlotte's instincts and gotten far away from Serenity House. He'd gotten her out, but he hadn't done a very damn good job of keeping her safe. He shifted the box to one arm, so he could nonchalantly reach for his gun.

"Don't move," a raspy voice warned him, "or I'll kill you."

Chapter Six

"You don't want to kill me," the man told her.

Timmer was right. She didn't want to kill him. But he was the only thing that stood, literally blocking the door, between her and freedom. And she suspected that she needed to leave before the other man returned.

What had he been saying about a case and a missing witness? And why had his mentioning those things had her heart beating heavy with dread and fear?

"I won't kill you," she promised, "as long as you do what I tell you. Hand over your gun and don't try to stop me from leaving."

"You can't leave," he said.

"Why did you go to the trouble of breaking me out of that place?" she asked. "Why take me out of one prison cell if you only intended to put me in another?" That was why she'd been determined to not get on that plane to only the devil knew where—the devil who claimed to be the father of her unborn child. She shuddered.

"This isn't a prison cell," he replied.

"Then let me leave."

"And go where?" he challenged her. "Do you have any idea where we are?"

"Too close to that horrible hospital." She shuddered again.

"Do you even know which state we're in?"

"We're in the U.S.?" The question slipped out, revealing too much of her ignorance. Hell, talking to him at all when she should have been running from him was showing her ignorance. She couldn't trust him—not when she couldn't remember who he was to her—besides that he was an old lover.

He nodded, his head moving against the barrel of the gun she held on him. She eased back a little, not wanting to hurt him. "We're in Michigan."

Michigan. She'd been in Michigan before. Hadn't she?

"And," he continued, "this place is a temporary shelter."

Despite her earlier threat, he moved. His eyes must have adjusted to the faint light as thick clouds moved away from a sliver of the moon. He set the box down on a table and rummaged inside it. If he'd been looking for a weapon, he would have pulled the gun from the waistband of his pants. Instead he pulled out a small box and a wad of paper, and he moved again—to the fireplace. The paper rustled then caught the flame from the match he struck. The paper ignited the logs that had been left in the hearth.

Warmth and light spilled from that wide brick hearth, tempting her to leave the bone-chilling cold of the open doorway and approach it. But then she'd be approaching him, too.

"We'll stay here," he said, "until we figure out our next move."

"Our next move should be getting out of this place," she said. They needed to leave before the older man returned or those guards from the hospital tracked them down.

"We have no vehicle," he pointed out.

She shouldn't have let the other man leave with the car, but she hadn't wanted to deal with him and his insistent questions, either. That was why she'd faked the faint. "I can walk."

"You're not strong enough," he said.

Pride lifted her chin. "I'm strong—"

"You just—" He stopped himself and laughed. "You didn't really faint. You staged that whole thing, so you could get the jump on me. I helped you escape Serenity House. Why won't you trust me?"

Serenity House? That was the name of the psychiatric hospital? How ironic when she'd felt anything but serene there.

"Because I don't know who you are," she reminded him.

"My name is Aaron Timmer."

She shrugged. "Your name means nothing to me." But that was a lie. *Aaron* felt right, like it fit him—like she had once fit him.

He sighed with obvious resignation. "You really don't remember anything."

"I need more than your name," she explained. "I need to know who you are. What kind of person can break in and out of a secure facility and steal an ID badge and fight off trained guards…?"

"A trained bodyguard," he replied.

"Bodyguard?" she asked, the title striking a chord within her. "For hire?"

"Yes, I'm a professional bodyguard. I used to have my own security business." He sighed again. "Well, with a partner, but that didn't work out. Now I protect only one person."

"Me?"

"No."

She smiled. "Good. Because if you were responsible for protecting me, you're not that great at your job."

He flinched as if she'd struck a nerve.

She nearly apologized, but then she didn't know the whole story. Didn't even know if what he was telling her was just a story and not the truth.

"If you're someone else's bodyguard, why are you here?" she asked. "Why did you come looking for *me?*"

AARON HAD ANSWERED her earlier questions because he wanted to jar her memory—wanted to say something that would have her remembering everything. So he'd been honest with her. But being honest now would gain nothing. She didn't know how he'd felt about her. Because she'd left the palace the morning after they'd made love, he hadn't even had time to figure out how he'd felt about her before she and the princess had disappeared.

"Why did you track me down?" she repeated her question. Then she drew in an audible breath and asked, "Or aren't I the woman you were looking for?"

"You're the woman I was looking for," Aaron assured her.

Her brow furrowed in skepticism. "I'm Princess Gabriella?"

"No," he said, correcting her. She was nothing like the princess, who he'd found to be rather timid despite having lived her life in the bright glare of the media spotlight. "You're Charlotte Green."

Her brow furrowed even more with confusion and skepticism. "You convinced the other man that I wasn't."

"I wasn't sure he can be trusted."

"I'm sure he can't," she said.

"You remember him?"

"I don't have to remember him to realize that he can't be trusted," she said. "I'm not sure I can trust you, either."

"I'm telling you the truth. You're Charlotte Green." He had no doubt. She may have forgotten who she was but she hadn't forgotten *what* she was. She wasn't just defending herself as she'd taught Princess Gabby; she was using her talent and experience to protect herself. She'd even used it to protect him back at Serenity House. "You're a bodyguard, too."

"I'm a bodyguard." She said it as if trying on the job title to see if it fit.

"Now," he said. "Before you went into private security, you were a U.S. Marshal."

"That's why that other man was talking about a case and a witness," she said. It was as if she was trying to fit together puzzle pieces to get a picture of her forgotten past.

He studied her face, looking for any flicker of recognition—to see if she remembered any of what he was telling her. "He thinks you know where she is."

"I don't know…" She lifted her free hand and rubbed her swollen temple as if her head was throbbing. "I don't remember…"

"That's okay," he assured her with a twinge of guilt for overwhelming her with information. It was obviously too much for her to process all at once. "He was talking about an old case. You may not know anything about that witness anymore."

"But the other guy—*Trigger*—" she uttered his nickname with such derision it was almost as if she did remember him "—said that the witness was a friend of mine."

"I haven't known you long," he admitted, "but it seems like you tend to become friends with the people you protect."

"Do you get close to the people you protect?" she asked.

He glanced back at the flames flickering in the hearth, and with a flash of pain he remembered another fire. "Sometimes too close and then it hurts too much when you lose them."

"Who's lost?"

He wouldn't talk about his old case with her. That wasn't her memory to recover, and it was one he wished he could forget. "Princess Gabriella."

"Is that who you were protecting?" she asked.

Aaron shook his head. "No, you're her bodyguard. Do you know what happened to her?"

She swayed as if her legs were trembling, as if she were about to pass out again. Or for real this time. Because she still tightly clutched the gun, he walked slowly and carefully toward her—trying to be non-threatening. But she didn't let him get close. Instead she moved around him to stand in front of the fireplace. She trembled yet, shivering.

Cold air blew through the open door, stirring sparks in the fire. So she stepped back from the hearth, as if afraid of getting burnt.

Aaron shut and locked the door, but because his kick had broken the jamb, he also moved a bureau in front of it to keep the wind from blowing it open again.

"Are you okay?" he asked, as he joined her by the

couch in front of the fireplace. "Is your memory coming back?"

She shook her head and grimaced. "No. It's almost like it's slipping farther away. If you're so sure I'm Charlotte and not the princess, then you're saying I had plastic surgery to look exactly like her? That's why you and that other man—that Marshal—didn't know for certain which one of us is which?"

Firelight flickered across her face, illuminating her perfect features—her breath-stealing beauty. "When you started protecting Princess Gabriella, you had plastic surgery to look like her. When I met you, you had already had it done—the two of you are pretty much identical." But only Charlotte had stolen his breath—not the princess.

"So identical that you couldn't tell us apart? What makes you so certain that you're right now?" she challenged him.

"I was wrong to doubt myself before," he said, self-disgust overwhelming him. "I should have known immediately that you were Charlotte."

"Why should you have known?" she asked.

He had to *tell* her. He just hoped she wouldn't laugh as she had at her old partner. Or worse yet deny that it had ever happened. "I should have known who you were right away because we were lovers."

LOVERS.

Those images—of his naked skin rippling over hard muscles—flashed through Charlotte's mind again. He wasn't lying to her. But maybe he didn't know the truth. "How can you be sure?" she asked.

He chuckled. "No one hit me on the head. I haven't lost my memory. We made love." He glanced down at her stomach, as if trying to gauge if the child she carried was his.

Was he the father? Another man claimed the baby was his. But she couldn't be any more certain that he was right than she could be sure of anything in this crazy situation.

"Why would Princess Gabriella's bodyguard have plastic surgery to look exactly like her?" she prodded him. This was one answer she knew but needed to draw him to the same conclusion she had.

"To protect her," he automatically replied, probably thinking she was stupid in addition to having amnesia.

"How?" she persisted. "By *fooling* someone into thinking that she was the princess even though she wasn't? By stepping in for the princess in the case of danger?"

He gave a slow nod, his blue eyes narrowing.

"Well, then," Jane said, bringing home her point, "when the bodyguard is pretending to be the princess, isn't the princess pretending to be the bodyguard?"

His jaw dropped open, as if he were appalled at the thought of being fooled into making love with the wrong woman. "No. I would have known. You're very different from the princess."

"You told the other guy that Charlotte taught the princess how to act like her."

"Just how to shoot and defend herself," he clarified, "but you're not Princess Gabby."

"How can you be so certain," she wondered, "when *I* don't know which woman I am?"

A muscle twitched in his jaw as if he was clenching it. "I wouldn't have gotten involved with a client."

"I thought you weren't the princess's bodyguard."

"I wasn't. I'm her father's bodyguard, so I wouldn't

have gotten involved with his daughter." His gaze dropped from hers as he made this claim.

She'd struggled to trust him before, but now she knew she shouldn't. "You're lying to me."

"Not lying—leaving something out."

Somehow she suspected she could relate—that she'd kept secrets of her own and had kept them so well that she couldn't even remember them now—when she so desperately needed to remember.

"What are you leaving out?"

"Something that happened before I met you." He uttered a ragged sigh. "Something that has nothing to do with you."

He sounded as if he believed that, but still she doubted him. He might not be aware of it, but she felt as though she had had something to do with it—something to do with whatever had his shoulders slumping even now with a heavy burden of guilt and regret. Guilt and regret overwhelmed her now. Her legs weakened and began to shake.

He reached for her, his hands on her arms steadying her. "Sit down," he advised, as he helped her settle onto the couch on which he'd laid her earlier. "You're probably starving. Let me get you something to eat."

"I don't need food," she said even as her stomach growled and the baby shifted inside her.

He headed back to the box and ripped open a plastic bag and then passed it to her. "It's just crackers. But there's soup in here, too. I can see if the stove works or heat it over the fire."

More out of reflex than hunger, she ate a couple of crackers. "This is fine," she assured him. "What I really need is my memory back. Since you didn't know for certain if I was Charlotte or the princess, you didn't know where *either* woman was."

"No," he said. "You've been missing for the past six months."

"I disappeared in Paris?"

"You remember?"

She shook her head. "You mentioned it in the car. It sounded ominous."

His jaw tensed again. "The hotel suite was trashed. There was evidence of gunshots. And blood. You must have been attacked."

She touched her swollen temple. "This isn't six months old."

"Do you have other scars or bruises?"

"Lots of them," she said. Either she'd been assaulted or tortured...maybe from someone trying to find out where the princess was. She had to be Charlotte. How would a princess, no matter how good her teacher, know how to shoot as she had? And the very thought of her being a princess was really utterly ridiculous...

He grimaced as if feeling the pain she must have felt when she'd gotten all those marks on her body. "You had some scars and bruises before you disappeared."

"I did?" She lifted her hand to her cheek, but the skin was smooth. It hadn't always been. She could almost remember running her fingertips over the ridge of a jagged scar.

He reached out and ran his fingertips along her cheekbone, as well. "You remember the scar..."

Her skin tingled from his fleeting touch. And she involuntarily leaned closer, wanting more—wanting to be closer to him. "I don't know if it's memory or instinct," she admitted. "Like with the gun, I didn't necessarily remember how to shoot—I just *knew*."

"That's how I know you're Charlotte. You can be sure of that, too," he said. "Princess Gabby has never even been in so much as a car accident. She would have no scars."

"We don't know that anymore," she said. "We don't know what happened to her." She could be dead, and that horrible thought overwhelmed Charlotte with grief. The princess must have been her friend. "How could I have failed to protect her?"

"You don't know that you failed her. You don't know that she's gone," he said, trying to offer her hope—which she feared might prove false. "Until the hotel in Paris called about the damaged suite, we thought that you two had run away."

She snorted derisively. "I must be at least thirty years old. I doubt we would have run away like teenagers." Then she remembered what Aaron had said when he'd first come into her room at the psychiatric hospital. "You thought I would be mad at you about some announcement the king had made…?"

He contorted his mouth as if biting the inside of his cheek—as if trying to grapple with what he'd done. Or what he'd allowed to be done. "The king is old-fashioned."

"He's a king—that's pretty archaic."

"To us Americans, yes," he agreed, "but in St. Pierre, he is the absolute authority. The ruler. He treats his daughter the same way he does his country. From the day she was born, she was betrothed to the prince of a neighboring island."

Anger flared inside her. "That is barbaric."

"I think she was resigned to marry Prince Demetrios," Aaron said. "But then the night of the ball…"

His pupils enlarged, darkening his pale blue eyes, as he remembered something.

The night they'd made love?

"What happened the night of the ball?" she asked.

"The king cancelled Gabriella's betrothal to Prince Demetrios."

"That's great—"

"And promised her to another," Aaron continued as if she hadn't spoken at all. "He changed her engagement to Prince Malamatos, whose country has more resources and wealth."

A curse spilled from Jane's lips—a curse she doubted a princess would know. "The king sounds like a selfish son of a bitch. Why would anyone work for him?"

"He's a powerful man who's used to getting what he wants."

"But his daughter disappeared before he could arrange her marriage," she said. "He must be furious."

"At first he was," Aaron admitted. "But then when the hotel notified us, he was devastated. He loves his daughter."

She snorted in derision of a man claiming to love someone he tried so hard to control. Jane's heart swelled with sympathy and concern for the princess. "But if Gabriella was alive, wouldn't you or her father have found her before now?"

"It took me six months to find you," he said with a heavy sigh of frustration.

"But you weren't looking for me," she said. "You were looking for the princess."

"The king and his other bodyguard—they're looking for the princess—I was always looking for you."

Her pulse stuttered and then raced. "Because we were lovers?"

"I know that blow you took gave you amnesia, but…"

"It bothers you to think that I forgot." She needed to tell him the truth—that one of the few memories she had was of him.

"And I haven't been able to get you—and that night—out of my mind." He reached out again, to touch her belly.

The baby shifted, kicking against his palm. If she believed the conversation between the guard and whoever he'd called, this baby wasn't Aaron's. She belonged to another man. She needed to tell him—needed to be honest with him about the little she did remember. But before she could open her mouth, his lips pressed against hers.

And whatever thoughts she'd had fled her mind. She couldn't think at all. She could only feel. Desire overwhelmed her. Her skin tingled and her pulse raced.

He deepened the kiss, parting her lips and sliding his tongue inside her mouth. He kissed her with all the passion she felt for him.

She moaned, and he echoed it with a low groan. Then his palms cupped her face, cradling the cheek she'd touched looking for a scar. And he pulled back.

"I'm sorry," he apologized, and his broad shoulders slumped as if he'd added to that load of guilt and regret he already carried. Or, actually, she had added to it. "I shouldn't have done that…"

"Why did you?" she wondered aloud. With a bruised face and ugly scrubs stretched taut over her big belly, she was hardly desirable.

Those broad shoulders lifted but then dropped again in a slight shrug. "I wanted you to remember me—to remember what we once were to each other."

Confession time had come. "I remember," she admitted, "that we were lovers."

"You remember me?"

"I remember making love with you." And after that kiss she wanted to do it again—wanted to cling to the one good memory she had of her life before waking up in that horrible hospital.

Desire heated his blue eyes. "I haven't been able to forget—not one single detail of that night. But you have amnesia—"

"That's all I remember. You—just you..." She pulled him back to her and kissed him desperately. He was the one connection to her past—to who she was. She needed him close—as close as a human being could get to another.

He kissed her, too—with his lips and his tongue and with a passion that matched hers.

Putting aside her weapon, she slid her hands over him—as she had in that vivid memory. In the dreamlike vision, he had worn a tuxedo. She'd undone his bow tie and all the studs on his pleated shirt. Now she had only to pull his scrub shirt over his head and push down his drawstring pants.

But he groaned and pulled back again. "We can't do this..."

"Why not?" she asked and then teased him. "Worried that I might get pregnant?" Or was he disgusted that she was? To find out if that was the case, she pulled off her shirt.

But the passion didn't leave his face. Instead his pale blue eyes softened with awe, and he reached out trembling hands, running his palms over her belly.

She needed to tell him that the child probably wasn't his. But before she could open her mouth, he was kissing her again. His hands moved from her stomach to her breasts. When his thumbs flicked over her nipples, she cried out with pleasure. Her desire for him was so intense that she lost all control—lost all sense of time and place as she had lost her past. He was that one link to who she was—her anchor in a storm of emotion and doubt. She needed him like she needed air.

She pushed him back onto the couch. Then she wriggled out of her pants and straddled him, taking him deep inside her. She cried out again, passion overwhelming her.

"Charlotte," he said with a deep groan. Muscles tensed in his shoulders and arms as he held her hips. He thrust gently, as if trying not to hurt her.

But she was beyond pain. Pleasure was all she felt in his arms, with him buried deep inside her. And finally he joined her in ecstasy, groaning gruffly as he filled her. She collapsed onto his chest, which heaved with pants for breath. But instead of relaxing like she had, his body tensed.

"Someone's here."

She tensed, too, as she heard gravel crunching beneath footsteps on the driveway. "It's probably that Marshal coming back."

"No. We have a signal he's supposed to give if it's him. Someone else is here."

"Maybe the owner of the cottage…" But she doubted it. They'd been found. And they might not even have time to get dressed and armed before the person, who rattled the door now, caught them.

Chapter Seven

Damn it. Damn him!

Aaron cursed himself for doing it again—for letting his emotions distract him. And his emotions for Charlotte were stronger than he'd ever had before. For anyone else. After helping her pull on her clothes, he pressed her down in front of the couch, even though the thin fabric and wooden frame would provide little protection from a barrage of bullets.

But he wouldn't give the intruder time to aim his gun. The minute the door opened he vaulted over the couch and tackled the dark figure, dragging him to the floor. He threw a punch, eliciting a grunt of pain. But the man swung back, striking Aaron in the jaw.

To block more blows, he locked his arms around the intruder's. Trying to break free of Aaron's hold, the guy bucked and rolled them across the floor toward the fire. The wood floor was hard beneath Aaron's bare back, scratching his skin. He'd only had time to pull on his pants before the stranger had broken the lock on the door. As they wrestled, Aaron's bare foot struck the hearth. Pain radiated up his leg, distracting him so that the man loosened his grip and swung his fist again.

In the light of the fire, Aaron recognized him. But

just as he said his name, "Whit," his former partner's dark eyes widened with shock before closing completely as he slumped forward—collapsing onto him.

Charlotte stood over the man, clenching the barrel of her gun in her hand. She'd struck Whit's head with the butt of the weapon, just as she had probably been struck when she'd lost her memory. "Who is he?"

"You don't recognize him?" Even if she had amnesia, Princess Gabriella probably would have. The young woman had seemed fascinated by her father's other bodyguard.

She studied the man's face before shaking her head. "No. Should I?"

"You've known him as long as you've known me," Aaron said, trying to prod her memory. But if making love hadn't brought it back…

"And how long is that?" she asked. Maybe the heat from the fire flushed her face or maybe she was embarrassed that she didn't remember how long she had known her lover.

"We met you just a couple of months before you and the princess disappeared," he replied. "His name is Whit Howell."

"And who is he?"

Aaron got up from the floor and stood over his old friend's unconscious body. "He is also one of the king's bodyguards."

"You work with him?"

He had sworn to himself that he never would again. But he had needed a real job—something more challenging than guarding white-collar secrets for corporations or vaults for banks. Choking on the self-disgust welling up in his throat, he just nodded.

"So we can trust him?" She dropped on her knees

beside Whit and felt for his pulse. Her breath shuddered out in a ragged sigh. "I didn't kill him."

"Good." Relief eased the pressure he hadn't even realized was squeezing his chest. No matter what he had become, Whit Howell had once been his friend. "But we really shouldn't trust him."

"Why not?"

Aaron shrugged. "It's kind of like your former partner—nothing I can prove—"

"If I could remember, I probably could prove that I can't trust that man," she said, glancing through the open door. "Your friend has a car out there. Grab his keys and let's get the hell out of here before the other guy comes back."

Aaron shook his head. "We can't leave yet." Maybe she was wrong about Trigger and the guy would come through with a subpoena for Serenity House's records. But he needed another answer right now and only one man could give him that. "I want to talk to Whit and find out how the hell he found me."

"If you two work together, didn't he know where you were going?"

"No. I made sure he didn't know," Aaron said. He had used a family emergency as his reason for leaving St. Pierre. Maybe Whit had checked out his story and discovered his lie. But how the hell had Whit tracked him down—not just to Michigan—but to this very cabin?

She glanced again out the open door. But darkness enveloped them in the impenetrable cocoon of night; morning was hours away yet. "We can take him with us and question him when he wakes up."

Aaron lifted Whit from the floor but just to drop his heavy body onto the couch. "I don't want him coming along with us. I don't want him to know where we're going." He already knew too much about Aaron's whereabouts.

She expelled an unsteady breath. "You *really* don't trust him."

"Not as far as I can throw him." He pointed toward the box. "There're some smelling salts in there. Can you find them?"

"Smelling salts?" She arched a golden-brown brow, as if offended. "You planned on me fainting?"

"You did," he retorted.

"Not for real."

The thought flitted unbidden into his head: What else had she faked? Amnesia? Desire? He shook off the idea; he didn't have time to deal with the consequences.

"There are some clothes in the box, too," he said. "You should probably change into something warmer." Spring nights were cold in Michigan, as a bitter gust blew through the open door.

She glanced down at the wrinkled scrubs and nodded. Then she lifted out the bundle of clothes. "Looks like some of these are yours."

"Yeah." Another cold gust blew through the open door, sending sparks shooting up the chimney. He caught the shirt and jeans she tossed at him.

"Here are the salts," she said, passing over a bottle. "I'll take these." She held on to a sweater and pants. "And change in another room."

"Why?" It wasn't like he hadn't already seen every inch of her. Again.

She pointed toward the man on the couch. "I didn't kill him, remember? He could come around even before you use those on him."

And Whit did. When a door to another room closed

behind her, the man shifted on the couch and groaned, struggling to regain consciousness. Aaron dragged on his jeans. He grabbed up the ID badges from Serenity House that he'd dropped on the floor in front of the couch when he'd torn off his clothes earlier. He might not need them again. But just in case he did...

As his head popped through the collar of the heavy knit shirt he pulled over his head, he came face-to-face with Whit. The guy's dark eyes were open and staring up at him. His brow furrowed with pain and confusion.

"Who hit me?" he asked, with another groan. "And what the hell did he hit me with?"

"Charlotte hit you with the butt of a gun," he replied matter-of-factly. After all, Whit wouldn't have followed him if he hadn't discovered he was chasing down a lead to her whereabouts.

"You found Charlotte?" Whit scrambled up from the couch and peered around the dimly lit room, as if looking for the female bodyguard. "And she's armed?" He slid his hand into his jacket, reaching for his own gun.

Aaron caught his arm. "What the hell's wrong with you?"

"What's wrong with you?" Whit asked. He pointed at the scratch on Aaron's forehead. "Did she do that? Did she shoot you?"

"It's nothing," he said, touching the mark on his head to remind himself. He'd forgotten all about the shard from the broken vase hitting him. "And she didn't do it. She isn't dangerous."

Whit uttered a bitter laugh. "There's no one more dangerous for you." He shook his head with disgust. "This is why you shouldn't have given me the slip back on St. Pierre. Family emergency—my ass."

"You were supposed to stay there and guard the

king," Aaron reminded him. As if he'd needed another reminder of why they were no longer business partners. "Who's protecting him? You didn't bring him with you?" He grimaced at the thought of the king in the line of fire. It was bad enough that Charlotte had been.

Whit shook his head. "He's still on St. Pierre, ensconced in the palace, with Zeke Rogers reinstated as head of his security in our absence."

"Zeke?" Aaron hadn't trusted the former mercenary and apparently neither had Charlotte since she'd recommended the king replace the man. "Is that wise?"

"With the guys we brought on as backup palace security, the king is safe," Whit assured him.

Were Aaron and Charlotte safe now that Whit knew where they were? Aaron asked the question that had been nagging at him since Charlotte had hit Whit over the head. "How did you find me?"

"Stanley Jessup."

Disappointment tugged at Aaron. Obviously the other man hadn't forgiven him. "He had promised me that he wouldn't tell you where I was."

It had been the most important of all the favors Aaron had requested of their former client.

"I forced it out of him," Whit defended the media mogul. The legendary businessman had never been forced into doing anything he hadn't wanted to—except for burying the ashes of his only child. "I told him you were playing white knight again, and that you were probably going to get yourself killed."

Even though Aaron had only gotten the scratch on his head and some bruises on his stomach, he couldn't deny that he had had some close calls. "None of that was Charlotte's fault. She's a victim in all this."

Whit shook his head. "No. Gabby is the real victim in all this. Did you find *her?*"

"No."

A muscle twitched in Whit's cheek, as if he'd tightly clenched his jaw. "Did Charlotte tell you what she did with her?"

Aaron hadn't been hit with anything other than that shard of glass or porcelain, but his head was beginning to ache. "What do you mean? What would Charlotte have done with Princess Gabriella? Do you think she's hidden her because of the king arranging another marriage for her?"

That muscle twitched in Whit's cheek again. "I thought so—at first," he admitted. "But even though Gabby might have been upset with her father, she loves him too much to make him worry this way. If she was all right, she would have contacted somebody by now."

"What makes you think Charlotte has anything to do with the princess not being able to contact anyone?" he said, wondering about Whit's suspicions. Was it Whit's cynicism talking or his own guilty conscience?

"She was the last one to see Gabby alive, so of course she had something to do with her disappearance. And I'm going to find out exactly what," Whit vowed, his dark eyes raging with anger and determination. "Where the hell is she?"

"She can't tell you anything," Aaron said, edging between Whit and the door which Charlotte had shut behind herself. Everyone wanted information from Charlotte. He wanted only Charlotte.

Whit was no longer the man who never gave in to—hell, even appeared to—have emotions. The anger bubbled over into pure rage. "She is damn well going to tell me what she did to Gabby!"

"She can't tell you anything!" Aaron shouted to get through to the stubborn man. He had never seen Whit so out of control. Maybe Charlotte had hit him too hard, like she had been hit too hard. "She doesn't remember."

Beneath the blond hair falling over his brow, furrows of confusion formed deep ridges. "Doesn't remember? What the hell are you talking about?"

"She has amnesia."

Whit stared incredulously at Aaron like he had just announced a spaceship landing on the island of St. Pierre. "What the hell—"

"She has a concussion," he explained. "She doesn't remember *anything.*"

Whit snorted. "That's damn convenient. What doesn't she remember?"

"Anything. She doesn't remember anything." But him. "She doesn't even know who she is—if she's Charlotte or Gabby."

"And you fell for that?" Whit asked with a grimace of disgust.

"Why would she lie about something like that?" he asked because he had wondered, as well.

"Because the woman has lied to you about *everything,*" Whit said. "Hell, she was lying to you before you even met her."

"What the hell are you talking about?" Aaron's stomach churned with a sick feeling of foreboding. "What has she lied to me about?"

That telltale muscle twitched in Whit's cheek. "Josie."

He fisted his hand, tempted to strike Whit again for even daring to mention the name of the woman who had died under their *protection.* "Josie? She didn't even know Josie Jessup."

"When Charlotte was with the U.S. Marshals, she staged Josie's death and relocated her," Whit said matter-of-factly, as if he was speaking the truth and not the wild fantasy that it had to be.

Aaron shook his head. "No. We were there—we both saw that house blow up."

"But we didn't see Josie in the house when it blew up," Whit pointed out. "Her body was never recovered."

"But her DNA…"

"Charlotte planted it and had a coroner identify the remains of a cadaver as Josie," Whit explained. "It was her last case before she discovered who her own father was. Then she realized she wouldn't ever have to work again if she played her cards right."

Aaron couldn't accept what Whit was saying. "Josie is dead."

"Nope," Whit corrected him. "She and Charlotte let you believe that."

"*You* let me believe that!" And of all the people who had known about Josie going into the witness relocation program, his best friend should have been the one to tell him the truth. *Then.* Not now…

Now it was too late—to undo the damage that had been done to their friendship—too late to restore the trust that Aaron had lost.

"When you saw how much he'd been suffering, you would have told Stanley Jessup," Whit said. "And no one could know where she was."

"Do you know?"

"Charlotte is the only one authorized to know her whereabouts," Whit replied. "Not even Charlotte's partner with the U.S. Marshals knows."

So Josie had to be the witness that Trigger had wanted to question Charlotte about—the one he claimed had gone missing. But how could he know that if he'd never known where she was?

"But I don't care about Josie," Whit said.

The admission surprised Aaron because he'd thought the other man had been as attracted to the American princess as he had been. Well, he'd thought that until Whit had talked him into leaving her momentarily unprotected. Now Aaron knew why he had—if he believed what the other man was telling him. Now. More than three years after the fact.

"I care about Gabby," Whit admitted. "I want to know what Charlotte did to her. Let me talk to her! Now!"

Aaron was afraid that talking wasn't all Whit intended to do to Charlotte. And Aaron hadn't found her only to lose her again.

But then had he ever really had her? Betrayal struck him like a fist in the gut. Did he have any idea who she actually was?

THIS MAN, THIS stranger who'd broken into the cottage—he knew Charlotte. He knew her better even than the man with whom she'd made love because Whit Howell knew all her secrets. All the secrets she hadn't really wanted to remember.

Aaron had been in love with another woman—so in love with her that he'd turned on his best friend. He'd given up his business. His life. He had been so in love with Josie Jessup that he would have never been able to fall for another woman.

No matter what feelings Charlotte might have had for him, they would never be returned. And now she heard the suspicion in his voice as he questioned his emotional friend.

"Why do you think Charlotte would hurt the princess? They were so close. She had surgery to look like her, to protect her!"

Charlotte closed her eyes, and the image was there—of her face. But it wasn't her face at all. The golden brown eyes were wide and full of innocence and naïveté. And the skin was so smooth, completely free of lines of old scars or stress. Princess Gabriella St. Pierre had spent her life so sheltered that she'd been completely unaware of what the world was really like.

It would have been so easy to take advantage of that youth and innocence. So easy to dupe her...

"Charlotte Green had surgery, so she could take over Princess Gabriella's life and her inheritance."

Aaron's derisive snort permeated the door behind which Charlotte stood. "That might have worked if everyone wasn't aware that she'd had that surgery. Everyone in the king's inner circle—his business associates, lawyers and financial advisors—knows Princess Gabriella has a doppelganger."

"Charlotte isn't just a doppelganger."

"No," Aaron agreed. "She's her bodyguard and her friend."

"She's her *sister*."

"No."

Charlotte silently echoed that denial. Sisters grew up together or were at least aware of each other's existence. Charlotte hadn't been until her mom had finally conned the wrong person and wound up dead, leaving behind documents that Charlotte had never seen before, documents that had proved that her mother's outrageous lies had actually been the truth.

"Why do you think they looked so much alike?" Whit asked.

"The surgery—"

"Hadn't changed her height or build or coloring," Whit pointed out. "Even before the surgery they'd looked eerily similar."

"How do *you* know?" Aaron asked and then bitterly answered his own question, "Oh, that's right, you met her before…when you helped her stage Josie's *death*."

Jealousy kicked Charlotte in the stomach just as the baby did. Why had she given in to her attraction to him even though she had known that he had already given his heart to another? She patted her belly soothingly.

Apologetically…

"She's good at staging murder scenes," Whit said.

"Like Paris?"

"Maybe that wasn't staged," Whit said. "Maybe that was a real murder scene. Maybe she killed Gabby."

"I don't think—"

"No, man, you don't!" Whit accused him. "You *feel*. And you let those feelings cloud your judgment. That's why you couldn't know about Josie."

"Why couldn't I know about *Charlotte?*" he asked, his voice gruff with anger. "Why didn't you tell me that she's the king's daughter, too?"

"Because King St. Pierre didn't want anyone to know."

Charlotte flinched, feeling rejected all over again. Her father hadn't wanted his dirty little secret to come out. But he'd been happy to use her to protect the daughter he had wanted. The one he had loved.

"And that's why she did this," Whit explained. "With his legitimate heir dead, he'll be forced to acknowledge his illegitimate one—if he wants to continue his reign in St. Pierre."

"Charlotte wouldn't do something like that," Aaron protested, but his argument had weakened, his voice lower now with doubt.

She had to nearly press her ear against the wood to hear him.

"You don't know Charlotte Green at all," Whit said, almost gently. "You have no idea what she's capable of…"

But Charlotte finally did—as all of her memories came rushing back over her. They struck her like blows. And as the pain overwhelmed her, she wanted to strike back.

FISTS CLENCHED AT his sides, Aaron struggled for control. He wouldn't hit Whit—despite his gut-wrenching need to pummel the other man until he took back every last word he'd uttered.

"You have no proof to back up all these wild accusations." His head reeled from them, making him wonder if he had been hit harder than a graze. "Why should I believe you?"

"Because I always had your back," Whit said. "Because we were closer than friends—we were like brothers."

"Until Josie…" Losing her had cost them their friendship. But then they hadn't really lost her.

"There was nothing between me and her, you know," Whit said.

Aaron had thought there'd been, and he'd resented Whit for acting on the attraction Aaron had struggled to ignore. Because he'd wanted to be professional, had wanted to keep her safe. And all these years he'd thought he'd failed. "It doesn't matter now."

Because he realized those feelings for Josie hadn't been real. He'd liked her, had admired her beauty and brains, but he hadn't loved her. He'd only loved one woman, but now that might have been a lie, too.

If he were to believe Whit...

"What you're saying is wrong," Aaron pointed out. "None of it makes sense."

"Greed always makes sense," Whit insisted, his words an unwitting reminder of how much money had mattered to him. His background was completely opposite Aaron's; Whit had grown up poor with a single dad who'd struggled to support them. Whit had been denied all the things he'd wanted. Had he gotten sick of going without all the things that money could buy—all the things he'd always considered so important?

"But if she'd intended to pull the switch, why had she talked the king into hiring us?" Aaron wondered.

"Maybe the king's head of security had been on to her," Whit suggested. "Maybe she thought we would be easier to dupe than the guard who'd known Gabriella her whole life."

At Serenity House, Aaron had had his doubts about her identity. And she and the princess had disappeared just a couple of months after he and Whit had been hired. "I can't believe this..."

"Let's ask her," Whit suggested. "Get her out here to explain herself."

She wouldn't be able to explain what she couldn't remember. But was Whit right? Had her claim of amnesia just been a trick? Was it all a trick? His legs didn't feel quite steady as he walked across the room to that closed door. "Charlotte?"

She didn't reply. She had probably heard every word of their conversation—why hadn't she come out earlier to explain herself? He reached for the knob, but it wouldn't turn. She'd locked him out. Like he had the front door, he kicked the door until it broke free of the jamb.

Cold air, flowing through an open window, hit him in the face like a shotgun blast.

"She's gone?" Whit asked, leaning against the broken jamb behind Aaron.

He shut his eyes as dread pummeled him. "Tell me you didn't leave the keys in the car."

Whit cursed profusely. They both turned toward the front door—just in time to see the flash of a gun as it fired directly at them.

He'd been such a fool—such a damn fool to fall for her lies. To fall for her. And now he was about to become a dead fool…

Chapter Eight

As he had just minutes ago, Aaron knocked Whit to the ground again. Bullets flew over their heads and filled the room. Stuffing burst from the holes in the couch and wood splintered—in the furniture and the walls behind them. And the sound was deafening, rattling the windows and shaking the pictures off the walls.

It wasn't a handgun firing at them—more likely a machine gun or some other automatic rifle. Even if they could get off a shot, they were outgunned.

"We have to get the hell out of here!" Aaron said. When he'd first found the cabin, he had scoped it out and knew all the exits. He dragged Whit across the floor with him, toward the back. It was the one he'd left unlocked earlier. But instead of reaching up to turn the knob, he just kicked it open as he had the others.

"She took my car, man," Whit reminded him, as they rolled across the back porch and tumbled down the steps.

Aaron kept low to the ground as they edged around the corner of the cottage. How long before the shooter stormed inside and discovered them gone? Minutes? Seconds? "And your gun?"

"I have my gun on me." It glinted in that sliver of

moon. He had it drawn, clutching it tightly in his hand. "She had her own. She hit me with it," Whit reminded him.

"That's not her gun shooting at us." Where was Charlotte? They hadn't heard the car start; she may not have driven off before the gunman arrived. She could have been somewhere out there—in the line of fire? Or kidnapped again. "We have to make sure she's okay."

"She's okay," a female voice whispered. "This way…"

Aaron turned to follow the shadow moving toward the trees, but Whit caught his arm.

"Don't trust her," he warned, lifting his gun so that the barrel pointed toward her.

Aaron knocked the gun down. "She's not the one shooting at us."

That person had moved to the back of the building. More shots rang out, hitting the ground near them.

They ran toward the woods. Aaron easily caught up to Charlotte. She wasn't as strong as she wanted to be, and her gait was unsteady. He caught her around the waist, almost carrying her through the small thicket of brush.

"I parked the car over here," she said.

It idled in the dark, its lights shut off. The engine was quiet. No wonder Aaron hadn't heard it drive up or drive away.

"You stole my car," Whit accused as he opened the driver's door and slid in behind the wheel.

As she scooted across the backseat in front of Aaron, she nodded. "I took it. But when I saw the other car driving toward the cottage, I came back." She turned to face Aaron, her gaze steady, as if she was trying to tell him something else. "I came back…"

Before she could explain herself, the back window exploded behind her. Aaron pushed her head down below the seat.

Whit slammed the car into Drive and pressed hard on the accelerator. Gravel sprayed from under the wheels as the car fishtailed, nearly careening into the trees surrounding it.

Aaron checked Charlotte. Shards of glass caught in her hair, cutting his fingers as he brushed them out. "Are you all right?"

"Do you care?" she asked, and she drew back, settling into the corner and probably for more than protection. Obviously she'd heard quite a bit of his discussion with Whit before she'd climbed out the window and stolen the only means of escape.

But she came back, he reminded himself. And somehow he suspected she meant more than physically.

"What the hell is this road?" Whit grumbled as the car bounced over deep ruts.

As well as the cabin, Aaron had scoped out the area surrounding it before he and Trigger had gained access to Serenity House. "It's the public access road to a lake."

"A lake?" Whit repeated. "So if I keep going we're going to hit water?"

And the road was unlit, the surrounding woods dark, blocking out that faint sliver of moon. They might not even see the lake before it was too late and the car was going under.

"Turn around," Charlotte advised.

But bright lights came up fast behind them—blinding in the rearview mirror.

"Get down," Aaron said, as he pulled Charlotte onto the floorboards behind the front seats. He covered her with his body, protecting her from flying glass and gunfire.

But if they were forced off the road into the lake, he wasn't sure he would be able to save her then. He wasn't sure he would be able to save himself in dark, cold water.

But hell, he already felt as though he was drowning—going under from all the information Whit had given him—from all the secrets his old partner had revealed. Aaron was already drowning in emotion, so water couldn't hurt him much more.

SHE HAD ALREADY hurt him enough—with all the secrets she'd kept from him. She couldn't accept this, too—his using his own body to protect hers. But maybe he wasn't really protecting her—maybe he was protecting the child he thought was his.

And there was one more secret she'd kept from him. "I'm sorry," she murmured, turning her face into his neck as he crouched over her.

His heart thumped fast and hard in his chest; she felt each beat of it against her back—beating in rhythm with hers. They would have been perfect for each other—if he hadn't already loved another woman.

But Charlotte was used to that—used to being rejected for someone sweeter and prettier—someone more uncomplicated and open. Her own father had rejected her in favor of her sister, choosing Gabriella as his heir even though Charlotte was his firstborn.

She covered the rounded swell of her belly. She didn't care who the father of her child was; she wouldn't reject her. Charlotte would never deem a baby unworthy of her love.

But Aaron probably would—were he to learn the

truth. She needed to tell him—needed to tell him *everything*. Because she remembered…

But she couldn't talk into his neck as they huddled in the backseat. She had to wait until they got to safety. If that was even possible…

"You have to do something," Aaron ordered his former friend. "If we go in that water, we'll be sitting ducks. He'll just wait until we surface to shoot us dead."

"You don't think I know that?" Whit snapped, his voice gruff with frustration.

"We're braced back here," Aaron said. "Put on your seat belt and then slam on the damn brakes. Hard."

"He'll rear-end us," Whit said.

"Yeah," Aaron agreed. "And maybe he'll knock himself right through the windshield or at least the hell out."

Charlotte nodded her approval of the plan. They were safer on land than in the water—had more options for escape.

But then the car screeched to a stop, and the other car struck them with a sickening crunch of metal. Despite Aaron holding her tight, she shifted against the seats and her shoulder jammed into the console.

"Are you okay?" Aaron asked.

She managed only a nod.

Then Whit shoved the car into Reverse and stomped on the accelerator. Bumper ground against bumper, as the pursued became the pursuers.

Aaron rose up, and his gun glinted in the headlamps of the other car. But instead of becoming a target again, he took aim and fired. Again and again.

If he didn't hit his target, he would become one. And the driver of the other car had a clear shot at him. Charlotte reached up, trying to pull him down—trying to protect him as he had protected her.

The metal crunched against metal again. Rubber burned, enveloping the cars and woods in a thick, acrid smoke. Charlotte blinked furiously against the sting, fighting off the threat of tears so that she could see—so that she could make sure Aaron was all right.

But there was another crash that flung Aaron's body into the back of the front seat. He grunted and struggled for the grip on his gun. But it flew into the front, leaving him unarmed and vulnerable.

Charlotte pulled her weapon from the back of her jeans, but by the time she surged up—it was too late. There was nothing she could do...

"Is HE REALLY gone?" Whit asked, as he stood over Aaron's body. Instead of gazing down at his friend, he stared off down the road in the direction the other vehicle had disappeared.

Aaron scrambled to his feet. He'd had to crawl out of the crumpled rear door of the backseat he'd shared with Charlotte. The trunk was totally crushed, and the quarter panels had buckled. "For now."

"Do you think you hit him?" Whit asked.

Aaron shook his head. "If I did, it wasn't fatal or even painful enough to stop him."

"It got him to leave though," Whit remarked.

"He'll be back." Every time the mysterious gunman had fired at Aaron, the man had come back for another round.

Whit moved back toward the open driver's door. "Then we should get the hell out of here."

Aaron wanted to make sure Charlotte was okay first. He reached back and helped her out of the twisted metal. "Are you all right?"

He found himself reaching out automatically to her

belly, placing his hands on her to check her baby as if he had the right. As if the baby was his...

Was it?

They'd used protection that night—and they had only been together just that one night. Until tonight...

And letting her distract him had nearly taken all their lives. The baby moved beneath his palms, kicking against her belly.

"I'm fine," she said. "But Whit's right. We need to get out of here before he comes back."

"We're going to need time to find a safe place," Aaron said. He couldn't risk her and her unborn child getting into the line of fire again.

"Got it," Whit said.

Doubt knotted Aaron's stomach muscles. Over three years ago he had lost his trust of this man. And learning that Whit had lied to him hadn't exactly worked to regain that trust. "You just got here." Hadn't he? "How do you already know of a safe place to stay?"

"Stanley Jessup."

"He found you a place?" All he'd given Aaron was the name of the hospital where Princess Gabby might have been committed. Okay, he'd given him a hell of a lot.

"His place."

"Stanley Jessup has a place here?"

Whit nodded. "He rented something. He's here. Guess he wanted to see for himself if this story was as big as that freelance reporter claimed it would be."

It was a hell of a lot bigger, and Aaron didn't even know the half of it. The woman who did was, of course, keeping quiet. Keeping her secrets...

So many damn secrets...

And he had so many questions. He kept them to himself during the bumpy and rigorous ride in the damaged car to the cottage Stanley Jessup had rented. It was nothing like the cabin Aaron had found in the woods near Serenity House.

The contemporary tower of metal and glass sat on a dune overlooking Lake Michigan. Waves rushed to the dark shore below, breaking apart on the rocks. While Whit had gone inside the house, Charlotte stood on the overlook deck, her arms propped on the railing.

Aaron joined her on that deck that overlooked the beach far below. But he kept a careful distance from her. "Don't you have anything to say?" he wondered out loud.

Like sorry?

Charlotte shrugged. "I've been waiting for the inquisition. It sounded like your friend has a lot of questions for me."

"More like a lot of accusations." He glanced toward the house, where a shadow moved behind one of the walls of glass. "Is that why you ran?"

Or was it because she'd gotten caught in a web of her own lies?

"Does it matter why I left?" she asked. "I came back…" Her tone was just as distant as it had been before.

"It matters to me," he said. Why she'd left and why she'd returned…

Even knowing how much she'd lied to him, she mattered to him. Self-disgust over what a lovesick fool he was turned his stomach.

"I was overwhelmed," she said. "It all came back. All my memories."

"Had they ever really been gone?"

She sucked in a breath, as if offended that he wouldn't

trust her. Given what he'd learned, how the hell could he trust her? No matter what she told him now...

"I didn't remember anything," she insisted. "But you..."

His heart—his stupid, traitorous heart—clenched in his chest. "I can't believe you," he said. "I can't believe anything you tell me now."

"But you can believe *him?*" she asked. "Hasn't he lied to you, too?"

He found himself defending his old friend. "Because you made him."

"Does anyone make Whit Howell do something he doesn't want to do?" she asked with a bitter chuckle.

No. But she didn't need the confirmation. She already knew.

"So you do remember everything now?" he asked.

"No," she replied with a shaky sigh of frustration. "There are still holes in my memory."

"Paris?" They needed to know what had happened there, if they were ever to learn Princess Gabriella's fate.

"I remember someone bursting into the suite, guns blazing. I remember fighting for my life. And then I woke up in that damn hospital." She touched her stomach. "Pregnant..."

That was a hell of a hole. How many months had she lost?

He drew in a breath, bracing himself for the answer before he even asked the question. "Do you remember who the father of your baby is?"

Her reply was a flat, unemotional "No." As if it didn't matter to her.

And it mattered like hell to Aaron. "So it might not be mine?"

She shook her head. "She's probably not."

He had known about the child for less than twenty-four hours but losing her—losing the possibility that she was his—hurt like hell. The loss twisted something inside Aaron, tied his emotions up in a tight knot.

"When Mr. Centerenian, that guard, called whoever the hell his boss is, he referred to the person as the father," she explained.

That breath he'd drawn in to brace himself stuck in his lungs, hurting his chest. "So you knew that I wasn't the father before I broke you out of Serenity House? Before we…" He couldn't call it making love—not now that he had confirmation that only his feelings had been involved.

"I was confused and scared. I had no idea what was going on. I didn't even know who I was. You were the only one I recognized, making love with you was the only thing I remembered."

She turned toward him and closed the distance between them. Wrapping her arms around him, she clung to him as if she cared—as if his feelings might not have been all one-sided. "I needed you…"

Aaron released the breath he'd held, but the pressure in his chest didn't ease. And the rest of his body tensed with attraction to her. No matter how many secrets she'd kept from him, no matter how many lies she'd told him—he still wanted her.

But he resisted the urge to wrap his arms around her and hold her close. Because he couldn't think with desire overwhelming him. He couldn't be objective when his emotions got involved; Whit had been right about that. *Damn him!*

So Aaron caught her shoulders in his hands and eased her away from him. "But now you have your memory back," he reminded her. "You don't really need me anymore."

He suspected Charlotte Green had never needed anyone. She was tough and independent. And those very traits that had drawn him to her were what would keep them apart.

"I still don't know who committed me to that horrible hospital."

That same person was the father of her child. "You have no idea who it could be?"

She had been in the princess's world longer than he had. She would know all the king's enemies. Not that he couldn't think of a few after the king's announcement at the ball the night before the princess and her bodyguard had left for Paris. But had the person who'd committed Charlotte to Serenity House realized she was Charlotte or had he mistaken her for Princess Gabriella?

She shook her head. "All I know for certain is that it wasn't me. I don't have some master plan to take my sister's place as princess of St. Pierre. I don't want that kind of life."

"You don't want a life of wealth and privilege?" he asked skeptically. "You just wanted her face?"

She skimmed her fingertips across her cheek that used to be marred with that horrific scar.

Aaron had only seen that one photograph of her face before the surgery, but the scar had haunted him, reminding him of the pain she must have endured when the injury had been inflicted. That snapshot had been of her and her aunt, their arms around each other—both looking, as Whit had said, eerily similar to Princess Gabriella, even before the surgery.

She tapped her cheek. "I did this to protect her—to keep her safe. I wouldn't have done anything to hurt

Gabby. Not like her father continuously hurt and betrayed her."

"*Her* father? But the king is your father, too."

She shook her head. "He's my employer. Not my father. And if not for Gabby, he wouldn't even be that. I wanted to protect her."

Maybe Whit was right again. Maybe Charlotte had hidden Gabby from the king—to thwart his plans to marry off the young princess. He studied her face, looking for any sign that she might be lying when he asked, "Where is she?"

She shook her head. "I don't know..."

Aaron shouldn't believe her—given how easily and often she'd lied and kept information from him in their brief past. But he wanted to believe her. He needed proof to do that. "I'll go back to Serenity House."

He had almost gotten into the administrator's records once. With more time, he could break into the system. Or maybe there was another way he could find out. He pulled his cell from his pocket and checked the call log. He hadn't missed any, though—not even during the shoot-out. "Trigger was going to try to get a warrant for their records. I'll see what he found out—"

Charlotte knocked the phone from his hand. The cell flew over the railing and dropped far to the beach below, breaking apart on the rocks.

Staring down at the pieces of metal and plastic glinting in the faint light of that crescent moon, he murmured, "What the hell—"

"Don't you get it?" she asked with impatience. "He can't be trusted."

"You remember him?"

"I remember that Trigger is actually short for Trigger *Happy*. He's a loose cannon. And there's another reason I didn't tell him where Josie is," she said. "He can be bought and the people looking for her have deep pockets."

He gasped. "She's still in danger?"

She turned away, looking out at the waves rushing toward the shore. "Too many people now know she's still alive."

He glanced toward the house but no lights had come on inside. Whit must not have woken Stanley Jessup yet. "So we can tell her dad the truth?"

"No," she said. "You shouldn't have been told, either. Every person that learns the truth puts her in more danger."

Aaron nodded.

He didn't like that he'd been lied to—that people thought he'd failed to protect his client. But if lying to him had kept her safe, he would make peace with the fact.

"Do you think that could have been Trigger shooting at us tonight?" he asked. It would explain why he hadn't called; why he hadn't come back...

She nodded, and her tangle of golden hair fell across her face. "If Mr. Centerenian hadn't found us, it could have been Trigger. He's one of the few who knew where we were."

"The only one who wasn't there when the shooting started," Aaron pointed out.

"But how did Whit know where we were?" she asked.

"Stanley Jessup told him," he reminded her.

"But he knew *exactly* where we were," she pointed out. "He knew we'd already broken out of Serenity House and broken into that very cabin to hide out. How did he know that?"

Aaron had wondered that himself and had fully intended to find out how—but then the shooting had started. "You think that Whit could be working with Trigger?"

"Or someone else he's had following you," she suggested, "maybe from the minute you left St. Pierre."

"But they shot at him, too."

"But he didn't get hit, did he?"

"You're saying I shouldn't trust the man I've known for so long." When sometimes he felt like he'd only known her ten minutes.

"Do you trust him?"

"Damn it…" His curse was his admission. He couldn't trust Whit. When she'd staged Josie's death, Charlotte hadn't known Aaron. But Whit had—he'd known how much it'd hurt him—how much it had hurt him to think he'd failed her. But he'd let him suffer anyways.

Whit was not really his friend.

"I should contact the authorities myself then," he said since he couldn't trust that the U.S. Marshal had.

"Serenity House might be the biggest employer around here. Someone at the sheriff's office could tip them off," she pointed out. "Then they'd have time to destroy the records."

She was smart, since Dr. Platt had insinuated as much when he'd been listening to her conversation with the private guard. He needed to accept that he could trust no one. "I'll go to Serenity House alone."

"No," she said. "I'm going with you."

"We barely got you out of that place," he reminded her. "We can't risk taking you back there."

"I know who I am now," she said. "I know how to take care of myself."

Even when she hadn't known who she was, she'd still known how to defend herself. And him.

"What about your baby?" he asked. Her baby. Not his. Why did it hurt so much to lose what he'd never really had? What he hadn't even realized he'd wanted? "Don't you want to take care of him?"

"Her," she corrected him—almost automatically. Every time she'd talked about the baby, she'd referred to her as a girl.

"You had an ultrasound," he realized. "You know what you're having?"

"If I had an ultrasound, I don't remember it," she said. "But I know…" She was already connected to her child.

"Then you know you have to stay here—where she will be safe." He didn't wait for her agreement. He didn't care what she said. She damn well wasn't going back to Serenity House with him.

Hoping that Whit had left the keys in his car again, Aaron headed toward the driveway. That sliver of moon led him toward the banged-up vehicle. It had a sticker on the crumpled rear bumper that identified it as being from the same rental company as Aaron's car. Whit wasn't going to get back his security deposit, either. With the rear quarter panels nearly pushed into the tires, it was a wonder that the thing was drivable at all.

But it had to make another trip. Aaron needed to discover the truth about how Charlotte had wound up in Serenity House. And he figured he was only going to trust it was true if he learned it for himself instead of trusting what someone—anyone—told him.

Charlotte had raised more doubt in his mind. About her. But mostly about Whit.

Could he trust what his former business partner had

claimed? And how had the man found him at the abandoned cabin tucked away in the woods?

Sure, he'd been with him when the shots had been fired. But that didn't mean he didn't have an accomplice—either the Marshal or some mercenary he'd hired. Had he wanted to kill Aaron and take Charlotte for ransom since he was one of the few who knew she was really royalty?

Had Whit known where to find them because he was the one who'd put her in Serenity House?

Aaron opened the door and the dome light glinted off the keys hanging from the ignition. After what had happened at the cabin, Whit really should have been more careful. Aaron slid behind the wheel and reached for the keys. But he didn't turn them. Because the barrel of a gun pressed against his temple.

He really should have been more careful.

Chapter Nine

In the rearview mirror, Aaron met Whit's gaze. "This is the second damn time that someone I thought I could trust pressed a gun to my head and threatened to kill me."

"I haven't threatened you."

Aaron pointed toward his head. "Guess it's kind of implied by the gun to my temple."

Whit pulled it away. "I thought you were her. I figured she'd give you the slip on the beach and try to steal the car again."

"Sure, she stole it. But she came back," Aaron reminded him.

"Probably to make sure we didn't get away from the guys she hired to kill us."

Aaron snorted. "She speaks highly of you, too."

"So she's talking now?" Whit scoffed. "Passing all the blame off on me?"

Aaron turned around to face his old partner. "She doesn't know who's to blame."

Whit snorted now. "Yeah, right."

"You didn't see her in Serenity House," Aaron said, flinching as he remembered how scared and confused she'd been. That was why he'd momentarily mistaken her for Princess Gabriella. "She was tied down to a bed. She had been beaten up and bruised. She didn't do that to herself."

"So who did it?"

Possibly Whit. He knew, as few people did, that Charlotte Green was a royal heir. "I'm going back to Serenity House to find out."

"You're just going to walk inside and politely ask them for the princess's records?" Whit scoffed. "At least I'm assuming they thought she was the princess since that's the tip the freelance reporter passed on to Stanley Jessup."

"How did the reporter get that tip?" Aaron hadn't bothered asking Jessup who his source was because the media mogul was a die-hard newsman and fanatic defendant of the First Amendment. He would never reveal a source.

"Someone on staff at Serenity House tipped off the young reporter," Whit explained. "Do you want me to wake up Stanley and get the reporter's contact information? He's some young kid fresh out of community college, but he's got great investigative skills. He's been following you around since you got here."

The kid was very good because Aaron usually figured out when he was being tailed. But maybe three years of being bored out of his mind in corporate security had dulled his instincts. "So that's how you knew where I was tonight?"

Whit nodded. "What? Did you think I planted a GPS chip in you like a dog?"

Aaron chuckled.

"I thought about it," Whit teased, reminding Aaron of the friend he had once trusted with his life. "But I thought you'd notice. And you probably wouldn't believe that you were abducted by aliens, and they implanted it."

Aaron snorted with derision. "I'm not that big a fool."

"You are if you think you're going to just waltz right back in there." Whit crawled over the console and dropped into the passenger seat. "I checked that place out. It's got higher security than most federal penitentiaries."

"That's why whoever kidnapped Charlotte put her in that place."

Whit stared at him with respect. "So how'd you get her out?"

Aaron pulled one of the ID badges from his pocket, grateful now that he'd grabbed them from the cabin. He suspected they hadn't been deactivated—just that during their escape someone had sounded an alarm that sealed all the doors and gates.

"I used this to get out, and I'll use it to get back in. It's like a key that'll let me through all the locked doors and gates." He dug deeper into his pocket. "I should have a couple more of these." He'd taken three.

"We only need one more," Whit said, holding out his hand—palm up, "for me."

Aaron's pocket was empty. "I must have lost them back at the cabin…"

"When we were getting shot at," Whit finished for him. "It's okay. Instead of splitting up and having me play the diversion tactic, we'll have to stick together at the hospital."

He was tempted. But he'd be a fool to trust anyone again. "Like I told Charlotte, it'll be better if I just go in alone."

"And she agreed to that?" Whit asked skeptically.

Aaron nodded. "She knows it's not safe for her to go back there."

"It isn't safe for you, either," Whit pointed out. "I should be the one to go back in alone. Let me do this…"

Aaron shook his head. "No."

Whit uttered a ragged sigh of resignation. "You still don't trust me."

"Right now I don't know who to trust," he replied, "not after years of being lied to."

The sigh became a groan. "God, man, I would have told you the truth if I could have. But you wouldn't have been able to watch Stanley Jessup suffer like he had and not tell him that his daughter wasn't dead. And the people after her needed to see him suffer to believe she was really gone. Don't you get that?"

Anger and resentment overwhelmed Aaron. "I get that you didn't trust me to do my job—to protect our client, and you let me suffer these past three years thinking that I'd failed."

"It wasn't like that…"

"It was exactly like that," Aaron retorted. "You didn't trust me. So how can you expect me to trust you?"

"Then don't let me go in alone," Whit negotiated. "But let me go in *with* you. We have always worked well together—in Afghanistan and running our own security business. Hell, look what we did tonight. You pulled me out of the line of fire."

"And you drove us here, to safety," Aaron had to admit.

Whit uttered a wistful sigh of nostalgia. "It was like old times…"

Aaron chuckled. "Yeah, getting shot at—running for our lives. It sure was like old times."

Whit chuckled. "I didn't say they were all good times."

"Okay, you can come along," Aaron allowed.

"You've finally decided you can trust me again?"

Aaron turned the keys in the ignition and pointed at the lightening sky. "I'm sick of arguing about it. We're wasting time. Our best chance of getting inside and finding the records is going to be now—before the more heavily staffed first shift starts."

The rental car's ignition whined but didn't turn over. However, another engine fired up, breaking the quiet of the late night. Lights momentarily blinded Aaron until the car passed them. And as it passed, Aaron recognized the profile of the woman driving the sports car.

"Charlotte..." She must have taken a car from the garage of Stanley Jessup's rental home. "I thought she agreed to stay here. Out of danger..." Aaron turned the keys again, but the engine refused to start. "Now she's going off with no backup..."

"Damn her," Whit said, pounding his fist against the dash. "She's getting away."

"She's not getting away," Aaron said. "She's going back to Serenity House. She's risking getting caught all over again."

Whit pounded the dash again—this time right in front of Aaron. "She told you she was staying here, too. Why would you believe anything *she* tells you?"

But, Aaron realized, she'd never actually said the words—had never agreed not to go back to Serenity House. Whit's pounding the dash must have knocked something loose because the car finally started.

"We have to beat her back there." Or she would walk alone into danger—just as she had so many times before.

Whit shook his head. "How many times do I have to tell you that you can't trust Charlotte Green?"

"I know I can't trust her," Aaron admitted. But he didn't want to lose her, either. And if she walked back into Serenity House alone, he worried that he would.

SHE HAD BEATEN them to Serenity House. The car she'd borrowed from the garage was faster than the battered rental. As damaged as Whit's car had been, she'd have been surprised if it had started up again let alone been functional enough to follow her. And even though she hadn't known exactly where she'd been going to get back to the horrible hospital, she'd found street signs that had guided her.

She bypassed the front lot to drive around the fenced-in grounds and the building to pull the borrowed Camaro into the employee lot in the back. She parked far from the gate that led to the building. If she were to be discovered, she wanted to be close to the street so no one could block the car from leaving.

Night shift must have been skeletal because there weren't that many cars in the lot. Or maybe, after her escape, some of the employees had quit for fear of getting involved in a police investigation. Maybe she should have gone to the authorities as Aaron had wanted.

But if Serenity House had influence over them, the police might have brought her right back here. Because of the holes in her memory, she didn't know if she had been legally committed to the hospital. Maybe a judge had ordered her confinement. And the authorities would have to uphold the judge's order.

That was why she'd had to go back. She couldn't stand one more minute of not knowing how she had wound up here. But she had a sick feeling that she wouldn't like what she learned. What if the king had orchestrated her disappearance?

What if he'd resented her intrusion into his life and her interference with Gabriella? He had spent years denying her existence. When she'd showed up to protect his real princess, he had agreed begrudgingly. And only because of all the attempts that had already been made to abduct the princess. Since the day she'd been brought home to the palace, Gabriella St. Pierre had been the target of kidnapping and extortion plots.

His enemies had wanted to use Gabriella for leverage—forcing King Rafael to agree to their political or business demands. And everyone else had wanted to hold the princess ransom for money because her father would have willingly paid a huge sum for her safe return.

If Charlotte had been kidnapped by mistake—which might have been the case—he wouldn't have paid a dime for her return. He would have just let her rot. Here.

Why had she wound up in a psychiatric hospital? Had it all just been a case of mistaken identity?

She turned off the car and reached into her pocket, pulling out one of the security badges she'd stolen from Aaron. Growing up with a con artist mother had had some benefits. She'd taught Charlotte to pickpocket at an early age. Not that Bonita had relied on pickpocketing to support herself. She'd just used the wallets she'd *found* to meet the men she'd wanted to meet.

Charlotte flinched with a twinge of guilt that she'd used Aaron to get what she'd wanted. Of course she'd wanted to hug him, had wanted to apologize for keeping so many secrets from him. But now that he knew his beloved Josie was alive, he wanted nothing to do with Charlotte. So when he'd pushed her away, she had pulled the badges from his pocket. She'd only intended to take one, but the lanyards had been tangled together. She had left him one…if he could get here to use it.

But dawn was already burning away the night with a low-hanging fog. Getting in now, before the day shift began, was Charlotte's best bet to go unnoticed. Because she'd been cold, she had kept on the scrubs under the warmer clothes Aaron had packed in the box for her.

He was such a considerate man—always more concerned about others than himself. It was no wonder that, even knowing his heart had already belonged to another, she'd begun to fall for him. He had reminded her of her missionary grandparents and her aunt. Always trying to save the world and uncaring of their own comfort or needs.

Her mother had been the exact opposite. And Charlotte had grown up worrying that she would become more like her than the others—since her father was also a selfish bastard. How could he have made that announcement at the ball? Cavalierly passing Gabriella from one man to another like a possession with no thoughts or feelings of her own…

Just as Charlotte had been imprisoned here—with no concern for her comfort or her feelings. She stepped out of the vehicle and peeled off the sweater and then wriggled the jeans down her legs. The exertion zapped what she had left of her strength, which had already been diminished by being restrained to a bed. And either the pregnancy or the concussion had stolen the energy she used to have.

Her legs trembled beneath her weight. Maybe she just wasn't accustomed to standing anymore. Or maybe she dreaded going back inside the hospital that had served as her prison. She tucked the stolen gun in the waistband of her pants and tugged the shirt down over it. At least now she wasn't unarmed.

But if she was caught…

She wouldn't be just tied down to that bed again. She would be taken to that airfield and whisked away on a private plane to some other prison. One from which she would probably find no escape.

And no one to help her.

If she were taken again, would Aaron even look for her this time? Or was he so angry over her lies and lies of omission that he would consider it good riddance if she went missing again?

Or would he think that she'd just taken off on her own? That she'd duped him yet again?

She glanced back toward the street, wanting to wait for him. Wanting him to come for her. But she had no way of knowing if he was coming—if he were even able or willing to come after her.

And she couldn't wait any longer. This was her last shot to find out who had abducted her—to find out the identity of the father of her baby.

"WE'RE TOO LATE," Aaron said as he pulled into the employee lot and parked beside the Camaro, which was in a space farthest from the building. Even once he'd gotten Whit's rental car started, he should have known it would never catch up to the faster vehicle Charlotte had taken. "She's probably already inside."

She must have taken the extra two badges from him when she'd hugged him. God, he'd been a fool again—to think that she'd actually been apologizing to him for all the secrets she'd kept from him.

But she'd only been playing him to get what she wanted. Access to Serenity House. After what she'd gone through—being tied down and beaten—why would she want to go back inside?

And would he be able to get her out again?

He shut off the vehicle and turned toward the three-story brick building. Lights shone in only a few windows, the rest of the rooms eerily dark.

Serenity House had been anything but serene earlier that evening—it had been like a war zone with gunfire and fighting and yelling. Hell, there had even been the vehicle knocking down the fence. But as they'd passed the front entrance, he'd seen that gate and fence had been repaired, so it appeared as though nothing had happened. And now it seemed that hardly anyone was around—guards, staff or patients.

Whit stared at the black Camaro as if trying to determine if it was the one that had raced past them earlier. "I have to admit that I'm surprised she came here at all. I figured she'd just keep driving."

"She wants to find Princess Gabriella every bit as much as you do," Aaron said. That had to be the reason she would risk going back inside. Now he understood why she'd been so protective of the princess. She hadn't been just doing her job. She'd been guarding her sister.

Whit shook his head. "I doubt that…"

"She said she doesn't want to take Princess Gabriella's place."

"She's said a lot of things."

"Actually she hasn't," Aaron said, compelled to defend her. "It wasn't that she lied to me. She just didn't tell me things."

"A lie of omission is still a lie," Whit persisted.

"I guess you'd know."

Sick of arguing with his old partner, Aaron stepped out of the car and slammed the door. "We have to find her."

Despite her skills, Charlotte needed him. She wouldn't be able to get in and out of Serenity House alone. Remembering the shots that had been fired at him earlier in this lot, Aaron moved cautiously toward the building.

Whit's footsteps followed him, the other man sticking close and keeping his voice low. "She's already beaten us to whatever we might find here."

"You don't know that." She could have been stopped at the gate. Maybe the ID badges they'd taken had been deactivated. Maybe they wouldn't open the locked gates and doors.

Disappointment and frustration made Whit's whisper gruff. "Princess Gabriella isn't here."

Aaron had already checked that out; he knew it was true. Obviously Whit had learned the same from Stanley Jessup's young reporter's source. "But maybe whoever put Charlotte here took Princess Gabriella, as well."

"I doubt both of them survived what happened in Paris," Whit replied.

"We don't know what happened in Paris."

"She does…"

Aaron was done arguing. He ignored the other man and hurried toward the gate.

"Stop," Whit ordered in a harsh whisper.

Recognizing the urgency in Whit's voice, Aaron froze and crouched lower to the pavement, wary of getting shot at again. He turned back to Whit, who was pointing toward one of the few other cars parked in the lot.

Like the fog rising up from the ground, steam covered the windows, but it didn't conceal the dark shadows of two people sitting inside the front seat.

Had Charlotte already been grabbed—before she'd even made it to the building?

With just a look and a jerk of his head, Aaron communicated with his old partner. They each took a side of the car—Whit on the driver's side and Aaron the passenger's. That was probably where Charlotte would be sitting if she were inside the vehicle.

He could only see the shadows through the fogged-up windows. He couldn't tell if the passenger was actually Charlotte. And he had no clue who the driver was. The U.S. Marshal? One of the guards?

Neither shadow moved. They must not have noticed him pass behind the vehicle on his way across the lot. Why were they just sitting there—long enough to steam up the windows?

Were they talking? Arguing?

He heard neither, nothing except for the mad pounding of his own pulse in his ears. Foreboding chilled him more than the cool gusts of wind. Something wasn't right. It had to be Charlotte…

Whit moved as silently and quickly as Aaron did. Each had his weapon clenched in his hand, the barrel glittering in the first light of dawn streaking across the sky.

Maybe he could grab her and pull her to safety before the driver even realized they were sneaking up on them. With his free hand, Aaron grabbed the handle and jerked open the door. And the passenger fell out—onto him. Blood—thick and sticky—dripped from the woman's body—saturating his shirt. And he realized it wasn't steam fogging up the windows but a spray of blood.

They were too late.

Chapter Ten

"This is why you don't want to help me," a soft voice murmured from the cover of the enveloping fog.

Startled, Aaron jerked—knocking the body off him so that it dropped onto the asphalt and rolled over. With the hole in her face from the bullet she'd taken in the back of her head, the woman was nearly unrecognizable but for the gray hair.

But she wasn't Charlotte, who stepped from the fog and approached the car.

"You're all right," Aaron said, breathing a sigh of relief that she hadn't been in the car—or entered the hospital yet.

She shook her head in denial, but he figured she was referring to her emotional state rather than her physical condition.

"It's Sandy. The nurse who took care of me," Charlotte said, identifying the woman. "She tried to help me, and look what she got for her trouble. Dead."

"Driver's dead, too," Whit informed them. He flipped open a wallet he'd taken off the body. A curse whistled between his teeth.

"What?" Aaron asked.

"It's that kid," Whit replied, "the young investigative

reporter who approached one of Stanley Jessup's editors with the story about Princess Gabriella being here."

"The nurse must have been his source," Aaron said, leaning inside the car to see that the reporter had also been shot in the back of the head like the woman.

They had probably been meeting in the parking lot to discuss what she'd witnessed that evening when someone had executed them. He suspected that their killer had been hiding in the backseat, like Whit had back at Jessup's rented cottage.

"That's why they were killed, Charlotte," he told her, trying to ease her guilt. She hadn't asked to be kidnapped and held hostage in this place. "It had nothing to do with you."

She shrugged off his reassurance. "It had everything to do with me. It wouldn't have happened if I hadn't been here. They would both still be alive."

He couldn't absolve her of guilt she was determined to hold on to—just as Whit hadn't been able to absolve him three years ago when he'd thought Josie had been murdered on their watch. The only thing that might help her was learning the truth.

"Then we need to find out who put you in here," he said, "because that's who's really responsible for these deaths."

"We don't know that," Whit said, his dark gaze narrowed with suspicion as he stared at Charlotte. Maybe he'd taken her claim of responsibility literally.

As Aaron lifted the nurse's body back into the car, he noted that her skin was already cold. "She's been dead awhile," he said. "They were probably killed shortly after Charlotte and I broke out of here. And our only lead to finding out who is behind all this is in that hospital."

He gestured back at the three-story building. But Whit continued to study Charlotte. He obviously thought she was a more viable lead. But if she knew who'd put her in this place, she would have no desire to go back inside.

Instead she drew in an audible breath and started across the lot toward the building.

He caught her arm. "You can't go back in there."

She pointed back at the car with the blood-spattered windows. "It's not any safer out here."

"She's right," Whit miraculously agreed. "We should all stick together."

Aaron figured his old partner just didn't want Charlotte getting away again before he'd had a chance to interrogate her. But, even though they didn't trust each other, maybe they would all be safer if they stayed together.

Because wasn't the saying *to keep your enemies closer...*

CHARLOTTE ACHED WITH the desire to throw her arms around Aaron's neck and cling to him. She was afraid, but her inclination had less to do with fear and more to do with relief. When she'd first realized that was blood dripping down the car windows, she'd thought that Aaron might have been inside—that he might have beaten her there using some back roads and...

Her breath hitched with a sob she held inside. She'd learned at an early age that tears were a waste of time. They had never swayed her mother from doing what she'd wanted and had never made the selfish woman care about her. She doubted crying would make Aaron care, either.

He was already in love with another woman. But

why hadn't he pressed her for Josie's whereabouts? Ironically, she was close. That was why Michigan had sounded familiar to Charlotte because she had brought Josie here for her new life.

It would be even more ironic if this was where Charlotte lost her life. But Aaron was determined to keep her safe. That was why he was still here—because it was his job. Even more than that, it was his honor. He was the kind of man who enjoyed playing white knight to helpless damsels. He was a true hero—in wartime and peace. That was why Charlotte had been so drawn to him.

But she was no damsel in distress, so she should have known that they could never be…

"Are we doing this?" Whit asked, breaking the silence that had fallen between them as she stared up at Aaron's handsome face.

His gaze was locked with hers, as if he was trying to figure out what she was thinking. Or plotting…

Aaron nodded. "Yeah, we're doing this."

"What's the plan?" Whit persisted.

"We go in the employee entrance, but we bypass the locker room and cafeteria and take the back stairs up to the administrator's office."

Whit whistled in appreciation. "You know the layout of the place."

"I interviewed here and then worked a day before I even tried getting inside her room," Aaron explained.

A grin tipped up a corner of his sexy mouth. "And then I got tossed out on my ass after I got caught coming out of her room."

"I thought you weren't coming back," she remembered with a flash of the panic she'd felt then. "I thought you'd been shot."

"Not yet," Aaron said with a glance back at the car where two people had been shot. "But we have to make this quick. Get in, get into the administrator's records, and get the hell out!"

"Good plan," Whit mused.

The first test was getting past the lock at the security gate. They all breathed a sigh of relief that a swipe of the card turned the light from red to green.

"I thought they might have deactivated them." Aaron spoke aloud the fear she'd been harboring, too. "Guess they didn't think we'd be stupid enough to come back."

But they were wrong. It probably was very stupid to return to the place they'd barely escaped the first time.

No one accosted them between the employee entrance and the stairwell to the second floor and the office suites. But the administrator's office was not empty. A light glowed behind the frosted glass in the door, and a machine buzzed inside, the floor vibrating with the low drone of it.

"She's shredding papers," Charlotte said, her stomach lurching with a sick feeling of hopelessness.

"The records are online," Aaron assured her—giving her hope as he had in the parking lot. Trying to make her feel better.

He was such a damn good man. That was why she reached for the door handle, trying to enter first. Whoever had put her in this place wanted her baby; she doubted anyone would shoot at her. But Aaron apparently wasn't willing to take that chance. He held her back, and with a nod at Whit, the two men burst through the door with their weapons drawn.

The woman standing behind the desk wore a power suit and had an air of authority—even with her ash-blond hair falling out of the bun on top of her head and dark circles blackening the skin beneath her eyes. She had to be the administrator. She confronted them with a hard stare and slight smile—more triumphant than fearful. She had definitely suspected that they would come back.

"It's too late," Dr. Mona Platt, per the nameplate on her desk, said. "I wiped the hard drive. Everything's gone..."

Charlotte shook her head. She would not be denied. She had gone too long without knowing what had happened to her. "Everything's *not* gone," she pointed out. "You're still here."

"I'm not going to tell you anything," the woman stubbornly insisted.

"You'll talk to us or the police," Aaron threatened her.

"What will I talk to the police about?" Dr. Platt asked, waving her hand over the paper shredder. "There is nothing to talk about."

Charlotte's anger flared, energizing her as her pulse raced. "You held me captive in this place!"

The woman's thin lips pursed into a tight line of defiance and denial. "I don't know what you're talking about."

"You restrained me to a bed," Charlotte accused, "and had a guard posted outside my door with a gun."

"We do not employ armed guards at Serenity House," the administrator replied prissily.

Aaron snorted at that claim.

Charlotte pointed to the bruise on her head. "Mr. Centerenian nearly killed me with that gun!"

"Mr. Centerenian was not employed by Serenity House."

"Who was he employed by?" Whit threw the question out there. "Who paid him and who paid for this woman's stay here?"

"I cannot violate doctor-patient confidentiality clauses," Dr. Platt persisted. "Or the privacy law."

"I am the patient!" Charlotte snapped. "So you're going to damn well tell me who paid you to keep me here!"

"I will not—"

Charlotte lifted her gun and pointed the barrel directly at the woman. "You will tell me!"

"You won't shoot me."

"I wouldn't be so sure of that," Whit warned the doctor. "She can't be trusted."

"And since I was confined to a psychiatric hospital, I must be out of my mind." She moved her finger to the trigger. "I could probably use an insanity plea to get out of jail time."

"Then you'd wind up spending the rest of your life in a place like this," Dr. Platt threatened.

"At least I'll be alive…"

The woman's eyes narrowed with her own temper. "You should be thanking me."

A laugh, at the woman's audacity, burst out of Charlotte's lips. "God, lady, you should be committed here yourself instead of running the place. What the hell do you think I should be thanking you for?"

Dr. Platt pointed toward Charlotte's belly. "You should thank me for your baby. You owe me for its life."

"What the hell are you talking about?" Aaron asked the question before Charlotte could.

She pressed her palm over her stomach, as if her hand alone could protect her baby from this crazy woman. "You—you did this? You impregnated me?"

The doctor shook her head, knocking more brittle

blond strands of hair loose from the bun. "I was supposed to—with special sperm. But you were already pregnant. I didn't tell *him* that, or he would have had me terminate it. You have me to thank for your baby."

"My baby..." But it wasn't just *her* baby. It was Aaron's baby, too. Even though they had used protection that one night they'd been together, it must have failed...because he was the only man she'd been with recently. In a long while, actually. She turned toward him, and when she met his gaze, she knew he *knew*.

AARON WAS GOING to be a father. The baby was *his*.

The thought stole his breath away for a moment.

Whit had no such problems. "Who is *he?*" he demanded to know.

"The father?" Dr. Platt asked with a sniffle of disinterest. "I don't know." And she obviously didn't much care. She turned toward Charlotte. "Do you remember? Or are you still suffering from amnesia?"

If the look on Charlotte's face was any indication, she knew—with as much certainty as he knew. The baby was his. But that wasn't Whit's question.

So the tenacious Mr. Howell repeated it. "Who is the man who paid you to make her pregnant with his sperm? Who brought her here?"

"That guard—the one with the gun—Mr. Centerenian is the one who brought her here," Dr. Platt replied. "And he hired a private nurse, too, who only took care of the princess."

"The princess..." Whit murmured the words.

"I am not Princess Gabriella," Charlotte replied.

The woman laughed now. "And you don't think you belong here? You've either still got amnesia or you're crazy."

"Who I am is Charlotte Green," she said, "bodyguard to Princess Gabriella."

When Dr. Platt continued to stare at Charlotte like she was crazy, Aaron said, "It's true. She's a former U.S. Marshal and professional bodyguard." The woman didn't need to know that she was also royalty. "This man—Mr. Centerenian—brought you the wrong woman. He and his boss kidnapped the wrong woman."

Dr. Platt shrugged. "It doesn't matter to me. None of these outrageous claims of yours has anything to do with me or Serenity House."

"It has everything to do with you," Aaron argued, because she was the only one who could tell them what they needed to know. "You took money to hold a woman hostage. You're an accessory."

"That man brought her here," she stubbornly repeated. "I had no idea that she had been kidnapped."

Whit swore. "Bullshit!"

"That gorilla with the gun is not the one giving the orders," Aaron said. "And he's not the one paying you. I hope his boss paid you a hell of a lot for what you're going to wind up giving up for it."

She arched a brow, her interest finally piqued. "Giving up?"

"Your hospital," Aaron said.

"Your freedom," Whit added.

"Your life," Charlotte murmured. "If I have anything to say about it…"

She didn't mean it. Aaron was almost certain that she didn't. That she was just upset. Understandably so for all she'd had to go through.

"You're threatening me," Dr. Platt accused, as if she were the victim.

Charlotte stepped closer to her, and even though she

was six months pregnant and weak, she was a far more dangerous woman than the administrator realized. "I'm not just threatening," she warned the woman.

Aaron put his hand on her arm, pulling her back before she vaulted over the desk and throttled the administrator. He told both women, "We need to know who that man is."

And if Charlotte killed Dr. Platt, they might never figure it out. Or at least be able to prove it.

"You're already in trouble here," Aaron pointed out, "so you might as well tell us what you know."

"Come on," Whit urged her.

Aaron felt them coming before he heard them. There were enough of them that there were vibrations on the floor beneath his feet. He reached for Charlotte even before the door burst open and the armed men stormed into the office. He pushed her behind him, taking cover behind a filing cabinet, and raised his weapon.

The administrator didn't have magical powers, but somehow she had summoned the guards as silently as she had last time Aaron had been in her office. Maybe she had a secret button somewhere on her desk, or maybe she had a remote alarm in her pocket.

Or maybe she hadn't summoned them at all because the first bullet they fired went through her forehead, spattering her brains on the wall behind her. There was no need to check her for a pulse; there was no way she could have survived that shot.

Then the guards swung their weapons toward them, and the office erupted with gunfire. Aaron fought hard to stay between Charlotte and the men as he returned fire. But she moved around him, taking her own shots. Aaron was so concerned about her that he hadn't even noticed that Whit was down. He'd been hit.

Aaron's heart slammed against his ribs as he noticed the blood. And in that moment of distraction, one of the guards lunged toward him with gun blazing…

Chapter Eleven

"Her guards don't have guns, my ass," Whit murmured as Aaron carried him from the building. Sirens wailed in the distance.

Charlotte's hand shook as she swiped the badge through the lock on the gate. "Maybe we should wait for the police," she said, "or at least for an ambulance."

Whit had lost a lot of blood. But that hadn't stopped him from saving her and Aaron. He'd taken out the last guard. But none of the men who had stormed into the office had been the one who'd struck her with the gun and stolen her memory. Where was Mr. Centerenian?

"We should wait for an ambulance," Aaron agreed.

Whit shook his head. "It's a through and through, and I can move my arm so it didn't hurt anything in my shoulder."

"Then you should be able to walk," Aaron grumbled, but he continued to carry his friend across the lot. And they were friends again.

Enlisting Whit to help her stage Josie Jessup's death and forbidding him to tell Aaron had destroyed their friendship. Whit had obviously resented—maybe even hated her—for it. And for three years Charlotte had re-gretted what her job had cost the two men. That was why she'd convinced the king to hire them both for bodyguards. She'd wanted them to work together again.

But she had never imagined how well they would have to work together. They had kept each other alive in that office, and they'd kept her alive. She wasn't certain who else had survived. Not the administrator. But some of the guards might have.

And Mr. Centerenian was out there, somewhere. So she clutched her weapon close and kept a watchful gaze on the area around them. She hoped she wouldn't have to use her gun, though, because if she had to, she would need to make the one bullet she had left count.

"Put him in Jessup's car," she ordered as she fumbled for the keys and unlocked the doors. "We need to get out of here fast."

They all squeezed into the sports car, Whit bleeding on the leather seats in the back. Charlotte passed the keys to Aaron, who drove.

"He's lost a lot of blood," she whispered, leaning across the console. Warmth radiated from Aaron, chasing some of the chill from her body. "We should take him to the hospital."

"No," Whit protested from the back. "Just take me to Stanley Jessup's. And make sure nobody follows you this time."

Aaron cursed him, but he took the route toward the lake and the house sitting high on the dune above it. "If you die, you stubborn ass," he threatened, "it's on you."

"Actually it'll be on you," Charlotte remarked with a faint chuckle as Aaron carried his friend into the house.

"I'm fine," Whit promised.

Charlotte reached for the door just as it opened, and she came face-to-face with an older man. His hair was thick and wavy and pure white despite the fact that he wasn't even out of his fifties yet. And his gaze was green and piercing. She didn't need an introduction; she knew exactly who he was. Her stomach flipped, and then the baby kicked as if in protest of Charlotte's lurch of guilt.

"What the hell happened?" the older man bellowed. "Did you shoot him, Aaron?"

Aaron chuckled. "No. Can't say I haven't been tempted, though. Where can I put him? He's all dead weight."

"I'm not dead yet," Whit weakly murmured.

"Over here," Stanley Jessup said, leading them toward a den. "Lay him down on the couch and I'll call for a private doctor."

The media mogul understood the need for discretion. Over his head, Aaron met her gaze—as if trying to convince her to tell the man about his daughter.

She was tempted. Never more so than now that she carried a child of her own. But she couldn't risk Josie's safety. Not even to ease her conscience.

"Do you need a doctor, too, your highness?" Mr. Jessup asked, his voice gruff with concern.

If only her own father had ever cared about her like a virtual stranger cared...

She shook her head at the self-pitying thought as much as in reply to his question.

"This isn't Princess Gabriella," Aaron said.

"I told you I wouldn't run the story until she got out of danger, but the story's too big..." His gaze focused on her rounded belly. "I can't sit on it anymore. The young reporter who has a source at the hospital is ready to run with his story."

Thinking of the horrific fate that had befallen that

poor kid and the nurse who had tried to help her, Charlotte sucked in a breath of pain and guilt.

"I'll call the doctor," Stanley interrupted himself. He grabbed a cell from his pocket and punched in some numbers. Then he lowered his voice as he issued commands to whoever answered his call.

"Are you all right?" Aaron asked, his focus on her rather than his bleeding friend now. "You're extremely pale."

His concern was back. But was he concerned about her or was he concerned about his child? *Of course, it's the baby.*

She was worried about the baby, too, and what could have happened with all the bullets flying. She could have easily been shot, just as Whit had. Fortunately for her—*unfortunately for Whit*—the guards had been more focused on firing at the men than at her. She suspected they'd had orders not to harm her baby. Because whoever had employed them mistakenly thought the baby was his...

The administrator had been right. But unfortunately Charlotte hadn't had the chance to thank her before the woman had been killed.

She should have listened to Aaron and stayed behind the first time he'd brought her to this house. But she hadn't wanted to be alone with Stanley Jessup almost as much as she'd wanted to learn who had kidnapped and imprisoned her in the mental hospital.

Having spent most of her professional life in dangerous situations, she hadn't had any qualms about risking her life again. After all, she had survived all those previous dangerous situations, so she'd proven that she could take care of herself.

But it wasn't just her anymore. She had someone

else to think about now—someone who wasn't a client or a witness but someone who was actually a physical part of her. Someone whose life depended on Charlotte staying alive and healthy.

As the enormity of that responsibility struck her, her knees began to shake, and she started trembling all over in reaction.

"Charlotte!" Aaron called out to her, his voice sharp with alarm. Then he repeated his earlier question, "Are you all right?"

"I—I need to sit down," she said. "Just rest for a little while, and I'll be fine." But before she could find a chair to sit on, Aaron swung her up in his arms. Black spots swam across her vision and dizziness threatened to overwhelm her. She clutched at Aaron's broad shoulders and his neck, holding on to him tightly.

"Where's a bedroom?" he asked Jessup, who'd just slipped his cell phone back in his pocket.

Even knowing that Aaron was only concerned about the baby and her health, Charlotte's pulse jumped at his question—at the idea of Aaron wanting to carry her off to a bedroom. But now that he knew how much she'd kept from him—that she'd kept Josie from him—she doubted he would ever want her—*Charlotte*—again.

Her head pounded with frustration and exhaustion, and she closed her eyes as the hopelessness washed over her. She did just need some rest—just a little—to get back her energy and her will to fight.

"Top of the stairs," the older man directed them. "There's a nice guest suite a couple of doors down the hall on the right."

She didn't care if it was nice or not. Hell, anything was nicer than Serenity House. She expected to fall asleep the minute her head hit the pillow. But when

Aaron laid her down on the bed, she tensed—unwilling to drop her arms from around his neck. She wanted to cling to him again—wanted to make sure that they had both really survived the shoot-out at Serenity House.

"After he takes care of Whit, I'll have the doctor come up to check you out," he assured her.

"You can't tell him…" she murmured as sleep tugged at her lids, bringing them down.

"I'm sure since Stanley Jessup called him, the doctor will be discreet. He won't be spreading any rumors about Princess Gabriella being pregnant."

"Gabby isn't…" Actually she didn't know that; she hadn't seen her sister in months. She had no idea how she was, and the panic must have shown on her face.

Because Aaron assured her, "Don't worry about Gabby or the doctor."

She shook her head, frustrated at his misunderstanding. "No doctor." She didn't need a doctor. She just needed sleep.

And Aaron. She needed Aaron. He was the father of her child, but she had to accept that was all he would ever be to her.

As if he couldn't stand her touch or feared she was picking his pockets again, he pulled away, albeit gently, from her grasping arms. He headed toward the door with the explanation: "I need to check on Whit. Make sure he stopped bleeding."

They had pressed a makeshift bandage, of his own handkerchief, to his shoulder, but the thin swatch of fabric hadn't done much to stem the blood loss.

So much blood…

Charlotte shuddered as she recalled the horrific crime scene they'd left. So much devastation.

Who was responsible?

"I need to talk to Mr. Jessup, too," Aaron continued with a heavy sigh.

Fighting to stay awake, she murmured, "You can't tell him about Josie…"

"It's been almost four years now," Aaron said. "What makes you think she might still be in danger?"

She placed her hands over her belly to soothe the baby's frantic kicking. Or was that her stomach churning with jealousy? And guilt churned along with that jealousy. Trigger had been telling the truth—she and Josie had become quite close. Charlotte should be worried about her friend—not Aaron.

"Trigger," she reminded him. "He wants to know where she is."

"You're sure it's her whose whereabouts he wanted to know?"

"My last case." Seeing how close Josie had been to her father had compelled Charlotte to want to get to know her own father.

It hadn't taken her long to realize that King St. Pierre would never be the father Stanley Jessup had been to his daughter. But Charlotte had stayed because of the bond she'd formed with her sister. It wasn't just outside dangers that she'd wanted to protect Gabriella from…

But now she focused on another friend. "There must be a reason Trigger wants to find Josie now. Somebody might have figured out she's alive and hired him to find out where she is."

"We haven't seen Trigger since we broke out of Serenity House," Aaron reminded her. "I don't think Josie's in danger."

"We can't be sure. Don't tell her dad."

"I won't," he promised, as he closed the blinds to shut

out the morning sun. "Don't worry. Just sleep. You're safe here. No one will hurt you."

It was too late. Someone already had. Aaron had with how easily he walked away, leaving her alone and aching for him.

Aching for a love that would never be hers...

HER LAST LUCID thought wasn't for her own safety but for someone else's. How could he have doubted—even for a minute—that her intentions weren't honorable?

Sure, he'd let Whit and all his cynicism and doubts get inside his head, but he had never considered Charlotte with his head.

He had always connected with Charlotte with his heart. That was how he'd known—no matter how morbid the crime scene in Paris was—that she wasn't dead. Because he would have known...

"She's not the princess," he told Stanley Jessup again, as he joined the older man at the bottom of the contemporary metal and glass staircase. It was a wonder he hadn't slipped carrying Charlotte up them. But then he'd been totally focused on her—on protecting her and their unborn child.

The media mogul snorted. "How big a fool do you think I am? That girl's the princess."

She was a princess. Just not the princess that Jessup thought she was.

"That girl is the princess's bodyguard," he divulged. It wasn't like it was a secret that could be kept any longer. "She had plastic surgery to look exactly like her."

Stanley Jessup whistled in appreciation of Charlotte's dedication. "Even you guys wouldn't have gone to those extremes to protect someone."

"She did." Because Princess Gabriella was her sister.

But that was a story Stanley Jessup didn't need to have because he wouldn't be able to *not* print it.

"Are you sure?"

"I've seen them both together. To people not that familiar with them, they're virtually identical." But if you really knew them, they were nothing alike.

So who had kidnapped Charlotte thinking that she was Gabriella? Someone who hadn't known either of them that well. And where was Princess Gabby?

"Doesn't matter who she is," Jessup said. "There's a hell of a story here. She was held hostage in that hospital for months, apparently. Whit got shot in that place."

Aaron glanced into the den where the doctor treated his old friend. The former war hero cursed profusely and creatively as a needle penetrated his skin, stitching up the wound.

Jessup reached for his phone again. "I'll call that young reporter and get him over here to brief us with what he knows."

Aaron shook his head. "That won't be possible."

"You need to get over this need for confidentiality," the media mogul scoffed. "There's really no such thing anymore."

"I'm not talking about the story," Aaron said. "I'm talking about the reporter. He can't come here." He swallowed hard on regret. "I'm sorry…"

The older man groaned. "I've heard that tone from you before. Heard that damn from-the-depths-of-your-soul apology. What happened?"

"I don't know for certain," he admitted. "But we found him and his source…"

"Dead?"

He nodded.

"Who did that?"

"Probably the same men who shot Whit." Four of them had stormed the administrator's office. Two had looked like the Serenity House guards he'd fought earlier—probably why they'd been so determined to shoot him. If not for Whit, Aaron might have been lying on the couch. Or in a morgue. "We left before the police arrived but we need to know what they know."

"And since you left the scene of a crime, you can't very well just waltz into the sheriff's office and ask?"

Aaron shook his head. "Only two of the men shooting at us were hospital guards." Despite Mona Platt swearing her security force was unarmed. "I don't know if the other two men worked for the hospital or someone else." Since they'd shot her first, and fatally, he heartily suspected someone else.

"The sheriff's office?"

Aaron shrugged. "We can't trust anyone." He had learned that the hard way. He couldn't even trust the woman who carried his baby. He still felt as though she had secrets, things she'd remembered but hadn't shared with him.

GUNSHOTS ECHOED INSIDE her head and blood spattered everything, blinding her with red. She shifted against the bed, fighting to awaken from the nightmare.

But it hadn't been just a dream. It was real. All of it had happened. All the death. The destruction. The senseless murders.

She could see Whit again, taking the bullet—getting knocked to the floor as blood spurted from his shoulder. But then it wasn't Whit she was seeing. It wasn't a blond man with dark eyes. Instead it was a dark-haired man with eerie light blue eyes that were wide, staring up at her in confusion as the life seeped away with the blood that pooled around him.

"Aaron!" she screamed his name, jolting awake with her heart pounding frantically with terror.

"It's okay," a deep voice murmured. And strong arms wrapped around her in the dark. "I'm here."

She clutched him close, realizing quickly that he wore no shirt. His skin was bare and damp beneath her fingers. And water trailed from his wet hair down his neck and chest. "Are you…"

Naked?

"I'm here," he assured her. He pulled her closer, so that her body pressed tightly against his. Rough denim covered his lower body. He must have only had time to pull on his jeans when he'd heard her scream.

"I thought it was you," she said, "who got shot. I thought you were dead."

"I'm fine," he said, skimming his hand over her hair—probably trying to tame the tangled mess. "How are you?"

Still trembling in reaction to her awful dream and filled with shame that she had let so many people believe their loved ones were dead. Maybe that was why she'd been so compelled to quit after Josie's case.

"Charlotte?" He eased back and tipped up her chin, his blue-eyed gaze intent on her face. "Are you all right?"

She nodded. "I'm just not quite awake yet. And it seemed so real…"

"It was real," he said. "The shooting was real. It just wasn't me."

"It was Whit," she said, remembering. "Is he okay?"

Aaron chuckled. "Sleeping off the painkillers the doctor gave him. But he'll be fine. We were lucky," he said, his voice gruff with emotion, "that we all survived."

"You told Mr. Jessup about the reporter?"

He nodded.

"I'm sorry." She pressed a kiss to the rough stubble on his cheek. "I know how hard that can be…"

Even if the people she'd told hadn't always lost their loved ones to death, they had lost them all the same. Her lips were still on his face, but he turned his head until they brushed across his mouth.

And he kissed her.

He knew Josie was alive, but he kissed *her*. Dare she hope that he cared? But then he pulled back.

"We need to talk," he said, "about the baby. About us…"

"Us?" She couldn't give in to the hope lifting the pressure from her chest. "When you learned how many things I'd kept from you—" *Josie* "—I didn't think you'd be able to forgive me."

"I don't know that I have," he admitted.

And he didn't even know that she still kept one secret from him.

"I feel like you're holding something back yet," he said.

Maybe he did know.

"Aaron…"

"But I know this isn't the right time for us to talk," he said. "We still don't know what happened to Princess Gabby. Or who kidnapped you. Or who shot all those people and had us shot at…"

She had leads. Thoughts. Suspicions. But when she opened her mouth, he pressed his fingers across her lips.

"So I don't want to talk," he said. "I want to celebrate

that we're alive." And he replaced his fingers with his mouth, kissing her deeply.

She moaned.

And he pulled away. "I'm such an idiot. You're exhausted. You've been through hell…"

"But none of that stops me from wanting you." She was surprised, though, that he wanted her since he knew that the real love of his life was still alive. But maybe he'd accepted that he couldn't be part of Josie Jessup's life without putting her in danger, so he'd decided to make do with the mother of his child.

"Charlotte…" he murmured her name with such regret.

He couldn't love her. She had to remind herself of that—so that she wouldn't fall even deeper for him than she already had.

"I shouldn't take advantage of you," he said, "like I did back at that cabin—"

She pressed her fingers over his lips now. "If anything I took advantage of you back there."

"You didn't even know who you were then."

"But I knew who you were." Strong and loyal and trustworthy. He would be a wonderful father—a far better father than she had ever known.

"I wish I knew who you are," he murmured wistfully.

"I told you—"

"I know your name," he said, "but I don't think I've ever really known you. And I'm not sure if you'll ever let me know the real you."

She didn't want him to just know her. She wanted him to love her. So she made herself vulnerable to him in a way that she never had for any other man. She didn't trust him enough to give him the words of love, but she showed him her love. With her lips and her tongue.

He lay back on the bed and groaned. He let her bring him to the brink before he turned on her. Pulling off her clothes, he kissed every inch of skin he exposed. And he pressed her back into the pillows and used his mouth to bring her beyond the brink—until pleasure tore through and she moaned his name again.

He joined their bodies, thrusting gently inside her— as if afraid that he might harm their unborn child. His slow and easy strokes drove her up again, with tension winding tight inside her. She clutched at his back, then slid her hands lower, grasping his tightly muscled butt. But he refused to rush. And each slow stroke drove her a little crazier—until she just dissolved with pleasure and emotion.

Then he groaned and filled her. "Charlotte…"

She was the woman whose name he uttered when pleasure overwhelmed him. She wanted to hope it meant something—that it might indicate they could have a future. But she had had her hopes dashed too many times to entertain any now. He flopped onto his back beside her and curled her against his side. But she couldn't look at him—couldn't let him see how much she cared. So she gazed around the room. The curtains were still drawn tight over the blinds—shutting out whatever light might be outside. "How long did I sleep?"

"Probably not long enough," he said. "You were exhausted. I should have let you go back to sleep instead of…"

"I must have spent months in that bed in Serenity House," she reminded him. "I shouldn't ever be tired again."

"But, even before what we just did, we had quite a night," he pointed out. "A night we were damn lucky to have survived."

And that was the only reason they had made love—in celebration of that survival, and for a wonderful while, she had been able to replace the pain and fear with pleasure. But now it all came rushing back along with her nightmarish memories of the night.

Her breath shuddered out in a ragged sigh as she remembered it all. "That was just one night? You got caught in my room and then came back to break me out all in the same night?"

"Yes."

Now she remembered something else—the guard's phone call. "Mr. Centerenian's boss is coming here tonight—to some private airfield. The guy who kidnapped and tried to impregnate me is going to be here."

"The guy who thought he was kidnapping and impregnating Princess Gabriella," Aaron pointed out. "This has nothing to do with you."

"She's my sister," Charlotte said with pride. "It has everything to do with me." It was her responsibility to keep the real princess safe.

Aaron shook his head. "I'll take it from here. I'll figure out which airfield they'll be using, and I'll meet him there."

"You're not going alone."

She didn't want to risk the baby's safety again, but she didn't want the baby's father putting his life at risk without backup he could trust, either.

"Absolutely not," he said. "I will not let you put yourself and my baby in danger again."

Chapter Twelve

Aaron momentarily took his gaze from the airfield to glance at the woman sitting in the passenger seat. She had come along. While he had admitted to himself and to Whit that he didn't know her as well as he should, he was already intimately familiar with her stubbornness.

If he had forbidden her to join him, she would have stolen another car from the garage and tracked down the airfield on her own. At least now, going together, it would be easier for him to protect her.

But she hadn't come along thinking that he would keep her safe. If anything she might think she needed to protect him...

But more likely she didn't trust him to tell her what he discovered on his own. And she wanted to know who'd locked her up in a psychiatric hospital. But what were all her motives? To keep Gabriella safe? They didn't even know where she was. Or so that Charlotte could take revenge on the person who had stolen nearly six months of her life?

Studying the dark airfield through the car windows, Aaron wasn't certain they would discover anything. They had been parked outside it since night had first begun to fall, and there were no lights illuminating the single runway or the steel hangar beside it. There was no vehicle parked near the hangar, either. They had parked Stanley Jessup's car on a farmer's access road to his fields that surrounded the small, private airport.

"This place looks deserted," he mused aloud.

He had no more than uttered the words when lights flashed on—bright beams of light pointing up into the night sky—to guide a plane to ground.

"He was here—that guard from the hospital—he's been here the whole time," Aaron said with a glance at Charlotte. "You knew it?"

She nodded.

"But there's no car anywhere around here..." So they'd shut off the Camaro's lights and waited in the dark for him to drive up.

"You said it's the only private airfield in the area," she reminded him. "He's here..."

Aaron nodded with sudden realization of how they'd missed him. "He must have parked his car inside the hangar."

Charlotte reached for the door handle. "We need to get inside there, too."

Aaron grabbed her arm, stopping her from stepping out. "No. *We* don't."

"We can't let him get on that plane and just fly away," she said. "He's the only lead we have left."

The reporter was dead. The nurse. The administrator. And if any of the armed men from the office had survived, they weren't talking yet. Stanley Jessup had developed a source in the sheriff's office. The small town was overwhelmed and bringing in state and federal authorities to take over the investigation. While that would be better for him and Whit and Charlotte, it would take too long for the investigation to yield any results.

"I will go," he clarified. "You will stay here."

"So he can sneak up on me, grab me and force me onto the plane?" She shuddered at the thought.

"You're armed," he reminded her. "I doubt he could force you to do anything." And that was part of the reason he'd agreed to let her come along with him. She really could take care of herself.

So was she more worried about him? That he'd take a bullet without her being there to protect him? Maybe she had feelings for him, too. Or was she just trying to keep alive the father of her baby?

"We decided to stick together," she reminded him. "That's what kept us alive in the administrator's office—sticking together."

"Glad Whit didn't hear you say that." They'd snuck out of the house while the other man had still been sleeping off his painkillers. Hopefully they would be back before he ever woke up.

Her lips curved into a faint smile. "He's in no condition to be here with us."

Aaron pressed his palm over her stomach. "Neither are you."

"I'm pregnant," she said. Then she dragged in a shaky breath and repeated, "I'm pregnant." She expelled the breath and said, "I'm not sick or injured."

Now he moved his hand to the bruise on her temple. "You were hurt," he pointed out the yet to heal injury. Thinking of the pain she'd endured, the fear over her lost memory and months of imprisonment, his stomach clenched as if he'd been punched in the gut again. "And you're lucky to be alive."

"I am alive," she said.

But what about Gabriella? Learning her fate was

probably what compelled Charlotte to put herself at risk again.

"And now I remember who I am," she added. "And I know what I know—how to take care of myself."

"And others..." He patted her belly again and nodded. "Let's get in there while the plane's landing." When the guard was distracted with the plane, they would be able to get the jump on him.

CHARLOTTE WINCED AT every snap of twig and rustle of grass beneath their feet as they moved stealthily toward the hangar. It was so damn quiet, and so damn black but for those lights beaming into the sky. She stumbled in the dark, would have tripped and gone down, but for Aaron catching her arm and steadying her.

She waited for him to use her clumsiness as a reason to insist on her returning to the car. But instead he kept his hand on her, keeping her close to his side.

Heat and attraction radiated between them. He may not trust her. Hell, he may not ever be able to forgive her, but he did want her. He'd proven that back at the house—proven it in a way that had her still feeling boneless and satiated.

The man was an amazing lover. If only he could really love her—*deeply* love her...

She shook off the wistful thought. It must have been the hormones—due to the pregnancy—that had her hoping for things she knew weren't possible. She had never been the romantic type.

She had always been a pragmatic person. She knew how the world really worked—her mother had made certain of that.

Now she had to make certain that the threat against

Princess Gabriella was gone. She clasped her weapon tightly in her hand.

Aaron reached for the handle to the back door of the steel hangar. He tested the lock and nodded.

The idiot guard wasn't as careful here as he'd been at the hospital. Mr. Centerenian would have never left the door to her room unlocked.

Charlotte lifted her weapon and nodded that she was ready. Aaron opened the door and stepped inside first, keeping his body between her and whoever might be in the hangar. Like her, he probably doubted that there was only one man meeting the plane—after all the men who had stormed into the administrator's office.

But the hangar was quiet and filled with light from the door open onto the field. One man stood there, staring up at the sky. A cigarette tip glowed between the fingers of his left hand. A white bandage swaddled his right hand.

"It's him," she whispered.

The man tensed and dropped his cigarette. Then he reached for the gun in the holster beneath his jacket. Before he could withdraw it, the drone of an engine broke the quiet. Mr. Centerenian turned his attention to the lights in the sky.

The plane was coming. The plane that Charlotte was supposed to leave on—to God knew where. A brief moment of panic clutched her heart. But she reminded herself that she wasn't going to be leaving—at least not on anyone's terms but hers.

As the guard stepped outside the hangar to watch the plane begin its descent, they moved through the shadows and edged closer to that wide-open door. But Charlotte clutched Aaron's arm—holding him back from going any farther. They ducked down below the side of the black SUV parked inside the hangar—keeping it between them and the guard.

She held tightly to Aaron's arm, making sure he stayed down. They couldn't be detected before the plane landed, or the guard might wave it off. And then they might never learn who had orchestrated her kidnapping. She had to know...

Her heart beat with each second that passed before the tires touched down on the airstrip. Calling it such was generous. It was obviously used mostly for crop dusting—not private planes coming from foreign countries. That had to be where Mr. Centerenian's boss came from. Was it someone working for her father? Dread welled up inside her at the thought. The plane bumped along the rough runway before finally coming to a stop.

The engine wasn't killed though; it continued to drone on even as the door lifted on the side. "Get her!" a voice yelled from inside the plane. "We can't stay here."

"I—I can't get her," Mr. Centerenian yelled from the entrance to the hangar. Obviously he was afraid of being too close to his boss when he gave him the bad news. "She got away."

"You lost her?"

He shook his head in denial of any culpability. "No. She got away from the hospital. She escaped."

"You were there so that would not happen," the boss reminded him—his voice terse with anger and frustration. "You need to find her! Now!"

"What are they saying?" Aaron asked, his breath warm as he whispered in her ear.

She shivered. "They're talking about me." And until he'd asked, she hadn't even realized the men had been speaking another language. Charlotte had been multilingual since a very young age.

Her grandparents had been missionaries. Whenever Charlotte had gotten in the way of her mother's latest scam, she'd been left with her grandparents—in whichever country they were working in—trying to take care of starving children and orphans.

Her mother had resented their concern for other children—had resented that they'd spent all their time and money trying to take care of everyone else in the world. At least her aunt had understood, and after her grandparents died, Aunt Lydia had taken over their good work.

And in her own way, Charlotte had thought she was honoring her grandparents, too—by taking care of people in trouble, by protecting them like they'd wanted to protect all those underprivileged children.

The plane engine cut out. "We are not leaving here until we find her," the man ordered the guard. He stomped down the steps to the ground. He wore a silk suit, and his hair was as oily and slicked back as the creepy guard who worked for him.

A breath whistled between Aaron's teeth as he recognized the guy the same time Charlotte did. Prince Linus Demetrios had been promised Princess Gabriella's hand in marriage. They had been betrothed since the day she'd been born—until the king had rescinded that promise. The day of the ball at the palace—the night she and Aaron had made love—the king had promised Gabriella to another man, a wealthier, more influential prince from another neighboring country.

And sometime during that night, someone had slipped a note under Gabby's door that she would die before she would ever marry Prince Tonio Malamatos. That was why Charlotte had whisked them off to Paris the next morning—under the ruse of meeting with designers to begin work on the princess's wedding gown.

"She could be anywhere," the guard protested. "Surely she must have contacted the authorities by now. They'll be looking for us!"

"Princess Gabriella is mine," the prince said. "We're not leaving without her and my baby."

Despite Aaron's arm on her shoulder, trying to hold her down, Charlotte jumped up. "This baby is not yours!"

"Gabby!" The prince hurried forward, his arms outstretched as if to hug her close.

She lifted the gun and pointed it directly at his chest. He had to be the one who'd threatened her sister as well as kidnapping Charlotte. "I am not Gabby, either."

"Yes," the prince insisted. "You are my sweet, sweet Gabriella."

She shook her head. "'Fraid not."

"She kept saying that," the guard related. "Kept saying that we'd grabbed the wrong woman."

Prince Demetrios shook his head, but his swarthy complexion paled in the bright lights of the airstrip. "No. That's not possible."

"I'm Charlotte Green," she said. "You know that— now that you see me."

His voice lacked conviction even as he continued to insist, "It can't be..."

"You've seen us together," she reminded him, "at the ball." Because Gabriella had thought she could trust him. As well as being engaged since birth, they had been friends that long, too. She'd felt horrible over what her father had done.

One of his heavily lidded eyes twitched as anger

overwhelmed him. "I prefer not to remember that night and all its betrayals."

Now she wanted to calm him down, to make him see reason. If he hadn't kidnapped her, she might have almost felt sorry for him. In one night he'd lost the life he'd known—the one he'd planned—just like she had when she'd lost her memory. "Gabby and I had nothing to do with the king changing his plans."

"Suddenly my country—my wealth—was not sufficient for his daughter," the prince griped with all wounded pride. "For you..."

"I am not Gabriella," she said again, her voice sharp with irritation. "I am her bodyguard." And her sister. "You know we look exactly alike. I had plastic surgery to look like her, so that I could protect her from situations like this, from her getting abducted."

"Where is she?" Aaron asked the question. "What have you done with her? You must have mistaken her for Charlotte. Did you kill her?"

"Of course not! I would never kill anyone," he protested. "That was not part of the plan."

"What was the plan?" Aaron asked. "To kidnap and rape a woman?"

That eyelid twitched again. "I would never harm the woman I love. I was helping her. Her father put her in an impossible situation, and I gave her a way out. Since she's carrying my baby, the king cannot possibly make her marry another man."

"She's not carrying your baby," Aaron said. "She's carrying mine."

The prince sucked in a breath of outraged pride. "That is not possible."

"She was already pregnant when you grabbed her in Paris," Aaron explained. "She's carrying my baby."

Charlotte's heart warmed with the possessiveness in Aaron's voice. He had claimed her baby. If only he would now claim her...

"It doesn't matter whose baby I'm carrying," she said. "I'm not Gabriella."

The prince turned toward his guard. "Could it be? Did you grab the wrong woman in Paris?"

The guard shook his head. "There was only one woman in that suite."

ONLY ONE WOMAN. Aaron couldn't even consider the implications of that claim. "There was so much blood, so much destruction," he said. "The authorities believe someone died there."

The guard nodded. "I lost a friend because of this woman. I could not hurt her then...because I had my orders to not harm the princess." He lifted the gun he clutched in his nonbandaged hand. "But if she's really not the princess..."

"I'm not," she said, "but I am the woman holding a gun on your boss. And I'm not so sure that you're going to be all that accurate shooting with your left hand. So if your bullet misses, mine won't."

The prince shuddered at her cold pronouncement and so did Aaron. She would have no qualms about pulling that trigger—about taking the life of an unarmed man.

"You're not my sweet Gabriella," the prince said, his voice choked with disappointment. "Where is she?"

"Where you will never get to her," Charlotte vowed with a conviction that had disappointment clenching Aaron's heart in a tight fist.

He realized that she had known all along—or at least as soon as her memory returned—exactly where Princess Gabriella was. Obviously because she had stashed her there…

Charlotte pushed the barrel of her gun against the prince's skinny chest. "You're going to be locked up for the rest of your life."

Maybe she didn't know—maybe that was simply what she meant—that he wouldn't be able to get to Gabriella through the prison bars he would be behind.

"I told you that I harmed no one," Prince Demetrios insisted.

"You were the one who killed my friend," the guard said, clutching that gun tightly. The murderous intent in his eyes revealed how much he wanted to pull that trigger, how much he wanted to take Charlotte's life—after having already taken her freedom and her memory.

"There are a stack of bodies back at Serenity House," Aaron said, "thanks to you."

The prince turned toward his employee. "Mr. Centerenian? What are they talking about?"

The guard tensed. With guilt? But he claimed, "I have killed no one…*yet.*"

"That nurse was killed." Charlotte addressed the prince instead of his employee. "The one you hired to take care of me. Sandy…"

"And the young reporter the nurse tipped off about your kidnapping," Aaron added. "And the administrator you paid to impregnate the princess with your sperm."

"She didn't do it," Charlotte hastened to add when the prince's dark gaze lowered to her stomach. "Is that why you ordered her and the others killed? To cover your tracks?"

"Bullets were flying everywhere," Aaron said. "It was a wonder that Charlotte wasn't hit, too." Or him. It was bad enough that Whit had been.

The prince shook his head—his pride appearing every bit as wounded as it had over losing his fiancée. "I am not a killer," he said.

"You didn't pull the trigger yourself," Charlotte agreed.

"But you must have had your goon do it," Aaron finished for her.

The prince glanced toward his guard again. Even he must have begun to suspect him. "I told you to take her and to keep her safe."

Aaron gestured toward the bruise on her head. "He did that to her. He nearly killed her—despite your orders. You don't think he could have hurt anyone else?"

The prince glared at his employee. "I did not tell you to kill anyone."

"You are a fool," the guard remarked with pure disgust. "You will spend the rest of your life in prison. You do not understand that you can't leave loose ends."

"So you shot them?" Charlotte asked. "You killed all those people."

"The reporter and that stupid nurse," the guard agreed. "And now all of you. I will not spend my life in prison for some lovesick fool."

And he raised his gun and fired.

Chapter Thirteen

"Nice shot," Charlotte remarked, as the guard clasped his other hand. Aaron had used a bullet to knock the gun from the guard's hand.

But the man didn't stop—he charged at Aaron and tackled him to the cement floor of the hangar. His breath audibly whooshed out of his probably almost crushed lungs. Mr. Centerenian was much larger than Aaron but more fat than muscle. Aaron was the more experienced fighter. He tossed him off with a kick and a punch. Then the guard swung back. But Mr. Centerenian screamed in pain when his bloodied fist connected with the cement floor since Aaron had rolled out of his line of fire.

The two men continued to grapple with each other. But another man made his move, stepping back from Charlotte and heading toward the plane.

She caught him by the back of his jacket. "You're not going anywhere...except behind bars."

The tall man turned slowly toward her. Then he moved, as if to lunge at her.

But she lifted her gun and pressed it into his chest again. "I told you that I will shoot you," she said. "Given what I went through—the months I lost—because of you, I really should kill you."

"I thought you were Gabriella…"

"And that makes me want to pull this trigger even more," she said. Anger and dread surged through her with the thought of Gabby enduring what she had. The pain. The confusion.

First her father had betrayed the princess. And now the man she had considered a lifelong friend had betrayed her, too. Despite Gabby having grown up with the palace and the money, Charlotte was really more fortunate; she had learned early to count on no one. To trust no one.

She'd also learned that it was safer to love no one. But she'd messed up there. First she'd fallen under the spell of her sister's sweetness. And then Aaron's irresistible charms…

"Is she all right? Is she safe?" Prince Demetrios asked, his pride forgotten as he pleaded for information.

Gabby had considered him a friend when it seemed obvious now that he'd been more of a stalker.

"I need to know," he asked, his voice cracking with emotion. "I have loved her my whole life. I need to know that she's all right."

Whatever sympathy she'd fleetingly felt for the man was gone. She cared only about making sure Gabby was safe now. "And I need to know everything you know. I need to know every damn thing that you were behind."

"I told you," the prince said, his voice rising so that he sounded more like a whiny child than a grown man. The king had been right to end this betrothal—for so many reasons. "I only wanted Gabby—wanted us bound together for life."

"And instead so many people lost their lives," she mused and glared at him with condemnation.

"I didn't know that Mr. Centerenian shot the nurse and a reporter."

"And the administrator," Charlotte added.

"And my friend." Aaron jerked the beaten guard to his feet and shoved him toward the prince. "Make him tell us everything."

"I did," Mr. Centerenian insisted. "I told you that I cleaned up the mess he left. I killed the nurse and the man she kept sneaking away to meet. I did not kill anyone else."

"Then you hired those men to kill the administrator," Aaron said. "And try to kill us."

"No," the guard protested. "I knew Dr. Platt would not talk. And she had promised to get rid of any evidence that could lead back to the prince or me."

"Someone killed her," Aaron said. "So you didn't need to worry about that evidence after all. Or about her testifying against you."

"I told you—she would not talk."

Charlotte believed that—the woman had seemed quite stubborn. But she'd obviously had her price. Prince Demetrios had found it; someone else might have been able—if they'd had deep enough pockets. "I don't know about that. But I do know that, with all those bullets flying in that office—" she patted her stomach "—we could have been killed, too."

The prince gasped in horror. He was a sick man. But apparently he was not a killer.

"I had orders to not harm you," Mr. Centerenian said, "or I would not have been paid."

She touched the bruise on her temple now.

"Kill you," he amended himself. "I could not kill you. But had I known who you really were…"

She would have been dead. But even with all those bullets flying, none had come close to her. Maybe the shooters had just had qualms about killing a pregnant woman. Or maybe they'd had orders. At any rate, she believed someone other than Mr. Centerenian and Prince Demetrios had hired them.

Why?

"WHAT ABOUT THE parking lot?" Aaron asked the guard as an officer loaded him into the backseat of a state police cruiser.

He had called the authorities from the phone they'd found in the hangar. And the only reason he and Charlotte weren't being loaded into cruisers themselves for questioning was because of the threats of Stanley Jessup's influential lawyer. They had called the media mogul, too.

The older man had gone above and beyond all the favors Aaron had asked of him. Well, except for telling Whit where he was. But he had only confided in the other man because Whit had convinced him that Aaron was in danger.

Stanley Jessup was a hell of a lot more forgiving than he would have been. If someone had failed to protect his daughter, Aaron wouldn't have cared if the guy put himself in danger. Hell, he would have preferred it. Instead Stanley kept helping them—with doctors, lawyers and a safe place to stay.

But no place would ever be really safe if there was another shooter out there.

He asked the guard again, "You shot at me in the parking lot, right?"

Mr. Centerenian shook his head and then boasted, "I would not have missed had I been shooting at you."

Aaron could have pointed out that he had missed him in the hall. That he'd hit a vase instead of him. But this man didn't matter anymore. He apparently wasn't behind the shooting in the administrator's office.

So who was?

The prince was being loaded into the back of a separate police cruiser. Charlotte stood beside him, facing the prince instead of Aaron.

"You said that you'd tell me where Gabriella is," the prince implored her. "We had a deal…"

"The deal was," she corrected him, "that you would tell me everything you know—"

"And I did," he interjected.

"And I would tell you that she was all right—not where she is," Charlotte reminded him of the details of their agreement. "She's all right."

"But you won't tell me where she is?"

She shook her head, and the long waves of golden-brown hair rippled down her back. "I won't tell anyone where she is."

But she knew. Aaron heard the certainty in her voice. All this time he and Whit had been concerned about Princess Gabriella and Charlotte had known exactly where she was.

Whit was right. Again. When was he going to learn that he couldn't trust Charlotte Green?

"Don't ask me," she said as she stood beside him, watching the police cars leave the airstrip.

"I know better than to think you'd tell me anything," Aaron admitted. "But you should tell the king. He's been out of his mind worrying about her."

"Of course he has."

Aaron winced at his insensitive remark. "I'm sure he's been worried about you, too," he amended himself. "It's just that I didn't know then that you're his—"

"Bastard?" She shrugged, as if she didn't care, but he suspected she cared a lot. "Doesn't matter. I don't matter. Only the legitimate heir matters. Gabriella is the only child he can profit from—using her to further his empire with money and power. That's why I won't tell him where she is."

"But aren't you using her, too, then?" Aaron pointed out her double standard. "To get back at him for never acknowledging you?"

Her eyes, the same golden-brown of her hair, darkened with anger. "I wouldn't use Gabby. I only want to keep her safe."

"Is she?" Aaron wondered. "We don't know who's behind the shooting in the administrator's office."

"If we believe Mr. Centerenian and the prince's claims that it wasn't one of them," she said.

"We shouldn't," Aaron agreed. "We shouldn't believe or trust anyone." That fact had been driven home to him time and time again—with every lie and omission Charlotte had uttered.

Charlotte nodded. "And that's why I won't tell the king where Gabby is."

"That's the reason you're telling yourself," Aaron agreed. "To justify not telling him. But we both know that's not the real reason."

"Let's forget about my reasons," she said, "and focus on the reason that someone would have been shooting at you in the parking lot—"

"So I wouldn't be able to come back for you," he pointed out. That was what he'd figured at the time. Now he wasn't so certain…

"The guard said he didn't do it."

"And we trust what he said?"

She shrugged. "He admitted to two murders. Why wouldn't he admit to trying to kill you? What difference would it make at this point?"

"It would answer the rest of our damn questions," he said. "Well, not all of our questions."

Because she refused to tell him where Princess Gabriella was…

"If we figure this out, if I'm sure she's safe," Charlotte said, "I will consider revealing her location."

He nodded. "So we'll figure this out. If not the guard, who else would want to shoot at me?"

"And Whit," she said. "He was hit in the administrator's office."

"You were shot at, too," he reminded her.

"You stood between me and gunmen, kept me behind the filing cabinet," she said. "So no one really shot at me." But she had shot back.

If she hadn't, he and Whit probably wouldn't have made it out of that office alive. They probably would have wound up as dead as the administrator had.

"Just because you didn't get shot, doesn't mean you weren't the target," he pointed out. "But if you weren't, the shooting seems like more work of the prince."

Or was there someone else out there that Aaron had been too naive to consider? Just like he had been naive to think that Charlotte had finally started being honest with him.

"What about Trigger?" she asked. "Where has he been since he dropped us at that cabin?"

"Maybe the guard got rid of him like he had the reporter and the nurse," Aaron said. But then why wouldn't he have admitted it as he'd admitted to the other two murders?

Charlotte shook her head. "I doubt it. Trigger is like a cat with nine lives. He's out there. Somewhere."

CHARLOTTE SHUDDERED AT the thought. She hadn't liked working with the older man. Mostly because he had been a first-class jerk and a male chauvinist. But also because she hadn't trusted him.

Trigger had reminded her too much of her mother— both were totally concerned with their own welfare and no one else's.

If he'd ever had a daughter, he would have sold her, too. She'd suspected he would have sold a witness's location, and that was why she hadn't told him where Josie Jessup had been relocated.

She had only told one person where Josie was— just in case something ever happened to her. And she'd thought the two women would be good friends.

Had Trigger figured that out? Had he figured out where she'd stashed Gabriella? And if they'd convinced the man that she was Gabriella, then he would think that Gabriella was Charlotte Green, his ex-partner.

"I have a bad feeling," she said.

"You're not feeling well?" Aaron asked, reaching for her arm to steady her. "We should get you back to the house."

He led her toward the car and helped her into the passenger's seat.

No matter how angry he was at her—and she suspected he was furious since she hadn't told him she knew where Princess Gabby was—he was still courteous with her. Because of the baby?

"I may have put Gabby at risk," she admitted, hating herself for what she'd done. "And not just Gabby but Josie, too."

"What have you done?" he asked.

"I told Gabby where Josie is," she admitted. "If Trigger finds her…" He wasn't beyond torturing her to discover where the witness was hidden—especially not if he was being paid handsomely to find her.

"You're the only one who knows where Gabby is," he said.

Now she couldn't tell him what she had done. Aaron would probably never forgive her for putting the life of the woman he loved in danger. And she knew better than to reveal a witness's location to anyone. But she had never felt closer to another human being than she had her sister.

Until now.

To soothe herself more than her baby, she rubbed her hands over her belly. Aaron had given her this child, but yet she didn't feel as close to him. Because one woman—a woman she herself considered a friend— had always stood between them.

"Josie's fine," Aaron said. "She's safe."

His empty assurances hung in the air between them as he drove the distance back to Stanley Jessup's rental house. He pulled the car up next to the dark house and turned off the engine. "We'll ask Whit to help us get to the bottom of who is behind the other shootings."

After his taking a bullet for Aaron back in the administrator's office, she now trusted the king's other bodyguard—as much as she let herself trust anyone. But would Gabriella?

The man had hurt her…because he had let her go. He had just stood there, the morning after the ball, and had silently watched her leave for Paris, to design her wedding gown to marry another man. Like Charlotte with Aaron, Gabriella had hoped for more with Whit Howell.

"I'm not sure we should include Whit," she said, remembering that Gabby had claimed to want nothing more to do with him.

"The doctor said the bullet didn't strike anything vital," Aaron assured her. "Once the painkillers wear off, he'll be fine—determined to go again."

"But maybe he shouldn't…"

He studied her face in the darkness. "You still don't trust Whit?"

She held her breath, unwilling to admit her real problem with Howell—sisterly allegiance.

"You trusted him enough to involve him in faking Josie's death."

And not Aaron. She needed no further assurance that he would never get over not knowing that Josie hadn't really died.

"I can understand you not trusting me back then," Aaron said, surprising her with his words and his closeness as he leaned across the console separating their seats. "You didn't know me that well."

She hadn't known Whit then either, so she'd trusted Josie's judgment on which one of her bodyguards to include in her plan. Josie hadn't wanted to put Aaron in the untenable position of having to lie to her father. She'd said he was too nice to have to deal with that burden. They hadn't realized that they'd given him a far heavier burden of guilt to carry in thinking that he'd failed to protect Josie.

"But you know me now, Charlotte." His hands covered hers on her belly, and he entwined their fingers, binding them together just as their baby did. But then he leaned even closer, and his lips brushed over hers with teasing, whisper-soft kisses.

Her breath caught in her throat as desire overwhelmed her. The man's kisses stole away her common sense as effectively as that blow to her head had stolen her memories. All he had to do was touch her and she wanted him, the need spiraling out of control inside her.

But it was more than want. More even than need. It was love.

Aaron pulled back and asked, "So why do you still not trust me?"

Because he could hurt her more than anyone else ever had. Because she wanted more from him. She wanted his love. But he wasn't talking about their relationship.

"I get why you didn't tell me about Josie," he said. "But you should have told me about Gabriella." He stepped out of the car and slammed the door behind himself.

Gunshots echoed the slam. The windows burst, glass shattering as bullets hit them.

Shards struck Charlotte, stinging her skin, but she didn't duck yet. Because she was looking for Aaron. He'd disappeared. Had he been hit?

Her door creaked open, and a strong hand grasped her arm, pulling her from the car. Just like Paris, she was getting grabbed again. And just like Paris, she wouldn't go without a fight.

Chapter Fourteen

Aaron grunted as her elbow struck his chin. "Stop it," he said. "I'm trying to help you."

It was probably too late for him to help Whit. He couldn't believe he hadn't realized it before. He should have known…

Charlotte gasped in shock, and her struggles ceased. "You're all right?"

He nodded, his chin rubbing against her silky soft hair. Physically he was fine. For the moment…

"Trigger must have followed us," she said, whispering since the gunshots had stopped. "He must have found this place."

"I'm not so sure it's Trigger." He had a horrible feeling that it was someone else.

She peered around the car, looking for the shooter. "Who else…?"

"Maybe a man who lost his daughter…"

"The king?" She shook her head in rejection of that idea. "Rafael doesn't care enough about either me or Gabriella to—" She gasped and turned to him with wide eyes. "Josie's father?"

"I was a fool to ask for his help," Aaron said. "It must

have brought all those feelings rushing back—all his pain and resentment."

"No…" She shook her head, her brow furrowing with confusion. "It doesn't make any sense…"

"Stanley Jessup gave me the tip that brought me here," he reminded her. Sure, Aaron had asked the man to flush out any leads to Princess Gabriella's whereabouts. And in doing that, he might have given the grieving father the perfect opportunity to take his revenge.

Charlotte expelled an unsteady breath. "And he came, too."

"And more than that, he told Whit that I was here—getting us both in the same place." Another gunshot rang out, pinging off the metal roof of the sports car. "It has to be Jessup."

Charlotte shook her head. "No, it has to be someone else." She ducked low as shots pinged off the fenders. "Josie talks about her dad all the time." Her voice carried a faint trace of wistfulness. "She told me what a good man he is…"

"Josie was the center of his universe," Aaron said. "She meant everything to him." His baby wasn't even born, and he could identify with those feelings. Maybe because he already had those feelings for Charlotte. If something had happened to her…

She clutched her gun in her hand, but she seemed reluctant to aim it in the direction from which the shots had come. Maybe she was reluctant to take a shot and hurt a man who had already been through so much pain. "But I didn't think he blamed you two for what happened—or what he thinks happened to Josie."

"I blamed us," Aaron reminded her. "I ended my partnership—my friendship—with Whit."

For no reason. Whit had only been doing his duty—keeping Josie safe. And now Aaron might never have the chance to regain the friendship he had stupidly and stubbornly given up.

"I have to get in that house," he said, fear and desperation clawing at him as it had when he'd stood outside that burning house over three years ago and thought he'd been too late to save Josie. "I have to make sure that Whit—that Whit is…"

She must have picked up on his hopelessness because she squeezed his arm reassuringly. "Whit Howell is resourceful," she reminded him. "And he's smart. Maybe he figured it out in time."

"Whit was out," Aaron said, and he hated himself for really doing what he'd thought he and Whit had done three years ago—leaving someone alone and vulnerable who had needed his protection. While he hadn't actually failed Josie, he had failed his friend—the man who'd risked his life to save Aaron's more than once. "He was out cold on those painkillers—a sitting duck for Stanley Jessup to take his revenge."

The gunfire continued to come, bullets striking the car and the asphalt driveway near them. "But why is he shooting at *me?*" Charlotte asked. "Do you think Whit told him how I was involved?"

"No." He shook his head. "If he knew his daughter was still alive, he wouldn't be shooting at all," he told her. "Maybe he's using you to try to flush me out."

Or maybe Jessup intended to take Aaron's family from him the way that he thought his family had been taken from him.

"Let's flush *him* out," Charlotte suggested, raising her gun. "You need to get in that house. You need to check on Whit." Even though she hadn't always seemed to trust his friend and vice versa, she was concerned about him—enough to risk her own safety. She rose up and fired off a round of shots in rapid succession, giving Aaron the time and the cover to sprint toward the house.

Keeping low, he ran toward the windows of the den and, heedless of the glass, jumped through them. A hard fist struck his jaw, knocking him down onto the floor. He hit the hardwood with a bounce and popped up again to strike back. He swung his gun like a bat, hitting out with the handle. Blindly—because he couldn't see anything but a big shadow in the total darkness.

The man's eyes must have adjusted better to the dark because he caught Aaron's weapon and tried to wrest it from his grasp. Aaron was stronger, though, and retained control of the gun. He twisted it around and pressed the barrel against the temple of the man.

"Just shoot me then, you son of a bitch," the guy said with a snarl of rage and hatred.

Aaron uttered a deep laugh of pure relief. "You're alive!"

"Yeah," Whit grumbled, almost as if he wasn't entirely convinced that he lived yet. "But I feel like crap from the painkillers, and then I get attacked. By you…"

"I didn't think it was you," Aaron explained. "I thought you got shot again."

"The gunman's out there," Whit said, as more gunfire shattered the night. His voice dropped with suspicion. "Where's Charlotte?"

"She's not the shooter." But he'd left her alone with him. Panic clutched Aaron's stomach. "She's out there. She covered me, so I could get in here to check on you."

Whit snorted. "So you both thought I was dead? Some confidence—"

He grabbed Whit, inadvertently clutching his bad

shoulder and eliciting a cry of pain from his friend. But he didn't have time to apologize—not with Charlotte out there alone. "Where's Stanley?"

"He went down to the police station to help you out," Whit said. "He thought you guys might get booked no matter what his lawyer said to the authorities."

"Are you sure he really left?" Aaron asked. "You weren't still out of it?"

Whit shook his head. "No. I was clearheaded—even offered to go with him, but he said no."

"He wanted you here," Aaron said, "so that he could take his revenge on us together."

Whit snorted again. "Revenge?"

"Because of Josie."

Whit lifted a hand to his head, as if trying to clear it of the aftereffects of the painkillers. "But Josie's not dead."

"Her father doesn't know that," Aaron pointed out. "He thinks she's dead and he probably blames us. He hired us to protect her, and we failed."

Whit opened his mouth again but only a groan escaped. And Aaron hadn't even grabbed his shoulder again. "But it doesn't make any sense…"

"In *his* eyes we failed," Aaron said.

"In your eyes, too," Whit admitted. "It was what you thought. You don't think that's really Stanley Jessup out there?"

Aaron was afraid that it was, and he was afraid that he had left Charlotte out there alone with the madman.

WITH ALL THE shots flying, Charlotte had no way of knowing if Aaron had made it safely inside the house. She had heard breaking glass. Was it from bullets or from a body flying through a window?

It was too dark for her to see anything. And tonight there wasn't even a sliver of the moon that had been out the previous evening. She could see nothing of the house. Or the gunman.

Was it only one? Was it Stanley Jessup?

Josie had been so convinced that her dad was a good man. But he had made enemies—with the stories he'd run on all his media outlets. Good men didn't make enemies, did they?

But then even if he was a good man, he could have let his grief and loss drive him over the edge. If all that mattered to him now was vengeance, he wouldn't rest until both Whit and Aaron were dead.

Maybe Whit was already dead.

Aaron would be devastated if he was. Just as he had blamed himself for Josie's death, he would blame himself for Whit's. Maybe even more so because they had been estranged, their friendship destroyed because of her.

She was the one whom Aaron needed to blame. Not himself. The burden of guilt should be hers to bear—not his.

If he wanted to kill the person responsible for him losing his daughter, Jessup should be trying to kill her—not them. She moved around the back of the car and kept low behind the hedges that lined the driveway. She made it to the garage. Her foot struck some shells, sending them skittering across the asphalt.

This was where the man had been standing when he'd fired round after round at the Camaro. And at her and Aaron. Where had he gone?

She clutched her gun in her hand and spun around, looking for him.

"Over here, Charlotte," a gruff voice murmured.

Whose voice? Whit's? It wasn't Aaron because her pulse didn't quicken. Charlotte's heart didn't warm with hope and love. And the baby didn't move in her womb in reaction to her father's voice.

"You looked." The voice was closer now and clearer as the man taunted her. "When I said your name, you looked. I knew it was you." He hid yet in the shadows. "Just from the way you held a gun, I knew it was you."

"Trigger."

All of her lies had destroyed Aaron's trust so much that he had begun to suspect everyone of having ulterior motives. But her gut—and maybe the baby moving inside it—had convinced her it was her old partner.

"That Timmer guy made me doubt myself though," he admitted. "So I went back to Serenity House and talked to the administrator—flashed my U.S. Marshal badge to get her talking."

"She wouldn't have told you anything," Charlotte said, remembering how stubborn that woman had been.

"She didn't realize she was telling me anything," he said, his voice still taunting her from the darkness. "She just answered my questions about your scars. Well, her face answered them with her reaction. She just confirmed what I already knew though."

She didn't bother trying to deny who she was. She just asked, "Did you hurt the man inside the house?"

"What man? The old, rich guy left a while ago," he said.

So maybe he didn't even know about Whit. Maybe that could work to their advantage. If the men realized she needed help in time...

Before it was too late...

"I waited here for you and Timmer to come back," Trigger said. "My source with the state police department told me that they let you two go but arrested some royal subject and his goon bodyguard. So I figured you two would be heading back."

"Then you waited for us and started shooting?" she asked. "What if you'd hit me? How was I going to tell you what you wanted to know then?"

"They don't call me Trigger for nothing," he said with unearned arrogance. "I know how to handle a gun. I only shoot what I mean to."

She could have argued that point with examples. But she just nodded—regardless of whether or not he could see the motion in the dark. "What about those men in the administrator's office? Weren't you worried about them shooting me?"

He chuckled. "What would make you think I had anything to do with that? Didn't they kill that woman?"

"After you questioned her about me," she pointed out. "You spooked her. That's why she was destroying records when we got to her office. That's why you killed her, so she wouldn't admit that she already talked to a U.S. Marshal. Were you trying to get rid of any trace that you'd even been there? That you'd even tracked me down?"

"That lady didn't really matter one way or the other," he said offhandedly. "I told the guys to take the shot if they got it."

How had a lawman become so callous about life? Was it that they had faked so many witnesses' deaths that he didn't realize that some deaths were *real?*

"And me?" she asked.

"They weren't supposed to shoot you," he assured her. "I just paid them to get rid of the men with you."

"Those men are better than you realized," she said with pride. "Or maybe you knew how good they are and that's why you hired the guys but stayed out of the line of fire yourself." Even now he stubbornly stayed in the shadows, so that she couldn't get a clear shot at him. He was both a bully and a coward.

He chuckled again. "They can't help you now."

Her heart slammed into her ribs. Had he killed them? Was it already too late for her to save the man she loved? Was it too late for her to tell Aaron that she loved him?

Her feelings probably wouldn't matter to him. But she needed to say the words—needed to let him know how much he meant to her. And she needed the chance to tell him.

It didn't matter that she didn't have the shot. She lifted her gun to fire into the darkness.

"I wouldn't do that," Trigger warned. And he finally stepped from the shadows. Or at least he dissipated the darkness when he screwed back in the bulb of the porch light under which he stood. His gun wasn't pointed at her though.

She could have taken the shot. But Trigger was Trigger *Happy*. His finger was already pressed to the trigger of his gun while the barrel of it was pressed against Aaron's temple.

"I know you, Charlotte," he said. "There was no way in hell you would tell me what I want to know to save yourself. I could press this gun to your head and you would let me pull the trigger before you'd ever give me the location of the witness."

She nodded. "True. I won't reveal the location of a witness." Any witness, but most especially one with whom she'd bonded like she had Josie. It was no wonder that Aaron had fallen for the woman. She was smart and funny and sweet. And she deserved to live her life in peace—not with the constant threat of danger.

"But I think if it comes down between his life and hers, you'll pick his," Trigger said.

Aaron laughed. "You don't know her as well as you think you do."

"I think you're the one who doesn't know her," Trigger said. "She loves you. Even when she didn't really know who *she* was, Dr. Platt confirmed the amnesia wasn't a trick, Charlotte knew that she loved you."

She had wanted Aaron to know her feelings, but she'd wanted to be the one to tell him. And how had Trigger so easily recognized what had taken her so long to realize?

"I saw it on her face," he continued talking to Aaron. "She won't let me kill you."

The guy was a hell of a lot smarter than Charlotte had given him credit for.

"So before I pull this trigger," Trigger warned her, "you better tell me what I need to know. Where is Josie Jessup?"

Need to. Not want to know…

This was about more than money to Trigger, which made him even more desperate and dangerous. He would pull that trigger.

"Don't tell him," Aaron said. "Let him shoot!"

Charlotte flinched with the realization that the man she loved still loved another woman—so much that he was willing to give up his life for hers.

But Charlotte wasn't willing to make that sacrifice.

Aaron might never be hers. But he belonged to someone else—he was the father of the baby she carried.

And he would be a good father—the kind of father a little girl needed.

"I'll tell you," she said. "I'll tell you what you want to know."

IT WAS A trick. Charlotte Green wouldn't give up the location of a witness. Not for her own life. And not for anyone else's.

Aaron knew that as well as the U.S. Marshal did. The older man tensed and buried the barrel of his gun even deeper into the skin of Aaron's temple.

"You're going to tell me?" Trigger asked, his voice cracking with suspicion. "Really?"

"Let him go," she negotiated, "and I'll tell you."

Trigger laughed. "You always treated me like I'm an idiot. You really think I'm going to take your word that'll you tell me where she is once I release my leverage?"

"Do you think it matters?" Aaron asked. "Do you really think she's going to give you Josie's real location? She could tell you anywhere. Could set you up to walk into a booby-trapped house and get your head blown off. You just said she thinks you're an idiot." He snorted. "Sounds like she's right to think that."

"Aaron—" she protested.

It probably wasn't his smartest move to goad the man holding a gun to his head. But then he'd never been all that smart where Charlotte was involved.

Apparently neither had Trigger since the guy actually thought she loved Aaron. Sure, she was attracted to him. Their attraction was so strong that the air between them fairly sizzled when they got close. But love was something else. Love implied need. And Charlotte

Green had never needed anyone. She took independence and self-sufficiency to an extreme.

"You better not give me the wrong location," Trigger threatened. "Because I'm bringing him with me and if your directions don't lead me to Josie Jessup, he'll get that bullet in his head."

That had no doubt been his plan all along—to put a bullet in his head and one in Charlotte's, too. He couldn't leave behind any witnesses.

But he couldn't kill Charlotte until he knew for certain she'd given him the correct location.

Charlotte lifted her hands above her head, as if she were being held up. "All right, I'll tell you the truth."

She met Aaron's gaze, hers dark with frustration. And something else...pain.

How had he hurt her? He was trying to help her. Didn't she realize?

"Ironically she's not that far from here," she said. "She's in Michigan, too." She named a city just a few hours north of where they were. Then she added a number and a street name.

Trigger grabbed Aaron's arm and jerked him along with him, dragging him toward his vehicle. But the gun never left his temple. It would no doubt leave a mark even if the guy didn't shoot.

"You can't take him with you," Charlotte protested. "I gave you what you wanted."

"But as the man pointed out, you can't be trusted, Charlotte." He pushed Aaron through the passenger's side of his car, keeping his gun barrel tight against his temple. "He's my insurance that you're telling the truth. If you are, I might let him live."

The barrel vibrated as the man laughed with amusement over his own sick joke. "And if you are lying to me," Trigger said, "I'll be back. I'll find you again. And the next person I'll take away from you will be your kid."

Charlotte gasped with obvious fear, and her palm protectively covered her belly.

"It'd be a shame for him to be raised without a father anyway," Trigger said, turning the proverbial knife. "Look what it did to you."

Aaron saw the pain cross Charlotte's face, and he wanted to hurt Trigger for hurting her. He wanted to make the man suffer as he was making her suffer.

Didn't she realize that Aaron had a plan? Didn't she trust him?

No. She wouldn't tell him where Josie was. She wouldn't even tell him where Princess Gabriella was. He doubted she had given Trigger the real location. Maybe that was the reason for the pained look on her face.

Guilt.

She thought she had sealed his death warrant.

Aaron tried to catch her attention, tried, with his gaze, to convince her not to worry. But then he did have a gun pressed to his head. And the U.S. Marshal's real nickname wasn't just Trigger. But Happy…

He was laughing yet, still amused by his sick joke. He shoved the barrel harder into Aaron's skin. "Start the car, damn it!"

He obliged, turning the key and shifting it from Park to Drive.

"And no crazy stunt driving like the other night," Trigger warned, pressing a hand over the bump on his forehead.

"That wasn't me," Aaron assured him. "That was my friend. Whit."

Trigger's brow furrowed. "The guy who got shot at the administrator's office?"

Aaron nodded, knocking the barrel a little loose.

"I'm glad the son of a bitch got shot then."

Aaron pressed on the accelerator, easing the car away from where Charlotte stood, staring helplessly after them.

"She really loves you," Trigger remarked. "Didn't think the ice princess had it in her. But she gave up the witness location."

"How do you know it's the real one?" he asked again, wanting the guy to be doubtful and nervous.

"You better hope it is," Trigger threatened, "or you'll be paying the price for her lies."

"Maybe you'll be paying the price," Aaron remarked. "It could still be a trap. That place is three hours away—gives her three hours to have authorities in place to grab you."

"We're not going there," Trigger said, fishing a phone out of his pocket. "All I needed was to get the address. I don't need to go there."

Aaron glanced into the rearview mirror where Charlotte's figure was getting smaller and smaller. She stood there when she needed to be getting on the phone, needed to be getting Josie to safety.

Unless she'd done as Aaron had suspected, given Trigger a false address.

"So this person who must be paying you a pretty penny, he or she won't be upset if you send them into a trap?"

"What?"

"Like I said, you really don't think Charlotte Green gave up the actual location of a witness…especially one she considers a friend?"

Trigger glanced back, too—just distracted enough that he gave Aaron a chance to reach for the gun. But they barely grappled with it before a shot rang out— shattering the windshield.

And ending a life…

Chapter Fifteen

The gunshot shattered the eerie silence that had fallen once the car pulled down the driveway of the rental house. Brake lights flashed on that car, and a horn blared.

A scream tore from Charlotte's throat. He'd shot Aaron. He'd shot him.

She'd thought Aaron had had a plan. That was the only reason she'd let them pull away. Otherwise she might have risked a shot; she would have tried to hit her old partner. But with his finger already on the trigger, there was no way he wouldn't have pulled it—even if just by reflex.

But at least then she would have had the satisfaction of taking out the Marshal herself. A satisfaction she still intended to have.

Tears streaming down her face like rain off a rock, she ran down the driveway—heading toward the stopped car. She bypassed the driver's side. She couldn't see Aaron—like she'd seen those other shooting victims. Instead she headed toward the passenger's side, jerked open the door and pointed her gun inside. Her finger trembled as she moved to squeeze the trigger.

"You can't kill him twice," a male voice remarked. The man sprawled in the backseat.

And Trigger slumped over the dash, a bullet in his head and his blood sprayed across the shattered windshield.

"Aaron!" she screamed his name, trying to peer around the other man to the driver's side. But it was empty—no one sitting behind the wheel.

Then warm hands closed over her shoulders, twirling her toward him—pulling her tight against a strong chest. "Shh..." a deep voice murmured into her ear.

She shivered and trembled in reaction to the horror she had just endured over thinking him dead. "You're alive!"

"I'm fine," he assured her.

But blood had spattered the side of his face when Whit had killed Trigger. Seeing it on his face had her stomach lurching with fear over what could have happened, over how that blood could have been his.

She pulled back and swung her palm at him, striking his shoulder hard enough to propel him back a couple of steps. "You're an idiot! How could you do that? How could you risk your life that way?"

"We had a plan," Whit said. His face twisted into a grimace of pain as he crawled from the backseat and joined them on the driveway.

"What kind of plan?" she asked, anger eclipsing her earlier relief. "A suicide pact?"

Whit pointed toward the front seat. "Only one who wound up dead was the bad guy."

She stared hard at the king's blond bodyguard. Even though she had worked with him to stage Josie's murder, she hadn't trusted him. Maybe because he'd agreed to keep a secret from a man he'd claimed was his best friend.

"I'm really not a bad guy," he said.

She threw her arms around him, hugging him tight. He grunted with pain.

And Aaron protested, "Why are you hugging him? I'm the one who risked my life."

"You're not helping your cause with that," Whit said, as he awkwardly patted Charlotte's back. "I think that could be why she's pissed at you."

"Well, I'm not exactly thrilled with her, either," Aaron admitted.

"Lovers' spat?" Whit teased.

"She doesn't just know where Josie is," Aaron said. "She knows where Princess Gabriella is too."

Whit's hands clenched on Charlotte's shoulders, pulling her back. "You know? Have you known all along?"

She uttered a shaky sigh and stepped back—away from both angry men. "Just since my memory returned."

"Since then?" Whit seemed more appalled than Aaron had been.

Aaron had just seemed betrayed. It would be a miracle if he ever trusted her again. And now that he knew where Josie was…

She expected him to leave soon. She glanced inside the car again. "We need to call the police."

"And probably Stanley Jessup's lawyer," Aaron added. "To help us explain everything that's happened and how a U.S. Marshal wound up dead."

"I had to shoot him," Whit said, "or he was going to kill you."

That feeling of panic and loss struck Charlotte again. She had nearly lost him. Not that she still wasn't going to lose him. He would be a part of his child's life. But he probably wouldn't be a part of hers.

And that was fine. She had never envisioned for herself the fairy-tale, happily-ever-after ending.

"You saved my life," Aaron said, and patted his friend's shoulder in appreciation.

Whit groaned in pain. "Damn it! Stop doing that!"

"I'll leave the two of you alone," Charlotte said, "to bond again." But she didn't make it two steps before Whit stopped her, with his hand on her arm.

"You're going to tell me where Gabby is."

She shook her head. "I haven't talked to her in six months. I need to make certain she still is where I sent her. And I have to find out if she's ready to see anyone yet."

"It's been six months," Whit reiterated. "Why would she need more time before she would want to see anyone?"

"She felt betrayed," Charlotte reminded him. "She's hurt and she's scared. And it may take more than six months for her to get over it." Because she suspected it would take more than six months for Aaron to get over her betraying him.

"I'll call her," she offered. Actually now that the threat against Gabriella was gone, Charlotte couldn't wait to see her sister again. They had so much to talk about—like the fact that Gabby was going to be an aunt.

Hell, she didn't even know that Charlotte was her sister. The king had forbidden her to tell the younger woman the truth. He hadn't thought Gabby was strong enough to handle that, but he'd had no problem passing her from potential bridegroom to potential bridegroom.

Charlotte should have ignored his threat to fire her if she told the truth. Because, by keeping that secret, she had betrayed the princess just as everyone else had. Charlotte was done keeping secrets; it was time for her to be honest with her sister. It was too late for her to be honest with Aaron.

As she headed toward the house, she felt both men watching her. With resentment...

And her heart ached with loss. Aaron was alive, but he would never be hers.

"GOD, THAT WOMAN is infuriating!" Whit exclaimed, staring after Charlotte.

"Yes, she is," Aaron agreed wholeheartedly, as he rubbed the blood off his face.

Whit slapped him on the shoulder now. "You're a lucky man."

"What?" His friend must have lost more blood that he'd thought. "Are you okay?"

"Yeah," Whit assured him, "I'm just a little jealous. Okay, a lot jealous."

He studied his friend's face. Dawn was approaching, lightening the dark sky, so that he could see more clearly now. Apparently more clearly than Whit could see. "You're not making any sense."

"She loves you," Whit said.

"What?" he asked. Whit must have heard Trigger's claims and believed the madman.

Whit slapped his shoulder again. "Is that one more thing she kept from you? Her feelings?"

"She doesn't love me," Aaron insisted. "She doesn't even trust me." And how could you love someone you couldn't trust? The thought made his heart ache with loss.

Whit blew out a ragged breath. "She gave up Josie's whereabouts for your life."

Aaron shook his head. "No. She must have made up that address she gave him—just to buy us all some time to get Trigger under control."

Whit shook his head. "No. That is really Josie's address." Whit must have had the window cracked when he'd crouched down in the backseat of Trigger's car.

"No one but Charlotte knows where she stashed Josie," Aaron reminded him. That was why the U.S. Marshal had gone to such extremes to get the information from her. "So how would you know if she told me the truth or not?"

"I followed her the day that she moved Josie," Whit admitted.

"You really cared about her?"

"Not as much as you did, but yeah," Whit said. "She was an amazing lady."

"Is," he corrected him even though he was still getting used to the idea himself of Josie Jessup being alive. He'd wasted more than three years on guilt and anger.

"You never acted on your feelings for her," Whit said with absolute certainty. They hadn't taken shifts but had watched her together.

"She was a client," Aaron reminded him. "We were paid to protect her." And he would never cross that line.

"Her protection was why I followed Charlotte that day—to make sure that no one else followed them."

And that was why Aaron had struggled to understand why Whit had talked him into leaving the safe house the day it had exploded. Because he had always been vigilant about protecting their clients.

Whit nodded. "I had to make sure that Josie would be safe."

"Charlotte made sure of that," Aaron pointed out. So he could no longer resent her for keeping that secret from him. She'd just been doing her job. Actually she'd gone above and beyond because Josie had become a friend of hers. No matter how tough and independent she acted, Charlotte allowed herself to get close. To be vulnerable…

"Charlotte was kind of a client, wasn't she?" Whit asked, as if testing his former partner. "Being the king's daughter and all."

"I didn't know that she was," he reminded Whit and himself of another secret to which he hadn't been privy. And his resentment returned.

"Doesn't matter if you knew that or not, I guess," Whit continued. "As the princess's doppelganger bodyguard, she was still part of the job detail."

Wondering where his friend was heading with his comments, Aaron only nodded his agreement.

"And yet you acted on your feelings for her," Whit said.

Aaron arched a brow, wondering how Whit knew.

"Her kid is yours, right?"

Aaron nodded and then grinned with overwhelming, fatherly pride. "Yes."

"So your feelings for her are obviously stronger than your feelings were for Josie," Whit concluded.

"Josie was a friend," Aaron said.

"And Charlotte?"

His everything. "I don't know what she is. Or how she feels."

"She loves you."

Aaron's heart warmed with hope, but he didn't dare believe Whit's declaration. He wouldn't believe it until Charlotte herself told him her feelings.

But he suspected that was another secret she wasn't willing to share.

GABRIELLA HADN'T ANSWERED. But the phone hadn't rang and rang, either. Instead Charlotte had heard a message that the number she'd dialed was no longer a working exchange. It probably meant nothing more than that the minutes had run out on the disposable cell Charlotte had given her.

But who had Gabriella been calling? No one else knew where she was. And the few who'd thought they had, had actually mistaken Charlotte for the princess.

Unless Gabriella had used those minutes trying to reach her. When the men had burst into the hotel suite in Paris, she had destroyed her phone—making certain that there had been no way those men could track down the real princess. "Where are you?" she asked aloud, her voice echoing in the eerie quiet of the bedroom where she and Aaron had made love just hours before. The sheets were still tangled and scented with the sexy musk of Aaron's skin. Of their lovemaking…

She trembled with need. But it was a need she suspected would go unanswered. He was probably already on his way to Josie.

"Here you are," a deep voice murmured.

She glanced up to find him in the doorway, leaning against the jamb and studying her. "You were looking for me?" she asked and then realized his probable reason why. "Are the police here?"

"On their way," he confirmed. "So is someone else."

So instead of going to her, he was bringing Josie to him? That was even more dangerous.

"You called her? You can't do that," she said. "Someone could have traced the call. You could have put her in danger."

"Her who?" he asked, his brow furrowing with confusion. He still bore the round mark of the barrel of

Trigger's gun on his temple. "I don't know where Gabriella is."

"Not Gabby," she said, "Josie. You can't call Josie."

"Of course I can't," he agreed. "I don't have her number," he said.

Relief shuddered through her, and she hated herself that she wasn't just relieved her friend was safe but relieved that Aaron hadn't immediately tried to contact her. She hated this petty jealousy. It had to be the pregnancy hormones making her so emotional and crazy—because she had never acted like this before. But then she had never been in love before, either.

"I didn't even know I really had her address until now," he said.

She waited for him to leave then—to rush off to the woman he really loved. But he stayed where he was, staring at her so intently it was as if he was trying to see inside her.

"What?" She self-consciously lifted trembling fingers and ran them across her cheek. But the scar wasn't there anymore. She had nothing to run her fingertips along like she used to.

"Why did you give him her real address?" he asked, all narrow-eyed curiosity.

She shrugged, but the tension didn't leave her shoulders. She knew why she had. "I couldn't risk your life."

"But by telling him, you risked hers."

Guilt and regret clutched at her. She hated that she'd done that—hated that she'd been so weak.

"Why would you do that?" he asked.

"I—I shouldn't have done that," she regretfully admitted. "I shouldn't have told him."

"Trigger is dead," he assured her—a slight shudder moving his broad shoulders as he must have relived that moment when Whit had shot the man holding a gun to Aaron's head. "It doesn't matter now what you told him."

She released a shuddery breath. "True. It doesn't matter."

"Except it does," he said. "To me."

He was asking a question she was too afraid to answer. Earlier she'd thought that she should tell him her feelings—that she should because if something had happened to him, she would want him to know that she loved him.

But Trigger was dead. The prince and his henchman arrested. Nothing was going to happen to Aaron. But something bad could happen to her. She could tell him she loved him, and he could reject her.

So she cast around for any reason that she could keep her feelings to herself, like the fact that he loved another woman. "Now that you know where she is, are you going to go see her?"

"And risk someone following me?" He shook his head. "I wouldn't put a friend's life at risk."

Like she had.

"A friend?" The question slipped out, and she hoped it didn't reveal her jealousy. "Is that all Josie is to you?"

He nodded. "We were friends when she *died.*"

"Just friends?" she asked. "You gave up your business because of what happened to her."

"What I thought happened to her," he said. "I didn't think I was too good at my job then so giving it up seemed like the right thing."

"And Whit?"

"I guess, subconsciously, I knew he was keeping something from me," Aaron said. "So I didn't trust him.

I didn't want anything to do with someone I couldn't trust."

And that was her reason for not telling him her feelings. He didn't trust her. After all the secrets she'd kept from him, she didn't blame him; she wouldn't trust her, either.

Since she had given up a witness's location, no one could trust her. Maybe it was good that she hadn't gotten in touch with Gabriella. The princess was safer without Charlotte knowing exactly where she was.

Sirens in the distance drew her attention. And she remembered something else he'd said. "Who, besides the police, is on their way?" she asked. "Stanley Jessup's lawyer?"

They would probably need him to help clean up and explain the mess they'd made in this small Michigan town. She doubted anyone would believe their convoluted tale of doppelgangers and kidnappings and amnesia and royalty.

"King St. Pierre is on his way," Aaron said.

Panic struck her. She was in no condition to deal with that man. Not now. Maybe not ever again. "What?"

"I called him," Aaron explained. "He needs to know what's going on."

"Why?" she asked. "So he can fire all of us?"

"You're his daughter."

She laughed. "Not to him, I'm not. I'm just an employee—like the two of you. You two were hired to protect him, and instead you came here—"

"He wanted us to find the princess," Aaron said. "He was all right with using his old security detail again. Why did you want them replaced?"

"I wanted you and Whit to work together again," she said. But she couldn't take all the credit with a clear conscience. "Actually Josie suggested it. She felt bad that her needing to disappear caused a rift in your friendship."

He grinned with obvious affection for the other woman. Just friends? Really?

"But I didn't entirely trust his current people, either," she admitted. "Especially Zeke Rogers." The former mercenary had given off a bad vibe. "The king hadn't done a very good job vetting them."

Kind of like how he hadn't done a very good job of vetting future sons-in-law—putting Gabriella and Charlotte in danger.

"Rogers headed up the king's security detail for years," Aaron said.

"That's why he should have had them more thoroughly checked out," she said. "He didn't know their backgrounds—their vulnerabilities."

"He knows ours now," Aaron said with a heavy sigh. "Guess that Whit and I can start up our business again if he fires us."

"He will," Charlotte warned him. "You found him the wrong daughter."

Just like she was the wrong woman for Aaron. She couldn't tell him her feelings. But it was okay. She had her baby. She would give her all her love.

Chapter Sixteen

Aaron waited for it but the words didn't come. So he asked the older man point-blank, "You're not firing me?"

Using Whit's gunshot wound as an excuse, Aaron had taken the meeting alone with the king. The gray-haired man paced the den of Stanley Jessup's rental home. His gaze kept going to the blood smeared on the leather couch. "Why would I fire you?"

"I followed this lead on my own," he sheepishly reminded him. He'd put himself in danger because he'd trusted the wrong people and hadn't trusted the right ones.

The king absolved him of any culpability, just as Stanley Jessup had. "You didn't think you could trust anyone."

"But shouldn't I have trusted you?" Aaron asked. Maybe he wanted to get fired. Because if Charlotte wasn't working at the palace, he had no reason for being there.

The king shrugged but even that had a regal edge to it. "Charlotte doesn't trust me."

"She probably won't tell you where Gabriella is," Aaron admitted. "But it's just to keep her safe." He believed that now, where before he'd thought it might have been out of spite that she wouldn't tell her father where his chosen daughter was.

But given how the first man to whom Rafael had promised his daughter had nearly killed Charlotte, he didn't trust the man's judgment. Even if arranging marriages was fine in his realm, Aaron hated to think of anyone marrying for any reason but love.

That was why he hadn't already asked Charlotte. He didn't want to marry her just because they were about to have a child together. He wanted to marry her for the reason his own blissfully happy parents had married— true love.

"You are a loyal man," the king praised him. "I will not fire you or Whit Howell. I believe it is my good fortune to have you as part of my security detail."

"And what about Charlotte?" he asked. Would he fire her as she suspected?

"She is not just a bodyguard," the king said. "She is my daughter."

Aaron was surprised by the man's admission. "You're claiming her now?"

Rafael St. Pierre's shoulders sagged with his heavy burden of guilt and regret. "I should have always claimed her."

"You should have," Aaron wholeheartedly agreed. "You don't deserve her."

"Do you?" the king asked, calling him on his hypocrisy. "I'm assuming you're the father of her baby?" No matter how busy the man had been ruling his country, he must have remained aware of what was going on with his daughters.

Aaron nodded. And now he realized the purpose of

this meeting. Today the king was just a father asking a man his intentions toward his pregnant daughter.

It didn't matter that Aaron, like Charlotte, was in his thirties. Heat rushed to his neck, and nerves mangled his guts—and he was every bit as nervous as a teenager who'd gotten his young girlfriend pregnant.

"I love her," he said. "And I'd like to marry her. But I don't know if she'll have me."

The king was not going to get away with arranging a marriage for his oldest daughter. But if he were to do that, he would undoubtedly choose someone with more wealth and means than Aaron had.

But no one could offer her the love that Aaron could. "I don't know if she can trust anyone to love her."

"Because of me." The king readily took the blame, his shoulders sagging even more with the additional burden. "I will talk to her for you."

Aaron flinched. "Championing me may not help my situation at all." If that had even been the man's intentions...

"She will not listen to me," Rafael agreed, "because she hates me."

Aaron shook his head. "If she hated you, she wouldn't be so hurt that you rejected her."

"I had more reasons for treating her how I did," the king said in his own defense. "But I really had no excuse for putting my country before my child."

Aaron couldn't absolve the man of his guilt—not when his actions had so badly hurt the woman he loved.

"Charlotte deserves to come first," he admonished the man.

The king studied Aaron's face through narrowed eyes. His eyes were a darker shade of brown than his daughters' warm golden brown. "Does she come first with you?" he asked.

"Yes," he answered from his heart.

"Does she know that?" the king wondered.

Given the way she'd treated him earlier, Aaron doubted it.

"Not yet." But he would make certain that she would have no doubts that she was the only woman for him.

CHARLOTTE WAITED OUTSIDE the door to the den where the two most important men in her life were locked inside together.

"Are you worried?" Whit asked and pointed toward the closed door. "About what's going on in there? Do you think your daddy is getting out the shotgun to force Aaron to the altar to make an honest woman of you?"

At the outrageous thought, she uttered a short, bitter chuckle. "I doubt that's happening."

"You don't think your father would defend your honor?" Whit asked.

"No."

"Do you want me to defend your honor?" Whit offered sweetly. "I could rough up Aaron for you."

"Since you only have one arm working right now," she reminded him, "I don't like your chances."

He shrugged then grimaced at his own gesture. "Well, I offered. So what do you think they are talking about in there?"

"Gabriella." That was the only daughter the king would worry about and rightfully so. "I'm worried about her, too," she admitted. "I couldn't reach her on the phone earlier."

All his teasing aside, Whit anxiously asked, "But she should be fine, right?" He nodded in response to his own question. "Of course she's fine. We neutralized all the threats against her."

"She's Princess Gabriella," Charlotte said. "There will always be threats against her."

A muscle twitched in his cheek as he tightly clenched his jaw.

"People will want to kidnap her for her father's money or his power," she said. "She's always in danger. And then there was that note shoved under her door the night of the ball."

"What note?" he snapped, as if he should have seen it himself. As if he'd been with Gabby...

"It threatened her life," she said. "It promised that she would die before she would get the chance to marry Prince Malamatos. It was why we left for Paris the next morning." When Charlotte would have rather stayed and explored her burgeoning feelings for Aaron. But then those feelings had burgeoned even when she'd been away from him.

He expelled a ragged sigh. "That was why you left? It wasn't because she was excited to get a dress for her wedding?"

Charlotte chuckled again—this time with real mirth over Whit's ignorance. "Gabby had no intention of marrying either man her father promised her to."

"That's why you put her in your unofficial relocation program," Whit said with sudden understanding.

"I wanted her safe and happy." And now she wasn't sure she was either anymore.

"So are you going to track her down and make certain she's all right?" Whit asked with an eagerness that revealed his true feelings for the princess.

"No," she said.

He jerked with surprise. "I thought you cared about her?"

"I do," Charlotte insisted. "But I'm not going to track her down, because you are."

He nodded. "Of course, in your condition, you shouldn't be doing a lot of traveling."

She could have pointed out that her condition was a lot healthier than his at the moment. But she skipped it. "I'll tell you where I sent her, and you'll find her and make sure she's all right."

"I'm probably the last person she wants to see," Whit admitted with a heavy sigh of regret.

Charlotte wasn't so sure about that. "Just find her and keep her safe." She pressed a paper into his hand with Gabriella's last itinerary.

Whit clutched the piece of a paper in a tight fist. "If I hadn't already told Aaron he was a lucky man, I'd tell him again."

"Why is Aaron lucky?" she asked.

"Because he has you," Whit said. Without waiting to talk to his employer or friend again, the man turned and headed out the front door.

Before Charlotte had a chance to point out that in order for Aaron to be lucky, he'd actually have to want her. And he'd already said that he couldn't be with someone he couldn't trust.

The door to the den opened, but only one man stepped out. Her father. She braced herself for his anger. For his demands.

She hadn't braced herself for a physical confrontation, for the man throwing his arms around her and pulling her close.

"I thought you were dead," he murmured, his voice cracking with emotion.

Tears stung her eyes at his seemingly genuine and heartfelt relief that she was alive. "I'm fine."

"And I will be forever grateful for that," her father said. "I never should have let you become Gabriella's bodyguard."

She flinched. Here was the rejection she'd expected. The firing she'd anticipated.

"I shouldn't have allowed you to put yourself at risk," he said. "I should have had protection for you, too. But I have remedied that situation. You now have your own bodyguard."

"Who?"

"Me," Aaron said, as he joined them in the hall.

She laughed. "I don't need a bodyguard."

"Then consider him a bodyguard for my heir," the king said.

Charlotte clasped her hands to her belly, as if to protect the child. "You haven't claimed me. How can you claim my baby?"

"That's something else I'm going to remedy," he promised. "I'm claiming you as my daughter. As my firstborn."

She nodded with sudden understanding and soul-stealing disappointment. "Of course. Having me as your legal heir will take Gabriella out of danger."

The king groaned with frustration. "This isn't about her. This is about you—about my finally doing right by you."

"Then don't lie to me," she said. "Don't claim feelings you don't have."

"I've always had the feelings," he said. "I just denied them—for the sake of my wife while she was alive and then for the sake of my honor and my kingdom. But I realized, when I thought you were dead, that none of that mattered anymore."

His wife had been dead for years. But for him to say his honor or kingdom didn't matter...

Could he be telling the truth? Could he actually care about Charlotte?

"Maybe you shouldn't publicly claim her," Aaron said. "As her bodyguard, I think we can keep her safer if no one else knows she's related to you."

The king turned to Charlotte. "I don't want to wait another day to declare you as mine. But I don't want you in danger, either."

"Or is it your heir you're worried about?" she asked. "I think she's a girl. You still won't have that boy you want."

The king shook his head and turned back to Aaron. "I can't get through to her. She's too stubborn." His voice cracked with more of that emotion that seemed to overwhelm him. "I wish you luck with her."

"What did my father mean by that?" Charlotte asked once she and Aaron were alone again in the room they'd shared. "Is he talking about you being my bodyguard? Because that's ridiculous. I don't need a bodyguard."

She needed Aaron though. She needed him for her lover, her friend—her soul mate. But if she couldn't have him as those things, she wouldn't settle for less.

"No, you don't need a bodyguard," Aaron agreed with a slight chuckle. "You need a husband."

"Why? Because I'm pregnant?" She snorted derisively. "That's archaic—kind of like a man arranging a marriage for his daughter." She groaned with sudden realization of the conversation that must have taken place in that den. "He arranged for you to marry me, didn't he?"

"He gave his blessing," Aaron admitted.

And now Charlotte fully understood Gabby's horror at being auctioned off, like a side of beef, for money and power. Aaron could give the king neither of those for her hand, though. But then she had never been the daughter that mattered. He must have been bluffing about claiming her. Maybe he had prearranged with Aaron to reject that idea under the ruse of keeping her safe.

They could keep her safe from danger. But not from pain...

"What did you promise him in exchange for his blessing?" she wondered aloud. Because the king was too shrewd and too mercenary to give up something without receiving something in return—just like her mother had been. No wonder Bonita had been his mistress for so many years—after they'd met at a charity ball at which her missionary parents had been guest speakers.

"I did make him a promise," Aaron admitted, "that I would love you and cherish you the rest of our lives."

Her heart shifted, kicking inside her chest like the baby kicking inside her womb. Her legs trembled and she dropped onto the edge of the bed. "Why would you make a promise you can't keep?"

Why would he give her foolish heart such hope when he couldn't possibly really want to marry her?

AARON DROPPED TO his knees in front of Charlotte and took her hand in both of his. "I don't make promises I can't keep," he said. "You know that. You know me. If you accept my proposal, I will spend the rest of my life loving you. Will you marry me, Charlotte Green?"

"No."

He felt as though she'd kicked him. But as her father

had warned, she was stubborn—and totally convinced that she was unlovable.

"Why not?"

"Because it's not the nineteenth century," she said. "And we don't need to get married just because I'm pregnant."

"I don't want to marry you because you're pregnant," he said. "I want to marry you because I love you."

She still refused to believe him, to believe in herself. "No, you don't."

"Have I ever lied to you?" he asked.

She stilled and shook her head. "No, but…I've lied to you. And you said you wouldn't be with someone you can't trust."

"You lied or kept secrets to protect people." And maybe to protect herself if Whit was right and she actually loved him, too. "Except when you told Trigger where to find Josie. Why did you do that?"

"I told you that I couldn't risk your life."

"Why not?"

She groaned as if in pain, as if she were being tortured for information. And then she made the admission in the same way—begrudgingly, resentfully. "Because I love you."

He fought the grin that tugged at his mouth. He wanted to rejoice in her love. But he couldn't accept it until she could accept his—his love and his proposal. "You can love me but I can't love you?"

"You love Josie Jessup," she said.

"As a friend." He'd already told her this. But it was easier for her to believe that he loved Josie than that he loved her.

"You mourned her like a lover."

"I mourned her because I felt guilty," he admitted.

Then, with sudden realization, he repeated, "I mourned her. But I didn't mourn *you*."

She flinched with pain, and he realized that this had been her problem all along, why she had fought to hide or probably even admit to her feelings for him. She had believed him in love with another woman. She'd felt second best again, like she had to her sister.

"I didn't mourn you because I knew you weren't dead," he explained. "Everyone else tried to convince me that you were. Whit—"

"My dad?"

He nodded.

"You have more respect for my skills," she said.

He shook his head. "You're amazing, but that wasn't the reason. I knew that I would have felt it if you had died. Because there's this connection between us—this bond that I've never had with anyone else—not Josie. Not Whit."

He entwined his fingers with hers. "I knew you were alive because I could feel your heart beating. Thousands of miles separated us, but I could feel your heart beating in my heart. We are that connected."

Her breath caught, and her beautiful eyes shimmered with tears. "Aaron..."

"Do you feel it, too?" he asked. "Do you feel this connection between us? Between our souls?"

She nodded. "You are my soul mate."

"So I am going to ask you again," he warned her. "Will you marry me? Will you make me the happiest man in the world for the rest of our lives?"

"Yes, I will," she said with a smile of pure joy.

She wound her arms around his neck and pulled him close. And just as he'd said, her heart pounded against his—inside his, as if they were one. He felt her happiness, too, as it filled him with the warmth of joy and love and relief that she had finally accepted his proposal. But more important, he knew that she had accepted his love.

Her mouth pressed quick kisses to his lips and his cheek and the side of his nose. "I will marry you," she clarified, as if he could have mistaken her intentions. "And I will spend the rest of my life making you happy."

"You already have," he said. "By giving me your love and our child."

"Our child…" Those tears shimmered even more brightly in her eyes. "*You* gave me our child," she said. "You gave me the family I never had. You have already made me the happiest woman in the world."

A thought occurred to him and Aaron chuckled with sudden amusement.

"What?" she asked, her smile still full and bright. She looked more like her sister now—younger and more carefree and optimistic.

"It's a good thing Whit didn't hear any of this," he shared his thought. "He would tease us mercilessly for being hopeless romantics."

She chuckled, too, but then she said, "We might not be the only ones."

"Whit? A hopeless romantic?" He snorted at the ridiculous notion. He had never met a more cynical person—until he'd met Charlotte. If she could let herself fall in love…

Maybe it was possible that Whitaker Howell could find happiness, too.

"Since I will no longer keep any secrets from you," she vowed, "I need to tell you that I sent him to find Gabriella."

Aaron tensed with concern for his fiancée's sister. "Do you think she's in danger?"

"As the king's daughter, she's always in danger," she reminded him.

It was why Aaron preferred that the king not acknowledge her now or maybe ever. He hated the thought of people coming after her because of her father. But then Trigger had already come after her because of who she was. Charlotte could take care of herself though. Despite what she had taught her sister, he wasn't so sure that Princess Gabriella could protect herself.

In that interest of full disclosure to which she now endearingly subscribed, she warned him, "Going to her may put Whit in danger, too."

"He can handle himself." Even after a bullet had ripped through his shoulder, the man had saved their lives.

"He can handle armed gunmen and thugs," she agreed. "I'm not sure he can handle Gabby. She might hurt him. I don't know that she can go against her father's wishes to marry another man."

It hadn't occurred to him that Whit might have been so concerned about Gabby because he'd developed feelings for her. For so long he had believed his friend hadn't possessed any feelings. "Well, I don't know if Whit can protect himself from a broken heart."

Aaron hadn't been able to protect himself from that pain—when he'd thought Charlotte could never trust him and therefore never love him.

As if she'd felt that pain, sadness momentarily dimmed her eyes. "I'm sorry I hurt you," she said, "with all my secrets."

"You had your reasons."

"Not anymore," she said and repeated her earlier vow. "There will be no more secrets between us."

There would be nothing between them anymore but love.

* * * * *

MILLS & BOON

THE HEART OF ROMANCE

A ROMANCE FOR EVERY READER

MODERN

Prepare to be swept off your feet by sophisticated, sexy and seductive heroes, in some of the world's most glamourous and roma... locations, where power and passion collide.

HISTORICAL

Escape with historical heroes from time gone by. Whether your passi... for wicked Regency Rakes, muscled Vikings or rugged Highlanders, a the romance of the past.

MEDICAL

Set your pulse racing with dedicated, delectable doctors in the high-p... sure world of medicine, where emotions run high and passion, comfo... love are the best medicine.

True Love

Celebrate true love with tender stories of heartfelt romance, from the rush of falling in love to the joy a new baby can bring, and a focus o... emotional heart of a relationship.

Desire

Indulge in secrets and scandal, intense drama and plenty of sizzling h... action with powerful and passionate heroes who have it all: wealth, st... good looks…everything but the right woman.

HEROES

Experience all the excitement of a gripping thriller, with an intense r... mance at its heart. Resourceful, true-to-life women and strong, fearle... face danger and desire - a killer combination!

To see which titles are coming soon, please visit

millsandboon.co.uk/nextmonth

JOIN US ON SOCIAL MEDIA!

Stay up to date with our latest releases, author news and gossip, special offers and discounts, and all the behind-the-scenes action from Mills & Boon...

 @millsandboon

 @millsandboonuk

 facebook.com/millsandboon

 @millsandboonuk

It might just be true love...

GET YOUR ROMANCE FIX

Get the latest romance news,
exclusive author interviews, story
extracts and much more!

blog.millsandboon.co.uk